'Unforgettably evoked . . . You can almost smell the hot strong breath of the land in this brave gallimaufry of Greek myth and pre-colonial Igbo cosmology'
Evening Standard

'Almost every page [of *An Orchestra of Minorities*] trumpets the gifts of a writer who can make his language soar, wheel and pounce'
Spectator

'Rich and vivid . . . Obioma's absorbing tragicomedy painfully probes the perils of victimhood'
Observer

'At once funny, furiously inventive and disturbing, *An Orchestra of Minorities* is an uncomfortable but engrossing read'
Mail on Sunday

'A tale of mythic nature and epic scale at times recalling Homer's *Odyssey* – a sweeping story about destiny and the power of choice'
Vanity Fair

'Astonishing . . . remarkable, mythic'
Alice Walker on *The Fishermen*

'Awesome in the true sense of the word: crackling with life, freighted with death, vertiginous both in its style and in the elemental power of its story . . . A truly magnificent debut'
Eleanor Catton on *The Fishermen*

Also by Chigozie Obioma

The Fishermen

Chigozie Obioma was born in 1986 in Akure, Nigeria. He has lived in Nigeria, Cyprus and Turkey and currently resides in the United States, where he teaches at the University of Nebraska-Lincoln. His first novel, *The Fishermen*, won the inaugural FT/OppenheimerFunds Emerging Voices Award for Fiction, an NAACP Image Award for a Debut Author and the Art Seidenbaum Award for First Fiction (*Los Angeles Times* Book Prizes); and was shortlisted for the 2015 Man Booker Prize. Translation rights sold in twenty-six languages. Obioma was named one of *Foreign Policy*'s 100 Leading Global Thinkers of 2015. His stories and articles have appeared in many publications including *The Millions*, *Virginia Quarterly Review* and *Guardian*.

Praise for *An Orchestra of Minorities*

'Chigozie Obioma's frenetically assured second novel is a spectacular artistic leap forwards ... Few contemporary novels achieve the seductive panache of Obioma's heightened language, with its mixture of English, Igbo and colourful African-English phrases, and the startling clarity of the dialogue. The story is extreme; yet its theme is a bid for mercy for that most fragile of creatures – a human'
Eileen Battersby, *Guardian*

'The chances that Chigozie Obioma's second novel would match, let alone surpass, *The Fishermen* were slim. Happily, his follow-up, *An Orchestra of Minorities*, is a triumph ... In an era of copycats, *An Orchestra of Minorities* is an unusual and brillian[

The Eco

AN
ORCHESTRA OF
MINORITIES
CHIGOZIE
OBIOMA

ABACUS

First published in the United States in 2019 by Little, Brown and Company
First published in Great Britain in 2019 by Little, Brown
This paperback edition published in 2019 by Abacus

5 7 9 10 8 6 4

Excerpts from this book were published in the *Guardian* in 2016 under
the title 'The Ghosts of My Student Years in Northern Cyprus'

ISBN 978-0-349-14318-7

Printed and bound in Great Britain by
Clays Ltd, Elcograf S.p.A.

Papers used by Abacus are from well-managed forests
and other responsible sources.

Abacus
An imprint of
Little, Brown Book Group
Carmelite House
50 Victoria Embankment
London EC4Y 0DZ

An Hachette UK Company
www.hachette.co.uk

www.littlebrown.co.uk

To J.K.
We've not forgotten

If the prey do not produce their version of the tale, the predators will always be the heroes in the stories of the hunt.

—Igbo proverb

In a general way, we may visualize a person's chi as his other identity in spiritland – his spirit being complementing his terrestrial human being; for nothing can stand alone, there must always be another thing standing beside it.

—Chinua Achebe, 'Chi in Igbo Cosmology'

Uwa mu asaa, uwa mu asato! This is the primal factor in determining the state of a newborn's true identity. Even though humans exist on the earth in material form, they harbour a chi and an onyeuwa because of the universal law which demands that where one thing stands, another must stand beside it, and thus compels the duality of all things. It is also the basic principle on which the Igbo concept of reincarnation stands. Do you ever wonder why a newborn child sees a particular individual for the first time and from that moment develops hatred for that person without cause? . . . It is often because the child may have identified that individual as an enemy in some past existence, and it might be that the child has returned to the world in their sixth, seventh or even eighth cycle of reincarnation to settle an ancient score! Sometimes, too, a thing or an event can reincarnate during a lifetime. This is why you find a man who once owned something but loses it may find himself in possession of something similar years later.

—Dibia Njokwuji of Nkpa, voice recording

Chart of Igbo Cosmology

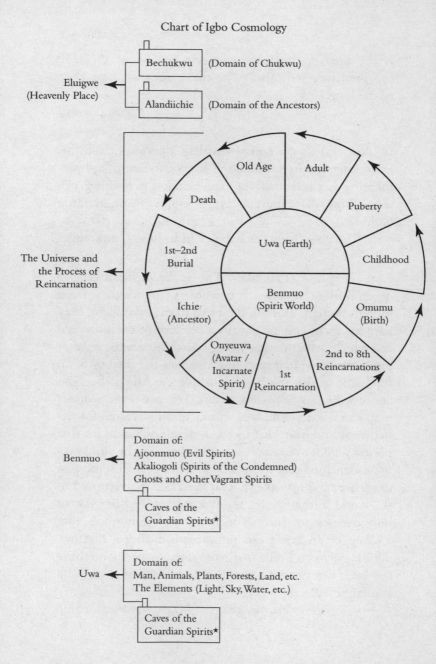

*Exists in both realms.

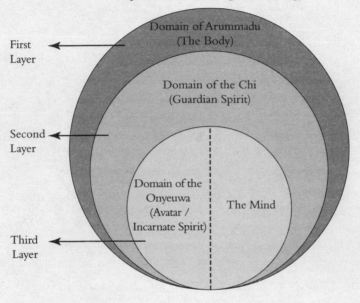

Composition of Man in Igbo Cosmology

Domain of Arummadu
(The Body)

First
Layer

Domain of the Chi
(Guardian Spirit)

Second
Layer

Domain of the
Onyeuwa
(Avatar /
Incarnate Spirit)

The Mind

Third
Layer

ONE

First Incantation

OBASIDINELU—

I stand before you here in the magnificent court of Bechukwu, in Eluigwe, the land of eternal, luminous light, where the perpetual song of the flute serenades the air—

Like other guardian spirits, I have gone to uwa in many cycles of reincarnations, inhabiting a freshly created body each time—

I have come in haste, soaring untrammelled like a spear through the immense tracts of the universe because my message is urgent, a matter of life and death—

I stand knowing that a chi is supposed to testify before you if his host is dead and his host's soul has ascended into Benmuo, that liminal space crowded with spirits and discarnate beings of every hue and scale. It is only then that you request that guardian spirits come to your dwelling place, this grand celestial court, and ask you to grant the souls of our hosts safe passage into Alandiichie, the habitation of the ancestors—

We make this intercession because we know that a man's soul can return to the world in the form of an onyeuwa, to be reborn, only if that soul has been received in the domain of the ancestors—

Chukwu, creator of all, I concede that I have done something out of the ordinary by coming here now to testify while my host is still alive—

But I am here because the old fathers say that we bring only the blade sharp enough to cut the firewood to the forest. If a situation deserves exigent measures, then one must give it that—

They say that dust lies on the ground and stars lie in the sky. They do not mix—

They say that a shadow may be fashioned from a man, but a man does not die because a shadow has sprung from him—

I come to intercede on behalf of my host because the kind of thing he has done is that for which Ala, the custodian of the earth, must seek retribution—

For Ala forbids that a person should harm a pregnant woman, whether man or beast—

For the earth belongs to her, the great mother of mankind, the greatest among all creatures, second only to you, whose gender or kind no man or spirit knows—

I have come because I fear that she will raise her hand against my host, who is known in this cycle of life as Chinonso Solomon Olisa—

This is why I have hastened here to testify of all I have witnessed and to persuade you and the great goddess that if what I fear has happened is true, to let it be understood that he has committed this great crime in error, unknowingly—

Although I will relate most things in my own words, they will be true because he and I are *one*. His voice is my voice. To speak of his words as if he were distinct from me is to render my own words as if they were spoken by another—

You are the creator of the universe, patron of the four

days – Eke, Orie, Afore and Nkwo – that make up the Igbo week—

To you the old fathers ascribed names and honorifics too numerous to count: Chukwu, Egbunu, Oseburuwa, Ezeuwa, Ebubedike, Gaganaogwu, Agujiegbe, Obasidinelu, Agbatta-Alumalu, Ijango-ijango, Okaaome, Akwaakwuru and many more—

I stand here before you, as bold as a king's tongue, to plead my host's cause, knowing that you will hear my voice—

THE WOMAN ON THE BRIDGE

CHUKWU, if one is a guardian spirit sent for the first time to inhabit a host who will come into the world in Umuahia, a town in the land of the great fathers, the first thing that strikes the spirit would be the immensity of the land. As the guardian spirit descends with the reincarnating body of the new host towards the land, what reveals itself to the eye astonishes. Suddenly, as if some primordial curtain has been peeled off, one is exposed to an interminable stretch of leaf-green vegetation. As one draws closer to Umuahia, one is enticed by the elements around the land of the fathers: the hills, the thick, great forest of Ogbuti–ukwu, a forest as old as the first man who hunted in it. The early fathers had been told that signs of the cosmic explosion that birthed the world could be seen here and that from the beginning, when the world was partitioned into sky, water, forest and land, the Ogbuti forest had become a country, a country more expansive than any poem about it. The leaves of the trees bear in them a provincial history of the universe. But beyond the exaltation of the great forest, one becomes even more fascinated with the many water bodies, the biggest of which is the Imo River and its numerous tributaries.

That river weaves itself around the forest in a complex circuit comparable only to that of human veins. One finds it in one part of the city spouting like a deep gash. One travels on the same road for a short distance and it appears – as if out of nowhere – behind a hill or an enormous gorge. Then there, between the thighs of the valleys, it is flowing again. Even if we miss it at first, one only needs to tread past Bende towards Umuahia, through the Ngwa villages, before a small, silent tributary reveals its seductive face. The river has a distinct place in the mythologies of the people because in their universe, water is supreme. They know that all rivers are maternal and therefore are capable of birthing things. This river birthed the city of Imo. Through its neighbouring city runs the Niger, a greater river which was itself the stuff of legend. Long ago, the Niger overran its boundaries in its relentless journey and met another, the Benue, in an encounter that forever changed the history of the people and the civilisations around both rivers.

Egbunu, the testimony for which I have come to your luminous court this night began at the Imo River nearly seven years ago. My host had travelled to Enugu that morning to replenish his stock, as he often did. It had rained in Enugu the previous night, and water was everywhere – trickling down from the roofs of buildings, in potholes on the roads, on the leaves of trees, dripping from orbs of spiderwebs – and a slight drizzle was on the faces and clothes of people. He went about the market in high spirit, his trousers rolled up over his ankles so as not to stain the hems with dirty water as he walked from shed to shed, stall to stall. The market seethed with people, as it always was even in the time of the great fathers when the market was the centre of everything. It was here that goods were exchanged, festivals were held and negotiations between villages were conducted. Throughout the land of the fathers, the shrine of Ala, the great mother, was often located close to the market. In the imagination of the fathers, the market was also the one human gathering that attracted the most vagrant spirits – akaliogolis, amosu, tricksters and various vagabond discarnate beings. For in the earth, a spirit without a host is nothing. One must inhabit a physical body to have any effect on the things of the world. And so these spirits are in constant search for vessels to occupy, and insatiable in their pursuit of corporeality. They must be avoided at all costs. I once saw such a being inhabit the body of a dead dog in desperation. And it managed, by some alchemical means, to stir this carrion to life and make it amble a few steps before leaving the dog to lie dead again in the grass. It was a fearful sight. This is why it is considered ill advised for a chi to leave the body of its host in such a place or to step far away from a host who is asleep or in an unconscious state. Some of these discarnate beings, especially the evil spirits, even sometimes try to overpower a present chi, or ones who have gone out on a consultation on behalf of their hosts. This is why you, Chukwu, warn us against such journeys, especially at night! For when a foreign spirit embodies a person, it is difficult to get it out! This is why we have the mentally ill, the epileptic, men with abominable passions, murderers of their own parents and others! Many of them have become possessed by strange spirits and their chi are rendered homeless and reduced to following the host about, pleading or trying to negotiate – often fruitlessly – with the intruder. I have seen it many times.

When my host returned to his van, he recorded in his big foolscap notebook that he'd bought eight adult fowls – two roosters and six hens – a bag of millet, a half bag of broiler feed and a nylon bag full of fried termites. He'd paid twice the usual price of chickens for one, a wool-white rooster with a long tapering comb and plush of feathers. When the seller handed him the fowl, tears clouded his eyes. For a moment, the seller and even the bird in his hands appeared as a shimmering illusion. The seller watched him in what seemed to be astonishment, perhaps wondering why my host had been so moved by the sight of the chicken. The man did not know that my host was a man of instinct and passion. And that he had bought this one bird for the price of two because the bird bore an uncanny resemblance to the gosling he had owned as a child, which he'd loved many years ago, a bird that changed his life.

Ebubedike, after he bought the prized white rooster, he embarked on the journey back to Umuahia with delight. Even when it struck him that he'd spent a longer time in Enugu than he'd intended and had not fed the rest of his flock for much of that day, it did not dampen his spirit. Not even the thought of them engaging in a mutiny of angry cackles and crows, as they often did when hungry, the kind of noise that even distant neighbours complained about, troubled him. On this day, in contrast to most other days, any time he encountered a police checkpoint, he paid the officers handily. He did not argue that he had no money, as he often did. Instead, before he came to their stations, where they had laid down logs studded with protruding nails to force the traffic to stop, he stretched his hand through the window clutching a wad of notes.

GAGANAOGWU, for a long time my host raced through rural roads that tracked through villages, between tumuli and mounds of the ancient fathers, through roads flanked by rich farmlands and deep bushes as the sky slowly darkened. Insects dashed against the windshield and burst like miniature fruits until the glass was covered with small mucks of liquefied insects. Twice he had to stop and wipe the mess off with a rag. But soon after he began again, the insects would rage against the pane with renewed force. By the time he arrived at the boundary of Umuahia the day had aged, and the lettering on the rusting pole with the WELCOME TO ABIA, GOD'S OWN STATE sign was barely visible. His stomach had become taut from having gone a whole day without eating. He stopped a short distance from the bridge that ran over the Amatu River – a branch of the great Imo River – and pulled up behind a semi whose back was covered with a tarp.

Once he stopped the engine, he heard a clatter of feet in the van bed. He climbed down and stepped over the drainage ditch that encircled the city. He walked over to the clearing where streetside sellers sat on stools under small fabric awnings on the other side of the drainage, their tables lit with lanterns and candles.

The eastern darkness had fallen, and the road ahead and behind was blanketed in a quilt of gloom, when he returned to the van with a bunch of bananas, a pawpaw and a polythene bag full of tangerines. He put on his headlights and drove back on to the highway, his new flock squawking in the back of the van. He was eating the bananas when he arrived at the bridge over the Amatu River. He'd heard only the previous week that – in this most fecund of rainy seasons – the river had overflowed and drowned a woman and her child. He didn't usually put stock in the rumours of mishaps that passed around the city like a weighted coin, but this story had stayed in his mind for some reason which even I, his chi, could not understand. He was barely at the middle of the bridge thinking of this mother and child when he saw a car parked by the railings, one of its doors flung wide open. At first all he saw was the car, its dark interior and a speck of light reflected on the window of the driver's side. But as he shifted his gaze, he caught the terrifying vision of a woman attempting to jump over the bridge.

Agujiegbe, how uncanny that my host had been thinking for days about a woman who'd drowned, and suddenly he found himself before another who had climbed one ledge up the rails, her body bent over as she attempted to throw herself into the river. And once he saw her, he was stirred within. He pulled the van to a halt, jumped out, and ran forward into the darkness, shouting, 'No, no, don't. Please, don't! Don't do that. *Biko, eme na!*'

It seemed at once that this unexpected intervention startled the woman. She turned in swift steps, her body swaying lightly as she fell backwards to the ground in obvious terror. He rushed forward to help her up. 'No, Mommy, no, please!' he said as he bent over.

'Leave me!' the woman cried at his approach. 'Leave me. Go away.'

Egbunu, rejected, he drew back in frantic steps, his hands raised in the strange way the children of the old fathers use to signify surrender or defeat, and said, 'I stop, I stop.' He turned his back to her, but he could not bring himself to leave. He feared what she would do if he left, for he – himself a man of much sorrow – knew that despair was the disease of the soul, able to destroy an already battered life. So he faced her again, his hands lower, stretched before him like staffs. 'Don't, Mommy. Nothing is enough for somebody to die like that. Nothing, Mommy.'

The woman struggled up to her feet slowly, first kneeling, then raising her upper body, all the while with her eyes fixed on him and saying, 'Leave me. Leave me.'

He glimpsed her face now in the pupillary light of his van.

It was full of fear. Her eyes seemed somewhat swollen from what must have been long hours of crying. He knew at once that this was a deeply wounded woman. For every man who has himself suffered hardship or witnessed it in others can recognise its marks on the face of another from a distance. As the woman stood trembling in the light, he wondered whom she may have lost. Perhaps one of her parents? Her husband? Her child?

'I will leave you alone now,' he said, lifting his hands up again. 'I go leave you alone. I swear to God who made me.'

He turned towards his van, but because of the gravity of the sorrow he'd seen in her, even the momentary shuffling of his feet away from her seemed like a grievous act of unkindness. He stopped, conscious of the rushed sinking in the pit of his stomach and the audible anxiety of his heart. He faced her again.

'But Mommy,' he said. 'Don't jump it, you hear?'

In haste, he unlocked the back of the van and then unlatched one of the cages, and with his eyes looking through the window, whispering to himself that she should not go, he took two chickens by their wings, one in each hand, and hurried down.

He found the woman standing where he'd left her, looking in the direction of his vehicle, seemingly transfixed. Although a guardian spirit cannot see the future and thus cannot fully know what its hosts will do – Chukwu, you alone and the great deities possess the spirit of foresight and may bequeath certain dibias this gift – I could sense it. But because you caution us, guardian spirits, not to interfere in every affair of our hosts, to allow man to execute his will and be man, I sought not to stop him. Instead, I simply put the thought in his mind that he was a lover of birds, one whose life has been transformed by his relationship with winged things. I flashed a stirring image of the gosling he once owned into his mind that instant. But it was of little effect, for in moments like this, when a man becomes overcome by emotion, he becomes Egbenchi, the stubborn kite which does not listen or even understand whatever is spoken to it. It moves on to wherever it wishes and does whatever it desires.

'Nothing, nothing should make someone fall inside the river and die. Nothing.' He raised the chickens above his head. 'This is what will happen if somebody fall inside there. The person will die, and no one can see them again.'

He lunged towards the rails, his hands heavy with the birds, which cackled in high-pitched tones and stirred with agitation in his grip. 'Even these fowls,' he said again, and flung them over the bridge into the gloom.

For a moment, he watched the birds struggle against the thermal, whipping their wings violently against the wind as they battled desperately for their lives but failed. A feather landed on the skin of his hand, but he beat it off with such haste and violence that he felt a quick pain. Then he heard the sucking sound of the chickens' contact with the waters, followed by vain plonks and splashes of sound. It seemed the woman listened, too, and in listening, he felt an indescribable bond – as if they had both become lone witnesses to some inestimable secret crime. He stood there until he heard the woman's gasps. He looked up at her, then back at the waters hidden from his sight by the darkness, and back at her again.

'You see,' he said, pointing at the river as the wind groaned on like a cough caught in the dry throat of the night. 'That is what will happen if somebody fall inside there.'

The first car to approach the bridge since his own arrived with cautious speed. It stopped a few paces from them and honked, then the driver said something he could not hear but which had been spoken in the White Man's language and which I, his chi, had heard: 'I hope you are not hoodlums oh!' Then the car drove away, gathering speed.

'You see,' he repeated.

Once the words had left his mouth, he resolved into a calm, as it often happens at such times when a man, having done something out of the ordinary, retreats into himself. All he could think of was to leave the place, and this thought came upon him with an overwhelming passion. And I, his chi, flashed the thought in his mind that he'd done enough, and that it was best he left. So he rushed back to his van and started it amidst the mutiny of voices from the back. In the side mirror, the vision of the woman on the bridge flashed like an invoked spirit into the field of light, but he did not stop, and he did not look back.

2

DESOLATION

AGUJIEGBE, the great fathers say that to get to the top of a hill, one must begin from its foot. I have come to understand that the life of a man is a race from one end to the other. That which came before is a corollary to that which follows it. This is the reason people ask the question 'Why?' when something that confounds them happens. Most of the time, even the deepest secrets and motives of the hearts of men can be uncovered if one probes deeper. Thus, Chukwu, to intercede on behalf of my host, I must suggest that we trace the beginning of everything to the harsh years preceding that night on the bridge.

His father had died only nine months earlier, leaving him with a pain that was exquisite beyond anything he'd ever felt. It may have been a little different had he been with others, as he was when he lost his mother and when he lost his gosling and when his sister left home. But upon his father's passing, there was no one. His sister, Nkiru, having eloped with an older man and feeling her conscience seared by their father's death, distanced herself even more. Perhaps she'd done this for fear my host might blame her for their father's death. The days that followed the demise were of utmost darkness. The agwu of pain afflicted him night and day and made of him an empty house in which traumatic memories of his family lurked like rodents. In the mornings on most days, he'd wake up smelling his mother's cooking. And sometimes during the day, his sister would reveal herself in vivid pictures, as if she'd been merely hidden all along by a drawn curtain. At night, he'd feel the presence of his father so intensely he'd sometimes become convinced that his father was there. 'Papa! Papa!' he'd call into the darkness, turning about in frantic steps. But all he'd get back would be silence, a silence so strong it would often restore his confidence in reality.

He walked through the world vertiginously, as if on a tightrope. His vision became one from which he could see nothing. Nothing gave him comfort, not even the music of Oliver De Coque, which he'd play on his big cassette player most evenings or while working at the yard. Even his fowls were not spared his grief. He tended to them with less care, mostly feeding them once a day and sometimes forgetting to give them food altogether. Their riotous squawking in protest was what often stirred him in those times, forcing him to feed them. His watch over his flock was distracted, and many times hawks and kites preyed on them.

How did he eat in those days? He simply fed off the small farm, a plot of land that stretched from the front of the house to the place where the motor road began, harvesting toma-toes, okro and peppers. The corn his father had planted he let wilt and die, and he allowed a collection of insects to foment the resultant decay as long as they did not also trample on the other crops. When what was left of the farm could not meet his needs, he shopped at the market near the big roundabout, using as few words as necessary. And in time he became a man of silence who went days without speaking – not even to his flock, whom he often addressed as comrades. He bought onions and milk from the provisions shed nearby and sometimes ate at the canteen across the street, Madam Comfort's restaurant. He hardly spoke there, either, but merely observed the people around him with a strained mercurial awe, as if in their seeming peacefulness they were all renegade spirits come into his world through a back door.

Soon, Oseburuwa, as is often the case, he became one with sorrow so much that he resisted all help. Not even Elochukwu, the only friend he kept after he left school, could comfort him. He stayed away from Elochukwu, and once Elochukwu rode his motorcycle up to the front of the compound, knocked on the door and shouted my host's name to see if he was in. But he pretended he was not in the house. Elochukwu, perhaps suspicious that his friend was in, rang my host's phone. My host let it ring on until Elochukwu, maybe concluding that he was indeed away, left. He refused all pleas from his uncle, his father's only surviving sibling, to come and stay in Aba. And when the older man persisted, he turned off his phone and did not turn it on for two months, until he woke up one day to the sound of his uncle driving on to his compound.

His uncle had come angry, but when he found his nephew so broken, so lean, so emasculated, he was moved. The old man wept in the presence of my host. The sight of this man whom he had not seen in years weeping for him changed something in my host that day. He discovered that a hole had been bored into his life. And that evening, as his uncle snored, stretched out on one of the sofas in the sitting room, it struck him that the hole became evident after his mother died. It was true, Gaganaogwu. I, his chi, was there when he saw his mother being taken out of the hospital, dead shortly after delivering his sister. This was twenty-two years ago, in the year the White Man refers to as 1991. He was only nine at the time, too young to accept what the universe had given him. The world he'd known up till that night suddenly became reticulated and could not be straightened again. His father's devotion, trips to Lagos, excursions to the zoo in Ibadan and the amusement parks in Port Harcourt, even playing with the video-game consoles – none worked. Nothing his father did repaired the chink in his soul.

Towards the end of that year, around when the cosmic spider of Eluigwe spins its lush web over the moon the thirteenth time, increasingly desperate to restore his son's well-being, his father took him to his village. He'd remembered that my host had been enticed by stories of how he'd hunted wild geese in the Ogbuti forest as a little boy during the war. So he took my host to hunt geese in the forest, an account of which I will give you in due course, Chukwu. It was here that he caught the gosling, the bird that would change his life.

His uncle, seeing the state my host was in, stayed with him for four days instead of one, as he'd planned. The older man cleaned the house, tended the poultry and drove him to Enugu to buy feed and supplies. During those days, Uncle Bonny, despite stammering, filled my host's mind with words. Most of what he said pivoted around the perils of loneliness and the need for a woman. And his words were true, for I had lived among mankind long enough to know that loneliness is the violent dog that barks interminably through the long night of grief. I have seen it many times.

'Nonso, ih if y-ou don't ge get y-y-yourself a-a wife s-su su soon,' Uncle Bonny said the morning he would leave, 'your aunt a-ah-ah me wi-will h-ave to get y-y-ou one our ourself.' His uncle shook his head. 'Be-be-be-because because you can't live like this.'

So strong were his uncle's words that, after he left, my host
began to think of new things. As if the eggs of his healing
had hatched in secret places, he found himself craving something he had not had in a long time: the warmth of a woman.
This desire drew his attention away from thoughts of his loss.
He began to go out more, to lurk around near the Federal
Government Girls College. At first, he watched the girls from
the roadside canteens with fitful curiosity. He paid attention to
their plaited hair, their breasts and their outward features. As
he developed interest, he reached out to one, but she rebuffed
him. My host, who'd been moulded by circumstances into a
man of little confidence, decided he would not try a second
time. I flashed in his thought that it was hardly possible to get
a woman at the first try. But he paid no heed to my voice. A
few days after he was turned down, he enquired at a brothel.

Chukwu, the woman into whose bed he was admitted
was twice his age. She wore loose hair, the kind which was
known among the great mothers. Her face was painted with
a powdery substance that gave it delicacy which a man might
find inviting. She looked by the shape of her face like Uloma
Nezeanya, a woman who, two hundred and forty-six years
ago, was betrothed to an old host (Arinze Iheme) but disappeared before the wine-carrying ceremony, taken away by
Aro slave raiders.

Before his eyes, the woman stripped and bared a body that
was buxom and attractive. But when she asked him to climb
her, he could not. It was, Egbunu, an extraordinary experience, the like of which I had never seen before. For suddenly,
the great erection he'd sustained for days was gone the very
moment it could be satiated. He was seized by a sudden acute
self-awareness of himself as a novice, unskilled in the art of
sex. With this came a flurry of images – of his mother in the

hospital bed, of the gosling perched precariously on a fence, and of his father in the hard grip of rigor mortis. He trembled, pulled himself slowly from the bed, and begged to leave.

'What? You wan just waste your money like that?' the woman said.

He said yes. He stood up and reached for his clothes.

'I no understand, look how your prick still dey stand.'

'*Biko, ka'm laa,*' he said.

'You no sabi speak English? Speak pidgin, I no be Ibo,' the woman said.

'Okay, I say I wan go.'

'Eh, na wa oh. Me I neva see this kain thing before, oh. But I no want your money make e waste.'

The woman climbed off the bed and switched on the light-bulb. He stepped back at the full glare of her female immensity. 'No fear, no fear, just relax, eh?'

He stood still. His hands yielded like one afraid as the woman took his clothes and put them back on the chair. She knelt on the floor and held his penis with one hand and clutched his buttocks with the other. He squirmed and trembled from the sensation. The woman laughed.

'Wetin be your age?'

'Thirty, ah-gh thirty.'

'Abeg talk true, wetin be your age?' She squeezed the tip of his penis. He gasped as he made to speak, but she clamped her mouth over it and swallowed it halfway. My host mumbled the word *twenty-four* in feverish haste. He tried to get out, but the woman curved her other arm around his waist and held him still. She sucked with plopping sounds, forcefully, while he screamed, gnashed his teeth and uttered meaningless words. He saw iridescent light tempered with darkness and felt a cold-ness within. The complex equation continued to erupt in his body until he let out a shout: 'I dey release, I dey release!' The woman turned away, and the semen barely escaped her face. He fell back into the chair, fearing that he might pass out. He would leave that brothel, shocked and exhausted, bearing the weight of the experience with him like a sack of corn. It was four days later that he encountered the woman on the bridge.

EZEUWA, he left the bridge that night, uncertain about what he had done, only knowing that it was something out of the ordinary. He drove home with a sense of fulfilment, the kind he had not experienced in a long time. In peace, he unloaded the new chickens, six instead of eight, and took the cages into the yard using the torchlight at the head of his phone. He unpacked the silo bag of millet and other things he'd bought in Enugu. Once he set everything down, he was hit with a sudden realisation. 'Chukwu!' he said, and rushed into the sitting room. He lifted his rechargeable lamp, pressed up the switch by its side, and a weak white light glowed from the three fluorescent bulbs. He turned the switch up even more, but the lighting did not improve. He moved forward and gazed down at it to see that one of the bulbs had died, its top end coated with a blob of soot. He ran to the yard with the lamp nonetheless, and once the half-light illuminated the cage, he screamed again, 'Chukwu, oh! Chukwu!' For he'd found that one of the chickens he'd thrown over the bridge was the wool-white rooster.

Akataka, it is a common phenomenon among mankind to attempt to flip precedence: to try to bring that which has gone forward back. But it always, always fails. I have seen it many times. Like others of his kind, my host ran out of his house back to his van, on which a black cat had climbed and sat gazing about like a watchman. He shooed the cat away. It gave a loud feline whine and dashed into the adjoining bush. He entered the van and drove back out into the night. The traffic was light, and only once did a big semi block the way while it was trying to pull into a petrol station. When he got to the bridge, the woman he'd seen only a while before was gone – her car, too. He reckoned that she had not fallen into the river, for if she had, then her car would still be there. But the woman was not, at this point, what he cared about. He rushed down to the shore, the nocturnal noise filling his ears, his torchlight swallowing the darkness like a boa. He felt the sensation of insects resolve into a concentric fold in the air and net his face as he approached the shore. He waved frantically to swat them away. The torchlight followed the movement of his hand and wavered upon the waters in a straight rod a few times, and then flashed across the riverbank for metres on end. His gaze traced the path of the light, but all he saw was empty banks and rags and dirt strewn about. He walked directly under the bridge, turning when he heard a sound, his heart palpitating. As he came near, the light revealed a basket. The main raffia plaiting had loosened into long, twisted fibres. He rushed towards it, in case one of the chickens had crawled into the basket to get away from the waters.

When he found nothing in the basket, he cast the light on the water under the bridge, down the distant reaches of the river as far as his torchlight could illuminate, but there was no trace of either chicken. He recalled the moment he threw them, how they'd fluttered their wings, how'd they tried in agonising desperation to cling to the bars of the bridge, and how they must have been unable to do it. He'd learned early on when he first began keeping poultry that domestic fowls were the weakest animals among all creatures. They had little ability to defend or save themselves from dangers large or small. And it was this weakness that further endeared them to him. At first he'd loved all birds because of the gosling, but he began to love only the weak domestic fowls after he witnessed the violence of a hawk attack on a hen.

After he had combed through the thick hide of night, as one would search for lice on the skin of a densely furred animal, he returned home in anguish. His action seemed to him all the more like something his hand had done out of concert with his mind. It was this, above all, that caused him pain. Sudden darkness often descends upon the heart of a person who discovers that he has unknowingly committed harm. Upon the discovery of the harm it has done, the man's soul kneels in complete defeat, submits to the alusi of remorse and shame, and in its submission wounds itself. Once wounded, a man seeks healing through acts of restitution. If he has soiled another's cloth, he may go to that person with a new cloth and say, there, my brother, take this new cloth in exchange for the one I ruined. If he has broken something, he may seek to mend or replace it. But if he has done that which cannot be undone, or broken that which cannot be mended, then there is nothing he can do but submit to the tranquillising spell of remorse. This is a mystifying thing!

Ezeuwa, when my host sought an answer to something beyond his understanding, I often ventured to supply it. So before he slept that night, I impressed on his mind that he should return to the river in the morning; perhaps he would still be able to find the fowls. But he paid no heed to my counsel. He thought it an idea that originated from within his own mind, for man has no way to distinguish between what has been put into his thoughts by a spirit – even if it is his own chi – and what has been suggested to him by the voice of his head.

I continued to flash the thought in his mind many times that day, but the voice of his head would counter each time and tell him that it was too late, that the chickens must have drowned. To which I responded that he could not know this. Then the voice of his head said, *It is gone; there is nothing I can do.* So when it was evening, and I could see that he would not go, I did that which you, Oseburuwa, caution guardian spirits to avoid doing except in extraordinary situations. I stepped out of the body of my host while he was conscious. I did this because I knew that my place as his guardian spirit was not only as a guide but also as a helper and witness to the things which may be beyond his reach. This is because I see myself as his representative in the realm of the spirits. I stand within my host and gaze at every movement of his hands, every step of his feet, every motion of his body. To me, the body of my host is a screen on which the entirety of his life is displayed. For while in a host I'm nothing but an empty vessel filled by the life of a man, rendered concrete by that life. It is thus from the place of a witness that I observe him live, and his life becomes my testimony. Yet a chi is constrained while in the body of its host. While there, it becomes nearly impossible to see or hear what is present or spoken in the supernatural realm. But when one exits one's host, one becomes privy to things beyond the realm of man.

Once out of my host, I was hit by the great clamour of the spirit world, a deafening symphony of sounds that would have frightened even the bravest of men. It was a multitude of voices – cries, howls, shouts, noises, sounds of every kind. It is uncanny that even though the separation between the world of mankind and the spirits is only leaf-thin, one does not hear even a faint whisper of this sound until one leaves the body of one's host. A freshly created chi on earth for the first time is immediately overwhelmed by this din and may become so frightened that it might run back into the fortress of silence that is its host. This happened to me during my first sojourn on earth as well as to many guardian spirits I have met at the resting caves of Ogbunike, Ngodo, Ezi-ofi, and even the pyramidal mounds of Abaja. It is especially worse at night-time, the time of the spirits.

Whenever I leave my host while he is in a state of consciousness, I make my visits rapid and brief, so that nothing will happen to him in my absence and he will not do anything I would not be able to account for. But because the road to anywhere in a disembodied form isn't the same as when one is borne by a human vessel, I had to slowly make my way through the crowded concourse of Benmuo, in which spirits of all kinds writhed like a can of invisible worms. My haste yielded fruit, and I got to the river within a period of seven battings of the eyelids, but I saw nothing there. I returned the following day, and by the third visit, I saw the brown fowl he had thrown over the bridge. It had bloated and now lay on the surface of the river with its legs facing up, taut and dead. The water had added a shade of imperceptible grey to the bird's barring, and its belly was naked of all plumage, as if something in the water had eaten it. Its neck seemed to have elongated, and its wrinkling was deeper and its body was swollen. A vulture sat on one of the wings of the chicken, which had flattened out over the surface of the water, peering down and about at the bird. I saw no sign of the wool-white rooster.

Ebubedike, in my many cycles of existence, I have come to understand that the things that happen to a man have already occurred long before in some subterranean realm, and that nothing in the universe is without precedent. The world spins on the noiseless wheel of an ancient patience by which all things wait and are made alive by this waiting. The ill luck that has befallen a man has long been waiting for him – in the middle of some road, on a highway, or on some field of battle, biding its time. It is the individual who reaches this point and is struck down who may be fooled into sullen bewilderment, along with all who may sympathise with him, even his chi. But in truth the man had died long ago, the reality of his death merely concealed by a silken veil of time, which would eventually be parted to reveal it. I have seen it many times.

While he slept that night, I stepped out of him, as I often did, so I could watch over him, because the inhabitants of Benmuo often become more active in the earth at night, while mankind sleeps. And from this position, I flashed the image of the chicken and the vulture into his subconscious mind, for the easiest way to communicate such a mysterious event to one's host is through the dream sphere – a fragile realm a chi must always enter with caution and great care because it is an open theatre accessible to any spirit. A chi must first eject itself from the host before stepping into its host's dream world. This also prevents the chi from being identified by the foreign spirits as a chi hovering in untenanted space.

Once I'd flashed the images before him, he twitched in his sleep, lifted one hand, and curved it into a weak fist. I sighed, relieved, knowing that he now knew what happened to his white rooster.

GAGANAOGWU, his sadness for drowning the fowls had suppressed every thought of the woman at the bridge. But slowly, as his sadness abated, thoughts of her began to line the boundaries of his mind and then gradually crowd in. He started to dwell on thoughts of her, what he had seen of her. All he'd been able to gather from the night vision was that she was mid-sized, not as fleshy as Miss J, the prostitute. She had worn a light blouse and skirt. And he remembered that her car was a blue Toyota Camry, similar to his uncle's. Then often, like a grasshopper, his thoughts would leap from her appearance to his curiosity about what she did after he left the bridge. He would blame himself for having left the bridge in haste.

In the days following, he tended to his poultry and the garden with light hands, consumed by thoughts of her. And when he drove about the city, he searched for the blue car. As weeks passed, he began to yearn for the prostitute again. Desire swelled like a storm and washed over the parched landscape of his soul. It drove him to the brothel one evening, but Miss J was busy. The other ladies mobbed him, and one of them dragged him into a room. This woman had a lean waist and a scar on her belly. With her he felt himself certain and sure, as if at the place of his last encounter his apprehensions and naïveté had been clobbered to a bloody death. He yielded to her without scruples, and even though I often avoid witnessing my hosts having sex because of its fearful imitation of death, I stayed put because it was to be his first. When he was done, she slapped him on the back, saying how good he was.

Yet, despite this experience, he was still drawn to Miss J, to her body, to the familiar sound of her sigh. It surprised him that even though he had done something more profound with the other woman, he'd found greater pleasure in the hands of Miss J. He returned to the brothel three days later and avoided the other woman, who ran heartily to him. Miss J, this time, was free. She regarded him only with faint recognition and set about undressing him in silence. Before they could begin, she answered her phone and told the caller to come in two hours, and when it seemed the male voice refused the bargain, she settled for an hour and a half.

They had begun when she spoke about the last time and laughed. 'You don open your eye now after I suck you that time, ba?'

He made love to her with an exuberance that fevered his soul and poured himself into the act. But once he slumped beside her, she pushed away his arm and rose.

'Miss J,' he called, almost in tears.

'Yes, na wetin?' the woman said. She started to strap her brassiere over her breasts.

'I love you.'

Egbunu, the woman stopped, clapped her hands and laughed. She turned on the light and crept back into the bed. She scooped his face in her hand, mimicked the calculated sombreness with which he'd uttered the words, and laughed even harder.

'Oh, boy, you no sabi wetin you dey talk.' She clapped her hands again. 'Look at this one, him say him love me. Nothing wey person eye no go see these days oh. Im see nyash wey tripam – na im be say im love me. Say you love your mama.'

She snapped her fingers as she burst again into renewed mirth. And for days, her laughter echoed through his being in many hollow places, as if it were the world itself that had laughed at him, a small, lonely man whose only sin had been that he was hungry for companionship. It was here that he first felt that befuddling emotion of romantic love, a kind of feeling that was distinct from what he felt for his birds and for his family. It was a painful feeling, for jealousy is the spirit that stands at the threshold of love and madness. He wanted her to belong to him and begrudged all the other men who would have her after him. But he did not know that nothing truly belongs to anyone. Naked he was born, naked he will return. A man may own something for as long as it remains with him.

Once he leaves it, he may lose it. He did not know at the time that a man may give up all he has for the sake of the woman he loves, and when he returns, she may no longer desire him. I had seen it many times.

So, broken by the things he did not yet know, he left the place and resolved never to return.

3

AWAKENING

IJANGO-IJANGO, over many sojourns in the human world, I have heard the venerable fathers, in their kaleidoscopic profundity, say that no matter the weight of grief, nothing can compel the eyes to shed tears of blood. No matter how long a person weeps, only tears continue to fall. A man may remain in the state of grief for a long time, but he will eventually grow out of it. In time, a man's mind will acquire strong limbs, strike down the wall, and be redeemed. For no matter how dark the night, it soon passes, and Kamanu, the sun god, erects his grandiose emblem the following day. I have seen it many times.

By the fourth month after the encounter with the woman on the bridge, my host almost ceased grieving. It was not that he was happy now, for even the hems of the garments of his brightest days were fringed with threads of sorrowful darkness. It was that he was alive again, open to the possibilities of happiness. He turned to his friend Elochukwu, who began visiting regularly and persuaded him to join MASSOB, the group that was sweeping young Igbo men with an old broom into a pile of dust. Elochukwu, who had been his friend and confidant in secondary school and who was always slender, had become brawny with biceps he displayed at every turn by wearing armless shirts or singlets. 'Nigeria has failed,' he would tell my host in the White Man's language, and then trail into the language of the fathers with which he mostly conversed with my host. '*Ihe eme bi go. Anyi choro nzoputa!*' At Elochukwu's insistence, my host joined him. In the evenings, at the big shop of a car dealer, they gathered wearing black berets and red shirts, surrounded by flags of a half-drawn sun, maps and images of soldiers who had fought for Biafra. My host would amble about with this group, shouting slogans at the top of his lungs. He would yell 'Biafra must rise again' with them, stamp his feet on the unfinished floor and chant 'MASSOB! MASSOB!' He'd sit among these men and listen to the dealer and the head of the movement, Ralph Uwazuruike. Here my host spoke, he made merry again, and many noted his broad smile and his quickness to laugh. These men, without knowing where he had been or where he was coming from, glimpsed the first marks of his healing.

Chukwu, because I had been present in a host during the Biafran War, I feared his dalliance with this group would lead him to harm. I put thoughts in his head that there may be violence in these engagements. But the voice of his head replied with certainty that he was not afraid. And indeed, for a long time he went with this group, moved only by an anger he could not define. For he had not himself experienced the grievances the men articulated. He did not know anyone who had been killed by people from northern Nigeria. Although many of the dark sayings of this group felt true to him – he could see, for instance, that indeed no Igbo had been president of Nigeria and perhaps none would ever be – none of it affected him personally. He did not know anything about the war except that his father had fought and had told him many stories about it. And while these men spoke, the vivid accounts of the war his father had given him would thrash about in the mud of his remembrance like wounded insects.

But he attended the meetings mostly because Elochukwu was the only friend he had. A neighbour's hand in the death of his gosling had shut his heart to friendships. After the incident, he had hovered over the grey field of humanity and determined that the world of man was too violent for his liking. He found solace instead among feathery creatures. He also went because it gave him something to do besides tending to the poultry and the small farm and because he'd hoped that while going from one point to another in the city, advocating for the actualisation of the sovereign state of Biafra, he might come across the woman he'd met at the bridge. Akataka, it was this last reason that was principal in his mind, the main reason why, even as the marches became increasingly dangerous, he persisted. But after a month of protests, clashes with police, riots and violence, and my intense persuasion through endless flashes of thoughts in his mind that he desist, he broke off from the group like a wheel unhooked from a fast-moving car and rolled into the void.

He returned to his normal life, rising at daybreak to the beautiful but mystifying music of the poultry – a symphony of crows, cackles and tweets that often melded into what his father had once described as a coordinated song. He harvested eggs, recorded the birth of new chicks in his foolscap record book, fed the flock, watched them graze about in the yard with his catapult at the ready to protect them, and tended to the ill and feeble ones. One day in that month, one of the days he worked the most without distractions, he planted tomatoes on the shorn part of the land. He had not tended to this part of the land in a long time, and the change he saw on it shocked him.

While weeding the area, he had found that red ants had not just encroached but also completely infested the land. They lay deep in the nerve of the soil, nestled in every clump. It seemed they'd fed on an old dead cassava head which, perhaps owing to their attack, had been unable to grow. He boiled hot water in a kettle and poured it on the loam, killing all the ants. Then he swept the mass of dead ants away and planted the seeds.

He returned to the yard afterwards and washed the tomato seeds that clung to his fingernails and blackened his thumbs. He then scooped bowlfuls of millet from a silo stacked in an unused room in the house and spread the grains on a mat. He unlatched the two large coops in which a dozen chickens grazed about, and they flocked out towards the mats of feed. Within the coops were two cages each of hens with their chicks and one of three large broilers surrounded by their eggs. He felt each one of the birds to try to see if they were all in sound health. There were about forty of the brown ones and about a dozen of the white ones. After he'd fed them, he stood in the yard watching to see which of them had shat so he could poke their excreta with sticks in search of worms. He was searching a grey glob of faeces dropped by the well by one of the broilers when he heard the voice of a woman hawking groundnuts.

Egbunu, I must say that it wasn't that he responded this way to every woman's voice, but her voice sounded strangely familiar to him. Although he did not know it, I knew that it reminded him of his mother. At once he saw a plump, swarthy woman who looked his age. She was sweating in the hot sun, and the sweat shimmered along her legs. She carried a tray filled with groundnuts on her head. She was one of the poor – the class of people who had been created by the new civilisation. In the time of the old fathers only the lazy, indolent, infirm or accursed lacked, but now most people did.

Go into the streets, into the heart of any market in Alaigbo, and you'll find toiling men, men whose hands are as hard as stones and whose clothes are drenched in sweat, living in abject poverty. When the White Man came, he brought good things. When they saw the car, the children of the fathers cried out in amusement. The bridges? 'Oh, how wonderful!' they said. 'Isn't this one of the wonders of the world?' they said of the radio. Instead of simply neglecting the civilisation of their blessed fathers, they destroyed it. They rushed to the cities – Lagos, Port Harcourt, Enugu, Kano – only to find that the good things were in short supply. 'Where are the cars for us?' they asked at the gates of these cities. 'Only a few have them!' 'What about the good jobs, the ones whose workers sit under air conditioners and wear long ties?' 'Ah, they are only for those who have studied for years in a university, and even then, you'd still have to compete with the multitude of others with the same qualifications.' So, dejected, the children of the fathers turned back and returned. But to where? To the ruins of the structure they had destroyed. So they live on the bare minimum, and this is why you see people like this woman who walk the length and breadth of the city hawking groundnuts.

He shouted for her to come up.

The woman turned in his direction and lifted a hand to hold the tray on her head in place. She pointed to herself and said something he could not hear.

'I want to buy groundnut,' he called to her.

The woman began walking down the curved dirt path, marked in many places by the tyres of his van and, recently, the four wheels of his uncle's car. The previous day's rain had moulded the red earth into small mud balls that clung to the tyres. And now, in the clearer day, the reddish earth still gave off an ancient smell and worms were strewn all over it, burrowing and leaving trails on the path. As a child he'd taken pleasure in crushing worms under his feet after bouts of rainfall, and sometimes he and his friends, especially the gosling-stealing Ejike, would store the worms in transparent polythene bags and watch them writhe in the airless, enclosed space.

She came wearing open-toed slippers, whose plastic straps as well as her feet were caked with dust. A small purse dangled over her bosom, held around her neck by a fabric lace. As she walked up, her feet stamping the dirt, he wiped his hand on the wall by his door. He stepped back into the house and looked around in haste. He noticed for the first time the big yarn of cobwebs that stretched across the ceiling of the sitting room, reminding him that so much time had passed since his father, who had maintained a high level of cleanliness, died.

'Good afternoon, sir,' the woman said, genuflecting slightly.

'Good afternoon, my sister.'

The woman set down the groundnut tray, reached for a side pocket on her skirt, and brought out a handkerchief that was soaked through and spotted with shades of brown dirt. With it she wiped her forehead.

'How much, how much is—'

'Groundnut?'

My host thought he caught a slight tremble in the woman's voice – the way people influenced by the bias of their own minds misjudge the actions of others. I listened as he did, but I did not hear any tremor in her voice. She sounded absolutely composed to me.

'Yes, groundnut,' he said, nodding. Fluid rushed up his throat, leaving a peppery taste in his mouth. His discomposure came from the strange familiarity of her voice, which, although he could not ascertain the source of the familiarity, drew him to her.

The woman pointed to a small canned-tomato tin in which groundnuts were stacked and said, 'Five naira for one small cup. The big one is ten naira.'

'The ten-naira one.'

The woman shook her head. 'So, Oga, you bring me here so you fit buy only ordinary ten-naira groundnut? Ah, abeg add some more na.' Then she laughed.

He felt the sensation in his throat yet again. He first felt it during the period of his mourning. He did not know that it was a kind of sickness related to indigestion which flares in the pit of the stomach of a person who is bereaved or in a state of extreme anxiety. I had seen it many times, most recently in the body of my former host Ejinkeonye Isigadi, while he was fighting in the Biafran War nearly forty years before.

'Okay, give me two of the big ones,' he said.

'Er-he, thank you, Oga.'

The woman bent to scoop groundnuts into the larger tin, and then emptied it into a small colourless polythene bag. She was pouring the second scoop into the same bag when he said, 'I no want only groundnut.'

'Er?' She dropped her head.

She did not immediately look at him, but he fixed his eyes on her. He let his eyes linger over her face, which was rough and covered with signs of privation. Some encrusted layers of dirt covered her face like patches of extra flesh, somewhat redefining it. Yet beneath these layers, he could see that she possessed striking good looks. When she laughed, her dimples deepened and her mouth formed into a pout. There was a mole above her mouth, but he did not look much at it or at her cracked lips, which she continually licked to give them a glossy texture. Down on her chest, though, was where his eyes rested: on the ponderous breasts that appeared separated by ample space. They were round and full and pushed against her clothes, even though he could see the signs of restraint – her brassiere straps – sticking out on both sides of her shoulders.

'*Ina anu kwa Igbo?*' he said, and when she nodded, he turned fully to the language of the eloquent fathers. 'I want you to come stay with me a little. I am feeling lonely.'

'So you don't want groundnut?'

He shook his head. 'No, not only groundnut. I want to talk to you, too.'

He helped her straighten up, and as she rose, he locked his mouth with hers. Agbatta-Alumalu, although he feared that she would resist him, his urge had been so strong that it had overcome his inner voice of reason. He drew back and saw her stunned and unresisting. He even saw a glint of joy in her eyes, and he pressed harder. He drew closer to her and said, 'I want you to come inside with me.'

'*Isi gi ni?*' she said, laughing even more. 'You are a strange man.'

She'd used a word for 'strange' that was not commonly used in the language of the old fathers as spoken in Umuahia but which he often heard used in the big market in Enugu.

'Are you from Enugu?'

'Yes! How did you know?'

'Where in Enugu?'

'Obollo-Afor.'

He shook his head.

She turned from him briskly, and folded her hands together. 'You really are strange,' she said. 'Do you even know if I have a boyfriend?'

But he did not speak. He put her tray on the dining table, on the edge of which was dried chicken shit. As he put his hands around her and gently pulled her close to him, she whispered,

'So this is what you really want?' When he said it was, she struck his hand lightly and laughed as he undid her blouse.

Chukwu, I had by this time known my host for many years. But I could not recognise him that day. He acted like one possessed, unrecognisable even to himself. Where had he, a hermit who yielded little to the world outside his own, found the courage to ask a woman to lie with him? Where did he – who until his uncle suggested he get a woman had thought little of women – find the courage to undress a woman he just met? I did not know. What I knew was that with this uncharacteristic bravado, he stripped the woman's gown off her.

She held his hand with a hard grip for a long time and covered her mouth with her other hand, silently laughing to herself. They came into his room, and as he closed the door behind them, his heart pounding more quickly, she said, 'Look, I am dirty.' But he barely acknowledged those words. He focused on his own slightly quivering hands as they pulled down her underpants. When he was done, he said, 'It doesn't matter, Mommy.' Then he pulled her into the bed in which his father had died, consumed by a kind of passion that bore close affinity with rage. That passion etched itself in the curious changes that appeared in the woman's facial expressions: one time of delight; one time of anguish, in which she gnashed her teeth; one time of exhilaration that culminated in a small laugh; one time in a shock that held her mouth in a perplexing O shape; one time of a restless peace in which the eyes are closed as if in a pleasant, exhausted sleep. These passed across her visage in succession until the very last moment, when he began to suddenly wither. He barely heard her saying, 'Pull out, abeg,' before falling beside her, his expiration complete.

The act itself is hard to describe. They spoke no words but mourned, gasped, sighed, gnashed their teeth. The things in the room spoke in their stead: the bed uttered a mournful cry, and the sheets seemed to engage in a slow, considered speech like a child singing a rhyme. It all happened with the grace of a festival – so quickly, so suddenly, so vigorously, yet so tenderly. And in the end, of all the expressions that had passed over her face, only joy remained. He lay beside her, touched her lips, and rubbed her head until she laughed. The terrors that had lurked in his heart were gone in this moment. He sat up, a drop of sweat falling slowly down his back, unable to grasp the full expression of what he was feeling. He could see in her a certain kind of gratitude, for now she took his hand and held it firmly, so hard that he squirmed silently. Then she began to speak. She spoke about him with an unusual depth of mind, as if she'd known him for a long time. She said that although he acted strange, something in her spirit assured her that he was a 'good' man. A good man, she emphasised again and again. 'There aren't many like that in this world any more,' she said, and even though he was now drained and exhausted and half asleep, he could feel the resignation in her voice. Then it seemed that she raised her head and looked down at his penis and saw that long after it had emptied itself on the bedsheet it was still hard. She gasped. 'You are still erect? *Anwuo nu mu o!*'

He tried to speak, but he only mustered a babble.

'Ehen, I see you are falling asleep so quickly,' she said.

He nodded, embarrassed by his sudden, unexpected exhaustion.

'I will go so you can sleep.' She picked up her brassiere and started to put it over her breasts, something the venerable mothers would not have used, for they either covered their breasts with clothes knotted at the back or left them bare, or, sometimes, merely covered them with *uli*.

'Okay, but please come tomorrow,' he said.

She turned to him. 'Why? You don't even know, or ask, if I have a boyfriend.'

His mind awakened to the thought, but his eyes remained heavy. He mumbled incoherently words she could not hear but which I heard to be the baffling statement: 'If you come, so do come again.'

'You see, you can't even talk any more. I will go. But what is your name, at least?'

'Chinonso,' he said.

'Chi-non-so. Good name. I am Motu, you hear?' She clapped her hands. 'I am your new girlfriend. I will return tomorrow, around this time. Good night.'

He heard, in his slouched awakening, the sound of the door closing as she left the house. Then she was gone, carrying with her her distinct smell, a fragment of which had stuck on his hands and in his head.

AGBATTA-ALUMALU, the fathers of old say that without light, a person cannot sprout shadows. This woman came as a strange, sudden light that caused shadows to spring from everything else. He fell in love with her. In time, it seemed that with one slingshot, she had silenced his grief – that violent dog that had barked relentlessly in this early night of his life. So strong was their bond that he was mended. Even my relationship with him improved, because a man is truly able to commune with his chi when he is at peace. When I spoke, he heard my voice, and in his will, shadows of my will began to lurk. If he had lived at the time of the old fathers, they would have said of his state that he had affirmed something, and I, his chi, had affirmed, too, as it is wholly true that *onye kwe, chi ya e kwe.*

No human who experiences such moments would ever

want them to end. But sadly, in uwa, things do not always happen in accordance with the expectation of man. I have seen it many times. It was thus no surprise to me that he woke up on the day it all ended as he'd been waking for many mornings, filled with the thoughts of this woman with whom he'd enjoyed four market weeks of bliss (three weeks in the calendar of the White Man). Things had appeared usual for him that morning, as they had been for those twenty-one days, because man is without the powers of prospicience. This, I have come to believe, is mankind's greatest weakness. If only he could see the faraway as clearly as he can see what is in front of him, or if only he could see the hidden as he can see what is revealed, if only he could hear that which is not spoken as well as what is spoken, he would be saved from a great many calamities. In fact, what is it that would be able to destroy him?

My host spent that Saturday waiting for his lover to come. He did not know that nothing would walk over that path between two rows of farmland, which ran for nearly two kilometres to the main road, that day. He'd sat on the front porch and fixed his eyes on it from early in the morning, but as the day began to wane, things he had never considered rose from some abyss and held court with him. He had not thought to get Motu's address. He did not know where she lived. When he had asked once, begging to drive her home, she had said that her auntie would punish her severely if she ever found out Motu was keeping a boyfriend. And this had been the extent of his knowledge – that she was a maid from a village in Obollo-Afor, serving her 'auntie' – an acquaintance not related to her by blood – in the city. She did not have a phone. He knew nothing else.

That day also passed and another came galloping in like a great baffling carriage with a loud toot and a majestic stride.

He rushed to welcome it, almost trembling from the weight of expectation. But when he unlatched the door, the porch was empty. Nothing except the rust of an old carriage and a mocking sound of dry metal. The following day came garmented in the colours of a familiar sky, one that reminded him of the time Motu and he made love in the kitchen and he'd heard for the first time the sound of air emit from a vagina. It was also the first day she took a bath in his house and put on the dress he had bought her: a gown made of sparkling blue ankara material, which she then washed in a bucket in his bathroom and hung on the laundry rope in the yard that was fastened between the guava tree and a stick half buried in the fence. Then they'd had sex, and she had asked him things about poultry. He had found himself telling her so much about his life that he became aware, as if by epiphany, how heavy his history had become. By sundown, he knew she would not come. He lay all day, empty, alone and stunned, listening to the raindrops fall into the bucket and hit the ground like drumbeats.

Oseburuwa, I myself became worried. It is hard for a chi to watch its host find happiness and lose it again. I listened keenly for this woman, and sometimes, while he worked at the farm or poultry, I'd leave his body and stand on the porch to see if I might see her passing the compound so I could flash it as a thought in his head. But I, too, saw no trace of her. Vain spirits mocked him with dreams of her that night, and he woke the following morning disturbed. They were somewhere, in a temple or an old church, looking at the murals and paintings of saints. He gazed at one image, of a man on a tree, closely, and when he turned, he did not see her. In her place was a falcon. It stared at him with its yellow eyes, its beak half open, its great talons firm on the edge of one of the seats. He did not speak at first, for he knew that it was she. Egbunu, you know that in the dream world, knowledge is not searched after – things are simply known. Thus, he saw that she whom he'd been waiting for had become a bird. As he made to take it, he woke up.

By the end of the second week, and with ideas falling into his mind as if an ancient mouth was constantly spitting into his head, he realised that something had happened and that it was possible he would never see Motu again. It was, Gaganaogwu, an awakening: that a man can find a woman who accepts and loves him, and that one day, she could vanish without cause. The weight of this realisation would have brought him down had the universe not lent him a hand that day. For one of the ways a man may be relieved of suffering is by doing something out of the ordinary, something he will always remember. That memorable action forces a staunch on the bleeding wound and helps the sufferer recover.

On that day, he was sitting on the floor in his kitchen, watching the brown chickens, all roosters, grazing alongside the brown hens and chicks and walking about the yard, feeding from mounds of marsh and corn which he'd spread on sacks. From the window, he caught sight of a hawk hovering over the birds, biding its time. He quickly unhooked his catapult from the nail on which it hung on the wall and picked out stones from the small raffia basket by the window. He shook off and blew small red ants off the stones. Then, closing one of his eyes and standing a short distance behind the door to conceal himself, he placed a stone in the rubber pocket of the catapult and held still, his eyes on the hawk. The bird had stopped at some point in mid-air, then raised itself further above so the chickens did not see it. Its wingspan then broadened, and in a moment, it plunged towards the compound with stupefying speed. He followed it, and as it attempted to grab a cockerel feeding near the fence, he released the stone.

True, he was adept in this art of stone archery, and he'd been slinging stones since he was a child, but it is hard to understand how he got the bird on its forehead. There was something instinctive about it, something divine in origin. It felt, Chukwu, as if this act itself had been rehearsed many years ago, before he was born, before you assigned me to be his guardian spirit. It was this act that began his fresh healing. For it seemed as if he'd carried out revenge against that primal force with whom he must reckon, that unseen hand that takes away whatsoever he possesses. That voice that seems to say, 'Look, he has been happy for so long, it is now time to send him back to that dark place where he belongs.' And from the end of that second week, he began to live again.

Rain poured in the days following with a relentlessness that reminded my host of one year in his childhood, while his mother was still alive, when rain destroyed a neighbour's house and the family came to take shelter with my host's family. During these wet days, it was hard for his poultry to come out of the coops into the yard. He, like them, kept away from most things and recoiled into the lone world he'd become accustomed to. Chukwu, he would live like this for the next three months after Motu's disappearance, avoiding even Elochukwu as much as he could.

IJANGO-IJANGO, the great fathers often say that a child does not die because his mother's breast is empty of milk. This became true of my host. He soon became used to the loss of Motu and began going out again to execute his daily tasks. It was thus without any expectations that he went out that day at the end of those three months to fuel his van at the petrol station near his house, expecting to return home afterwards the way he had left. He stayed on the long line at the petrol station and had finally made it to the pump, stepped out to open his fuel tank for the attendant when he saw a hand waving at him from the line of cars behind. At first, he did not see who it was, for he had to tell the attendant, who had put the nozzle in his tank, that he wanted to buy six hundred naira worth of petrol.

'That is, eight litres. No change. Seventy-five, seventy-five naira.'

'Okay, madam.'

As the woman tapped something on the pump station and the numbers began to roll out, he turned back and saw that it was the woman on the bridge. How, Chukwu, could he have thought that on such an inauspicious and unremarkable day that which he had been looking for for so long would appear again, suddenly, and reveal itself to him of its own accord? Although he kept a close eye on the pump, fearing he could be cheated, because he had heard about how people manipulated them, the shock of this encounter fastened itself to a branch of his mind like a viper. In a mix of haste and anxiety, he pulled over to the side of the station, near a culvert that descended to the street below. No matter which system of time he employed – the system of the fathers, in which four days make up a week, twenty-eight days a month, and thirteen months a year, or the system of the White Man, now commonly used by the children of the great fathers – nine months had passed since that night when he sacrificed two fowls to scare her back to life. As he waited for her, he searched back to all that had happened to him since that encounter. When she parked her car behind his vehicle and stepped out to meet him, he felt the craving that seemed to have disappeared long ago emerge as if it had been merely hidden all this while in the back pocket of his heart like an old coin.

4

THE GOSLING

ANUNGHARINGAOBIALILI, when a man encounters something that reminds him of an unpleasant event in his past, he pauses at the door of the new experience, carefully considering whether or not to go in. If he has already stepped in, he may retrace his steps and reconsider whether to re-enter. Like my host, every man is inextricably chained to his past and may always fear that the past might repeat itself. So, with Motu still fresh in his mind, my host attended his desire for this woman with caution. He observed that she'd changed so much – as if she were not the same woman who had been mired in grief the night he first met her, at the bridge. She was taller than he remembered from that brief encounter. Her eyes were framed by a delicate arc, and her forehead shone from the backwards pull of her permed hair.

She reappeared more beautiful than the image he'd stored in his mind for so long. She came up to him after fuelling her car and shook his hand and introduced herself as Ndali Obialor in the language of the White Man, as she'd done on the bridge. He told her his name, too. He found her intimidating, not only her presence but also her facility with this language, which he rarely used. He was curious how she had been able to recognise him.

'Your vehicle, the sign on it, OLISA AGRICULTURE,' she said, laughing. 'I remember it. I saw you a month or so ago, near Obi Junction. But you were driving very fast. I just believed I would see you again.' A car honked for her to step out of the way, and when it had passed, she said, 'I've been looking for you. To thank you for that night. Thank you, really.'

'Thank you, me also,' he said.

She'd closed her eyes while speaking, and opened them now. 'I am going to school now. Can you come to Mr Biggs?'

She pointed at the eatery on the other side of the road. 'Can you come there by six o'clock today?'

He nodded.

'Okay, Chinonso. Bye-bye. Good to see you again.'

He watched her retrace her steps back to her car, wondering if all this while he had been looking for her he'd seen her without knowing it.

He'd seen in the woman's eyes something – something he could not himself define. There are times when a man cannot fully understand his feelings, and neither can his chi. His chi is often at a loss at those times. Hence this mystery hung like a small cloud over him as he went home to prepare for the meeting with her later that day. What was clear to me and to him was that she was not like anyone else he'd met. The accent she affected was of a person who had lived in the foreign countries of white people. And there was a lushness to her demeanour and appearance that was nothing like the ramshackle outlook of Motu or the strange mixture of poise and feistiness of Miss J. And, Egbunu, when men meet those whom they esteem highly above themselves, they become measured in their actions, they check themselves, they try to present themselves before these people in a way that will earn them dignity. I have seen it many times.

So when he got home, he spread two sacks on the ground and poured millet and maize on them, then he unbarred the coops of the adult fowls. They rushed out and covered the sacks. In haste, he filled the water troughs and put them back in each of the cages. He brought out one of the suits he'd inherited from his father. With a sponge he'd cut a few days before from a grain sack, he brushed off a stain on the suit. Then he hung it to dry on a branch of the tree in the yard. He washed himself and was about to bring in the suit when it struck him that his hair was bushy. He had not cut it in nearly three months, since that day when Motu, insisting she could do it, cut it with scissors and he swept the yard in a frenzy afterwards, fearing one of his flocks would eat a strand of the hair. In haste, he drove to the salon on Niger Road, where he'd gone since he was a child. The man, Mr Ikonne, his barber, had suffered a stroke, and the man's eldest son, Sunday, now did it. When my host's turn came and Sunday began cutting his hair, the clipper went quiet suddenly. Seeing there had been a power outage, Sunday rushed to the back of the shop to put on the generator, but it would not start. My host glanced at himself in the mirror: half his head was cleanly shaved; the other half was full of tangled, bushy hair. He gazed about, stepped out of the swivelling chair, and sat back again. He was in flux, anxious, for the moving clock – the strange mysterious object with which the children of the fathers now measure time – showed that it was close to the hour when he should meet the woman.

Sunday came in a bit later, his hands black from working the generator, his shirt soaked in sweat, his trousers smeared with black dirt. 'I am sorry,' he said. 'The generator has developed a fault.'

My host's heart sank. 'Is it fuel?'

It was not, Sunday told him. 'It is the ignition. It is the ignition. I need to take it to a rewire. I am very very sorry, Nonso, we will finish the haircut any time NEPA restores power, oh. Or tomorrow after I repair the gen. *Biko eweliwe, Nwannem, oh.*'

My host nodded and said in the language of the White Man, 'No problem.' He turned back to the darkening mirror and gazed at his half-shaved head. Sunday unhooked a hat from the many on the wall and gave it to him. He wore it and headed for the restaurant.

EGBUNU, one of the most striking differences between the way of the great fathers and their children is that the latter have adopted the White Man's idea about time. The White Man reckoned long ago that time is divine – an entity to whose will man must submit. Following a prescribed tick, one will arrive at a particular place, certain that an event will begin at that set time. They seem to say, 'Brethren, an arm of divinity is amongst us, and it has set its purpose at twelve forty, so we must submit to its dictates.' If something happens, the White Man obliges himself to ascribe it to time – 'On this day, July twentieth, 1985, such-and-such happened.' Whereas time to the august fathers was something that was both spiritual and human. It was in part beyond their control and was ordered by the same force that brought the universe into existence. When they wanted to discern the beginning of a season or parse the age of a day or measure the length of years, they looked to nature. Has the sun risen? If it has, then it must be day. Is the moon full? If it is, then we must gather our best clothing, empty our barns and get ready to celebrate the new year! If in fact the sound we hear is thunderclaps, then surely the drought must have ended and the raining season must be upon us. But also, the wise fathers believed that there is a part of time that man can control, a means by which man can subject time to his own will. To them, time is not divine; it is an element, like air, that can be put to use. They can use air to put out fires, blow insects out of people's eyes, or even cause flutes to produce music. This is the same way that time can be subject to the will of man – when a group among the fathers says, for instance, 'We, the elders of Amaokpu, have a meeting at sunset.' That time is expansive. It could be the beginning of sunset, or its middle, or its end. But even this does not matter. What matters is that they know the number of those coming to the meeting. Those who arrive ahead of others wait, talk, laugh until everyone is there, and that's when the meeting begins.

It was thus following the prescribed tick of the clock that she got there before him. She looked even better than she'd looked earlier, wearing deep red lipstick that reminded him of Miss J and a dress that had leopard prints on it.

After he sat down and adjusted his cap to make sure it concealed every part of his head, she said, 'Eh, Nonso, I want to ask you: why did you go to that bridge at that very moment and stop?' As he made to answer, she raised her hand, her eyes closed. 'I really want to know, really. Why did you go there at that very time?'

He raised his head to look above her, to the ceiling, to avoid her eyes.

'I don't know, Mommy,' he said. He picked his words with care, for rarely did he have to speak in the language of the White Man. 'Something just pushed me there. I was coming from way back in Enugu, and then I saw you. I just say let me stop.'

He glanced out of the window, allowed his eyes to fall on a child rolling a motorcycle tyre along the road with a stick, trailed by other children.

'You saved my life that day. You will never—'

The ringing of her phone made her pause. She unwrapped it from a handkerchief in her purse, and on seeing the screen she said, 'Ah! I was supposed to go somewhere with my parents now. But I forgot before. I am so sorry, but I have to go now.'

'Okay, okay—'

'Where is your poultry? I would like to see it. What street?'

'It is number twelve Amauzunku, off Niger Road.'

'Okay, give me your number.' He leaned in towards her and listed the numbers in their order. 'I will come there one of these days. I will call you, later, so we can meet again.'

Because I could see in my host the beginning of the growth of that great seed that bears strong root downwards in the soul of a man and bears fruit upwards – the fruit of affection that becomes love – I came out of him and followed the woman. I wanted to know what she would do – if she would remain and not vanish, as the previous woman had done. I followed this woman in her car as she drove, and I saw on her face an expression of joy. I heard her say, 'Chinonso, funny man,' and then laugh. I was watching, curiously observing, when from within her something floated out, like a thick-formed steam rising. And within the batting of an eyelid, what stood before me was a spirit whose face and appearance were exactly like the woman's, save for her luminous body, covered with *uli* symbols, and her extremities, graced with beads and strings of cowries. It was her chi. Even though I'd been told many times at the caves of spirits that the guardian spirits of the females of mankind possessed more powers of sensitivity, I was astonished at how it was able to see me while still in the body of its host.

—Son of the spirits, what do you want from my host? the chi said in a voice as thin as that of the maidens who dwell on the road to Alandiichie.

—Daughter of Ala, I come in peace, I come not with trouble, I said.

Chukwu, I saw that the chi, who was clothed in the bronze skin of light with which you drape the guardian spirits of the daughters of mankind, regarded me with eyes that were the colour of pure fire. She had begun to speak when her host honked and pulled to a sudden stop, shouting, 'Jesus Christ! What are you doing, Oga. You no sabi drive?' The car that had veered in her way turned towards another street, and she continued on, sighing loudly. Perhaps now certain her host was fine, the chi turned back to me and spoke in the esoteric language of Benmuo.

—My host has erected a figurine in the shrine of her heart. Her intentions are pure as the waters of the seven rivers of Osimiri, and her desire is as true as the clean salt beneath the waters of Iyi-ocha.

—I believe you, Nwayibuife, guardian spirit of the dawn light, daughter of Ogwugwu, and Ala, and Komosu. I only came because I wanted to be sure that she desires him, too. I shall return with your message to comfort my host. May their union bring them fulfilment in this cycle of life and in the seventh and eighth cycles of life – Uwa ha asaa, uwa ha asato!

—Iseeh! she said, and without a moment's wait, she returned into her host.

Oseburuwa, I was greatly delighted by this consultation. And with this confidence, I returned to my host and flashed it in his thoughts that the woman loved him.

*

AKWAAKWURU, even with the thoughts I put in his head that she loves him, he was still afraid. I could not tell him what I had done. A chi cannot communicate with its host in such a direct way. The human would not understand even if we did. We can only flash thoughts in their minds, and if a host finds these reasonable, he may believe them. So I watched helplessly as he went about with an increased palpitation, fearing that, like Motu, she will be gone again. For days he paid curious attention to his phone, waiting for her to call. Then, on the fourth day, while he was sleeping on his sofa in the sitting room, he heard a car drive into his compound down towards his house. It was after sunset, and the shadows that had sprouted at the height of the day had already become old. When he looked through the window, he saw Ndali's car pulling to a stop. He cried, 'Chukwu!' He had eaten lunch not too long before, and the plastic bowl sat on the stool beside him, still containing water in which a small empty bag that had contained groundnuts and a plastic sachet of Cowbell powdered milk were floating. He dropped the bowl in the kitchen sink. Then he ran to his room and put on the trousers that lay on the bed. He glanced quickly in the mirror on the wall of his room, grateful that Sunday had finally cut his hair two days earlier. When he rushed back into the sitting room, his eyes fell on the blue box of sugar cubes that sat half closed on the centre table, beside a globular stain. And at the foot of the table, on the plastic bag containing thread, needles and a small sack of nails. She was knocking while he took these away. He returned again a moment later and looked about the house to see if there was anything he could clean, and when he did not see anything whose oddity he could very quickly fix, he ran to the door, still holding on to his chest to stabilise the heartbeat. Then he opened the door.

'How did you find me?' he said once she came in.

'Do you live on the moon, er, mister-man?'

'No, but Mommy, how? It is hidden, and the numbers are not even clear sef.'

She shook her head, wearing a gentle smile. Then she said his name with a slow, dragging enunciation, the way a child learning to speak might say it, No-n-so.

'Would you give me a seat?'

He threw his eyes about the room again and nodded. She sat on the big sofa near the window while he stood transfixed at the door. Then, almost at once, she rose and began walking about the sitting room. As she did, he became worried that she would perceive the smell that hung in the air. He observed her nose for any sign of her scrunching it or covering it. He noticed then, with even greater alarm, that there was a clearly perceptible stain on the wall. He feared it might be chicken shit. He went and stood in front of the stain, wearing a smile that concealed his distress.

'You live alone, Nonso?'

'Yes, I live here alone. Only me. My sister doesn't come, except my uncle who comes sometimes,' he said with haste.

Her nod did not translate into attention, for as he spoke, she stepped into the kitchen. The state of the kitchen made his heart sink. The arches around four sides of the ceiling had cobwebs that were blackened with soot, making it look as though spiders nestled in them. The sink was full of dirty plates, on one of which was a sponge hewn from a plaited-thread sack, a shrivelled green piece of soap trapped in its netting. Even more shameful to him was something he was not immediately responsible for: the tap on the sink. It had long atrophied into disuse, and its head had been removed and simply replaced with a piece of a black polythene bag. His kerosene stove, too, was dirty. It sat on a blackened slab of wood. It wore the singed skin of the chicken he'd roasted on its top levers, and around its top perimeter were grains of dried rice and what looked like a dried tomato skin. Even worse, at the far corner, behind the door that led to the yard, was a dustbin full of rubbish from which a putrid smell simmered.

Egbunu, he would have died if she'd lingered in the kitchen for a moment more after she turned on the light and roused the thread of flies gathered around the stack of unwashed plates. He was relieved when he saw the net door open slightly and its spring give way, creaking as it opened into the backyard.

'You have many chickens!' she said.

He walked up to her. She had one leg on the threshold, the other in the yard. She leaned back into the kitchen towards him.

'You have many chickens,' she repeated, as if in surprise.

'Yes, I'm a poultry farmer.'

'Wow,' she said. She stepped out into the yard, staring wide-eyed at the coops. Then, without saying a word, she returned to the sitting room and sat back on the sofa beside her purse. He followed her and caught a glimpse of her underpants as she sat down, briefly spreading her legs. He joined her, frightened because of the things she had seen. She did not speak for a while but kept looking at him in a way that so discomforted him that he wanted to ask her if she despised him because of the state of his house, but the words lay loaded in his mouth like a fodder in a cannon, awaiting the signal to fire. To prevent her from looking around the house again, he sought to engage her in conversation.

'What happened to you that night?' he said.

'I was going to die,' she said and dropped her eyes to the floor.

Her words softened his shame.

'Why?'

Without hesitation, she told him she'd woken up the morning of the day before to find the world she'd so carefully built crumpled into dusty ruins. She had been crushed for two whole days by an e-mail from her betrothed, which had announced that he had married a British woman. The blow, she told him, was unbearable because she had given that man five years of her life, gathered all her savings, and even stolen from her father to help him achieve his dream of getting a degree in film directing from a school in London. But barely five months into this move to Britain, he was married. With a voice filled with so much pain my host could feel it, she explained how nothing had prepared her for the blow she felt.

'Nothing to hold on to, nothing to even – nothing. Throughout that day before I saw you on that bridge, I was tired because I had tried, tried, tried to reach him, but nothing, Nonso.'

She had gone to the river not because she had any strength or will to kill herself but because the river was all she could think of after reading the e-mail for the umpteenth time. She did not know whether she would have jumped off the bridge if he had not come.

My host listened with a keen ear to her story, only speaking once – to ask her to ignore the chickens that had begun to squawk plaintively.

'What happened to you is very painful,' he said, although he'd not understood all of it. Her command of the White Man's language contained more words than he could comprehend. His mind had hovered, for instance, over the word *circumstances* like a kite over a gathering of hen and chicks, unable to decide how or which to attack. But I understood everything she said, because every cycle of a chi's existence is an education in which a chi acquires the minds and wisdom of its hosts, and these become part of the chi. A chi may come to know, for instance, the intricacies of the art of hunting because once, hundreds of years before, the chi inhabited a host who was a hunter. In my last cycle, I guided an extraordinarily gifted man who read books and wrote stories, Ezike Nkeoye, who was the older brother of the mother of my present host. By the time he was my current host's age, he'd come to be familiar with almost every word in the language of the White Man. And it was from him that I acquired much of what I now know. And even now, as I testify on behalf of my current host, I wear his words as well as mine and see things through his eyes as well as mine, and both sometimes meld into an indistinguishable whole.

'It is very painful. I am talking like this because I have suffered too much also. I no have father and mother. In fact, no family.'

'Ah! That is very sad,' she said, putting her hand over her wide-open mouth. 'I am sorry. Very sorry.'

'No, no, no, I am now fine. I am fine,' he said, even though the voice of his conscience was tugging at him for having left out his sister, Nkiru. He watched Ndali rest her weight on her thigh and tilt her body towards the small table centred between them. Her eyes were closed, and this made him think that she was sinking into pity for him, and he feared that she might cry for him.

'I am fine now, Mommy,' he said even more resolutely. 'I have a sister, but she is in Lagos.'

'Oh, junior or senior sister?'

'Junior,' he said.

'Okay, why I have come is because I have come to thank

you.' A smile washed across her tearful face as she pulled her bag up from the floor.

'I believe God sent you to me.'

'Okay, Mommy,' he said.

'What's this "Mommy" you keep saying? Why do you say it?'

Her laughter now made him conscious of his own feral laughing, which he'd tried to contain to avoid embarrassing himself.

'Really, it is strange oh!'

'I don't have a mother again, so every good woman is my mommy.'

'Oh, so sorry, my dear!'

'Am coming,' he said and went to the toilet to urinate. When he returned, she said, 'Did I forget to say that I love your laugh?'

He looked at her.

'I do. Seriously. You're a beautiful man.'

He nodded hastily as she rose to leave and let his heart take temporary flight at this extremely unexpected outcome of what he had been certain would be a disaster.

'I have not even offered you something.'

'No, no, don't worry,' she said. 'Another time. I have tests.'

He thrust his hand out to shake hers, and she took it, her face wide with smiles.

'Thank you.'

Guardian spirits of mankind, have we thought about the powers that passion creates in a human being? Have we considered why a man could run through a field of fire to get to a woman he loves? Have we thought about the impact of sex on the body of lovers? Have we considered the symmetry of its power? Have we considered what poetry incites in their souls, and the impress of endearments on a softened heart? Have we contemplated the physiognomy of love – how some relationships are stillborn, some are retarded and do not grow, and some fledge into adults and last through the lifetime of the lovers?

I have given much thought to these things and know that when a man loves a woman he is changed by it. Although she willingly gives herself to him, once he marries her she becomes his. The woman becomes his possession, and he becomes her possession. The man calls her Nwuyem, and she calls him Dim. Others speak of her as *his* wife and of him as *her* husband. It is a mystifying thing, Egbunu! For I have seen many times that people, after their beloveds have left them, try to reclaim them as one would attempt to reclaim property that had been stolen. Wasn't this the case with Emejuiwe, who, one hundred and thirty years ago, killed the man who took his wife from him? Chukwu, when you laid down your judgment after my testimony on his behalf here in Beigwe, as I am doing now, it was sad but just. Now, more than a hundred years later, when I saw my current host's heart lit with similar fire, I feared because I knew the potency of that fire, that it was powerful, so powerful that in time nothing might be able to quench it. As he walked her to her car, I feared it would push him in a direction in which I might be powerless to stop him from going. I feared that when the love had fully formed in his heart, it would blind him and make him deaf to my counsel. And I could see already that it had started to possess him.

OBASIDINELU, oh what substance does a woman bring into the life of a man! In the doctrine of the new religion the children of the fathers have embraced, it is said that the two become *one flesh*. What truth, Egbunu! But let's look at the times of the wise fathers, how indispensable the great mothers were. Although they did not make the laws that guided society, they were like the chi of society. They restored order and equilibrium when order became broken. If a member of a village committed a spiritual crime and vexed Ala, and if the merciful goddess – in her rightful indignation – poured out her wrath in the form of diseases or drought or catastrophic deaths, it was the old mothers who went to a dibia and consulted on behalf of the society. For Ala hears their voices above those of the others. Even when there was a war – as I witnessed one hundred and seventy-two years ago, when Uzuakoli fought against Nkpa and seventeen headless men lay in the forests – it was the mothers on both sides who marched and restored peace and pacified Ala. This is why they are called *odoziobodo*. If a group of women can restore equilibrium to a community on the verge of calamity, how much more one woman can do to the life of one man! As the great fathers often say, love changes the temperature of a man's life. Usually, a man whose life was cold becomes warm, and this warmth, in its intensity, transforms the person. It grows the small things in his life and puts shine on the spots in the fabric of his life. What the man did every day, now he does more cheerfully. Most people in their lives would come to know that something in them had changed. They may not need to speak of it to anyone. But their faces, the most naked of all features of human physiognomy, begin to wear a hue that anyone who pays attention soon notices. Say, if a man works in the company of other people, one of his colleagues may pull him aside and say to him, 'You look happy,' or 'What happened to you?' The stronger the affection, the more obvious it will become to others, and my host's affection for Ndali was tempered by his fear that he was unworthy of her. He resolved that if she ever gave in to him, he would give her the fullness of his heart.

In lieu of human co-workers, the fowls bore witness to my host's metamorphosis. He fed them ecstatically after the woman left his house that day. He found the sick rooster who'd developed a wry tail and took it to the edge of the farm, in front of the house and away from the sight of other fowls, and slaughtered it. He let its blood drain into a small hole in the earth, and then put it in a bowl and kept it in the refrigerator. After he'd washed his hands in the bathroom, he swept the large pens that were parted into halves by wooden walls. He chased a particular kind of lizard which the fowls did not like, the green-headed lizard, into a hole in the ceiling. Then he climbed up a ladder and stuffed a bunched-up rag with palm-oil stains into the hole. When he was done with it, he noticed that the chickens had upturned the basin of water from which they drank, and now it lay, leaning against the thatch wall, an eye-size pool of water anchored in it. Within the puddle lay a patch of sediment that stared back at him like a pupil. As he walked towards the bowl, he stepped on something he discovered to be the rib of a feather. It slid down in a straight line through the muddied earth, tripping him. He fell against the other empty basin, and it balled up into the air and emptied its contents – a mass of dirt, feathers and dust – on to his face.

Chukwu, if the chickens were humans, they would have laughed at what his face became afterwards: a rich patch of dirt and mud on his forehead and over his nose. Were I not myself a witness, I would have doubted what I saw in my host that day. For, despite his pain and feeling the spot on his head with his fingers repeatedly and looking at them to see if the wound would bleed, he was happy. He rose, laughing at himself, thinking of how Ndali had sat on the sofa and called him a beautiful man. He looked down where he'd fallen and saw a shaved part of the floor, which his shoes now wore like an encrustation. On the other side of the pen stood a hen on which he'd almost fallen. It had leapt hysterically out of his reach as he fell, raising dust and feathers with its violent wings flapping. He recognised it as one of the two hens that laid grey eggs. It stood crowing in protest, and others had joined. He left the coop and washed the dirt off himself, and all the while, even when he lay in bed later, Ndali remained in his mind.

Once he slept, as it often happens when he goes into the unconscious state of sleep, I became stripped of the barriers of his body. Even without stepping out of it, I am often able to see that which I'm not able to see while he is awake. As you know, you created us as creatures for whom sleep does not exist. We exist as shadows which speak the language of the living. Even when our hosts sleep, we remain awake. We watch over them against the forces that breathe in the night. While men sleep, the world of the ethereal is replete with the noise of wakefulness and the susurration of the dead. Agwus, ghosts, akaliogolis, spirits and ndiichies on short visits to the earth all crawl out of the blind eyes of the night and tread the earth with the liberty of ants, oblivious to human boundaries, unaware of walls and fences. Two spirits arguing may struggle and tumble into the house of a family and fall on them and continue to wrestle through them. Sometimes, they merely walk into the habitations of men and watch them.

That night, like most others, was filled with the din of spirits and the brass drum of the sublunary world, a multitude of voices emitting cries, shouts, voices, howls, noises. The world, Benmuo and Ezinmuo – its corridor – were soaked in them. And from a distance, the riveting tune of a flute riffled through the air, pulsing like an animate thing. It remained like this for a long time when, around midnight, something shot through the wall with uncanny speed. Instantly, it ringed itself into a luminous coil that was greyish and almost imperceptible to the eyes. At first it seemed to rise towards the roof, but slowly it began to diffuse and elongate like a serpent of shadows. Then it morphed into a most frightening agwu – with a roachlike head and a portly human body. I lunged forward at once and ordered it to leave. But it gazed at me with eyes filled with hate, then stared mostly at my host's unconscious body. Its mouth was sticky, glued together as if by some purulent secretion. It kept pointing at my host, but I insisted it leave. When it did not so much as stir, I became afraid that this evil creature would harm my host. I trailed into an incantation, fortifying myself as I invoked your intervention. This seemed to stop the being in its place. It stepped back, let out a growl, and vanished.

I had encountered spirits like this in my many cycles on earth, and I recall most vividly, while inhabiting Ejinkeonye during the war, that he'd slept in a half-destroyed, abandoned house in Umuahia, and while he was asleep, a spirit material- ised with such swiftness that I gave a start. I looked, but it had no head. It was waving its arms, stamping its feet and gesturing at the stump where its head had been. Egbunu, not even an akaliogoli, those creatures of dreadful forms, had inspired such terrors in a living spirit like me. Then, by some transmutative power, the creature's head emerged and hung in mid-air, its eyes glancing about. The headless creature would try to take the head with its flailing hands, but it would swerve that way and the other way, until finally the head floated away the way it had come, and the spirit followed it. I would find out the following day, through the eyes of my host, that the man had been an enemy soldier beheaded while raping a pregnant woman, and had become an akaliogoli. My host, Ejinkeonye, would watch the body of the man being burned the following morning, unaware of what had happened the night before.

I leapt up presently and tried to catch up with the spirit, to find out why it had targeted my host, but I could not tell which direction it had gone. I found no trace of it on the plains of the night, no footprints on the track of the air, no footfalls in the dark tunnelling beneath the earth. The night was full mostly of bright stars in the sky, and a multitude of spirits were about their business around the vicinity of my host's farm. No humans were about, nor was there even any trace of them except for the sound of cars racing past along some road in an unknown distance. I had the temptation to wander a bit, but I suspected that the agwu I had seen was a vagabond spirit in search of a human vessel to possess, and it could return to try to inhabit my host. So I made my way back to the compound as quickly as I could, projecting through the fence in the backyard, then through the wall into the room where my host lay still deep in sleep.

AKWAAKWURU, he woke to the wild noises of his crowd of fowls the following morning. One of them was crowing without cease, letting its voice ebb at intervals, then beginning again in a higher pitch than before. He pushed aside the wrappa he'd covered himself in and was starting to step out of the door when he realised he was naked. He put on shorts and a wrinkled shirt and went to the backyard. He emptied the last contents of a bag of mash into a bowl and set the bowl at the centre of the yard on an old newspaper page. When he unlocked one of the cages, the birds flung themselves at him at once, and in the batting of an eye, the bowl was covered in a goo of feathery beings.

He stepped back, his eyes scanning them for signs of anything out of the ordinary. He watched one of the hens especially, the one whose wing had caught an errant nail sticking out of one of the cages. The bird had tried to pull itself away from the nail so hard that it had almost ripped out its wing. He'd stitched the wing with a thread the previous week, and now the bird participated in the scramble for the mash with cautious gait, the red thread of the stitching visible beneath its wing. He picked up the hen by its legs. He checked its wings, tracing his fingers around the veins on the end. As he made to drop it, his phone rang. He ran into the house to get it. But by the time he got into the living room, the ringing had stopped. He saw that Ndali had just called him and sent a text message. He hesitated at first to read it – as if he feared that what he would read on the screen would remain for eternity unerasable. He dropped the phone back on the dining table, placed his palm on his forehead, and gnashed his teeth. I could see that he had become sick from the head wound of the previous day. From the top of the refrigerator, he took a sachet of paraceta-mol and ejected one of the remaining two tablets into his palm. He placed the medicine on his tongue, went into the kitchen, and washed it down with water from a plastic jug.

He picked up the phone again and read the message: Nonso, should I come and visit you in the evening? Chukwu, he smiled to himself, pumped his fist into the air, and shouted 'Yes!' He dropped the phone into his pocket and was almost back in the yard when he remembered he'd merely answered in speech as if she were there with him. He stood by the net door to the yard and typed 'yes' into his phone.

Lit with the prospect of meeting Ndali, he gathered some eggs and placed them in the egg-shaped holes on a plastic crate. Then he took hold of the wounded bird once more. Its eyes blinked with fear, its beak opening and closing as he rubbed its head and examined its wings to see if it could accommodate flight. He cleaned the mash tray and placed some mash on it.

Something like a half-broken toothpick stuck out of the feed. He picked it up and threw it behind him. Then, on second thought, fearing one of the fowls might find it there and swallow it, he rose and began looking for the stick. He found it just near one of the cages, the one for the small chicks. The stick was on the wet edge of the slab of wood on which he'd placed the cage. He picked it up and threw the stick over the fence into the dump outside his compound. Then he tucked the tray of mash into the bed of one of the two cages.

By the time he finished feeding the poultry, his hands were almost black with dirt. Dark grime lay in his fingernails, and the flesh of his right thumb looked barbed and was lined with welts. One of the eggs he'd picked was coated with a stiff encrustation of faeces, which he tried to scratch off with his fingers, and it was the crust of faeces that he now carried in his fingernails. As he washed his hands in the bathroom, he was thinking about how odd his work was and how lowly it seemed to be to one newly encountering it. He feared that Ndali may not come to love it or might even be irritated by it if she came to really understand the nature of his work.

Chukwu, as I said before, this kind of fear-induced rumination often occurs when people have been made self-conscious by the presence of others whom they hold in high esteem. They assess themselves by focusing on how others would perceive them. In such situations, there may be no limit to the self-defeating thoughts that may form in the person's mind, which – no matter how unfounded – may consume them in the end. My host did not, however, dwell on these thoughts for too long. He was, instead, in a haste to prepare for Ndali's visit. He swept the house and the balcony clean. Then he dusted the cushions and sofas. He washed the toilet bowl and sprayed Izal into it and cleaned out the rat faeces behind the water drum.

He threw away one of the plastic buckets, a paint bucket that had cracked in several places. Then he sprayed air freshener around the house. He'd just finished bathing and was creaming his body when, through the window, he saw her car coming towards the house, flanked on both sides by the plantations.

Ijango–ijango, my host felt his body lit with admiration at her appearance that evening. Her hair was dressed in a way the great mothers would have found strange but which made it shiny and attractive to my host. He gazed closely at the neatly permed hair, her wristwatch, the bangles around her wrist, the necklace with green beads that reminded him of his own mother's sister, Ifemia, who lived in Lagos and with whom he'd long since lost contact. Although he'd already begun to feel unworthy of Ndali because of his lack of exposure (he had never been to a club before, or to a theatre), he sank even lower in his own estimation when he saw her that evening. Although she engaged him with utmost geniality and affection, he stood with a strong feeling of unworthiness. So he attended their conversations like one forced to be there, saying only what was needed and what was prompted.

'Did you always want to be a poultry farmer?' Ndali said at one point, later than he'd expected, deepening his fear that in the end, she would not give herself to him.

He nodded, then it occurred to him that that might be a lie. So he said, 'Maybe, no, Mommy. My father started the idea, not me.'

'The poultry?'

'Yes.'

She gazed on at him, a restrained smile on her face.

'How? But how?' she said.

'It's a long story, Mommy.'

'God! Ah, I want to hear it. Please tell me.'

He looked up at her and said, 'Okay, Mommy.'

Ebubedike, he told her about the gosling, beginning with how it was caught when he was only nine years old, an encounter which changed his life, and which I must relate to you now. His father took him from the city to his village one day and told him to sleep, that in the morning he would take him into the Ogbuti forest, where a species of wool-white geese lived near a hidden pool in the very heart of the forest. Most hunters avoided this part of the forest for fear of deadly snakes and wild beasts. The pool was a tributary of the Imo River. I have seen it many times. Long ago, before Aro slave raiders began sweeping this part of Alaigbo, the river used to flow. But it was cut off by an earthquake which separated it from the rest of the river and made it into a stagnant body of water that became the home of the white geese. They had lived there for as long as anyone in the nine villages that surround the forest could remember.

When my host and his father, who carried a long Dane gun, got to this spot, they stopped behind the stump of a rotting fallen trunk covered by grass and wild mushrooms. Two stone throws from the trunk was the dead pool, half covered with leaves. Beside it was a riparian stretch of matted, damp land strewn with splinters of wood. It was here that a flock of white geese was gathered, grazing. As if alerted to the human presence, most of the flock whipped their wings and flew into the denser part of the forest, leaving only a mother goose and her offspring and another big goose in the field. The third goose leapt a few times and began floating across the distant waters until it reached the reef, then it vanished into the greenery. My host observed the mother goose with fascination. Its plumage was rich and its tails serrated downwards. Its eyes were wide and it had a brown beak with nares. When it moved, it spread its wings into a cascading flourish. The gosling beside it was different: its neck was longer and bare at the top, as if plucked. It tottered forward on its tiny feet after its mother, who'd begun moving away from the nestling. My host's father had brought his gun to bear and would have shot it if a perplexing vision had not suddenly presented itself. The mother goose, who had stopped in a place of soft earth so that her feet sank into the mud, was now waiting with her mouth wide-open. The gosling, clattering, approached and buried its head into the waiting mouth till part of its neck disappeared.

My host and his father watched in wonder as the gosling's head and neck probed into its mother's mouth. As the child fed, its mother struggled for balance. She dug her feet deeper into the clump of mud, fluttering her wings violently, stepping back with steady haste, her claws folding and unclasping. For a moment, it seemed to my host that the big goose's throat might tear open as the little bird gorged greedily within it. The movement of the gosling's beak could be glimpsed through the pale skin of its mother's throat. It came almost as a surprise to my host when the gosling disentangled itself and began sprinting away, fluttering its wings and full of life like one reborn. Its mother turned her head, gave a cry, and seemed to fall on her legs. Then she rose, caked in a half cloth of mud, and began racing in the direction where my host and his father were crouched.

The bird was close when his father took aim. The shot flung the goose backwards with a loud noise, leaving in its wake an explosion of feathers. The forest erupted into a hysteria of fleeing creatures and a chorus of fluttering wings. As the feathers settled, my host saw the gosling hurrying towards its mother's body.

'I did it, I finally shot an Ogbuti goose,' his father said, as he stood up and began running towards the dead goose. My host followed at a cautious pace, speechless. His father picked up the dead goose, exhilarated, and began walking in the direction from which they had come, the blood of the dead goose marking his trail. His father did not notice the gosling scampering along after him, making a shrilling sound which, many years later, my host would realise was the sound of a weeping bird. He stood still, listening to his father talk about how for years he'd longed to catch an Ogbuti forest goose – 'always said no one knew where they lived. How could anyone know? Only a few people will ever venture this far into the Ogbuti. People only saw them in the air. And, you know, it is very hard to shoot something in the air. This—' – until his father, turning abruptly, saw him standing back, afar.

'Chinonso?' his father said.

He looked up with a pout, his eyes near tears. 'Sir,' he said in the language of the White Man.

'What? What is it?'

He pointed at the gosling. His father looked down and saw the gosling moving its legs in the swamp, its eyes fixed on the two humans as it wept for its dead mother.

'Heh, why don't you pick it up and bring it home?'

My host walked towards his father and stopped behind the bird.

'Why don't you keep him?' his father said again.

He glanced at the bird, then at his father, and something lit up in him.

'Can I bring it to Umuahia?'

'Uh,' his father said, and turned back again to the path from which they had come with the dead goose, whose body was now half covered in crimson in his hand. 'Now catch it, and let's go.'

With hesitation, dragging his feet, he dived forward and caught the gosling by its thin legs. The bird mourned plaintively, beating its wings against the tender hands that held it. But he tightened his grip around its legs as he lifted it from the ground. He looked up at his father, who was waiting, blood dripping from the dead goose in his hand.

'It is yours now,' his father said. 'You have saved it. Take it and let us go.' Then turning, his father began walking back to the village, and he followed.

He then told her about how he loved the bird. The bird often flew into moods of rage, then calmed and lifted its spirit. It would sometimes make a mad dash towards nothing, perhaps intent to return to the forest from which it'd come. And when it saw no chance of escape it would circle back in defeat. He watched over it closely, with anxiety. He lived in perpetual fear that something bad would happen to the bird or that it might some day escape from him. This fear was most pronounced in the times when the gosling would, in anger, begin dashing about the house, from wall to wall, trying to break through it and flee. And after every such struggle, it would return to a chair or a table, its head bent as in some kind of prostration. It would hold its wings suspended as it cawed in fury or frustration.

'Yes,' he said in answer to her question: there were times the gosling was calm. He knew that it was in the nature of earthly creatures that even the most wounded of them is sometimes peaceful in captivity. These were times when the gosling slept in his bed, by his side, as though it were a human companion. When he first came to Umuahia with the gosling, the children of the neighbourhood flocked to see it. At first, he guarded it jealously, not allowing anyone to touch the raffia cage in which he kept the bird. He would even fight with some of his friends who lived around the neighbourhood and played football with him if they tried to touch it without his permission. One of them, Ejike, with whom he'd been best friends, was particularly enamoured of the bird. Ejike sought it more than the others, and, in time, my host allowed him to play with it often. Then one day, Ejike asked to take the gosling to his house so he could show it to his grandmother, saying, 'For five minutes, only five minutes.' Oseburuwa, I had seen the look in the eyes of this child, and I'd feared that in them, deep within, I could see the small flame of envy burning. For I have seen it many times in the children of men: that negative side of admiration that has caused many murders and dark conspiracies. I flashed it in my host's mind that he should not give away the gosling. But he would not hear me. He gave the bird to his friend, confident no harm would come to the bird.

Ejike took the gosling away. When by sunset he still had not returned it, my host became anxious. He went to Ejike's house and knocked on the door of the flat Ejike and his mother occupied, but heard nothing. He called Ejike's name many times, but received no answer. The door was bolted from within. But from the outside, he could hear the bird squawking and the sound of its wings as it glided about even with the twine that was wound around its legs. He rushed back home and sought his father. Together they went to the house, but even though this time Ejike's mother answered the door, she denied that they had the gosling.

This woman, whose husband had died, had once lured his father into her house and they had copulated. But not wanting to fill the place of his loving wife, for whom he would grieve for the rest of his life, his father had refused to continue the relationship. And this had put a wedge between him and the woman. Although my host did not know this, I did, for I'd heard his father talk about it to himself while my host was asleep. And one night, I'd seen his father's chi – a carefree chi who often floated with etheric flamboyance while lurking about the house – and it told me that it had left the body of its host because he was about to have sex with the neighbour. It said my host's father and the woman were fondling at the back of the house, in the yard. I had come to know this guardian spirit very well, as one often knows the guardian spirits of other members of a household. Peer into a household at midnight, and you'll find guardian spirits – usually of males – conversing or simply moving about the house, often developing a bond with each other over the lifetimes of their hosts. This is how I came to know a great many guardian spirits of the males and females of mankind.

So on this day, perhaps because of the hurt she still harboured, the woman slammed the door in the face of my host and his father.

There was nothing my host could do to Ejike and his mother after that. He was stunned for days and would sometimes descend into uncontrolled rage and dart towards the neighbour's house, but his father would call him back and threaten to whip him if he went back there. He listened every minute for the gosling, refusing to eat, and hardly sleeping at night. It was difficult for me, his guardian spirit, to watch him suffer. But there is nothing a chi can do to help a man in a circumstance such as this, as we have limitations. The old fathers, in their wisdom, say *Onye ka nmadu ka chi ya*, and they are right. A person who is greater than another is also greater than his chi. Thus, there is little a chi can do for a man whose spirit is broken.

Egbunu, Ndali was moved by this part of his tale. Although she spoke throughout his story, asking questions ('He said that?'; 'So what happened next?'; 'Did you see it?'), I've decided

not to relate them, as I must focus on this tale about this creature to whom my host once gave his heart. But in light of
the things that have now happened and the reason for which
I stand before you to testify about my host, I must relate her
speech at this point in the story in which my host's desire to get
back that which belonged to him had sent him to the edge of
madness. Shaking her head wearily, she'd said, 'It must be very
sad, a bird that is yours, which you suffered for, taken away just
like that. It must be painful.' He merely nodded and continued.
He told her that by the fifth day, he'd become desperate. He
climbed the tree in the backyard, and from there he gained a
view into the compound of the neighbour. He saw Ejike seated
on a stool behind their fenced house stroking the gosling. At
first, the goose had appeared dead, then he saw its wings flutter
as it tried to fly away from its captor who quickly stamped his
foot on the red leash fastened to its leg. The gosling struggled,
raised its leg again and again and flapped its wings, but the
twine held it still. It was as my host watched this that the cruel
idea came into his mind.

Chukwu, the moment I glimpsed the design of his heart,
I contested it. I flashed the thought in his mind to think of
the devastation and pain that would come to him should he
proceed. He considered it momentarily and even imagined
the bird bleeding from the gash inflicted by the stone on its
head, and it frightened him. Yet he brushed the thought away.
But as you know, a chi cannot go against the will of its host,
nor can it compel its host against his will. This is why the old
fathers say that if a man is silent, his chi also becomes silent.
This is the universal law of guardian spirits: a man must will
for his chi to act. Thus was I thrust into a difficult situation
in which I would watch helplessly as he did something that
would bring him anguish in the end. He returned with his

catapult, sat on a bowed branch, and concealed himself in its foliage. From there he saw the bird fastened to the leg of the stool on which Ejike had sat only a moment before going back into his house.

At this point in his story, my host saw that he was about to tell Ndali that he was capable of serious violence, so he paused the narration to lie to her and say that he'd stopped loving the gosling because it was no longer his. He told her that because it was attached to Ejike, he'd thought of killing it as revenge against its new master. When she nodded and said, 'I understand, go on,' he told her about how he shot at the bird with the stone without missing. It hit it on the shank, then it fell and let out what must have been a cry of pain. He rushed down the tree, his heart having become a beating drum. He ran into his room, and later, Ejike came rushing down with the bleeding bird, crying that it was going to die if it did not get treatment. Indeed, days later, after he had reclaimed the bird and brought it back into his house, he woke to find the bird lying in the centre of his room on its back, its small wings clasped tightly against its body, its head slumped by its side. Its two legs were firm and lifeless, their claws curving downwards with the early strain of rigor mortis.

Gaganaogwu, the death of the bird disturbed my host very much. He told Ndali how he'd mourned the loss and had become so harsh on himself that his father was forced to punish him. But it yielded nothing. Complaints began to tide in from his school of his inattention and constant truancy. Such was his revolt that he acted to provoke punishments, and he took them – especially the floggings – with a masochistic indifference that alarmed his teachers. They sent word to his father, who by then had grown weary of punishing him because he had changed from being a plump boy to a slender one. One

day, in a desperate attempt to save his son, his father took him
to a poultry farm outside the city. My host described the big
farm to Ndali in detail: the hundreds of birds before his eyes –
domesticated birds of different kinds. It was here, among the
smell of a thousand feathers and the clucking of hundreds of
voices, that his heart finally lifted within him and came back
to life. His father and he returned with a cage full of chickens
and two turkeys, and the poultry business began.

EBUBEDIKE, after he rendered the tale, they said nothing
for a while. In silence, he riffled back through the words he
had said to see if there was something that could cast him in a
bad light. And she sat there in deep thought, perhaps judging
his words. Discretion was at the centre of his self-esteem. It
was what must be kept alive to maintain him. It was therefore
paramount that he keep most of the details of his past hidden
and that his tongue retain its poverty even in the face of pressure. Pricked that he'd told her so much, he let his thoughts
shift to the tomatoes he'd planted the previous week, which
he had not yet watered, when she spoke suddenly.

'It is a good job,' Ndali said after what seemed like a long
contemplation.

He nodded. 'Do you like it, Mommy?'

'Yes, I do,' she said. 'You miss your family? In fact, what
about your sister?'

Simple as this question was, it took him a long time to produce an answer. I have dwelt amongst mankind long enough
to realise that they do not store information about those who
have hurt them as they do others. This kind is kept in tightly
sealed jars whose lids must be opened to remember them. Or,
in the worst cases – like the memory of his grandmother's rape
by enemy soldiers during the war – the jar must be smashed

to bits. Thus all he said was: 'She lives in, erm, Lagos. Me and her, actually, we don't talk. Her name is Nkiru.'

'Why?'

'Mommy, she left home before Papa died. She, you know, she – how I should say it? – abandoned us.' He looked up to meet her fixed eyes. 'She left because of a man no one wanted her to marry because the man is very old, old enough even to be her father. In fact, he take more than fifteen years to senior her.'

'Ah-han! Why did she do that?'

'I don't know, my sister.' He gave her a sharp look to see if there was a reaction to what he had just called her. Then he said, 'I don't know, Mommy.'

Egbunu, although this was all he'd tell her about his sister for the time being, when one prises such a lid open, one sees more than one can account for. There is often no way to stop this. 'Why would a child reject her parent?' his father would ask him, and he would say he did not know. To which his father would blink slow-moving tears. His father would shake his head and snap a finger over it. Then he would gnash his teeth tightly, making the sound of ta-ta-ta-ta-ta. 'It is beyond me,' his father would say with even more bitterness than before. 'Beyond any man at all – dead or alive. Oh, Nkiru, Ada mu oh!'

Because the memory of what he'd recollected weighed heavily on him, he wanted to change the line of conversation. 'I will get you something to drink,' he said, and rose to his feet.

'What do you have?' She stood with him.

'No, you sit down, Mommy. You be my visitor. You suppose sit don make I feed you.'

She laughed and he saw her teeth – how tender they looked, lined up almost delicately, like a child's.

'Okay, but I wan stand,' she said.

He shot a glance at her and arched his brow. 'I didn't know you can speak pidgin,' he said and laughed.

She rolled her eyes and sighed in the manner handed down from the great mothers.

He brought out two bottles of Fanta and handed one to her. He still bought crates of these drinks they call Fanta and Coke, as his father used to do for guests, even though he hardly ever had any guests. He stored some of them in the refrigerator and returned the empty bottles to the crates.

He pointed to the dining table, surrounded by four chairs. A half-burned candle sat on the used lid of a Bournvita tin, reshaped by a waterfall of wax that washed down the tin and formed a coating at its foot like the gnarled roots of an aged tree. He pushed this to the edge of the table by the wall and pulled out a chair for her on the side. He saw that she was looking at the calendar on the wall that had an image of the White Man's alusi, Jisos Kraist, wearing a crown of thorns around his head. The inscription beside the raised finger of Jisos marched on her lips but did not become audible. He'd opened the drink when she sat down, and as he made to return the opener, she grabbed his hand.

Ijango-ijango, even these many years later, I still cannot fully comprehend all that transpired in that moment. It seemed that by some mysterious means, she had been able to read the intents of his heart, which had all along cast themselves upon his face like a presence. And she had come to understand, by some alchemy, that the smile he'd carried on his face all along was his body's struggle to manage the solemn intransigence of its volcanic desire. They made love so heartily, so beauteously, for nearly an hour with a rare kind of energy. He was driven by a strange mix of unbelief and relief, and she by some feeling

I cannot describe. You know, Chukwu, that you have sent me out many times to dwell in people, to live through them, and to become them. You know that I have seen many people unclothed. But still the ferocity of their encounter alarmed me. It may have been because it was their first time, and they both could tell – for this was indeed his thought – that there was something ineffably deep between them, and indeed I was reminded of her chi's words: 'My host has erected a figurine in the shrine of her heart.' It must be why at the end of it, when both of them were drenched in sweat and he saw tears in her eyes, he lay by her, saying words which – although she, he and I alone could hear – were also heard in the realm beyond man as thunderous acclamations meant for the ears of man and spirits, the dead and the living, for the moment and for ever: 'I have found it! I have found it! I have found it!'

5

AN ORCHESTRA OF MINORITIES

GAGANAOGWU, the daily life of lovers often begins to share resemblances, so that, in time, each day becomes indistinguishable from the one that came before it. The lovers carry each other's words in their hearts when apart and when together; they laugh; they talk; they make love; they argue; they eat; they tend to poultry together; they watch television and dream about a future together. This way, time slips and memories accrue until their union becomes the sum of all the words they have said to each other, their laughter, their lovemaking, their arguments, their eating, their work with the poultry, and all the things they have done together. When they are not with each other, night becomes to them an undesirable thing. They despair at the masking of the sun and wait eagerly for the night, this cosmic sheet that has separated them from their beloved, to pass in fervent haste.

By the third month, my host realised that the moments he'd come to value the most were the times when Ndali tended the poultry with him. Although many things about poultry keeping — like the smell of the coop, the way the fowls defecate nearly everywhere, and the killing of the ones sold as meat to restaurants – still bothered her, she enjoyed tending to the flock. Even though she worked with my host without complaint, he remained worried about her perception of the work. He often recalled the university science lecturer at the poultry market in Enugu who had complained bitterly about the habit among poultry keepers of holding the birds by their wings, calling it cruel and insensitive. Although Ndali herself was training to be a pharmacist, sometimes wearing lab coats in some of the photos she showed him, she displayed no such sensitivity. She plucked with ease the overgrown feathers of the fowls. She harvested eggs whenever she visited in the early mornings or stayed over at his house. But even beyond the birds, she took care of him and his house. She poked her hand into the dark and secret places of his life and touched everything in it. And in time, she became the thing his soul had been yearning after for years with tears in its eyes.

In those three months, this woman he'd met on a bridge in a chance encounter, and who is the reason for my premature testimony this night, transformed his life. Without warning, Ndali arrived one afternoon with a new fourteen-inch television and an iron. For weeks before that she'd laughed at him as the only person she knew who did not watch television. He did not tell her that he had had one from his parents' time till recently, only weeks before he met her again, when in a rage at Motu's disappearance he smashed it to smithereens. When, later, he realised what he had done, he took it to the neighbourhood electronics repairman. After fiddling with it, the repairman told him, with much head shaking, that he should buy a new one. The cost of the bad part that needed replacement was the cost of a new set. He decided to let the TV remain with the repairman, in his small shop along the busy highway, surrounded by ziggurats of electronics in different states of dysfunction.

Even beyond bringing the new things, Ndali ensured that his house stayed clean. She mopped the floor of the bathroom constantly, and when a frog leapt in through the drainpipe after a heavy downpour, she brought in a plumber to cover the mouth of the pipe with netting. She scrubbed the white tiles on the walls of the bathroom, which he had not cleaned in many months. She bought him new towels and hung them not on the top of the door – *Because that must be dusty!* – or on the bent nail on the interior of the door – *Because the nail was rusting and now stained them* – but on a plastic hanger. As time passed, it seemed she improved something in his life on a daily basis, and even Elochukwu, to whom he now gave little of his attention, attested continually to the enormous change in his life.

Although my host appreciated these things, he did not give deep thoughts to them until the end of the three months, when Ndali travelled with her parents to Britain, the land of the White Man. The reason for this is that people do not see clearly what is positioned before them until they regard it from a distance. A man may hate another because of an offence, but after a significant passage of time, his heart begins to warm towards that individual. It is why the wise fathers say that one hears the message of an *udu* drum clearer from a distance. I have seen it many times. It was thus in her absence that my host saw all she'd done for him more clearly. It was during this time also that all the things she'd told him became more audible, and he noticed all that had changed in his life and how the past before her coming now seemed like a different age from the present. And it was during those days alone, thinking about these things, that the desire came to him with all the bolting powers of a persuasion that he wanted to marry Ndali. He rose to his feet and shouted, 'I want to marry you, Ndali!'

Ijango-ijango, I cannot describe the joy I saw in my host
that evening. No poetry, no language can fully describe it. I
had seen, long before his uncle came and asked him to find a
wife, that he had been seeking this – since the day his mother
died. I, his chi, was in full support. I had seen this woman,
approved of her care for him, and even received the testimony
of her chi that she loved him. And I was convinced that a wife
would restore the peace he had lost since his mother's death
because the early fathers, in their most gracious wisdom, say
that once a man builds a house and a compound, even the
spirits expect him to get a wife.

Two days after he made this decision, Ndali returned to
Nigeria. She called him once she arrived in Abuja with her
family, whispering into the phone. As she was speaking, he
heard the sound of a door opening somewhere in the house
where she was, and the call ended that instant. He was picking
eggs and replacing the floor of the main hennery with sawdust
when she called. When she reached Umuahia later that day, it
happened again. This time he'd just finished a meal at a restaurant he supplied eggs and chicken meat to, a place where
he ate every once in a while. They'd started to talk when she
ended the call abruptly at the sound of a door opening.

My host put down the phone and washed his hands in the
plastic bowl he'd filled with the bones from the bonga fish
served with egusi soup. He paid the daughter of the caterer,
whose habit of wearing a scarf that folded into the shape of
a bird's tail often reminded him of Motu. He picked up a
toothpick poking out of a plastic vase and walked into the sun.
He waved down a peddler, who went about carrying water in
small sealed bags, hawking his wares: 'Buy Pure Water, buy
Pure Water!' Agujiegbe, this buying and the selling of water
has always amazed me. The old fathers would never have

imagined, even in the time of drought, that water – the most abundant provision of the great earth goddess herself – could be sold the same way hunters sell porcupines! He bought one Pure Water and was tucking the ten-naira change into his pocket when his phone began to ring again. He removed it from his pocket, considered flipping it open to answer the call, but put it back in. He spat the toothpick away and bit open the bag and drank till the bag was empty, then he threw it into the nearby brush.

My host was angry. But anger, in a situation like this, often becomes a multiparous cat who bears litters of offspring, and it had already birthed jealousy and doubt in him. For as he walked back to his van, he kept wondering why he was giving himself to a woman who did not seem to care about him. I flashed the thought in his mind that there was no need to be annoyed with her and suggested that he wait till he'd heard her explanation and the full story.

He did not respond to my suggestion, but simply entered his van and drove past the large pillar along Bende Road, which bore the name of the town, still raging. He came by a rough intersection where a three-wheeled vehicle wedged itself between his van and another car and would have been run into had he not hit the brakes. The driver of the small vehicle cursed my host as he pulled to the shoulder of the road.

'Devil!' he shouted at the man. 'This is how you people die. You dey drive ordinary keke napep, but you dey do laik say na gwongworo you dey drive!'

His phone began ringing as he spoke, but he did not reach for it. He drove past the Mater Dei Cathedral, where he had not been for a long time, and, cutting through a small street, arrived at his farm. He turned off the engine, took the phone and dialled her number.

'What are you doing?' she shouted into the phone. 'What?'

'I don't . . .' he said, and breathed hard into the phone. 'I don't want talk to you by phone.'

'No, you must. What did I do to you?'

He wiped the sweat from his forehead and wound down the window.

'I was annoyed that you did it again.'

'What did I do again, er, Nonso?'

'You are ashamed of me. You did not phone because another person was coming into the room.' He could catch his voice rising, starting to turn loud and vehement, a tone she often complained about as harsh. But he could not stop himself. 'Tell me, er, who opened that door that time you ended my call?'

'Nonso—'

'Answer me.'

'Okay, my mother.'

'Er-er, you see? You are denying me? You don't want your family to know about me. You don't want them to know that I am your guy. You see, you are denying me in front of your people, Ndali.'

She tried to speak, but he pushed on, forcing her into silence. Now he waited for her to speak again, worried even more, not just because of what he'd betrayed in his tone but also because he'd referred to her by her name, something he did only when angry with her.

'Are you there?' he said.

'Yes,' she said after a pause.

'Then, talk naw.'

'Where are you now?' she said.

'My place.'

'Then, I'm coming there now.'

He dropped the phone into his pocket, and a silent joy

rose within him. It was obvious that she had not planned to meet him until after a few days, but he wanted her to come as soon as possible. For he missed her, and it was partly this that angered him. He'd also been annoyed by the anxiety that planted itself in him while she was away and became even more persistent after he developed the idea to marry her. As often happened to him – and to most of mankind – a questionable idea had formed in his mind with the power of a persuasion. At first people believe these ideas, but after a while their gaze becomes sharper and more penetrating so that they begin to see all the deformities of their plans. This was why, hours later, he became aware – as if it had been concealed from him all this while – that he was not rich, not particularly good looking, and not educated beyond secondary school. She, by contrast, was on the cusp of completing university and becoming a doctor (even though, Egbunu, she had told him many times that she was going to be a pharmacist, not a doctor). He needed her to come, to reassure him in some way again that he'd been wrong, that he was not beneath her but in fact her equal. And that she loved him. Although she did not know it, this was what she had done for him by agreeing to come.

He stepped out of the van and walked into the small farm, stopping halfway between the rows of the growing tomato plants to observe the ears of corn on the other side. Perhaps seeing him, a rabbit emerged and began hopping away into the cornfield in rapid, prodigious leaps, its tail swinging as it went. It would go a few steps, then stop, raise its head and glance about, and then run on again. He spotted a singlet – perhaps blown there by the wind from some compound – lying over one of the corn plants, bending it. He took up the singlet. It was covered with dirt, and on it was a black reticulated millipede. He shook off the millipede and was headed to dispose of the singlet in the dump behind the brick fence when Ndali arrived.

EZEUWA, the wise fathers in their cautionary wisdom say that whichever position the dancer takes, the flute will accompany him there. My host that evening had received what he wanted: that she come to him. But he had achieved it by protest and dictated the tune of the flautist. So when he went into the house, she was on her feet, her fingers splayed over her wearied face. She turned away once he came in, and with her eyes cast downwards, she said, 'I have come not to argue but to talk in a calm way, Nonso.'

Fearing that what she said might require him to focus on her for a long time, he asked to feed his flock first. He hurried out into the yard, wanting to return to her quickly. He opened the coop door, made of wood and netting. The chickens poured out, calling enthusiastically. They made a sprint with expectation towards the foot of the guava tree, where he'd spread sacks but had not poured feed. Once they began to peck, piping, he walked back into the house and put the main door against a wedge, so that only the net door was closed. He scooped up one last big cup of millet and tied up the nearly empty bag which he kept in one of the cupboards in the kitchen to prevent the birds from devouring it. He returned to the yard and poured the feed on the sack at the foot of the tree. At once the sacks were covered by a gathering of hungry birds.

When he returned to the sitting room, Ndali was seated and was looking at the camera she had brought from the White Man's country, which she called a 'Polaroid camera'. Her handbag was still by her side, and her shoes, which she referred to simply as 'heels', were still on, as if she was poised to leave soon. Egbunu, while one can often tell the state of a person's mind from the expression on their face, it is now difficult to tell with the daughters of the great mothers. This is because they now adorn themselves in ways unlike the mothers. They have shunned *uli*, the elaborate braiding, the wearing of beads and cowries. And now, a woman can cover her face with colours of all kinds all by herself, with a single paintbrush, and one in misery can wear so much colouring on her face that she might even look happy. And this was how Ndali appeared that day.

'So tell me,' she said once my host sat down. 'You want to meet my family?'

He'd settled into the weakest of the sofas so that his body sank low and he could barely see her complete figure, even though he was right in front of her.

Conscious of the anger in her voice, he said, 'That is so, if we want to marry—'

'So you want to marry me, Nonso?'

'That is so, Mommy.'

She'd closed her eyes as he spoke, and now she opened them, and they appeared reddish. She adjusted in the sofa so that her legs came forward towards him. 'You mean it?'

He gazed up at her. 'That is so.'

'Then you will meet my family. If you say you want to marry me.'

Egbunu, she said this as if it was a painful thing to say. And one could see then, without needing a diviner's eye, that there lurked in her heart something heavy which, concealed in the veiled compartment of her mind, she would not reveal. My host saw this, too, and this was why he drew her to sit by him on the big sofa and asked why she did not want him to meet her people. To this question she pulled herself from him and turned her face away. Then he saw that she was afraid. He saw it even though she had turned away from him, and all he could see were the big earrings that drooped down almost to her shoulders, forming a ring big enough for two of his fingers to slide through. For fear is one of the emotions that clothes the primal nudity of a person's face, and wherever it presents itself, every percipient eye can recognise it, no matter how adorned the face.

'Why is it making you sad, Mommy?'

'It is not making me sad,' she said almost before he finished speaking.

'Why, then, you fear?'

'Because it will not be good.'

'Why? Why can't I even know my girlfriend's family?'

She looked at him, her eyes firm against his own, unblinking. Then she turned away again. 'You will meet them. I promise you that. But I know my parents. And my brother. I know them.' She shook her head again. 'They are proud people. It will not be good. But you will meet them.'

Confounded by what he heard, he did not speak. He wished to know more, but he was not one who asked too many questions.

'When I go home, I will tell them about you.' She tapped her feet in an undecipherable act of discomfort. 'This night, I will tell them this very night. Then we see when I can take you home.'

Once she said this, as if she had relieved herself of a great burden, she leaned back into the couch towards him and drew a deep breath. But her words remained in his head. For words as strong as the ones she'd spoken – 'It will not be good'; 'So you want to marry me?'; 'You will meet them. I promise you that'; 'Then we see when I can take you home' – are not easily dispelled from the mind. They have to be broken down slowly, over time. He was digesting them when he heard a distinct sound from the backyard that startled him.

He leapt to his feet and was in the kitchen in the blink of an eye. He grabbed his catapult from the windowsill and opened the net door. But it was too late. The hawk had mounted its thermal by the time he got to the yard, flapping its wings violently against the updraft, with one of the yellow-white chicks clasped in its talons. Its wings hit the laundry rope as it lifted, rattling the rope so that two of the pieces of clothing he'd hung on it fell to the ground. He slung a stone at it, but it fell far away from the bird. He'd put another stone in the catapult when he saw that it was no use. The hawk had glided into an unreachable thermal and had started to gain momentum, its eyes no longer glancing downwards but ahead, into the colourless immensity of the sky.

Chukwu, the hawk – he is a dangerous bird, as lethal as the leopard. He craves nothing but flesh and he spends his life chasing it. He is an unspoken mystery amongst the birds of the sky. He is a soaring deity, borne on violent wings and merciless talons. The great fathers studied it and the kite, its close sibling, and made proverbs to explain its nature, one of which captures what had just happened to my host's chickens: Before every attack the hawk says to the hen, 'Keep your chicks close to your bosoms, for my talons are soaked in blood.'

My host was gazing at the fleeing hawk, full of rage, when Ndali opened the net door and entered the backyard.

'What happened? Why did you run out so fast?'

'A hawk,' he said without looking back. He pointed in the distance, but the sun forced his eyes into a squint. He held up his hand to shade them as he stared in the direction the bird had gone. But the image of the attack was still so clear in his mind, still so vivid, that he struggled to believe it had concluded. There was nothing he could do now to save one of his flock from being torn apart and eaten up. The chickens he reared with his own hands and sweat – one had been taken away from him, again, *without a fight.*

He turned about and saw that the rest of his flock – with the exception of the one whose chick had been stolen – was cowered in the safety of the coop. The bereft hen pranced about with a stutter in its gait, cawing with what he knew was the avian language of anguish. He did not speak but pointed in the direction of the empty sky.

'I can't see anything.' She cupped her eyes and turned to him again. 'It stole a chicken?'

He nodded.

'Oh, my God!'

He turned his gaze to the evidence of the attack: the ground stained with blood and strewn with feathers.

'How many did it take? How did it—'

'*Ofu,*' he said, then, reminding himself that he was talking with someone who preferred not to speak Igbo, he added, 'Only one.'

He set the catapult on the bench and followed the wailing hen around the yard. It eluded him at the first attempt to catch it. But he dashed forward with his two hands in front of him and clasped it by the wing closest to its left shoulder, then trapped it against the wall of the fence. Then he lifted it by its leg, gently feeling its spur. The hen went quiet, its tail upraised.

'How did it happen?' Ndali said as she picked up the fallen clothes.

'It just came—' He paused to stroke the hen's earlobe. 'It just land on them and catch the small one of this mother hen, Ada. One of her new chicks.'

He set Ada, the hen, back into the coop and closed the door slowly.

'Very sorry, Obim.'

He dusted his hands by slapping them against each other and went into the house.

'Does it happen all the time?' she said when he returned to the sitting room from washing his hands in the bathroom.

'No, no oh, not all the time.'

He wanted to leave his answer there, but Chukwu, I nudged him to unload what he bore in his mind. I knew him. I knew that one of the things that can heal the heart of a defeated man is the story of his past victory. It soothes the wound caused by the defeat and fills him with the possibility of a future victory. So I flashed the thought in his mind that hawks did not usually come here. I suggested he tell her it didn't always happen. And in a rare instance of compliance, he listened to me.

'No, it doesn't happen every time,' he said. 'It cannot always happen. *Mba nu!*'

'Er,' she said.

'I don't allow it. Not so long ago, in fact, one tried to attack my fowls,' he said, surprised by his sudden slide into the corrupted form of the White Man's language. But it was in this language that he told her the story of his recent victory, and she listened, transfixed. Not too long ago, he began, he'd let out the flock, almost all the poultry except the occupants of one of the cages of broilers, and had started to peel yams into the sink in his kitchen, looking out every now and then, when he noticed a hawk hovering in the air above the flock. He opened his louvres, grabbed the catapult, and pulled a stone from the windowsill. He blew the stone with his mouth to clear off the red ants on it. Then he unhooked one of the louvres to allow his hand enough space and wound the handles so that the louvres stood in straight horizontal layers over each other. Then he waited for the bird to strike.

The hawk, he informed her, might be the most watchful

of birds and can hover for hours on end, priming its target, making an effort to strike as precisely as possible – so one strike might be enough. So he, knowing this, waited for it, too. He did not take his eyes away from where it hovered for a second. It was why he caught it in that very moment when it made the daring plunge into the yard, picked up a small rooster, and attempted to mount the updraft. The missile knocked the raptor against the wall of the fence, making it drop the chick. The hawk slid down to the foot of the wall with a thud. It hoisted itself up, its head momentarily lost in its spread-out wings. It had been concussed.

He hastened out into the yard as the hawk tried to stand erect, then pinned it to the wall, unfazed by the violence of its beating wings and its riotous squawks. He dragged the bird by its wings to the cashew tree at the end of the compound, beside the rubbish bin. He could not, he emphasised, describe the anger he'd felt. It was with this great anger that he bound the hawk by its wings, its head blood soaking the strong fibres of the twine. As he tied the bird to the tree, he spoke to it and all of its kind – all who stole what people like him reared with their sweat, time and money. He walked into the house and returned with a few nails, sweat bleeding down his back and neck. As he stepped back into the yard, the hawk called with a strange fury, its voice piercing and ugly. He picked up a big stone from behind the tree and held up the bird's neck against the tree. Then he struck the nail into its throat with the stone until the nail burst out on the other end, spitting splinters and unbuckling a coat of old bark from the tree. He spread one wing, his hand and the stone now covered in the hawk's blood, and drove it, too, deep into the flesh of the tree. Although he saw that he'd done something extremely violent and unusual, so overwhelmed with rage was he that he was determined to complete what his mind had conjured up as the deserving punishment for the bird: a crucifixion. Thus he put together the feathery legs of the dead bird and nailed them to the tree. And it was finished.

He sat back into the chair now that he'd finished the story, entranced in his own vision. Although he'd been looking at her all the while, it seemed that he had just seen her for the first time since he began the tale. He became conscious of the weight of what he had told her. And he feared, now, that she must think of him as a violent man. In haste, he looked up at her, but he could not tell what she was thinking.

'I am amazed, Nonso,' she said suddenly.

'By what?' he said, his heart quickening.

'The story.'

Is that it? he wondered. Is that the way she would view him from now on? An irredeemably violent man who crucifies birds? 'Why?' he said instead.

'I don't know. But – in fact – I don't know. Maybe the way you tell it to me. But – I just see you, just a man who loves his fowls so much. So very much.'

Ebubedike, my host's thoughts swirled at this. *Love*, he thought. How could love be what she thinks about at this given moment after he'd just exposed himself as capable of such senseless brutality?

'You love them,' she said again, now with her eyes closed. 'If you didn't love them, you would not have acted this way in the story you just told me. And today also. You really love them, Nonso.'

He nodded without knowing why.

'I think you are really a good shepherd.'

He looked up at her and said, 'What?'

'I called you a shepherd.'

'What is that?'

'It is one who keeps sheep. Do you remember from the Bible?'

He was somewhat perplexed by what she'd said, for he had not given it much thought, just as men do not often give deep thoughts to the things they do every day, things that are routine to them. He hadn't considered that he had been broken by the world. The birds were the hearth on which his heart had been burned, and – at the same time – they were the ashes that gathered after the wood was burned. He loved them, even if they were varied while he was one and simple. Yet, like everyone who loves, he wished that it be requited. And because he could not tell even if his singular gosling once loved him or not, in time his love became a deformed thing – a thing neither he nor I, his chi, could understand.

'But I keep fowls, not sheep,' he said.

'It doesn't matter, so far you keep birds.'

He shook his head.

'It is very true,' she said, drawing close to him now. 'You are a shepherd of birds, and you love your flock. You care for them the way Jesus cares for his sheep with so much love.'

Although what she said had puzzled him, he said, 'That is so, Mommy.'

Agbatta-Alumalu, my host was so confounded by the things Ndali said that day that even long after they'd finished making love, eaten rice and stew, and made love again, he sat in the bed listening to the sound of crickets in the farm and barnyard while Ndali drifted off to sleep. His mind lay solidly on the cryptic things she had said about her family as if caught there, like a bird on birdlime. He was peering directly at the wall across from him, gazing at nothing in particular, when he was startled by her voice.

'Why are you not sleeping, Nonso?'

He faced her and slid downwards into the bed.

'I will, Mommy. Why did you wake?'

She shifted, and he saw the silhouettes of her breasts in the darkness.

'I don't know oh, I just wake like that. I did not sleep deep before oh,' she said, with the same weak voice. 'Er-he, Nonso, I have been wondering all day: what is the sound that the chickens were making after the hawk took the small one? It was like they all gathered – er, together.' She coughed, and he heard the sound of phlegm within her throat. 'It was like they were all saying the same thing, the same sound.' He started to speak, but she spoke on. 'It was strange. Did you notice it, Obim?'

'Yes, Mommy,' he said.

'Tell me, what is it? Is it crying? Are they crying?'

He inhaled. It was hard for him to talk about this phenomenon because it often moved him. For it was one of the things that he cherished about the domestic birds – their fragility, how they relied chiefly on him for their protection, sustenance, and everything. In this they were unlike the wild birds.

'It is true, Mommy, it is cry,' he said.

'Really?'

'That is so, Mommy.'

'Oh, God, Nonso! No wonder! Because of the small one—'

'That is so.'

'That the hawk took?'

'That is so, Mommy.'

'That is very sad, Nonso,' she said after a moment's quiet. 'But how did you know they were crying?'

'My father told me. He was always saying it is like a burial song for the one that has gone. He called it *Egwu umu-obere-ihe*. You understand? I don't know *umu-obere-ihe* in English.'

'Little things,' she said. 'No, minorities.'

'Yes, yes, that is so. That is the translation my father said. That's how he said it in English: minorities. He was always saying it is like their "okestra".'

'Orchestra,' she said. 'O–r–c–h–e–s–t–r–a.'

'That is so, that is how he pronounced it, Mommy. He was always saying the chickens know that is all they can do: crying and making the sound ukuuukuu! Ukuuukuu!'

Later, after she drifted back to sleep, he lay back beside her, thinking about the hawk attack and her observation about the fowls. Then, as the night prospered and his thoughts returned to the things she'd said about her family, the fear slithered in again, this time wearing the facial mask of a sinister spirit.

IJANGO-IJANGO, the ndiichie say that if a wall does not bear a hole in it, lizards cannot enter a house. Even if a man is troubled, if he does not become broken, he can sustain himself. Although my host's peace had been meddled with, he went about his business with serenity. He delivered twenty-nine eggs to the restaurant down the street and drove to Enugu to sell seven of the chicks and to buy a few more brown hens and six bags of feed. He had only bought a bag of mash when he came by a man playing *uja*, the flute of the spirits. The flautist trailed behind another man whose torso was painted with *nzu* and *uli* and camwood, and who clenched a strand of young palm leaf between his teeth. Behind the two men was a masquerade. A group of people were gathered as the *iru-nmuo*, wearing an antlered mask that bore the scarification of a slit-eyed ichie, danced to the sound of ancient flute music attended by a rattling twin gong. As you know, Egbunu, when one encounters an ancestral spirit – the corporeal manifestation of one or more of the great fathers – one cannot resist.

Gaganaogwu, I could not hold back! For I had lived in the days of the great fathers when masquerades were a frequent sight. I could not hold back the temptation to listen to the mystical tune of the *uja*, the flute crafted by the best among the people who live on the earth. I shot out of my host into a frantic crowd of spirits of all kinds and climes which were gathered around this area, making deafening noises, their feet ticking on the soft grounds of Ezinmuo. But what surprised me even more was what I saw above the other part of the bustling market. A group of small human-shaped spirits – of children killed at childbirth or conception or of twins killed long ago – stood playing at an elevation of about four hundred metres, the distance at which *ekili,* the mystical transport system of astral projection and bird flight, are rendered possible. This group of spirits was held above the human crowd by a force beyond the knowledge of man (except dibias and the initiated), so that it seemed as though they were on the ground. They were stamping their feet, leaping and snapping their fingers as they played the ancient game of *okwe-ala.* Their laughter was loud and cheerful, ringed with the hollow thread of the ancient language long lost among men. Chukwu, although I have witnessed things like this before, I was again mystified by the fact that, despite the dozen or so childish spirits playing, a market went on undisrupted below them. The market continued to teem with women haggling, people driving in cars, a masquerade swinging through the place to the music of an *uja* and the sound of an *ekwe.* None of them was aware of what was above them, and those above paid no heed to those below, either.

I had been so carried away by the frolicking spirits that the masquerade and its entourage were gone by the time I returned to my host. Because of the fluidity of time in the spirit realm, what may seem like a long time to man is in fact the snap of a finger. This was why, by the time I was back into him, he was already in his van driving back to Umuahia. Because of this distraction, I was unable to bear witness to everything my host did at the market, and for this I plead your forgiveness, Obasidinelu.

A short distance from Umuahia, my host received a message from Ndali that she would come that night briefly because she was preparing for a test the following day. When she came that night, wearing her lab coat, he was watching *Who Wants to Be a Millionaire*, a TV show she loved and had introduced him to.

She removed the coat and revealed a green shirt and denim trousers that gave her the appearance of a teenager.

'I am just coming from the lab,' she said. 'Please off the TV, we need to talk about coming to my family house tomorrow.'

'The TV?' he said.

'Yes, off it!'

'Oh? No vex, Mommy.'

He rose slowly to turn it off, but stopped at the intensification of a peculiar sound. He stood watching again.

'In fact let us go to the backyard, it is stuffy here,' she said.

He followed her to the yard, the air thick with the smell of the poultry. They sat on the bench, and she was about to begin speaking when she saw a long black bit of plumage stuck to the wall as if glued to it. 'Look, Nonso!' she said, and he saw it, too. He picked the feather off the wall and sniffed it.

'It is from that stupid hawk,' he said, shaking his head.

'Ah, how did it hang there like that?'

'I don't know.' He crumpled it and flung it over the fence, his anger erupting at the memory of the previous day.

She drew a deep breath, and, pushing herself forward, she spoke as if she'd been thinking about every word, and every one of them had been measured and planned for so long.

'Chinonso Solomon Olisa, you have been a great person, a godsend to me. Look at me, I have been through hell. You met me in the worst place. You met me, I was on the bridge. I was on that bridge because – because what? – because I was tired of the bad treatment. Because I was tired of being cheated and lied to. But God! He sent you into my life at the very appointed time. Look at me now.' She splayed her hands open for him to see. 'Look at me, look at how I have been transformed. If anyone told me or even my mum that her daughter would be working with poultry, touching agric fowl, who would believe it? Nobody. Nonso, you don't even know who I am or where I am from.'

She seemed to smile, but he could tell that it wasn't a smile. It was something her face had done to help her conceal the difficult emotion that was welling within her.

'So what am I saying? Why am I talking like this? I am saying that my family – my mother and father, and even my brother – may not accept you. I know it is hard to understand, Nonso, but look, my dad is a chief. *Onye Nze.* They will say I am not suited for a farmer. It is just that, they will say that . . .'

Egbunu, my host listened as she said the same thing over and over again to try to neutralise its effect. He was shaken by the things she'd said, for he'd been afraid of these things. He'd seen the signs. He saw it on the day at the watch shop on Finbarr's Street, when she'd told him that she was born overseas, 'in the UK'. Her parents and her older brother had been schooled there, and it was she alone who had chosen to do her schooling in Nigeria. 'But,' she had added, 'I will do my master's abroad.' He remembered another time. They were driving past the old part of the city, tearing through the storm wind that massed against it, when she asked if he had gone to university. He'd been struck by it, and his heart had begun to beat rapidly. 'No,' he'd said, as if with a dead tongue. But Ndali had simply said, 'Oh, I see.' He remembered how, afterwards, she'd pointed past a group of multi-storey buildings lined shoulder to shoulder on the side of the road around Aguiyi Ironsi Layout, a tall new solar-powered streetlight sticking up above one of them, and said, 'We live somewhere among those buildings.'

'I am not trying to make you afraid,' she said presently. 'Nobody can decide who I want to marry. I decide for myself. And I am no longer a child.'

He nodded.

'Obim, *igho ta go*?' she said, her head tilted sideways, her face anchored in the valley between smiling and crying.

'I understand, Mommy,' he said in the language of the White Man, surprised by her switch to the language of the old fathers. Although he'd heard her speak it on the phone with her parents, she hardly spoke it with him. She'd said she did not like to speak it except with her parents because, having lived abroad for a few years, she did not think she was fluent in it.

'*Da'alu*,' she said, and kissed him on the cheek. She rose and went into the kitchen.

Later, while they ate, she said, 'Nonso, you truly love me?' He was starting to answer when she said, 'That must be why you would want to marry me?' He murmured something that dissolved away in an instant because she quickly added, 'It must be because you love me.'

He waited for a moment before saying, 'It is.' He expected her to say more, but she went to the kitchen to wash the plates, carrying the single kerosene lamp in the house. It crossed his mind to put on the rechargeable lantern, but he remained seated instead, contemplating all she had said when she came back into the sitting room.

'Nonso, I ask again, do you love me?'

In the near darkness, although he wasn't looking at her, he could tell that she'd closed her eyes as she waited for his answer. She often closed her eyes whenever she expected a response to a question, as if afraid that what he might say might hurt her. Then, after he had spoken, she would try to slowly take in what had been said.

'You say yes, Nonso, but is it true?'

'It is so, Mommy.'

She returned to the room with the lantern, set it on a stool beside her, and turned it low so that their shadows sketched by the incipient darkness swelled.

'So you truly love me?'

'It is so, Mommy.'

'Chinonso, you always say you love me. But do you know that you need to really love someone before you marry the person? Do you know the meaning of love?' He was starting to speak. 'No, just tell me, first, do you know what love is?'

'I do, Mommy.'

'Is that truth? Really, is that the truth?'

'It is so, Mommy.'

'Then, Nonso, what is love?'

'I know. I can feel it,' he said. He opened his mouth to proceed, but he said, 'Eck,' and then fell silent again. For he feared that he could not answer her correctly.

'Nonso? Do you hear?'

'Yes, I feel love, but I cannot lie that I know everything concerning it, every single thing.'

'No, no, Nonso. You said you love me, so you must know what love is. You must know what.' She sighed and let out a tsk. 'You must know, Nonso.'

Gaganaogwu, my host was troubled by this. Although I, like every good chi, often allow my host to make use of the talent I have chosen for him from the hall of talents by interfering minimally in his decision-makings, I wanted to interfere here. But I was stopped by what he resorted to: the effective tool of silence. For I have come to know that when the peace of the human mind is threatened, it often answers with benign silence at first, as if stunned by a withering blow whose impact it must allow to dissipate. And when this dissipation had been completed, he mumbled, 'Okay.'

He leaned back into the chair and recalled what she had told him about one of her friends who laughed at a man who told her friend he loved her after just meeting her for the first time. He'd wondered at the time why she and Lydia, the friend, had thought it completely ludicrous and that it deserved mockery. This reminded him of when Miss J laughed at him when he said he loved her. At the time, he had been surprised, as he was now. He looked up at her silhouette, and it struck him for the first time that he'd not properly weighed what it would entail to be married. She would have to move in with him into the compound. She would ride with him in his van to deliver eggs to the bakery on Finbarr's Street and meat to the restaurants where he delivered live chickens every now and then. All that had come to belong to him would now also belong to her – everything. Did he hear himself say it correctly? Everything! And if, in time, he plants his seed in her, the child that will be born – even that child will belong to both of them! Her possessions, her car – he would benefit from her studies in the university, her family, her heart, and all that was her, hers, and all that would be hers would all be his, too. This was what marriage comprised.

In light of this new understanding, he said, 'Actually, I don't, I can say—'

She must have said the 'Okay' after she opened her eyes. 'But you . . .' she started to say, but fell silent.

'What? What?' he said in a frantic effort to prevent her from holding back that which she had prepared for release, for she often did this: pause on the verge of saying something, then draw back and seal it up again in the jar of thought, to be released later, and sometimes never.

'Don't worry,' she said almost in a whisper. 'You will come to my house next Sunday, then. And you will meet my family.'

Oseburuwa, you know that a chi is a font of memory – a moving accretion of the many cycles of existences. Each event, every detail stands like a tree staked into the bright darkness of its eternity. Yet it does not remember every event, only those which impact its host in memorable ways. I must tell you that my host's decision that night is one I will always remember. At first he'd waited for her to say these words he dreaded, that 'it will not be good'. But she did not speak. So, in a faltering tone, he said, 'That is so, Mommy. I will meet your family next week Sunday.'

6

'AUGUST VISITOR'

OBASIDINELU, you have sent me to live on the earth with humans in many cycles of existence, and I have seen many things, and I'm wise in the ways of humanity. Yet I do not fully understand the human heart. Every person lives as if oscillating between two realms, unable to anchor his foot in either. This is a strange thing. Let us consider, for instance, the intercourse between fear and anxiety. Fear exists because of the presence of anxiety and anxiety because humans cannot see the future. For if only a man could see the future, he would be more at peace. For one who plans to travel in a coming day may say to his companion, 'If we go to Aba tomorrow, we will encounter robbers on the highway and we will be robbed of this car and all our possessions.' To which the other may say, 'Surely we will not go to Aba tomorrow.'

Or suppose there is a young woman about to be married. If she could see the future, she could say to her father on the eve of the wedding, 'My father, I don't mean to disappoint our entire clan and soil our name. But I have come to find that if I marry this man, he will beat me every day and will treat me worse than a dog.' Can you imagine what fear this would create in her beloved father if he believes what she has seen is true? The father would snap his fingers over his head and cry, '*Tufia! Ya buru ogwu ye ere kwa la!* Anyone who has prepared such a spell, may it come to naught! You must leave the man at once, my daughter. Where is the bride price he has paid? Where is the young goat? Where are the three tubers of yam? Where is the bottle of schnapps and the crate of mineral? Return them all at once! God forbid that my daughter should marry such a man!' But Chukwu, they will not do such a thing because none of them can see the future. So without knowing it, the men of trade will embark on their journey on the planned day and get robbed and killed. The young woman will marry the man who will treat her worse than a slave.

I have seen it many times.

It is in this same way that my host drove his van to Ndali's house that Sunday not knowing what was in store. Unable to induce the day to arrive earlier and unable to stop it from coming, he'd waited anxiously for it. Time is not a living creature that can listen to pleas, nor is it a man who can delay. The day will come, as it has done since the beginning, and all that man can do is wait. Waiting in such a state of anxiety is tasking. Although one might feel a sense of peace while waiting, that peace is deceptive – the kind that could cause a man to think of roiling waters as calm.

He had not seen her in two days before that day, and he longed for her. He entered her street, trying to imagine what her family was like, what the house looked like. The electrical poles around the street were lower than they were in most other parts of Umuahia, and they seemed lined up close to each other, like laundry ropes. Small sparrows sat on a thick one that reared from the transmitter on the other side of the road, as if they were all in some agreement to stay on the cable. *Shepherd*, he thought suddenly. Is that nobler? Shepherd of birds? Is that what he would call himself at the meeting? Would that make things good and make things go well?

He arrived to find their house looming over the road in grandeur and prominence. He accessed this secluded part of the street called 'Layout' by serendipity. The road was well laid, and there was a pavement, beyond both sides of which were residential buildings. The house he was looking for, number 71, sat at the end of the layout, creating a dead end. Its walls were yellow, not quite as high as some of the others but rimmed around on the top with fine hoops of barbed wire. As if to demonstrate what might happen to a robber confident enough to attempt a break-in, a black polythene bag had been caught on the spike of one of the hooped wires. The morning wind pushed persistently at the bag, forcing it to cling to the wire by one of its handles, and its tumefied body to continue to wheeze at the pressure of the wind.

Oseburuwa, he did not know why he watched the bag for as long as he did – an object caught in something from which it could not get away no matter how much it tried. This intrigued him. He pulled up in front of the giant gate and turned off his engine. He looked at himself in the rearview mirror. He'd successfully cut his hair the previous afternoon. By the mirror, he fixed his tie, which was the colour of the shirt he wore. He'd pressed it with the iron Ndali had bought him, a strange technique in which the surface of a hot object is pressed against a cloth. He sniffed the suit and questioned whether he should have worn it. He had washed it the day before and hung it on the laundry rope. He'd hoped to take it in shortly afterwards but had fallen asleep. Once I heard the rain, I rushed out of the yard, but there was nothing I could do. A chi cannot influence a host who is not in a conscious state. So I had watched, helpless, as rain poured down on his laundry until the drumming on the asbestos roof woke him. Instantly, I flashed the thought of the suit jacket into his mind, and he ran out but found the suit already soaked. He brought it into the house and hung it on a chair in the living room. Although it was dry by the time he put it on, it had acquired a rank smell. He removed the suit jacket and held it in his hand in case Ndali became concerned with why he did not wear it.

Before he turned on the engine again, he looked at the metallic structure attached to the gate. It was of Jisos Kraist bearing a piece of wood with two outstretched arms. He was gazing at this when the small gate attached to the big one opened. A man stepped out of it wearing a uniform of faded blue and a black beret. The man's trousers were hiked unevenly – one to the knees and the other below the knee.

'Oga, what do you want?' the man said.

'I am a guest of Ndali.'

'A guest, er,' the man said, a weak frown on his face. The man ran his eyes over the van, ignoring his affirmative answer. 'From where you know Madam from, Oga?' the man said in the language of the White Man.

'What?'

'I asked how you take know my Madam?' The man had come to the van, planted his two hands on top of it, and bent his head to peer in at its only occupant.

'I am her boyfriend. My name is Chinonso.'

'Okay, sir,' the man said. He detached from the van. 'You be the man they are expecting?'

'Yes, na me.'

'Ah, welcome, sir. Welcome.'

The man hurried through the small opening in the gate, and he heard a rattling of metals and rods. One of the two big gates squeaked and swung open. Although he knew that Ndali's father was a titled chief and therefore rich, he did not expect that their wealth would be of this magnitude. He didn't at all expect to see the life-size sculpture of a menacing lion, one foot suspended in mid-air, the other ballasted into the floor of the fountain. From its wide-open eyes and mouth flowed a steady stream of water into a bowl of concrete. It took him a moment to recall that she'd said something about a figure whose photo her dad had taken during a trip to France and vowed to replicate in their mansion in Umuahia. He searched his mind carefully to see if he had been told about a basket-ball hoop. Had she mentioned the number of cars they had, or that their cars sat under a structure roofed with zinc? He could not remember. He counted: the black Jeep – 1, the white Jeep – 2, a car whose make he did not know – 3, Ndali's Audi sedans – 4, 5, 6. Oh, there's another shielded from view by the big wheels – 7! Yet another, a Mercedes-Benz, beside which he'd parked his own vehicle – 8. Looking carefully, he could see that was all. Eight cars.

He'd stepped out before he noticed that the gateman had been following him and had been standing beside his car wait-ing for him to get out.

'I can help you carry anything you bring inside, Oga.'

He noticed then that he'd forgotten the gift he had brought. He stopped, turned and rushed back to the car. Even though the image of him dropping the bag with the wine on the bench in the yard stood like a banner in his mind, he searched the van, the backseats, the front like a madman.

Egbunu, I must say here that this was one of the occasions in which I had wanted to remind him that he was forgetting the gifts. But I didn't because of your counsel: *Let man be man*. The role of the chi is to attend to higher matters, things which, by virtue of their magnitude, can affect the host in major or significant ways. It must also attend to supernatural matters which man, in his limitation, cannot handle. But this omission, as I look back now on the things that would result from that visit, strikes me with pangs of regret, and I begin to wish that I had reminded him.

'Oga, Oga, hope no problem?' the gateman said repeatedly.

'No, no problem,' he said with a slight trembling in his voice.

He thought for a moment if he should rush back home, but he recalled she'd begged him not to arrive late. The word flashed in his mind like fire: *punctuality*. He remembered her saying it: 'My dad likes punctuality.' I was relieved, Chukwu, as he hurried towards the house.

ECHETAOBIESIKE, the confidence he'd arrived with, like an egg in a calabash, was already broken by the time he sat at the table with the family. Ndali had met him at the door and told him, in frantic whispers, that he'd come late. 'Fifteen minutes!' Then she reached to his back and removed something he'd not imagined could be there: a feather. Even I had not seen it. He almost wept as she crumpled the white feather into her palm, pointing him towards the dining room. 'Is that all?' he said. In whispers she asked why he held the suit, and he raised it up towards her face, gesturing for her to smell it.

'Jesus!' she said. 'Don't wear that smelling thing. *Nyamma!* Give it to me.' She took it from him and folded it, then handed it back to him. 'Keep it in your hand throughout, you hear me?'

The grandeur of the living room defeated him. Never had he dreamt that such lighting could exist. He didn't know that someone could have a sculpture of the Madonna inside

a house. The marble on the flooring, and the design of the
ceiling, these were beautiful beyond words. There were chan-
deliers and mantelpieces, articles I had seen in homes when
my former host Yagazie was in Virginia, in that land of the
brutal White Man. If the house struck him with such awe, it
was without doubt that the people who owned it would do
even more damage to his composure. So when he saw her
father, the man appeared huge to him. The man's fair complexion was spotted with reddish blotches that reminded him
of the musician Bright Chimezie. He found some comfort in
her mother, for her face was the exact replica of Ndali's. But
when her brother walked down the stairs, he wished he'd not
come. He looked like black American musicians – with nicely
trimmed hair on the side of his face that traced down to his
jaw and a broad, pink-lipped mouth held between a heavy
moustache and beard. In response to his 'Good afternoon, my
brother', the man gave him only a grin.

They sat at the table as the maids served different foods
on trays. With every passing moment, my host noticed one
more thing that further damaged his confidence, so that by
the time the food had all been served and they began to eat,
he was already vanquished. When the first question came, he
struggled to form words and dithered for such a long time that
Ndali spoke in his stead.

'Nonso runs a poultry farm the size of this entire compound
all by himself,' she said. 'He has a lot of chickens – agric fowl –
and also sells them in the markets.'

'Excuse me, gentleman,' her father said again, as if she had
not spoken at all. 'What did you say you do?'

He made to speak, his voice starting to stutter, for he was
truly afraid, then he stopped. He looked at Ndali, and she
met his eyes.

'Daddy—'

'Let him answer the question,' her father said, turning to his daughter with a countenance that did not conceal his anger. 'I asked him, not you. He has a mouth, or not?'

He was worried by Ndali's confrontation with her father, and from under the table, he touched her with his leg to make her stop, but she pulled her leg away. In the small silence that descended, his voice broke out.

'I am a farmer, a poultry farmer. And I have land where I grow maize, pepper, tomatoes and okro.' He looked up at her – for he had come prepared to use a tool she had supplied him with – and said, 'I am a shepherd of birds, sir.'

Her father gave his wife what my host thought was a puzzled look that filled my host with the dread that he may have misspoken, and his feeling in this moment was like that of a man whose extremities were bound and was then thrust naked into the central arena of a village, with nothing to hide himself. Without intending to, he saw that he'd turned to her brother, on whose face he found the impression of muffled laughter. He became frantic. This thing Ndali had told him, how could it be wrong? She'd said it sounded fancier, and it did – to his ear, at least.

'I see,' the father said. 'So, gentleman, shepherd of birds, what education do you have?'

'Daddy—'

'No, Ndi, no!' her father said in a raised voice. A strained vein became visible on the side of his neck like a blow-induced swelling. 'You must let him speak, or this meeting is over. You hear?'

'Yes, Daddy.'

'Good. Now, gentleman, *ina anu okwu Igbo?*'

He nodded.

'Should I speak it, then?' the father said, and a piece of the chopped vegetable clung to his lower lip.

'No need, sir. Speak English.'

'Good,' the father said. 'What is your level of education?'

'I have completed secondary school, sir.'

'So,' the father said as he gathered pieces of chicken flesh on to the prongs of his fork. 'School cert.'

'It is so, sir. Yes, sir.'

The man gave his wife the look again. 'Gentleman, I don't mean to embarrass you,' the father said, letting his voice fall from the height to which he'd pitched it. 'We are not in the business of embarrassing people; we are a Christian family.' He pointed around to an étagère placed on the glass-covered bookcase on one side of the room, which held various paintings of Jisos Kraist and his disciples.

My host looked up at the étagère, nodded, and said, 'Yes, sir—'

'But I have to ask this question.' – 'Yes, sir.' – 'Have you considered that my daughter here is a soon-to-be pharmacist?' – 'Yes, sir.' – 'Have you considered that she is now completing her bachelor's in pharmacy and will so proceed to do her MPhil in the UK?' – 'Yes, sir.' – 'Have you considered, young man, what kind of future you, an unschooled farmer, will have with her?'

'Daddy!'

'Ndali, quiet!' her father said. '*Mechie gi onu! Ina num? A si'm gi michie onu!*'

'Ndi, what is this?' her mother said. '*Iga ekwe ka daddy gi kwu okwu?*'

'I'm letting him speak, Mommy, but do you hear what he is saying?' Ndali said.

'Yes, but keep quiet, you hear?'

'I do,' Ndali said with a sigh.

When her father began to speak again, the words came to my host again in a glut, each running into the other and the other.

'Young man, have you thought about it thoroughly?' – 'Yes, sir.' – 'Deeply about what kind of life you will have with her?' – 'Yes, sir.' – 'You have, I see.' – 'Yes, sir.' – 'And you think it is the right decision to marry such a woman who is so high above you, who wants to be her husband?' – 'I know, sir.' – 'Then, you must go and think about it again. Go and see if truly you deserve my daughter.' – 'Yes, sir.' – 'That is all I will say to you.'

'Yes, sir.'

Her father rose in a slow, heavy manner, with his body pitching against the table, and left. Her mother followed moments later, shaking her head with a countenance my host would reckon later to have been pity towards him. She headed first to the kitchen, carrying empty plates stacked together. Ndali's brother, who had not said anything but had made his resentment known by laughing at every answer my host gave, rose shortly after his mother. He lingered for a while on his feet while he took a toothpick from the casing, stifling a laugh.

'You too, Chuka?' Ndali said in a voice that dripped with sobs.

'What?' Chuka said. 'Er-er, er-er, don't even call my name here, oh. Don't tell me even a single thing! Is it me that asked you to bring a poor farmer home?' He laughed, jerking. 'Don't you mention my name again, there, oh.'

With that, he, too, headed his father's way, on a flight of stairs, the toothpick held between his clenched teeth, whistling a tune as he went.

Ijango-ijango, my host sat there, rendered inutile by shame.

He fixed his eyes on the plate of food in front of him, most of which he'd barely touched. From upstairs, he heard Ndali's mother say to her husband in the language of the eminent fathers, 'Dim, you were too harsh on that young man, er. You could have said these things in a way that didn't sound that harsh.'

He looked up at his lover, who remained where she was, rubbing her right hand over her left. He knew that she was feeling a pain that was as deep as his. He wanted to comfort her, but he could not lift himself. For such is the state a man enters when he has been disgraced: inaction, numbness – as if he has been tranquillised. I have seen it many times.

His eyes fell on the large painting of a man gently ascending into the sky over what seemed to be a village with the rest of the people of the village looking up in his direction and pointing at him. Because his mind sometimes bore strange convictions, he did not know why he thought for a moment that this man who was levitating into the sky was my host himself.

It was with a mighty effort that he rose and touched Ndali on the shoulder and whispered in her ear to stop crying. He pulled her gently up, but she struggled, her tears mixing with saliva that slid slowly down her dress.

'Leave me, leave me,' she said. 'Leave me alone. What kind of family is this, er? What?'

'It is okay, Mommy,' he said with his lips unmoved so that he wondered how the words had come out of him.

He rested his hands on her head and gently traced his fingers down her neck. Then he bent forward and, sinking his head towards her mouth, locked her in a kiss. Before they walked out of the house, he threw a gaze at the painting for one last time and noticed what had not occurred to him the first time:

that the people in the lower end of the painting were cheering at this man who was ascending into the sky.

CHUKWU, I have seen first-hand what shame can do to a man. As it often does, it filled my host with an oppressive fear, the fear that he would lose Ndali like most of the things that had once been his. It grew in the days following, during which she made efforts to force her family to reconsider, but failed. Those days stretched into weeks, and it became clear by the third that nothing would change their minds. When Ndali came back from a quarrel with her parents, he resolved to change things himself and do something. Rain had fallen all morning, but by noon the sun had risen. She came directly from school in Uturu, filled with bitterness. He was out on the small farm when she drove on to the path flanked on both sides by farmland. He was at the furthest end of the farm, where his father had erected a fence which had partly crumbled under the heavy rainfall of the year the White Man refers to as 2003. Two feet from the fence was a long gutter that ran through the street, and beyond this was the long main road. As he watched her step out of the car towards the house, it occurred to him that she had not seen him. He dropped his hoe, and the head of the yam for which he had been digging a hole, and ran to the house.

He entered still wearing his dirty visor, a soiled shirt, trousers, and farm slippers covered with loam and other weeds he'd pruned off the land.

He found her with her face buried on her wrist, facing the wall.

'Mommy, *kedi ihe mere nu*?' he said, for in the moment of tension, he reached for the language to which he was much accustomed. 'Why are you crying, why are you crying, Mommy? Er, what happened?'

She turned to embrace him, but he stepped away from her because of his farm clothes. She stopped an inch from him, her eyes deep red.

'Why are they doing this to me, er, Obim? Why?'

'What happened, er? Tell me what happened.'

She told him about how her father had asked her if she was still seeing him and had threatened her. Her mother had intervened, saying the man was being too harsh, but her father continued unhindered.

'It is well,' he said. 'It will be well after everything.'

'No, Nonso, no!' she said, slapping the wall with her palm again. 'It will not be well. How can it be well? I am not going back to that house again. I am not. Over my dead body. What kind of family is this?'

His heart swirled within him at her rage. He did not know what to do. The old fathers, in their magnanimous wisdom, say that a person saves himself in the process of saving others. If she cannot be saved from a situation such as this, which has held them bound like invisible leashes, then he, too, cannot be saved. And it won't indeed be well. He watched her walk a few paces towards the door, stop, and put her hand on her chest. Then she turned back to face him. 'I have – I have brought a few of my things, and I am staying here. I'm staying here.'

She opened the door and stepped out of the house. He followed her out to the front porch and looked on as she opened the boot of her car and returned with a shiny Ghana-must-go bag. Then, from the backseat, she took out a pair of shoes and a nylon bag. He watched her with a certain joy, inwardly happy that he finally had a companion.

But for much of that week, her phone rang again and again, sometimes for extended periods. And each time, Ndali would look at its face and say to my host, 'It is my dad,' or 'It is my mum.' And every time he would beg her to answer the call, but she wouldn't. For she was strong-willed like most of the great mothers. She would merely hiss at my host's entreaty and turn her attention to something else, like one beyond reproach or beyond the fear of reproach. My host admired this in her. Whenever she did this, at such moments he'd think about a similar trait in his mother.

In the middle of the second week, her parents came to look for her at school and waited outside her classroom, but she ignored them and walked away with her classmate Lydia. After she told him this, he began to fear that she was starting to resent her family for his sake. Even though he increasingly sought to salvage the situation as days passed, he could not deny that her love for him seemed to grow stronger in those days. For it felt as though she'd culled her love away from everyone else and bequeathed it all to him. It was during this time that twice, while they made love, she wept. It was during these days that she baked him a cake, wrote him a poem, and sang for him. And once, while he was asleep, she unhooked the catapult from the wall and rushed out to the yard with it and scared away a prowling kite. And part of him sought to prolong those days, for although they were not yet married, it felt to him as though they were. He wished that he would take the centre of her life, dwell around the boundaries, and seal up the limits. This woman, whom he'd always feared he could never have but who was now his, he could not afford to lose. Yet his fear of what she was doing grew alongside the blossoming of his affection for her, and her affection for him.

It was during this period that she travelled to Enugu with him. He'd woken early that memorable morning of life to find her dressed, in an ankara print gown and a calico head scarf, stirring tea in a cup while looking through the poultry record book on the table.

'Are you going somewhere, Mommy?'

'Good morning, dear.'

'Good morning,' he said.

'No, I'm going to Enugu too.'

'What? Mommy—'

'I want to come, Nonso. I am not doing anything here. I want to know everything about you and about the fowls. I like it.'

He was so taken aback that he struggled to find words. He looked on the dining table, and there he found one of the plastic crates, its dozen egg-holding cups nearly filled with eggs.

'Those ones are from the broilers?'

She nodded. 'I collected them around six o'clock. They are even still laying more.'

He smiled, for one of the things she loved the most about tending his poultry was collecting the eggs. She was fascinated by the phenomenon of egg laying, how rapidly it occurred in chickens.

'Mommy, okay, but Ogbete market is—'

'It is okay, Nonso. It is okay. I am not an egg. I have told you – I don't like you treating me like I'm an egg. I'm like you. I want to come.'

His eyes fell hard on her face, and he saw in her eyes that she meant it. He nodded. 'Okay, let me baff, then,' he said, and rushed off to bathe.

Later, they dropped off the eggs at the restaurant down the street, and he promised to come for his pay on his way back from Enugu. As they drove on the highway, he could tell that he'd never felt such joy while travelling before. On the bridge over the Amatu River, she revealed to him how after the night he first found her on that bridge, she was still greatly heartbroken. She went to Lagos to stay with her uncle for two months, and while there, she frequently thought of him. And every time she did she would laugh at how strange he was. He in turn told her about how he'd returned to the river to look for the fowls but couldn't find them, and how he had been angry at himself.

'I was thinking the other day,' she said, 'how a man who loves fowls so much could do that. Why did you?'

He looked at her. 'I don't know, Mommy.'

Once he'd said those words, it struck him that he might know why she loved him: because he'd rescued her from something. Just like his gosling, also taken under his care. This thought was enunciated so loudly in his mind that he looked at her to make sure she did not hear it. But her eyes were out the window, looking at the other side of the road, where the thick forest had given way to the scattered habitation of a village.

At the market in Enugu, he introduced her as his fiancée to a gleeful reception by his acquaintances. Ezekobia, a feed seller, gave them palm wine to drink, *the drink of the gods*. Some of them shook hands with him and embraced her. My host's face was lit with a flaming smile the entire time, for the blank wall of the future had suddenly become emblazoned with warm colours. It was almost full sun when they left the market, carrying the things they had bought.

He and Ndali purchased *ugba* from a roadside hawker near the garage where they parked the vehicle. Ndali, soaked in sweat, bought a bottle of La Casera. She had him try it, and it tasted sweet, but he could not describe what it tasted like. She laughed at him.

'Bushman. It is apple taste. I'm sure you have never eaten apple before.'

He shook his head. They had loaded a new cage, and two

bags of broiler feed, and a half sack of millet, and were now sitting in the van, about to return to Umuahia.

'I am not Oyibo. I will eat my *ugba* as correct African man.'

He unwrapped the food and began putting handfuls into his mouth and chewing in a way that made her laugh.

'I have told you to stop chewing things like a goat: nyum-yum-yum. *Tufia!*' she said, snapping her fingers in the air, laughing.

But he ate on, bobbing his head and darting his tongue about in his mouth.

'Well, maybe one day we will go abroad together.'

'Abroad? Why?'

'So you can see things, naw, and stop this bushmanliness.'

'Ha, okay, Mommy.'

He started the engine, and they hit the road. The van had just left the city when he began feeling uneasy. His stomach gave in to wild sensations, and he farted.

'Jesus! *Nyamma!*' she cried. 'Nonso?'

'Mommy, sorry, but I am—'

He was silenced by another release. He pulled hurriedly to the shoulder of the road.

'Mommy, my stomach,' he gasped.

'What?'

'You have tissue, tissue paper?'

'Yes, yes.' She reached for her bag, but before she could get the papers out, he grabbed a handkerchief from the pocket under the door handle of his side of the van and raced towards the bush. Chukwu, he nearly tore his trousers open once he was within concealable distance of the forest, and once they came off, his excreta slammed into the grass with an unaccustomed force. I was alarmed, for not since he was a boy had I seen this kind of thing happen to him.

When he rose up it was with some relief, his forehead wet as if he'd been in the rain. Ndali had come out of the van and was at the mouth of the bush, holding the half-used roll of tissue.

'What happened?'

'I wanted to shit badly,' he said.

'God! Nonso?'

She burst out laughing again.

'Why are you laughing?'

She struggled to speak. 'See your face – you are sweating.'

They had barely driven for fifteen minutes when he rushed out again. He had the tissues this time, and with so much force did he defecate that his strength was expended. For some time after he was done, he knelt down and clung to a tree. I had never seen anything like this happen to him. And even though I had learned to gaze into his viscera, I could not find exactly what was wrong with him, even though he was convinced he had diarrhoea.

'I actually have diarrhoea,' he told Ndali when he returned to the van.

Ndali laughed even harder, and he joined in.

'It must be that *ugba*. I don't know what they put inside.'

'Yes, you don't know.' She laughed even more. 'This is why I don't eat anyhow for anywhere. You are doing African man.'

'I'm feeling like tired.'

'Yes, drink water and my La Casera and rest. I will drive.'

'You will drive my van?'

'Yes, why not?'

Astonished though he was, he let her drive, and for a long time after they resumed the journey, he did not feel the urge. But when it came, he pounded his hands on the dashboard, and when she pulled up, he flung himself out of the door and tripped into the creepers. Then, picking himself up, he dashed into the bush as if unhinged. He returned to the van drenched in sweat, while she struggled to contain her laughter. He emptied the big Ragolis water bottle into his mouth and clung to the empty bottle. He told her a story his father had once told him about a man who had stopped like him to shit in a wild bush on the highway, and while at it, got swallowed by a python. His father used to play the song someone sang about it, 'Eke a Tuwa lam ujo'.

'I think I have heard the song before. But I'm afraid of all snakes – python, oh; cobra, oh; rattlesnake, oh; every snake.'

'It is so, Mommy.'

'How are you feeling now?'

'Fine,' he said. He hadn't gone for nearly as long as it would take to break five full kola nuts in four places, and they were almost in Umuahia. 'Almost thirty minutes now, I never go. I think it have stopped.'

'Yes, I agree. But I have laughed all my energy out, too.'

They drove past thick forests on both sides for some time in serenity, his mind splintered between thoughts. Then suddenly it came upon him with the force of a gust, and he dashed into the bush.

OSEBURUWA, she tended to my host until he was whole again. She went to the university the following day. When she returned, she joined him on the bench in the yard, plucking a sick fowl with bare hands so it could get some air into its skin. An old tray sat between them, full of feathers. He held on to one leg of the bird as he worked. She did this duty – the oddest thing she'd ever done in her life – with a curious mix of equanimity and laughter. While they worked, he forced himself to talk about his family, how he missed them, and the need for her to reconcile with hers. He spoke with great care, as if his tongue was a wet priest in the sanctuary of his mouth.

Then she told him that her parents had come to the school to look for her that day again.

'Nonso, I don't want to see them. I just don't want.'

'Have you thought of it very well? Do you know this is even making the situation worst now?'

She'd started to twist a feather from the leg of the bird when he said this. She drew back and sat on her legs on the raffia mat spread on the ground.

'How?'

'Because, Mommy, I am the one. It is because of me this is happening.'

The hen raised its freed leg and dropped a blob of faeces on the mat.

'Oh, my God!'

They laughed and laughed on until he released the hen and it hopped towards the coop, cackling plaintively. Egbunu, it might be the laughter that softened her heart, for when he explained afterwards that her action might make her family despise him the more, since it was for his sake this was happening, she sat in silence. And, later, as they lay in bed to sleep, she said, suddenly and over the rattling of the ceiling fan, that he had spoken the truth. She would return home.

Like a water-filled calabash sent off with an emissary to the land of a provoked enemy, she went home the following day, but returned three days later as a calabash smouldering with fire. Her father had sent out very many invitations for his upcoming sixtieth birthday party but had not invited him. Her father had said he was not qualified to be there. She left the house, her resolve firm that she would not return. She said this with feral rage, stamping her feet and shouting, 'How, just how can he do this? How? And if they refuse to invite you,' she said, 'I swear to God who made me' – she tapped the tip of her tongue with her index finger – 'er, I swear to God who made me, I will not attend myself. I will not.'

He said nothing, busied with the soft burden she'd laid on him. He was seated at the dining table, where he'd sat picking dirt and pebbles out of a bowl of white beans. Bean weevils escaped from the unpacked beans, crouched on the table, or perched on the adjacent wall. When he finished picking the beans, he poured them into a pot and set it on the stove. He took up the flashy invitation card from the chair on which she'd dropped it and began reading the words to himself.

This card is to invite mister _____ and miss _____ and your household to the birthday party of Chief. Doctor. Luke Okoli Obialor, the Nmalite 1 of Umuahia-Ibeku kingdom of Abia State of Nigeria. The event shall be at the Obialor compound on July 14, at Aguiyi Ironsi Layout . . .

She had gone to his old bedroom, where the wall was defaced with his childhood drawings, mostly of the God of the White Man, his angels, his sister and his gosling. She'd chosen this room as her study, where she read her books while in the house, and she slept with him in the bedroom that had once belonged to his parents. He read the invitation aloud from the sitting room so that she could hear him.

'Fourteen, at Lagos Street on the July 14, 2007. There will be food in abundance and music by His Excellency, the king of ogene music, Chief Oliver De Coque. The party will be held from four p.m. to nine p.m.'

'It is my turn, me too I will not care.'

'The emcee of the occasion will be none other than the inestimable Nkem Owoh, Osuofia himself.'

'I don't care; I will not go.'
'Come one, come all.'

IJANGO-IJANGO, the early fathers, wise in the ways of humanity, used to say that the life of a man is anchored on a swivel. It can spin this way or that way, and a person's life can change in significant ways in an instant. In the batting of an eyelid, a world that has stood can lie prostrate, and that which was flat on the ground just a moment before can suddenly stand erect. I have seen it many times. I saw it again after my host returned from an errand one afternoon a few days later. He'd gone out not too long after they had lunch to supply four of the large cocks to the restaurant at the centre of the city while Ndali studied. He'd become increasingly troubled by the gathering storms in his life, fearing again that something was watching him, looking for a time when he'd be happy enough to strike and steal his joy and replace it with sorrow. It was a fear that had lodged itself in his mind from the time his gosling died. This fear – as is common when it possesses a man's mind – convinced him with all the force of a persuasion that Ndali would be pressured to leave him eventually. And as much as I flashed thoughts in his mind continuously to contest it, it held firm. He went on fearing that, in time, she would give him up rather than lose her family. So biting was this fear that, as he drove back to the compound after the errand, he had to play Oliver De Coque's music on the van's cassette player to prevent himself from slipping into despair. Only one of the speakers was working, and sometimes, overwhelmed by the loud street noise, the music lapsed. It was those times, when Oliver's baritone voice quailed, that the weight on his mind came bearing down on him.

When he got home later, Ndali was sitting in the backyard, watching the fowls feed on the corn she'd spread on a sack, reading a textbook on the bench under the tree by the light of the rechargeable lamp. She had changed into a blouse and shorts that made her buttocks prominent. She had her hair oiled slick and now wore a bandanna over it. She stood up once she heard the net door opening.

'Guess, guess, guess, Obim?' she said.

She clasped her hand around him, almost stepping on one of the chickens, which fled frantically, its wings spread out, cawing.

'What?' my host said, surprised as much as I was.

'They said you can come.' She pressed her hands around his neck. 'My dad, they said you can come.'

He had not expected this at all, and it was thus with relief and mild incomprehension that he bellowed, 'Oh, that is good!'

'Will you come, Obim?'

He could not look at her, so he did not look at her. But she inched towards him, in slow steps, and took his jaw and lifted his face to face her. 'Nonso, Nonso.'

'Eh, Mommy?'

'I know what they did to you was not good. They disgraced you. But, you see, these things happen. This is Nigeria. This is Alaigbo. A poor man is a poor man. *Onye ogbenye*, he is not respected in the society. And, again, my dad and brother? They are proud people. Even my mum, even though she does not support my dad very much in this.'

He did not speak.

'They may be ashamed of you, but I am not. I cannot be ah—' She held his jaw and peered into his face. 'Nonso, what is it? Why are you not saying anything?'

'Nothing, Mommy. I will come.'

She hugged him. And in the silence, he heard the sound of the nocturnal insects emptying into the ear of the night.

'I will go with you to the party, for your sake,' he said again. And as he spoke, he saw that she'd closed her eyes and would not open them until he'd finished speaking.

7

THE DISGRACED

EGBUNU, the old fathers say that a mouse cannot run into an empty mousetrap in broad daylight unless it has been drawn to the trap by something it could not refuse. Egbunu, would a fish see an empty metal hook sticking out beneath water and cleave to it? How would it unless it is enticed by something on the hook? Isn't this similar to how a man is enticed into a situation he would not have liked to be in? My host, for instance, would not have agreed to attend Ndali's father's party had they not shown repentance and her father signed an invitation card with his name on it: 'Mr Chinonso Olisa'. Although I will acknowledge that he was persuaded in part by the determination to make Ndali happy at all costs and by a desire to see Oliver De Coque perform live, he was cautious even to the end. He decided to attend the party with only a part of him attuned to it, merely dragging along the other intransigent half. And I, his chi, had been unable to decide whether he should go. I feared that from what I knew of man, a feeling such as that which they had shown him – repulsion – does not easily expire. But I had seen the healing and equilibrium that this woman had brought into his life and desired that it would continue. For it is abominable for a chi to stand in the way of his own host. When a man affirms a thing, and if his chi does not desire this thing, all it can do is persuade its host. But if its host refuses, then the chi must not attempt to compel its host against his will; it must affirm the thing. This is again why the wise fathers often say that if a man agrees to something, his chi must agree too. The second reason for my ambivalence was because I had developed a strong faith in Ndali's love for him, mostly after encountering her chi, and I strongly believed that if he married her, he would become complete, as the old fathers often say that a man is not complete until he marries a woman.

The day before the party, they went to buy greeting cards for her father at the big supermarket near the Oando petrol station. At a roadside clothes shop on Crowther Street, he bought an isiagu tunic. Although Ndali had pointed out that the ones with the black lion-head prints were better looking, he was drawn to the red ones for some reason he could not understand. They had emerged from the shop and were walking towards a shopping complex, the speakers of a church blasting from an upstairs block on the complex, when he saw Motu in front of an open mechanic's workshop. She stood between a pile of motor tyres and a mechanic who, dressed in blue overalls and large dark goggles, was firing a rod with something that gave off radiant, glittering sparks of red flame. She was dressed in a flowing gown, the green one with red leaf prints, which he'd removed a few times before making love to her. She had just finished selling groundnuts to one of the men, and she was bunching a piece of cloth into an *aju* to place on her head before balancing the tray on it. It felt, Egbunu, that for an instant, he'd slipped from the hands of his present world like an oiled fish. He stood there, undecided as to what to do, wondering why she had left him. But Motu did not even turn. She put the tray on her head and walked in the other direction, towards a crowded market. He thought to call out to her but feared that she might not hear him over the great noise of the welding machine. His heart palpitating, he turned towards Ndali, who had continued to walk on without knowing he was no longer in tow. He had not realised that while watching Motu, he'd also focused on the fire from the mechanic's welder. And when he stirred away from it, his vision had become blurred, and for a moment it appeared as if the world and all that was in it had become covered in a thick, silky veil of yellow.

CHUKWU, Ndali did not return with him to his house that day. She went to help her parents prepare for the big next day. Aside from attending to a sick hen who had started to sprout a nacre-like substance on the sides of its beak, dabbing it with a clean towel soaked in warm water, he spent the rest of the day thinking of Motu. He wondered what had happened, whose hand it was that had stretched out and grabbed her away from his fold and stolen her away from him. He would have spoken to her, had he been alone. He thought long about why she left him, without warning, without provocation, when in fact it had seemed she loved him and he'd been firmly planted in her heart. Children of men beware: you cannot put your confidence in another man. No one is fixed beyond being blown sideways. No one! I have seen it many times. He was still deep in thought when his phone buzzed. He picked it up, tapped the message box, and read, They really want u to come Obim!!! even my brother. i luv u, gudnyt.

He arrived at her family's residence the following day to find that he was the first person there. Ndali came to meet him and asked him to follow her into the house. But he would hear none of it. He sat in a plastic chair under one of the two tarpaulin-covered pavilions erected for guests. Another pavilion stood separated from these two by a raised stage platform with a floor covered by a red rug. It was the High Table, where the party hosts and other dignitaries were to sit. There, the seats were arranged behind a long table near the stage, which was covered with embroidered cloth. A group of men soaked in sweat set speakers in place beside the table while two women dressed in identical blouses and skirts decorated big cakes with the moulded effigy of Ndali's father holding a staff.

He picked up a copy of the programme placed on his seat and was starting to read when he felt a chair behind him rattle. Before he could tell what it was, or even look back, a hand tapped his shoulder and a head bent towards his side.

'So you came,' the head said.

Things had happened so quickly that he was incapacitated by the ghastly thrill of sudden fright.

'You came after all,' the man, whom he now recognised to be Chuka, repeated. Chuka spoke the language of the White Man with a foreign accent similar to Ndali's. 'Some people, some people, they just have no shame. No shame. How can you – after all popman did to you that day – come here?'

Chuka placed his arm on my host's shoulder and pulled him closer. I heard the voice of my host's head shout, *Was he not close enough*? A sound in the upward direction in the distance caused him to raise his head and catch the sight of Ndali on what must have been the balcony of her room.

'Wave at her, tell her you are okay,' Chuka said. 'Wave at her!'

She was saying something he could not hear but which I made out to be a question as to whether or not he was fine. He obeyed the order he'd been given, and she waved back and blew a kiss into the air. He had thought her brother was concealing himself behind him, but now Chuka shouted, 'Your man and I are having a sweet talk!'

At that my host thought he saw something like a smile flash across his lover's face, an unmistakable sign that she believed her brother.

'Good. Thank you, Chuka,' she shouted back.

Chuka had spoken the language of the White Man to his sister, but now he continued his onslaught in the language of the fathers: 'I bu Otobo; otobo ki ibu. *Real, real* otobo. How should one position his neck or shape his mouth to pass a message into the head of an otobo like you? How? It baffles me.' He squeezed my host's shoulder so hard that he squirmed.

'Now, listen, *Church Rat*, my father said I should tell you that if we hear "phim" from you, or any noise at all, you will be in serious trouble. Do you know you are playing with fire? You are cuddling a consuming fire. You are romancing the child of a tiger, Nwa-agu.' Chuka drew a deep breath and released it on his neck.

'Ah, you dress in a respectable fashion, *Church Rat*,' Chuka said now, pulling up the isiagu on my host by its shoulder. '*Looks very good, sir.* Otobo. Eh, let me pass the message: no speaking, no doing anything. No phim. Don't make the mistake of coming out to join the family on the dance floor, or anything like that, no matter what my sister says. *I repeat*, no matter what my sister says. You hear me?'

Gaganaogwu, I had known my host at that point for twenty-five years and three moons, and I had never seen him that embarrassed. He was wounded as if Chuka had not said words to him but had lashed him with a whip. What pained him the most was that he could not retaliate. As a boy, he had not been afraid of fights: in fact, he had been feared, for although he did not court trouble, he fought with a fist of stone when provoked. But in this situation, he was incapacitated, hand-tied. So although bruised, he simply nodded in response.

'Good, *Church Rat*, you are welcome.'

For no particular reason, he would always remember those final words, a mix of the language of the fathers and the White Man's: 'Odinma, *Church Rat*, ibia wo.'

The early fathers often say that a planned war does not take even the crippled by surprise. But an unplanned one, that which is unexpected, can defeat even the strongest army. It is why they also say, in their cautionary wisdom, that if one wakes in the morning to find something as innocuous as a hen chasing him, he should run because he does not know whether the hen has grown teeth and claws during the night. Thus defeated, my host sat stunned for the rest of the party.

The guests started pouring in not too long after Chuka left him. The invitation card indicated that the event was to be held from 4 to 9 p.m. But the first guests arrived around a quarter after five. Ndali had bemoaned the fact that this would happen – 'You will see that they will all follow Nigerian time. This is why I hate attending events like this. If it was not because of my father, I tell you, just count me out.' He watched as the seats filled up all around him with guests who came wearing different attire, usually a man in flowing traditional cloth and his wife in an equally sparkling blouse, a wrappa wound around her waist, a fancy purse or handbag in her hand. Children sat in the last two rows of plastic chairs, with high armrests. By the time most of the seats were occupied, the air was filled with a cocktail of perfumes and body fragrances.

The man who sat by his left arm took up conversation with him. Without being asked, the man said that his wife was one of those cooking 'up there in the palace', pointing to the house of the Obialors. My wife, too, he said, intending to silence the man. But the man spoke on about the big attendance, and then about the hotness of the weather. My host listened with a dry indifference which, in time, the man seemed to notice. And when the seats next to him became filled with a couple, he turned away from my host to them.

Glad that he'd finally been left alone, my host evaluated what had happened: a hand had come, drawn him back so hard he'd almost fallen out of his seat. Then a mouth had asked him why he'd come, called him foolish, called him a hippopotamus, mocked his clothes, laughed at his love for Ndali, and inflicted the death blow: Church Rat. Had the seats been filled as they were now, none of that would probably have happened. These people had all come too late. So late were they that the celebrated entrance of Oliver De Coque – his favourite musician, the great singing bird of Igboland, Oku-na-acha-na-abali, the chief of Igbo highlife music – meant nothing. He sat as if benumbed as the guests rose to cheer the singer. Blood would have stirred within him as the emcee of the occasion and the famous home-video actor Osuofia introduced Oliver De Coque. But the words sounded like the words of a rambler. He would have laughed at Osuofia's jokes – for instance, the one he'd drawn right out of his famous movie, *Osuofia in London*, about how white people had mangled his name and called him Oso-fire. But the joke sounded like a child's gibberish, and it even surprised him that people laughed. The big fat man in front of him, how is he laughing like that? The woman beside the man, why is she rocking like that on the chair? He made no response at all to Osuofia's constant bellowing of 'Kwenu!' to which the people responded, 'Yaah!' And when, shortly after the introduction and the invitation of certain persons to the High Table, and after Oliver De Coque mounted the stage to the tune of

'People's Club', he sat dead as a log of wood. Even De Coque had come too late.

Much to his irritation, the man who sat next to him on the left had been dancing in his chair and had remembered him again. And the man would bend every now and again to comment about the attendance, the music, Oliver De Coque's genius, and whatever. But the log of wood merely nodded and muttered under his breath. And even this was said with much reluctance. The man did not know that he'd been asked not to make even the faintest of sounds, a phim. It struck him now, as he thought about it, that the order had come from the owner of the party himself, the very host, Ndali's father. In the midst of these thoughts, he heard something knock at the back of his chair. His heart flew out of him. When he turned, he found the culprit was the boy who sat directly behind him. The boy's foot had hit his chair.

EZEUWA, there are times when it feels like the universe, as if possessing the face of a laconic man, mocks man. As if man were a toy, a plaything given to the whims of the universe. Get down, it seems to say one time. And when a man sits, it orders him to stand again. It gives a man food with one hand and with the other compels him to vomit it. I have lived in the world for many cycles of life, and I have seen this mysterious phenomenon many times. How, for instance, might one explain that just shortly after my host had been startled by this boy (a mere boy!) and returned his gaze back to the great musician, a hand tapped him from behind again, and before he could stir, he hears, 'Obim, Obim, they will call us soon. Stand and come. Stand and come'? Well, the action must have come to him too quickly for him to think it through. And because she'd esteemed him highly before those present by calling him her darling, he'd risen and followed her in the glory of the moment. He would himself be taken in by her beauty, for she was dressed exquisitely. A long string of *jigida* cascaded down her neck, and she wore some of the beads on her wrists. This woman whom everyone around him was calling the daughter of the High One – Adaego and Adaora. Would it not be the worst disgrace to have, in the midst of all these people, remained seated? So he followed her to wild cheers.

The things they said as she and he left came to him like a big joke of fate. 'See him, a worthy man deserving of such a woman!' one man said. 'Nwokeoma!' another praised. 'Enyi-kwo-nwa!' one woman cried. A man standing in plain clothes by one of the tall standing fans at the end of every two rows gave him the greeting of chiefs by extending his hand against his. In shock, as much as with reluctance, he knocked the back of his hand against the man's three times. 'Congrats!' the man whispered. He nodded, and his hand, as if it had suddenly acquired a mind of its own, patted the man on the shoulder. It occurred to him then that things were happening too quickly – as if his body parts had mutinied against him and formed a defiant confederacy devoid of his control.

With every step, his hand locked in hers, Ndali led him further and further into transgression. But he could do nothing, for the whole party, spread around the spacious front area of the compound, had now turned to them, and Oliver De Coque himself had paused his music to give a passing greeting: 'See the future oriaku and her man walking by with great strides.' To which Ndali waved – and he waved, too – at the crowd of dignitaries, rich men and women, chiefs, doctors, lawyers, three men who had flown in from two of the white people's countries, Germany and the United States (one of whom had brought a white woman with yellow hair), Chuwuemeka Ike, one senator from Abuja, a representative of the state governor, Orji Kalu. He, a Church Rat – a man who raised domestic fowls for a living and cultivated tomatoes, corn, cassava and peppers, killed red ants and poked sticks into the faeces of yard fowls for worms – had waved at these dignitaries.

They passed so many people on the way into the house. Amongst them were two women who were looking in a mirror, applying powder to their faces; a man (one of the ones from overseas) in dazzling white *bariga* and a red *ozo* cap, smoking from a pipe; a policeman with an AK-47 who stood with his gun pointed upwards; two young girls of puberty age, in flowing gowns, looking in a phone under the shelter of the huge veranda with Roman columns; and a bow-tied boy whose shirt had been soaked in Fanta.

Once inside the house, Ndali pressed her lips on his sweating cheek. It was what she did in lieu of locking mouths with him whenever she had painted her lips a darker shade of pink or red.

'Are you enjoying yourself?' she said, and before he could speak, she said, 'You are sweating again! Did you bring a handkerchief?'

He said no. He wanted to say more, but she'd turned into the house, and he followed her. Once in, he found Chuka standing midway on the flight of stairs, visibly astonished to see him there. Words hung, dazed, on his lips as they passed Chuka.

'What is it, Obim? Nonso?' she said after they had passed Chuka, stopping again, this time in a small room where shelves of books split the room into four rows.

'Nothing,' he said. 'Water, can you give me water?'

'Water? Okay, let me bring it.' At the threshold, she said, 'My brother, did he do anything to you?'

'Me? No-oh, no, he didn't.'

She stayed her gaze on him for a moment, as if unbelieving, then she left the room. Once she was gone, he nearly wept. He sat without realising it on a small reclining couch that spun, rapidly, and faced the window. He saw now, from the vantage of a hawk paused on a thermal, the party. Osuofia was dancing, interrupting Oliver De Coque every now and then. Chukwu, this is how things sometimes happen to humans: a man becomes afraid of something like this, of being shamed in public, and this fear becomes his undoing. For the state of anxiety is a seed-bearing one. Every occasion pollinates it, and with every action, a seed is begotten. When a word is used that might elicit an unhealthy response, and in the presence of people, he may lose composure and his limbs may quiver. Thus, every inch of the way, propelled by the state of his fragile mind, he does things that worsen his situation rather than redeem it. He is punished by his own self, as if engaged in a continuing act of unintended self-flagellation. I have seen it many times.

Now firmly in this anxious state, he was so deep in thought that Ndali's footfalls startled him. He took the cup and drank until it emptied.

'Okay, Obim, let's go out now. They will soon call us.'

'Ndali, Ndali!' her mother called, with a clatter of feet in the living room.

His heart dropped. I felt pressured to do something, so I flashed in his mind that he be not afraid. *Do as much as you can to hold up against these people.* To this he tapped his feet on the floor, and the voice of his head said, *I will not be afraid.*

While I was communicating with my host, Ndali was saying to her mother: 'Ma, ma-Mommy! I'm coming out now.' To which the woman responded, 'Ngwa, ngwa, quick,' in a voice hardly audible over Osuofia's, which came from the speakers outside the house.

'Let's go now,' Ndali said, and she took his hand. 'It is our turn to sit at the High Table.'

He wanted to speak, but all he was able to muster was a muffled 'Oh'. As if something had wheeled him there, he found himself in the living room face-to-face with Chief Obialor, who was dressed in magnificent regalia – a red-coloured long and flowing isiagu – and brandished an ivory tusk. On his red cap were two kite feathers, tucked into both sides of the cap – the way the old fathers dressed. For they believed that birds were a symbol of life and that a man who has succeeded in this world has acquired feathers and, in the proverbial sense, become a bird. His wife who marched beside him wore similar prints on her body and beads around her neck – just as the great mothers did. She held a hand fan, and the bangles on her wrist were innumerable.

When Ndali and he came up to her parents, he bowed before them both in greeting as Ndali genuflected. Her parents smiled back as her father waved his staff and her mother waved her fan in the air. Chukwu, after all that would happen afterwards, my host would always remember how her parents had seemed to show no sign of displeasure at the sight of him during the encounter.

My host, in a state of internal fluster, merged with what was a procession, stepping slowly towards the door of the entrance to the mansion like one being dragged along by invisible ropes. He marched along with the man from Germany, a country of white people, and his white wife, who was dressed like the daughters of the great mothers. Beside them was Ndali's uncle, the famed doctor who'd sutured blown-out limbs during the Biafran War, waving his staff whose top bore an elephant figurine. Outside, Osuofia was shouting into the microphone, his voice amplified by the speakers: 'Now they are coming out, they are coming – the celebrant and his family!' My host followed them with the lightest foot, carrying his body as if it were a walking bag of pus kept alive only by Ndali's hand in his, until they entered the arena to the noisy cheering and applause of the crowd. He danced with them lightly, even as Chuka, with scorn on his face, constantly came within an inch or two of him. Increasingly, his fear was inflamed and he did not want to proceed. So he withdrew his hand when they began filling the seats in the front row under the awning where the dignitaries were seated behind the High Table and whispered 'No, I can't, can't, no' into Ndali's ear. She held on but as Osuofia began calling on her, she left him and sat in the very first row with her family members and other high-calibre guests. He hurried into the first empty seat behind them.

Egbunu, the slighted man – he is one who has felt himself disrespected by someone beneath him. Such a man has, by stroke of luck, or by hard work, or by strong bargaining by his chi, obtained good fortune or influence. And now, having measured his wealth or influence against those of others, he sees any raising of the hands by those of less estate as a slight to which he must respond. For to be challenged by a man of less fortune disrupts the equilibrium of his mind and infects his psyche. He must restore this quickly! He must strike at the thing that has caused that shift. This must be his response. Although such men were few in the times of the fathers – mostly because they feared Ala's wrath – I have seen it many times amongst their children. I had seen the sign of this state of mind in Chuka, so I was not surprised when, just as my host sat down, one of the cameramen came to him and whispered into his ear, 'Bros, Oga Chuka say make you follow me.'

Before my host could make sense of it, the man had begun walking away as if it were a given that he'd do as he'd been told. That in itself brought a lash of fear upon his back. If the messenger had relayed his message with such confidence, without any doubt that the order would be obeyed, how powerful must his master be? How mighty his wrath? He rose and followed the man as quickly as he could, thinking that everyone must have seen that he was the odd one at the High Table who was now paying for his brazen act of transgression. The man circled the house, past a gathering of women cooking stew and a mighty pot of rice. They walked swiftly past a group of sweating men unloading crates of drinks from the inside of a van. Then they passed through a small gate, beside which was a guard hut – a small room. The man turned and pivoted to the outpost. 'Enter here, Bros.'

It is in circumstances such as these that I often wish that a chi had more power and could defend his host through some supernatural means. It is at times like these that I also wish my host was wise in the ways of *agbara* and *afa*, like the dibia who was my host more than three hundred years ago. That man, Esuruonye of Nnobi, had reached the prime of human superabilities. He had been so strong, so potent in divination, that he was deemed *okala-mmadu, okala-mmuo*. Esuruonye was able to strip himself of his flesh and become a discarnate being. I saw him twice invoke the mystical *ekili* and ascend into the astral plane so that he was able to travel in the batting of eyelids to a distance that would have taken him two market weeks to reach were he to walk and a full day were he to go in a car. But my present host, like others of his generation, was helpless in a situation like this – as helpless as a cockerel in the eye grip of a hawk. He merely entered the house with the mysterious man who had given him the instruction.

Another fellow, with the build of a wrestler, stood inside the room, wearing a deep frown on his face. A blue sleeveless shirt hung around the man's body, embossed with the image of an explosive in motion, its coloured sparks like paint stains all over the shirt. 'Na the man wey dey disturb Oga's party be this?' the brawny man said in the broken version of the White Man's language.

'Na him,' the cameraman said from outside the small room. 'But Oga say make we no touch am. Just give am work make im do.'

'No problem,' the heavy man said. He pointed at a blue khaki shirt and pair of trousers, the kind my host had seen the gateman wearing, and said, 'Wear that.'

'Me?' my host, with a furiously palpitating heart, said.

'Yes, who else dey here? Look – er, Nwokem, I don't have time for questions, oh. Biko wear that thing may we go.'

Ijango–ijango, at times like these my host's mind always failed to provide an adequate answer to the questions. Should he argue with this man? Certainly not: he would get his head split open. Run? Certainly not. He possibly could not run faster than this individual. Even so, if he ran he faced the possibility of going back to the party to face more humiliation. The best thing to do was yield to the orders of this strange person who, without warning, had assumed lordship over him. So in submission, he took off his gown and new plain trousers and put on the regalia of the gateman.

Satisfied, the brawny man said, 'Follow me.' But what he meant was 'Walk in front of me.' The horsewhip the man took with him as they walked – what was it for? Could it come down on his back any time? The fear of the possibility of this was overwhelming. The man and he walked all the way back the way he and the cameraman had taken earlier, only now he was dressed differently – stripped of the regalia of the dignified, clothed in the garments of the lowly, and reduced to his true status. The phrase *where you belong* came into his head with such force that he was convinced someone had whispered it into his ear right then. As they passed, he saw that the food was being dished into plastic bags and that the van was driving away. He heard Ndali's father's voice, unmistakable over the speakers, as they passed behind the awnings, hidden behind the backs of people who stood on the edge of the pavilions, until they reached the gate.

'Join the gatemen,' the brawny man with the whip said, pointing to the gate. 'This is your job.'

AGUJIEGBE, it was here that Ndali would find him later, drenched in sweat, directing the surfeit of cars that poured in and out of the compound, finding parking spaces, settling disputes, and helping unload and take into the house some of the gifts some of the guests had brought (a bag of rice, tubers of yams, cases of expensive wines, a television in a box ...), and once, when the ribbons fastened around the statue of the lion snapped, he and one of his colleagues adorned the statue with new ribbons.

When she saw him, he had no words for her – for such is the kind of thing that gouges words from within a man, and leaves him empty. Thus he could not even answer the questions, 'Who did this to you? Where is your dress? Where – what?' He had merely said, in a voice that seemed as if it had grown old in the time he'd served at the gate, 'Please take me home, abeg you in the name of the almighty God.' The party was still in full swing and Oliver De Coque was making unintelligible sounds akin to those made by termites crawling on dead wood and the crowd was braying like senseless lambs. All of it, all of them were blown away as his van lurched out of the gate. Memories completely random, moments past – as if fanned by some orchestrated wind – blew into his mind and replaced them. He paid no heed to Ndali who wept all the way as he drove slowly through the noisy streets of Umuahia. But even in his tombed silence, he was well aware, as I could see, that she, like him, had been gravely wounded.

CHUKWU, what had been done to him was so painful that he could not shake a single detail of it out of his mind. Memories of the events persisted, like insects around a glob of sugarcane, crawling into every crevice of his mind, filling him with their black fragrance. And Ndali had cried much of the night until he made love to her and she slouched into slumber. Now the night had deepened, and he lay on the bed beside her. By the dim light of the kerosene lantern, he gazed into her face and saw that even in sleep, he could see signs of anger and sympathy – things that were often difficult to find on her face. His father had once told him that a person's true countenance at a given moment is that which remains on their face while in an unconscious state.

Earlier, while he worked at the gate during the party, he'd thought of how to repay her brother for what he had done to him. But he realised he could not have. What could he have done? Hit him? How can one hit the brother of the woman one loves so much? It occurred to him, again, that things could only go one way any time he met Chuka. He can only be hit; he cannot hit back. Like craven blacksmiths, Ndali's family had forged a weapon out of his desire, from his heart, and against this weapon he could not contend.

Yet, Egbunu, he knew that the only possible solution – that he should leave her and end it all – lay in the centre of the room of his thoughts, gazing at him with its dim face and cruel eyes. But he kept looking past it as if it were not there. And it persisted. He began to ponder instead the itinerant fear that now returned to him – the fear that in the end, Ndali would be frustrated and leave him. Ndali herself had raised this question earlier, just before she fell asleep.

'Nonso, I'm afraid,' she'd said suddenly.

'Why, Mommy?'

'I'm afraid that they will succeed in the end and make you leave me. You will, Nonso?'

'No,' he'd said, much louder than he intended to, vehemently. 'I will not leave you. *Never.*'

'I just hope you will not leave me because of them, because I will not let anyone choose who to marry for me. I'm not a child.'

He had said nothing else but instead recalled the moment when, while directing traffic at the gate, the man who'd sat beside him under the party tents had seen him on the way out and been bewildered. The man wound down the tinted glass of his Mercedes-Benz and cocked his head towards the front seat. 'No be you sidon there with me before?' He found no words. 'You are – what? A gateman?' He shook his head, but the man laughed and said something he could not make out, then wound up his window again and drove out.

'Are you sure, Nonso?' Ndali said, her voice tense.

'That is so, Mommy. They won't. They cannot,' he said, and his heart palpitated at the violence with which he'd spoken. He did not know, Egbunu, that fate was a strange language which the life of a man and his chi are never able to learn. He raised his eyes to her again and saw a tear sliding down her face. 'Nobody can make me leave you,' he said again. 'Nobody.'

8

THE HELPER

OSEBURUWA, I stand here testifying to you, knowing full well that you understand the ways of mankind, your creation, more than they can know themselves. You know, then, that the character of human shame is chameleonic. It appears at first, disguised, as if a benevolent spirit, by allowing reprieve whenever the humiliated is taken away from the presence of those to whom or by whom he has been disgraced – those from whom he must hide his face. The disgraced can forget his shame until he comes across those privy to it. Only then does shame strip itself of its dubious benevolence like a bodice and present itself in all its truthful colours: as malevolent. Yes, my host could hide from everyone else, from all of the people of Umuahia, and even from the whole world, and in doing so, all that had happened to him could amount to nothing. A pauper can disguise himself as a king in a place where his true identity is not known, and he would be received as such. Thus my host's peculiar dilemma was that Ndali had witnessed his humiliation. She'd seen him in the cloth of the night watchman, drenched in sweat, directing traffic. This was the blow from whose impact he could not recover. A man such as he, who knows his limitations, who is aware of his own capabilities – such a man is easily broken. For pride erects a wall around a man's inner self while shame pierces that wall and strikes the inner self in the heart.

Still, I have lived with mankind long enough to know that when a man begins to break, he tries to do something to salvage his situation as quickly as possible. It is why ndiichie, in their ancient wisdom, say that it is best to search for the black goat in daylight, before night falls and it becomes difficult to find it. So even before he vowed to Ndali that he would never leave her, he'd already begun to think of a solution. But he could not come up with anything he thought worthwhile, and for days he thrashed about like an injured worm in the mud of despair. On the fourth day of the following week, he called his uncle for advice, but the line was so bad my host could barely hear him. It was with much effort that he understood – in between the older man's stammering and the fragile connection – that it was best he leave Ndali. 'You sti-still a boy,' his uncle had said again and again. 'You still a bo-oy. J-j-jus twenty-six, er. Jo-jus-t forget about this wo-wo-wo-man n-ow. Th-ere are many many out there. Ma-ny many. Yo-yo-u see me? You ca-ca-n't convince them to a-cce-pt you.'

Ijango-ijango, I was happy that his uncle had given him this advice. I had thought of the same thing after his treatment at Ndali's family house. The wise fathers often say that when one is insulted, it extends to his chi. I, too, had been humiliated by Ndali's family. Yet I knew it was not of her making and hoped that she would find a way to resolve the crisis. So I did not reiterate his uncle's position. Also, it occurred to me that my host was one of those on earth with the gift of luck, one who would always get whatever he wanted. Before he was born, while he was yet in Beigwe in the form of his onyeuwa and we were travelling together to begin the fusion of flesh and spirit to form his human component (an account which I will render in detail in the course of my testimony), we made the customary journey to the great garden of Chiokike. We walked the gleaming paths between the luminous trees across from which plumes of emerald clouds hung in exquisite arrangement. Between them flew the yellow birds of Benmuo, emerging from the open tunnel of Ezinmuo, as big as full-grown men moving through the serrated tracks. A lump of herbage crowned the sides of the road leading up to the gate out into uwa. There was the great garden where the onyeuwas often go to find a gift which had returned there from unfortunate people who had either died at childbirth or infancy or had been miscarried. Even though we arrived to find the garden crowded, with hundreds of chis and their potential hosts combing through the plants and tangled copse, my host found a small bone. Some of the spirits immediately gathered and revealed that it was from some beast that dwells primarily in the great forest of Benmuo, where Amandioha himself lived in the form of a white ram. They told us that the finding of the bone meant that my host would always get whatever he wanted out of life if he persevered. This they said was because the beast whose bone he'd found, an animal exclusive to Beigwe, is never lacking in food as long as it lives in the forest.

Gaganaogwu, I can name numerous instantiations of this gift of luck at work in my host's life, but I do not want to stray too much from the testimony. At the time, I had confidence that the white bone would bring him some help. I was thus delighted when he decided it was best he try to win the support of her family. Worried that her continued stay away from her family on account of him was only going to escalate the crisis, he begged her to return.

'You don't get it, Nonso, you don't. You think they just

don't like you? Eh? Okay, can you tell me why? Can you give me one reason why they don't like you? Can you tell me why they treated you like this last Sunday? Or have you forgotten what they did to you? It was only six days ago. Have you forgotten, Nonso?'

He did not speak.

'No answer? Can you tell me why?'

'Because I am poor,' he said.

'Yes, but not that only. Daddy can give you money. They can open a big business for you, or even help expand the poultry business. No, not only that.'

He had not thought about these possibilities, Egbunu. So, riveted by her words, he looked up at her as she spoke.

'It is not that you are poor. No. It is because you don't have a big degree. You see, Nonso, you *see*? They don't think in those their big heads that sometimes people are orphaned. And Nigeria is hard! How many people who don't have any parents can go to university? Even – the public schools? Where will you find money to bribe even if your JAMB score is three hundred? Er, tell me, how will you pay school fees, even?'

He gazed at her, his tongue numb.

'Yet they say it, all the time: "Ndali, you are marrying an illiterate"; "Ndali, you are embarrassing us"; "Ndali, please, I hope you are not thinking of marrying that riffraff." It is, just, very bad. This thing they are doing, it is very bad.'

Afterwards, when she had retreated into his old room to study, he sat, folded into himself like a wet cocoyam leaf, worried that she had said a lot of things he hadn't thought about before. Why hadn't he considered that it might be possible to return to school, and that that could be the solution? He beat himself up, Chukwu, for what he hadn't thought of. He did not realise that he had grown up in adversity and had become

resigned to it. It had made him live a life unlike that of most
of his age-mates, a reclusive, provincial life, which developed
in its adherents a natural proclivity to be patient in adversity,
unhurrying and measured. If he was not stirred, he would not
act. His achievements, if there were any, were given to a slow
and sluggish emanation, and his dreams were long-limbed.
This was why his uncle had to arouse in him the desire for a
woman and now Ndali had inspired him to return to school.
And he began to see this sluggishness as a weakness. Later, after
she had gone to sleep, he sat alone in the living room, deep
in thought. He could register at ABSU and get a degree. Or
perhaps he could do a part-time study. Now that his discovery
of his love for birds had swallowed the initial dream to go to
university, he could even study agriculture.

These ideas came to him with so much power that joy
welled within him. They meant that there was genuine hope –
that there was a path to him getting married to Ndali. He
walked into the kitchen and fetched water from a blue keg,
and his thoughts were suspended by the recollection that they
were running out of drinking water. The keg was the only
one of the three he had with drinking water still left in it.
The family who owned two big tanks and sold water in the
street had been gone for two weeks, and many of the people
in the street either drove to get water from elsewhere or drank
rainwater, which they collected in bowls or basins or drums
while it rained. The water he scooped into his mouth had a
bad taste, but he drank one more cup of it.

As he sat down in the living room, the thought of leaving
Ndali reminded him of his grandmother, Nne Agbaso, how
she would sit on the old chair that used to be just at the end of
the living room – where now, piled up against the wall, were
video and audio cassettes, gathering dust – and tell him stories.

He imagined he could see her now, swallowing and batting her eyelids as she spoke, as if words were bitter pills she ingested when she talked. It was a habit she'd developed in old age, the only time he ever knew her. After she fell and broke her hip and could no longer continue to farm or even walk without a stick, she came from the village to live with them. During that period, she told him the same story again and again, and yet whenever he sat by her, she'd say, 'Have I told you about your great ancestors Omenkara and Nkpotu?' He would say either a yes or a no. But even when he said yes, she'd merely sigh, then blink and tell him how Omenkara had refused a white man's attempt to take his wife and was hanged in the village square by the district commissioner. (Chukwu, I bore witness to this cruel event and how it impacted the people at the time.)

He reckoned now that the story may have been his grandmother telling him again and again that he should not capitulate in the face of any situation. He thought now that he could choose to cower in the face of mere oppression and lose Ndali. No, he said aloud, struck by the thought of another man's mouth on her breasts. He trembled from the mere approach of such an idea towards the corridor of his mind. He'd dropped out after failing his first secondary school certificate exams, passing only three inessential subjects – history, Christian religious knowledge and agriculture. No mathematics, no English. His university matriculation exams had been worse. He took them around the time when his father's condition was deteriorating, leaving him to tend to the increasing demands of the poultry business alone. Agujiegbe, you know that all I've described here is the education of the White Man's civilisation. Like most people of his generation, he knew nothing of the education of his people, the Igbo and of the civilisation of the erudite fathers.

So after those strings of failures, he told his father he would not try any more. He could sustain himself and future family through the poultry business and small farm and, if possible, expand it or branch out into a retail business. But his father had insisted he return to school. 'Nigeria is becoming tougher and tougher by the day,' his father would say, scrunching his mouth, as he'd begun doing in the early beginning of his last days. 'Soon, someone who has a bachelor's degree would be useless, because everyone would have it. So what would you do without even a bachelor's? Farmers, shoemakers, fishermen, carpenters – everybody, I tell you, will need it. That is what Nigeria is becoming, I tell you.'

It was talks like this, as well as my frequent accentuation by flashes of thoughts that he should listen to his father – which I often buttressed with the proverb: what an old man sees squatting a child cannot see even from a treetop – that pushed him to take the external GCE. He studied and attended extra lessons at the building on Cameroon Street, where four young university students taught exam-preparatory sessions. And in the weeks of the exam, the extra-lesson centre turned into a miracle centre. One after the other, a few days before the subject exams, the teachers began to come to the class with leaked question papers. When the exams ended and the results came months later, he passed six of the eight subjects, even getting an A in biology, the one he'd been least prepared for. One of the papers, economics, was cancelled for most of the centres in Abia because of what the examination body said was 'widespread malpractice'. It was true. A copy of the exam paper had been in his hand for nearly three weeks before the actual exam day, and if the results had been released, he would have got an A in it, too. He would have returned to school at this time if they did not wake one morning that same month to find that his sister had vanished, plunging his father into a debilitating depression. All the peace that had returned after his father finished mourning his wife for many years vanished at once. Grief returned like an army of old ants crawling into familiar holes in the soft earth of his father's life, and months later, he was dead. With his father's body, every thought of school was buried.

OBASIDINELU, as days passed and Ndali continued to defy her parents, refusing to even talk with them, my host's fear grew. But, afraid he would bother her if he spoke up, he kept silent, shielding her from the turmoil in his head. But because fear does not leave until it is cast out, it curled around the trembling branches of his heart like an old serpent. It was there when he took her to the bus station the morning she was to go to Lagos for a conference. As the bus was about to leave, he embraced her, and putting his forehead against hers, he said, 'I hope I don't disappear before you return, Mommy.'

'What is that, Obim?'

'Your people, hope they don't kidnap me before you return.'

'Come on, why will you think like that? How can you even think they will do such a thing, eh? *O gini di?* They are not devils.'

Her anger at this suggestion flung him down. It made him look inward and question if he had been overestimating the situation, wonder if the long night of fear had been nothing but a skeletal dance of worry across the corridor of serenity. 'I was actually joking,' he said. 'Actually.'

'Okay, but I don't like that kind of joke, eh. They not devils. Nobody will do anything to you, oh?'

'That is so, Mommy.'

He tried not to think of the things that made him fear. Instead, he weeded the small farm and cleaned his room. Then he treated one of the roosters who had injured its foot. He'd found it the previous evening on the other side of the road. It had jumped the high fence of the yard, fallen into the bush behind, and stepped on what he believed may have been a broken bottle. It had reminded him of the gosling, how he'd once left it loose and it had made its way out of the house and sat on the fence. He ran out after it and found it on the fence gazing about with its head turning in agitation. With his heart pounding, fearing that it would fly away and never return, he beseeched it tearfully. It was morning, and his father was brushing his teeth (not with a chewing stick, as the old fathers did, but with a brush) when he heard his son's panicked shout. The man rushed out with the white froth dripping down his beard and his creamed brush in his hand to find his son anxious. He gazed up to the fence and the boy and shook his head. 'Nothing you can do, son,' he said. 'It is afraid. If you go close, it will run.' I, watching as well, had the same fears as his father, and I put the thought in his head, too. So he stopped crying, and in a voice as soft as a whisper, he began calling to the gosling, 'Please, please, don't ever leave me, don't ever leave me, I rescued you, I'm your falconer.' And, miraculously – or perhaps because the bird had seen something else across the fence, perhaps the neighbour's dog – the bird bristled and crouched into a spread of wings. Then it returned through a rushed updraft back to the yard, back to him.

He had hardly set the injured cock back into the coop when Elochukwu arrived. He'd texted Elochukwu early that morning, and Elochukwu had responded that getting an education was the best idea. 'If you go back and finish your studies, then they will surely accept you,' Elochukwu had said. Elochukwu dismounted from his motorcycle and stood with my host on the front porch overlooking the farm. My host gave

Elochukwu an account of the party and how he'd been humiliated by Ndali's family. And when he was done, Elochukwu
shook his head and said, 'It is well, my brother.' And my host,
looking up at his friend, nodded in acceptance. Egbunu, this
expression, very common amongst the children of the great
fathers and spoken mostly in the language of the White Man,
has often baffled me. A man in a situation in which his livelihood is threatened has just rendered an account of his travails,
and his friend – one he sees as a comforter – responds simply,
'It is well.' That expression instantly yields silence between
them. For it is a peculiar phrase, all-encompassing in scope.
A mother whose child has just died, when asked how she is
doing, replies simply, 'It is well.' It-is-well emerges from the
intercourse between fear and curiosity. It designates a tran-
sient state in which, although the unfortunate knows he is
experiencing something unpleasant, he hopes it will soon be
mended. Most people in the country of the children of the
fathers are always in this state. Are you hoping to recover from
an illness? It is well. Has something been stolen from you? It is
well! And when a man steps out of this condition of it-is-well
on to a new path towards a more satisfying state, he immediately finds himself in another situation of it-is-well.

Elochukwu shook his head again, repeated the phrase,
tapped my host on the shoulder, gave him a bag of books and
said, 'I am in a hurry, we are going to a rally at GRA.' Before
Elochukwu left, my host complained that he would not be
able to get a degree for at least five years, and that was if there
were no strikes, which could delay it and cause him to not have
a degree for probably even seven years. 'Start ti go du first,'
Elochukwu said, mounting his motorcycle. 'Once e start tiri,
ha ga hun na idi serious.' Elochukwu, who had himself nearly
completed a degree in chemistry and was not one to dwell on

words, finished the topic with, 'And if it doesn't work, just forget the girl. There is nothing the eye sees that can cause it to shed blood in place of tears.'

Not long after his friend left, rain began. It rained through that morning into the evening. As it poured down on Umuahia, unremitting in volume and unpredictable in temperament, he lay in the sitting room, studying one of the university matriculation exam preparatory books he'd received from Elochukwu.

Now, he read for a long time by the dim light from the cloud-washed sky that came through the parted curtains until his eyes began to close. He was almost asleep, anchored like a wind-borne leaf in the threshold between sleep and awakening, when he heard a knock on his front door. At first, he'd mistaken the knock for the rain pattering on the door, but then he heard a familiar voice say in the most forceful of tones:

'Will you open this door, now?'

Then the banging began again. He jumped up, and through the windows, he saw Chuka and two men, dressed in raincoats, standing on his porch.

Gaganaogwu, the effect of the sight of these men on him could only be described as hypnotic. In all the years I had been with him, I had never seen anything close to this happen to him. It seemed strange that only some time ago he had made a joke about something, a wild, far-fetched joke. And in daylight, his joke had materialised, and here was her brother at his doorstep with a gang of men? He let them in, steeped in terror, a pounding in his chest.

'Chuka—' he started to say as the men came in.

'Shut up!' shouted one of the men, the brawny one who'd led him to serve at the gate during the party. Even now, the man had come prepared – with that same whip.

'I can't shut up. No.' He stepped back as the men advanced and moved behind the biggest sofa. 'I can't shut up because this is my house.'

The man with the whip lunged forward, but Chuka raised his hand and said, 'No! I have said this before, no touching anybody.'

'Sorry, sir,' the man said, stepping back behind Chuka, who now walked into the centre of the room.

He watched Chuka unhood his raincoat, shaking his head as he did. Then Chuka swirled around to inspect the room, before sitting down with his raincoat on the couch, still dripping water. The men stood beside the couch, gazing at my host with a frown.

'I have come to ask you to send my sister back,' Chuka said in the same calm voice he'd spoken in before, and in the language of the White Man. 'We are not interested in making trouble with you. Not at all. My parents, her parents, are worried.' Chuka dropped his head to the floor as if in contemplation, and in the brief silence that ensued, my host heard the soft patter of rain dripping from Chuka's raincoat to the carpet.

'Once she is back from Lagos, we ask you to make sure she is back within two days,' Chuka said with his eyes to the floor. 'Within two days. Two days.'

They left the way they had come, slamming the door behind them. Although it was still daylight, the rain clouds had dimmed the horizon so much that they'd driven with their headlights on. He watched their car retreat from his farm path in reverse gear, like two discs of yellow light receding into the distance. When they were gone, he sank to his knees, and without any reason to which his mind could cling, he broke into a prolonged sob.

*

EGBUNU, if an arrow is pointed at the chest of a defenceless man, that man must do as he is told. To do any different in the face of indefensible danger is folly. The valiant fathers say that it is from the house of a coward that we point to the ruins of the house of a brave man. Thus the defenceless man must speak, with a soft tongue, effectual words to the one who bears the arrows: 'Do you want me to go yonder?' And if the man who endangers him answers that he should, he must do as he is told until he is cleared from the present danger. After Ndali's brother left, my host resolved to do all he had been told to do. He would persuade her to return home, and while she was gone, he would find a solution to his inadequacy, the main source of all the problems. He would go back to school and get an education and a job that would make him suitable for her. Chukwu, I have come to understand that, when a man is disgraced, his actions might be shaped by shame and his will by desperation. What once means much to such a man might begin to mean little. He could, for instance, stand in his yard and regard his poultry, this thing he had built for himself, these eight coops of nearly seventy birds, and see how lowly a business it was. The sight of feathers, which he'd normally sniff and twist in admiration, now may look like litter to him. What is he doing now, one may ask? Well, he is responding, Chukwu. His mind is preparing itself for change. It has weighed everything on a scale and determined that a return to loneliness, especially by losing Ndali, would be worse than anything else. She was the glittering, priceless article in a shop full of precious artefacts. The poultry, the birds, these weighed less. They could be got rid of if need be in order to get her. After all, he'd seen a man sell his land to send his child to school abroad. What has such a man done? He has decided that it would be better in the future to have a child who can be a doctor than to keep the land. Such a man has reasoned, perhaps, that with a rich son, the land can be recovered, or such a son can even buy him a bigger piece of land.

So by the time he'd finished these unbroken ruminations, by morning two days after Chuka came to his house, he rose and, even without feeding his flock and harvesting fresh eggs, went out and bought forms for the university matriculation exam from the Union Bank branch down the street. He waited in a long line in the old and crowded bank, a line that stretched to the entrance, and he had to plead for those in the line to make room so he could squeeze into the building. He left the bank tired and soaked in sweat.

Ijango–ijango, it is imperative that I tell you, in detail, about this walk back home, for it was during this walk that the black seeds of his undoing came to root in his life. When he got back on the road home, he walked for a while by a school bus, which had slowed down in the clotted traffic. He gazed at the uniformed children inside it, who were poised in different shades of slumber. A few had their heads resting against the seats, some had their heads tilted sideways against the head-rests, some had bowed their heads into their hands, and others were resting their heads against the windows. One or two of them seemed awake: an albino girl with sand-coloured hair and a sore on her purplish lower lip, gazing blankly at him, and a boy with a clean-shaven head. He lumbered on, carrying the file containing the forms under his armpit, past sheds and tables from which articles were sold, the sellers calling to him to buy their wares. One of them, a woman who sold used clothes piled on a jute sack, called to him, 'Fine man, come buy fine shirt, fine jeans. Come see ya size.' He had just passed the woman's shed when he felt something palpitating in his trouser pocket. He reached for his phone and saw that Elochukwu was calling.

'Er, Elo, Elo—'

'Kai, Nwanne, I've been calling you!' Elochukwu said, partly in the language of the great fathers and partly in the White Man's language.

'What, I was at the bank, so I silence my phone.'

'Okay, no problem. Where are you now, where are you? We are at your house, oh. Me and Jamike, Jamike Nwaorji.'

'Er, Chukwu! *Isi gi ni?* Jamike? No wonder you are speaking English.'

He heard a voice in the background and Elochukwu ask the person in the broken language of the White Man if he wanted to talk to him.

'Bobo Solo!' the voice said into the phone.

'Jisos! Ja-mi-ke!'

'Please, come, come, we are waiting for you oh. Come come.'

'I am almost there,' he said. 'I am coming, oh.'

He put the phone back in his pocket and began walking fast towards his house, his mind racing. He had not seen or heard anything about this man in a long time. And now Jamike, his old classmate from Ibeku High School, was at his house. He crossed the street and passed between the poor houses of the lower street, where a gulley had carved up the earth and dug up the yellow soil and swallowed the loam in many broken places. He ran, the file in his hand, until he reached his compound. At the entrance, he raised his head and saw Elochukwu and their old classmate standing on the porch. By the porch, leaning against its kickstand, was Elochukwu's Yamaha motorcycle. He walked towards them on the gravelled path flanked on both sides by the fields of the small farm. As he drew closer to the men, he stifled the urge to shout. At first, he did not recognise this person with a broad, mustachioed face. But then he found himself suddenly absolutely beyond repose, shouting,

'Jamike Nwaorji!' The man, in a red cap with a white bull's head embossed on it, and a white shirt and jeans, drew close and rammed his hand into his raised hand.

'I can't believe it, mehn!' the man said.

He recognised at once a tincture of a foreign accent in the man's voice, the way people who'd lived outside the world of the Black Man spoke, the way his lover and members of her family sounded.

'Elo here tell me that you are living in overseas,' he said in the language of the White Man, as they did in their school days, when it was a punishable offence to speak an 'African language'. So with the exception of Elochukwu, the language of the White Man was how he communicated with friends from school, even though nearly every one of them spoke the tongue of the august fathers.

'Na so, oh, my brother,' this man, Jamike, said. 'I have been living abroad for many, many years, mehn.'

'Er, let me go now, Nonso.' It was Elochukwu who had spoken. He tipped his black hat, which he'd begun wearing since he joined MASSOB, as he shook my host's hand. 'I was just waiting for you to come because when I saw him, I remembered your problem. Jamike can help you.'

'Er, you are going?'

'Yes, I gat do something for my Popsy.'

He watched Jamike, who had a smell that must have been from an expensive perfume, hug Elochukwu, who then hopped on his motorcycle, pumped the pedals twice, and a plume of smoke gushed up into the air. 'I go call una,' he said, and rode away.

'Bye-bye,' he called after Elochukwu, then turned to the man before him.

'Na wa oh, Jamike himself!'

'Yes, oh, Bobo Solo!' Jamike said.

They shook hands again.

'Let us go inside naw. Come, come.'

My host led the visitor inside the house. As they entered, he had a flash of how, two days before, Chuka had sat on the sofa where Jamike now sat, his raincoat giving him the appearance of a movie villain and his presence bearing as much threat to my host as this sudden recollection of it.

'Mehn, you get very big compound, oh. Only you live here?' Jamike said.

My host smiled. He sat down to face the visitor after parting the curtains to let in light to the room.

'Yes, my parents passed away, and you know that my sister, the small one that time?'

'Er, er—'

'Nkiru, she marry. So only me I am here now. And my girlfriend also. Ehen, where are you living now?'

Jamike smiled. 'Cyprus – you know the place?'

'No,' he said.

'I know that you won't. It is an island in Europe. A very small country. Very small, but very beautiful; very beautiful, mehn.'

He nodded, 'That is so, my brother.'

'Oh-ho. You remember our classmate Jonathan Obiora? He used to live here,' Jamike said, pointing at an old house in the distance. He removed his cap and tapped it on his lap. 'Bobo, do you want us to go drink beer and talk small?'

'Yes, yes, my brother,' he said.

Egbunu, when two people meet at a place such as this, and both of them have crawled out of each other's past, they often suspend the present as they try to drag all that has happened in the intervening period into the moment. This is because they are bound somewhat by where they had both been in that time long ago or by the same uniform they wore. It would occur to both of them that it is sometimes hard to tell how much time has passed until something or someone from that point in the past reappears, bearing the wear and tear of long travel. For my host, Jamike noted that he was much taller but still lanky. My host on the other hand was astonished at how Jamike's once small body and clean-shaven head had now given way to a towering figure only half an inch shorter than himself and a beard that cascaded down both sides of his head. After they have noted these differences, they will proceed to talk about where they have gone since the last time they met, what road they have taken, and how they have got to the point at which they find each other now. And sometimes these two may build new relationships and become friends. I have seen it many times.

So they left his compound and walked to the Pepper Soup place on the adjacent street and sat on one of the rows of benches on the earthen floor. The sun had increased in intensity and they were sweating when they entered the restaurant. They sat under one of the ceiling fans, beside a stereo from which a low tune slowly rose. He could barely wait to sit down, for during the short walk, Jamike had painted a portrait of the place where he lived, Cyprus, as a place where everything was in order. Electricity was constant; food was cheap; hospitals were plentiful and free, if you were a student; and jobs, 'like water'. A student could own a Jeep or an E-class Mercedes-Benz. In fact, Jamike said that he'd returned to Nigeria with a sports car which he had now given to his parents. On their way to the restaurant, he'd observed that Jamike walked with a certain ceremonial gait, employing the full weight of his body as he went along, as if his movement were a performance whose audience was everything within the ambit – the parked truck, the old pub, the cashew tree, the mechanic's workshop, the mechanic working beneath a pickup truck on the other side of the road, even the vacant sky. Jamike spoke with the same cadence, with a light swagger in his voice, so that every word he said struck deep into my host.

For a moment, they did not speak, and he let what Jamike had told him sink in while the latter replied to a message on his phone. He let his eyes hover over the calendar with the Star beer advert on the wall beside where they sat and on a poster of American wrestlers he knew and whose names flashed in his mind as he gazed at the poster: Hulk Hogan, the Ultimate Warrior, the Rock, Undertaker, and the Bushwhackers.

'So Elo said you want to start school? He said you are having some problems and I can be able to help you.'

My host threw himself up in thought, as if lifted from within by a monstrous hand. 'Yes, Jamike, yes, my brother. I have a problem.'

'Tell me, Bobo Solo.'

He wanted to speak, but the recollection of that name, which his mother used to call him, made him pause for a moment, for somewhere in the itinerant years long travelled into oblivion, he saw himself standing in the room, laughing as she laughed and clapped, singing, 'Bobo, bobo, Solo. Bobo, bobo, Solo.'

He took up the bottle of beer and drank to calm himself. Although it tasted strange to him – for he rarely drank – he felt obliged to take it. When a man receives a visitor, he eats and drinks that which the visitor eats and drinks. Then words burst out of him like wine from an uncorked bottle carrying in it an amalgam of emotions – fear, anxiety, shame, sorrow and despair. In the torrent of words, he told Jamike everything that had happened up till two days prior, when he'd been threatened at his home. 'This is why I told Elochukwu that I have to return to school quickly. In fact, I don't have choice. I love Ndali very much, my brother. I really really really love her. Ever since she came into my life, I have not been the same again. Everything has changed, Jamike, I'm telling you, everything has changed. Every single thing, from *a* to *zed*, have changed.'

'Ah, that is serious problem, oh, mehn,' Jamike said, sitting up in the chair.

He nodded and took another sip of the drink.

'Mehn, why don't you want to leave her?' Jamike said. 'Is this not easiest for you instead of this stress?'

Egbunu, my host was silent at this. For in this moment, he recalled his uncle's counsel and even Elochukwu's partial counsel. He knew because he'd heard from somewhere he could not recall that a person must reconsider their position if everyone else is saying something that contradicts their own position. And a part of him, a part that seemed to have resolved into a shadow, wanted to submit, to accept that the only way was to leave her. But another part was defiantly resolute not to, and it was this part that urged him with a ferocity he could not suppress. And I, his chi, I was in between, desiring that he have her but fearful for what it might cost him. And I have come to understand that when a chi cannot decide the best path on which to lead its host, it is best if the chi remains silent. For in silence the chi yields, fully, to the complete will of its host. It lets man be man. This is better, far better, than a chi who leads its host to a path of destruction. For regret is the poison of the guardian spirit.

He spread his hands over the table and said, 'That is not it, my brother. I can go if I want, but I love her very much. Jamike, I'm ready to do anything to marry her.'

Gaganaogwu, in the grave ills that would befall my host

later, I would look back frequently and wonder if indeed it was in these words that all that happened later was first hatched. A twitch appeared on Jamike's face after my host said those words, and Jamike did not respond immediately. He first looked around at the house, then nodded and sipped the beer before he said, 'Ah, love! You don hear D'banj's "You Don Make Me Fall in Love"?'

'No, I never hear,' my host said, continuing quickly so Jamike would not go on discussing the needless song, for he wanted to unburden his heavy mind. 'I love her so much I go do anything for her,' he said again, this time with much restraint, as if it had cost him much to say it. 'I want to go back to school now because before my father died, he was sick, and so I dropped out to help him grow his business. This is why I did not go to university.'

'I see,' Jamike said. 'I know you didn't drop out because you are not brilliant. You were brilliant, mehn. No be you score second, third, for class behind Chioma Onwuneli?'

'It is so,' he said, for he remembered days now long past. But it was the present and the future that he must reckon with. 'I have complete GCE. If I return to school, er, my brother, I am sure once they don't think I be illiterate again, them go accept. I strongly believe this.'

'Tha-that is very true, Bobo Solo,' Jamike said. His eyes watered, and he blinked. 'Very true.'

'It is so, my brother,' he said. He felt, for the first time in weeks, somewhat relieved, as if he'd solved his problems by simply recounting them.

'So since you say it is fast and quick to school in Cyprus, that I can get a degree within three years, I want to go there,' he said with relief, for it struck him that he'd said everything he said simply because he wanted to tell Jamike this.

'Very good, Bobo Solo! Very good, mehn!' Jamike lifted himself summarily out of the seat and slapped his hands. 'High five there, nwokem!' Then sitting back, Jamike gazed at his hands with his eyes, scrutinising the lines as though it were a foreign hand. 'Is that sweat?'

'It is so,' he said.

'Wow, wo-ow, wo-ow, Bobo! So you still sweat like Christmas goat?'

He laughed. 'Yes, my brother Jamike. I still sweat on my palms.'

'Bobo nwa.'

'Errrr,' he said.

'You have found the solution, mehn!' Jamike said, shaking his finger. 'You have found it. You can now go and sleep.'

He laughed.

'Cyprus is the solution.'

IJANGO-IJANGO, it is true, as the great dibias among the fathers often say: that in this world which you have created, if a man wants something very much, if his hands do not desist from chasing it, he will eventually possess it. At the time, like my host, I, too, had thought that the encounter with his old schoolmate was the universe lending him what he had been longing for. For he returned to his house later that evening with a slight tremor in his gait from the drink he'd shared with his friend and with a hive full of honey in his heart. When he went to sleep, the squawking of the hennery in his ears, he began to digest it all: the island on the Mediterranean Sea, as beautiful as the ancient Greece of the books he read as a child. The ease of admission into the universities. 'No JAMB!' Jamike had repeated again and again. 'You only need GCE, only GCE.' The timing of it: how it had happened exactly when he needed it. He could start in September, four or five weeks from now. The uncanniness of the possibility threatened to throw everything into unreality. How affordable it was: 'It is cheaper than all these Nigerian private schools,' Jamike had boasted. 'These nonsense schools we have here: Madonna, Covenant, it is better than them all.' And what is more? He need only pay the first-year school fees and campus apartment, and by the time he got to the second year – in fact, even the second semester – he would have earned enough from part-time jobs to pay the next school fees and board.

Even now, as he slowly drifted off to sleep, he saw Jamike dance with his words, a ritual dance whose effect was hypnotising. He let his thoughts linger on the auspicious suggestion from Jamike that it would be great and healthier for his relationship with Ndali if he went abroad to live for the first few years of their marriage. Jamike had insisted, in a most convincing way, that it would make her parents respect him even more. Then he considered the last thing Jamike had said about this country, which had only served to increase his hope: 'You can easily go to any other part of Europe, or US. By ship, very cheap. Within two hours! Turkey, Spain, many many countries. This will not only be the best opportunity to please Ndima—' He helped him say the name. 'Oh, sorry, Ndali. It is also an opportunity for you to experience a good life. In fact, look, if I be you, I will make all the arrangements without telling her. Look at all the big land, big house your father left for you. You can do it, mehn. Surprise her!' Jamike said this with almost a scowl on his face, as if angered by his own words. 'Surprise her, mehn, and you will see. You will see that you will not only gain her respect, but, I tell you' – Jamike licked his thumb with his tongue until a gasp of erhen erupted – 'I swear to almighty God, Ndali will love you die!'

These last words had come out of Jamike with such assurance and certainty that my host let out a laugh of relief. He laughed again now as he remembered it and stood up. He picked up his jeans, which lay on the chair by the bed, and took out the piece of foolscap on which Jamike had made notes. He'd brought out a pen and a book from his back pocket, the book folded through the centre from him sitting on it. With a glib smile, he detached a leaf from the book and said, 'I am a practical man, let us come down to practical,' then he began to scribble all he had said down.

2 semesters scool fees = 3000
1 years accomodation = 1500
Mantainanse = 2000
_____
6500 euro
_____

Gaganaogwu, the peace that came upon my host that night was like the pure unspotted waters of Omambala. After he'd gazed at the paper as many times as possible, he folded it. He switched off the light and walked to the window, his heart throbbing wildly. He could not see much outside even though the moon seemed to be bright. For a moment, the house across the road looked as if it were on fire, its roof a raging vermilion and smoke rising from it. But he soon saw that it was the streetlight cast on the building and the smoke was rising from some cooking hearth.

9

CROSSING THE THRESHOLD

AGBARADIKE, the great fathers in their discreet wisdom say that seeds sown in secret always yield the most vibrant fruit. So my host, in the days following his meeting with his old schoolmate, shielded from the world the inflorescence of joy that grew along the edges of his heart. In secret, his plans grew, unbeknownst to Ndali, who returned from her week-long trip to Lagos three days after he met Jamike. He hid his father's old briefcase, in which he stored the documents he collected, under the bed. He attached his heart to the bag as if it contained everything he owned, his very life.

As the contents of the bag increased, so did other joyful developments. He did not have to persuade Ndali to go back home after she returned. She went back by herself, deceived by Chuka's lies that their mother had taken ill. This resolved his fear that something else might happen if he was not able to persuade her to return as Chuka had warned, an encounter which – not wanting her to escalate issues with her family – he kept from her. When she came to see him exactly two weeks after he began his plans with Jamike, her mood was wholly changed. She had come from church that day, lighthearted.

'I can't even believe it, Obim,' she said, clapping her hands playfully. She sat on his legs. 'Can you guess what Daddy said?'

'What, Mommy?'

'I told them that you bought JAMB forms to go back to school. So they said that if you register at a school, that would be a good first step. It would show your seriousness to become somebody.'

Egbunu, he was stunned by this. It seemed to him that something he could not see had peered over his shoulder and looked into the pot of his secrets. For having resolved all along not to tell her about his plans, as Jamike had advised, not wanting her to stop him, he'd only told her about the form he'd bought. Yet he knew he could not hide it from her for too long. So as he took more steps in this direction each day, he'd assure himself that he would tell her about it. But by the end of the day, he would push it like a thing with wheels into the future and say not today but tomorrow. But if *tomorrow* Ndali came home with a fever after a long day at school, he'd say *Tomorrow, she will be home all day and it will be easier then*. But alas, that tomorrow would come with a phone call first thing in the morning that her uncle had suffered a stroke. *Over the weekend*, the voice in his head would resolve, perhaps on Sunday after church. And as if by some alchemic manipulation, today was that Sunday. Now that she had said something that touched the core of the very thing he'd been keeping secret, he resolved to tell. 'Mommy, consider it done!' he said.

'Er, Obim?'

'I say, consider it done,' he said even louder. He made her stand, and he rose, too, swaggering slightly. 'I have gone to school and come back.'

She laughed. 'How? Abi in spirit or in your dreams?'

'Just watch, er.'

He went into the room and retrieved the bag from under the bed in what was once his sister's room. He blew away a spider that lay on the fading coat of arms inscribed on the bag's leather skin and carried it with him back to the sitting room. He put the bag on the centre of the table.

'What is in the bag?' she said.

'Abracadabra – you will see.' He waved his hands over the bag while she bobbed with laughter. Then he opened it and handed her the documents. He'd arranged the documents in the order of lowest cost, so when she began from the last one, he said, 'No, no, Mommy, begin here, first.'

'Here?'

'Yes, that one.'

He sat down to watch her peruse the documents, his heart sounding a nervous beat.

She read the header on the paper aloud: 'Admission letter.' She raised her head. 'Wow, Nonso, you got an admission!' She rose to her feet.

He nodded. 'Just read on.'

She returned her eyes to the paper.

'Cyprus International University, Lef-lef-ko-sa?'

'Lefkosa.'

'Lefkosa. Wow. Where is this place? How did you get it?'

'It is surprise, Mommy. So just look, just look.'

She read through.

'Oh God! Business Administration? That is very good!'

'Thank you.'

'I can't believe it,' Ndali said. She threw her hands into the air, swirled into a half circle and faced him again, and kissed him.

'Read all first, Mommy,' he said, detaching himself. 'Then you can kiss me after. Read.'

'Okay,' she said, and looked at the book between the files. 'Your passport?'

He nodded, and she looked through it, with her face filled with light.

'Where's the visa?'

'Next week,' he said.

'You will go to where – Abuja?'

'Abuja.'

He saw a shade begin to grow over her face, and he stiffened.

'Read it all, Mommy, please.'

'Okay,' she said. 'Letter of accommodation,' she said, and glanced up at him. 'You have accommodation already?'

'Yes. It is so. Read, see, Mommy?'

But she dropped the documents back on the table.

'Nonso, you are planning to leave Nigeria and you are just telling me?'

'I wanted it to be surprise. Look, Mommy, your brother came here after you go to Lagos. No, no, listen first. He came with thugs to frighten me. Actually, I have no choice. I have to do something. Listen godunu first. Look, I luckily saw my former classmate who schools in this beautiful country, Cyprus. And he told me everything. How everything is cheap, school fees, and jobs easy to get. Degree, I can get within three years, if I do what he called summer schools. That is why I did this.'

'Who is this person you met?'

'His name? Jamike Nwaorji. He just went back to Cyprus – actually four days ago. He was my classmate in primary school and also secondary school.'

She took up the documents again, as he'd hoped, and went through the course curriculum, then returned her gaze back to the inscriptions on the softer foolscap.

'Wait oh, I still don't understand.'

'Okay, Mommy.'

'You are leaving Nigeria when you said you want to marry me?'

'It is not so, Mommy.' He opened his mouth to say more, but he could not form words, as the confidence that had been painstakingly constructed over the days and weeks prior, the confidence derived from the result of weighing everything on the scale and deciding he could give up everything for her, had suddenly flattened. To shore it back up, he moved closer to her and sat on the arm of the couch.

'How is it not so? This is a school abroad.'

He took her hand. 'I know it is abroad, but it is actually the best way. Imagine in two and a half years, I have a real, authentic degree? Imagine, Mommy? Even, you can always visit me. You graduate next year June, and by then I would actually also be going to my second year. You can come and stay with me.'

'Jesus! Nonso, are you saying . . . ' She clasped her palms over her head. 'Forget it, just forget it.'

'No, Mommy, no. Why don't you tell it to me, why?'

'Forget it.'

'Nne, look, I am doing this because of you, only because of you. Actually, I never even wanted to go back to school, but that is the only way I can be with you. The only way, Mommy?'

He put his hand on her shoulder and gently pulled her towards him. 'You know I love you. I love you very much, but see what they are doing to me. See how they disgraced me. They really disgrace me, Mommy. And who knows, maybe it is just the beginning. Just the beginning, and, you don't know, I don't know. I'm coming, Mommy . . . '

All evening, they had been hearing loud, excessive caws, but now it grew too distracting for him. He went to the kitchen, drew his catapult and a stone from the window sill, and ran out. All his chickens were in their coops, and just as he got close to one of them, a reddish cock leapt to the bars noisily, squawking in distress. It was fighting with one of the newest roosters, the one with a serrated comb and an abundance of wattles. The rooster had shown unusual belligerence even from the day he bought it. He unbarred the coop's net door and tried to catch it. But it hopped against the wall and tried to find something to hang on, but couldn't. He tripped and landed with his hands on the floor as the roosters leapt up and ran out of the coop with two others from the group of six cocks and cockerels. He pursued it, and it jumped on to the bench under the guava tree, and when he tried to catch it, it mounted the water drum, crowing aggressively. He was furious. He circled the well and then, moving as fast as he could, grabbed the rooster.

He was binding the bird to the tree with hempen twine when Ndali stepped into the yard. The low evening sun cast a shadow of her against the wall, a shadow so large that only half of it could be seen.

'Nonso,' she said, startling him.

'Yes, Mommy.'

'What have you done?'

'Nothing,' he said.

He turned and held her, his chest still pounding, but pressed against her chest, he felt that her pounding was far worse.

AGBATTA-ALUMALU, sometimes a man cannot fully understand what he has done until he has told another person about it. Then his own action becomes clearer even to himself. I have seen it many times. Although my host had spent the past hour explaining his rationale for selling the compound, and poultry, when he was done, he began to see the flaws in the decisions he had made. Again, Chukwu, you have established that the main roles of the guardian spirit are to watch over our hosts and make sure that preventable calamities do not befall them, so they can more easily fulfil their destinies, the reason for which you created them. We must never try to compel our hosts against their will. So even though I had worried that he was selling most of what he had, I had let him do this without interference. I did this also because I believed that the man who had come to him to help him had been a product of his gift of good luck, the bone from the garden of Chiokike.

But now, when he heard the gasps and saw the fright on Ndali's face, he became afraid that he had made hasty decisions. A coldness came upon his heart which, for the weeks past, had been warm with the joy birthed by hope. After he'd finished revealing everything he had done in secret, Ndali said, 'I have not words, Nonso. I am speechless.'

She went into his old room and closed the door while he sat in the sitting room, staring at the documents. He reread the agreement about the sale of the compound, and fear welled up in his mind. When his father bought the house, he was barely nine, and his mother was pregnant. His father had said they needed a bigger house as more children came. He thought he'd forgotten this bit of memory, but now he found it as fresh as yesterday. His mother holding him, he'd stopped in the empty room while his father and the seller went around the place. Then he'd broken free from his mother and ran to the backyard and stood under the guava tree, greatly fascinated by it. He tried to climb it, but his mother, although heavy with child, came running and calling him down. He heard her voice with startling clarity, as if she were behind him in the room. 'No, Bobo, no. Don't, I don't like people who climb trees.' 'Why?' he'd asked, turning his back to his mother, as he did when he wanted to disobey her. 'Nothing,' she said, and he heard her sigh, as she had begun doing as her belly bulged. Then, with the kind of resignation that he'd come to understand as a marker of finality, she said, 'If you do, I won't like you.'

He was thinking of this when Ndali emerged from the room and said, 'Nonso, let us go to Tantalizers, I'm hungry.' At first, he could not distinguish between the voices of the two women, but Ndali stepped further into the sitting room and stamped her feet on the floor. 'Nonso, I'm talking to you!'

'Er, Mommy, yes, yes, let us go.'

They walked slowly, a quietness between them, as if some authority beyond the will of man had ordered that words not be spoken. They went through the narrow street, between greying and moulding fences and street gutters clogged with waste. On the other side, separated by a potholed road, birds sat in chambers of an unfinished multi-storey building fettered by wooden scaffolding. He was gazing at the birds when, in a voice a little above a whisper, Ndali said that if she knew it would come to this, she would have left him.

'Why do you say that, Mommy?'

'Because I am not worth this sacrifice. All this – it is too much.'

He did not speak until they entered the restaurant, for he was disturbed by what she had said. The restaurant was alive with the chatter of people – a group of men in plain shirts, some office workers and two women – and a song was playing at a low tune on the speaker. He wanted to contest what she'd said vehemently and insist that she was worth it. But he didn't. For even though he now mostly regretted it and agreed that he had acted in haste, he knew, too, that he'd gone too far to turn back now. He had sold his compound, which he inherited from his father. Two semesters of school fees had been paid, along with the fees for a year's accommodation. And Jamike, who had now returned to Cyprus, had two thousand more euros which he had given Jamike to keep in an account for him for 'maintenance', so he wouldn't have to carry much money while travelling. In the bag was another six hundred euros, the last of the hard currency. Only the forty-two thousand naira he had in the bank was to remain, in addition to however much they would get from selling all the fowls.

When they sat down in a corner of the restaurant, she repeated her words again.

'Why do you say this?' he said.

'Because, Nonso, you have destroyed yourself because of me!' she said with what my host thought was anger. After she said this, she turned about to look around the place, for it seemed as though she realised that she'd spoken in a burst of emotion, and her words had been loud, so she whispered, 'You have destroyed yourself, Nonso.'

Chukwu, the effect of this unexpected proclamation on my host was severe. It felt as though something had riven through the landscape of his soul and split it in two. It was in an effort to hold himself together that he said, 'I didn't destroy myself anything, I didn't destroy myself.'

'You have,' she said. '*I gbu o le onwe gi.*'

Surprised by her switch to Igbo, he did not speak.

'How can you sell everything, Nonso?'

'I did it because I don't want them to separate us.'

'Yes, but you sold everything you have, Nonso,' she said again and turned to him, and he saw that she had again begun to cry. 'For me, for me, why, Nonso?'

He swallowed hard, for he saw now that the reality of what he had done, when expressed in words, bore a grave, crushing enormity.

'No, I will recover it all—' he said, but saw that she was shaking her head, her eyes diluted with tears. He stopped. He looked about, afraid that people around them would see her crying. 'I sold it to go to school, and to go overseas where I can make it. I will get it all back ten times. I will get a job there . . .'

The food arrived: jollof rice for him and fried rice for her, with meat pie on the side. And in the lull, I flashed in his mind to assure her in stronger words. I reminded him of all the things he'd considered to arrive at the decision. I reminded him of the man who sold his land to send his son to school. I reminded him, Ezeuwa, that he had reckoned that if he got the degree, and returned and married her, he could get a job by her father's influence and could buy new poultry and build a new coop. And the house? What was it even worth? He had not considered that it may be big but that Amauzunku was one of the worst places in Umuahia. So he could not wait for the waiter to go, and once the waiter was gone, he said, 'I will be paying for my life also, and for the woman I love. If I get the degree and I get a good job, I can buy a house ten times better, Mommy. Look at this dirty street. Maybe we can even go to another place, or even, in fact, even maybe Enugu. It is better, Mommy. Actually, it is better. It is better than me allow them to separate us.'

But Ndali simply shook her head in a way that he would remember for a very long time. She said nothing more. She ate little and wiped the steady tears that ran down her cheeks. Her sorrow troubled him, for he had not expected that she would react this strongly to his decision. He held her hand as they walked home, but as they drew near the house, she removed her hand. 'Your hand is sweating again,' she said. He wiped his palms on his trousers and spat into the gutter on the side of the road.

She began to walk alone, a distance from him. He was watching her walk, the swinging of her buttocks with every lithe step visible through the fabric of her tight skirt, when a man on a motorcycle raced past and called at her, 'Asa-nwa, how are you?' She hissed at the man and, laughing, the man took off, his vehicle whining. My host, his heart now cleaved, hastened to her. She turned and looked at him, but without a word. He glanced at the disappearing man, at the empty street behind him, as if the world had itself suddenly become empty. For it occurred to him that this might be what she most feared: if he left, other men would come to her. And he wished, then, that this had happened a few days before, when he had not yet sold his house.

As he began to reach for her clothes after they got home later that night, she thrust the camera into his hand, stripped bare, and asked him to take photos of her. His hand shook as he snapped the first photo, which instantly emerged printed from the top of the camera. It was a full image of her erect body, with her supple breasts staring at the camera, and the nipples taut and hard. The pictures were for him, she said. 'So that any time you feel like you want to do it, you can look at the pictures.' After he lay down by her side, he wondered if she had done it because of the man who had called to her. And a strange fear came upon him, one that possessed him through the night.

CHUKWU, the old fathers say that the god who created the itch also gave man the finger to scratch it. Although his joy had sprung leaks in response to Ndali's sorrow, once they returned home that evening and she asked him to make love to her, he felt better. She told him she was sad mostly because she would miss him, and he assured her that he would return frequently until she could join him. He said, the degree will be quick, and then he will be done. And he said these things so fervently because he was now afraid of leaving her alone in the interim, exposed to the prying eyes of other men. By the time he was to travel to Abuja the following week, his words had worked and she was no longer steeped in sorrow. She drove him to the bus station and returned to her parents.

It rained heavily the night before his trip to Abuja for his visa, and by morning the storm had caused the main road to close. A great pothole that formed in the centre of the road would have drowned every vehicle the size of the Abia Line luxurious bus. The route the driver took was longer, and by the time he got to Abuja, it was almost nightfall. He took a taxi to the cheap hotel where Jamike had suggested he stay, near Kubwa. They knew Jamike, too. They called him *Turkey Man*. 'He is a good man, nice guy,' the cashier, whose mouth smelt of something like vomit, told him. So taken by the man's words was he that as he took his travelling bag into the room, it occurred to him that he had not yet given Jamike anything in appreciation for his goodness. He'd only bought him beer during the four times they ran around to cyber cafes, the immigration office, the high court to swear an affidavit in lieu of a birth certificate, and to find a buyer for his house.

He became worried by this. He cursed himself inwardly for such an oversight, which may have been interpreted as ingratitude, and decided to call Jamike immediately. He scratched a Globacom phone card he'd bought from the vendor's tent outside the hotel and loaded the phone. After he dialled Jamike did not pick up, and then a foreign voice came on, followed by an English translation. He laughed at the words and the way they had been said. Then he tried again, and this time, Jamike picked up.

'Na who be the fool wey dey call me at this time of the night?'

He was struck as if with a rod to his back. He thought to remain silent so Jamike would not find out it was he who was foolish enough not to have remembered they were in different time zones, but he was too embarrassed to control himself in the way he wanted.

'I say who be that?'

'Am sorry, my brother,' he said. 'It is me.'

'Ah, ah, Bobo Solo!'

'Yes, me. I am sorry—'

'No, no, no, mehn. Na me suppose dey sorry. I just came in today. I was in—'

Jamike's voice disappeared behind a wall of indecipherable sounds, then emerged again with a discordant echo of 'ebi', then 'ommm', and then it went blank again. 'Jami, are you there? Are you there?' he said.

'Yes, Bobo Solo, you dey hear me?'

The talk was interrupted by a warning that the call would soon be disconnected. When it cleared, Jamike was saying, 'That's why I neva call you yet. But Solo, you don get the visa?'

'I am in Abuja now. Just today.'

'Oh boy! Bobo Solo, the main man!'

'That is—'

The ping went off again, and the call died. He put the phone on the only table in the room – on which sat the TV, a Bible, a laminated card listing the channels on the TV and, on the back, a menu from the hotel restaurant. At one corner of the room, near the closed curtain, a small cockroach clung to the wall, its antennae curved backwards. As he disrobed, the phone rang. When he looked at the screen, it was Ndali.

'I just wanted to see if you had a safe journey,' she said.

'Yes, Obim. But the road was very bad. Too bad.'

'Blame Orji Kalu, your governor.'

'He is a madman.'

She laughed, and as she did, he heard the voice of a rooster from some distance in the background.

'Where are you?'

'At your house.'

He hesitated. 'Why, Mommy? What are you doing there? I said you should go home after feeding them.'

'Nonso, I can't leave them here alone because you travelled. What am I, Oyibo or egg?'

Her words cut to his heart.

'I love you, Mommy,' he said. Words pooled together in his head, but he hesitated, overcome by the surprise of what she had done. 'You are feeding them yourself alone?'

'Yes,' she said. 'And I picked the eggs.'

'How many?'

'Seven.'

'Mommy,' he said, and when she said 'Eh?' he fell silent. For he could not tell why suddenly he'd become moved to tears. 'If you don't want me to actually leave home, I will come back tomorrow. I will return the money for the house and not sell it again. I will ask Jamike to send me back my school fees. Everything, Mommy. After all, actually I have not started school, you see?'

The words had come out with such rapidity that it surprised him to think he uttered them. For even as he spoke, a strange silence formed an integral part of his speech. He knew, once he'd said all that, that he had simply spoken for her sake. He waited for her to respond, his mind light as the feather of a pipit.

'I don't know what to say, Obim,' she said after a while. 'You are a good man, a very good man. I love you, too. I support your decision — because God has given me a good man.' He heard her deep sigh. 'Go.'

'I should go, Mommy? If you say no, I swear to God who made me, I won't go.'

'Yes. Go.'

'Okay, Mommy.'

'Do you know that the breeder laid pink egg again?' she said.

'Ah, Obiageli?'

'Yes. I fried the egg. Very sweet.'

They laughed, and later, long after the call, he wished he had not made the decision to leave. For the rest of that day, the joy that had filled my host's heart was sealed off from him by the partial veil of regret. I, his chi, felt he had made a good decision, and I was convinced that this sacrifice would further solidify Ndali's love for him rather than destroy it. Chukwu, if only I, too, could see the future; if only I could see that which was to come, I would not have thought this foolish thing!

By dusk the following day, when he got to the embassy, the joy returned again and filled his heart so much that, in the taxi back to the hotel, he wept as he looked at the visa in his passport and the Turkish Airlines ticket he'd bought from the place Jamike had suggested. As he returned to the hotel, it seemed to him that something divine had happened to him. Before he died, his father had once said he was sure that his wife, the mother of my host, was watching over her children. He remembered now that his father had said this after my host escaped what would have been a ghastly accident. It was four years ago when he'd boarded a bus to Aba to visit his uncle but had removed himself at the last minute. Just as the bus was about to set off, a passenger arrived carrying bush meat in a jute sack. My host had complained that he could not endure the smell for the duration of the journey. He left the bus and went to another. He would see the bus on the evening news later that day, damaged beyond recognition. Only two people, of all the nine occupants, had survived the crash. Something he did not know, and which even I could not discern, had brought the meat-carrying man and forced my host to leave the bus and escape an untimely death. He resolved now that the same thing may have brought Jamike to him – the hand of some benevolent god, to help him in this time of need. As I have mentioned before, I, his chi, thought it was a result of the good-luck gift he obtained at the garden of Chiokike.

The journey back to the hotel was long, clogged with traffic in various places. He closed his eyes and imagined the future. There were Ndali and he, together in a beautiful house overseas. With much effort, he imagined them with a child, a boy, carrying a big soccer ball. Inchoate and indistinct as these imaginations were, they soothed his spirit. For a long time he had been a lost man riffling through the crammed quarters of life, but now he had found fertile hope, in which anything could grow. At the hotel, he rang Ndali, but she did not answer. While he lay waiting for her to return the call, he dozed off.

ONYEKERUUWA, after he returned to Umuahia with the visa, his journey became more certain, and so, too, did the anxiety and fear that it engendered. The last week before his final trip passed at the pace of a leopard in pursuit of its prey. On the evening before he was to leave for Lagos, where he

was to board the flying vessel, he found himself fighting hard
to comfort Ndali. For her sorrow had grown in those last
days with a fecundity that amazed him, like a cocoyam in the
wet season. By that time they had loaded the van with the
remaining things he'd not been able to sell. Most were things
that had once belonged to his parents. Elochukwu, who had
joined them, took the red Binatone rechargeable lantern for his
possession. My host let him take it for free. Ndali would have
nothing for herself. She'd fought against his selling his things.
Since he was taking the van to keep in his uncle's garage in
Aba, she asked, why not keep his things with his uncle? Now,
as they began packing the contents of the last room, the living
room, into his van, she broke down.

'It is not easy for her,' Elochukwu said. 'You must realise
this. That's why she is feeling like this.'

'I understand,' my host said. 'But I am not going to Eluigwe.
I am not leaving this world.' He pulled her to himself and
kissed her.

'I am not saying that,' she sobbed. 'It is not that. It is just, the
dreams I have been having in these past few days. They are not
good. You have sold everything, because of me and my family.'

'So you don't want me to go again, Mommy?'

'No, no,' she said. 'I said you should go.'

'You see?' Elochukwu said, splaying his hands open.

'I will come back soon, and we will be together
again, Mommy.'

At this, she nodded and forced a smile.

'That is it!' Elochukwu said, pointing at her face. 'She is
happy now.'

My host laughed, then, holding her, locked mouths with her.

In such moments as this, Egbunu, when a person is about
to leave a companion for a length of time, they do everything

with haste and heightened intensity. The mind ingests these things and stores them in a special vial because these are the moments it will always remember. This is why the way she held his head and spoke into his face after they finished packing was one of the things he'd always recall of her, time and time again.

After he disengaged from her, he ran into the house in tears. Nothing remained of it but the walls. For a moment, he could almost not recognise any of the rooms. Even the yard looked nothing like it had ever been before. A red-headed lizard stood where his poultry had been only five days before, a crumpled piece of feather stuck to its digits. He'd realised, as they loaded the first things into the van, that in some way, a man's life could be measured by the things he possessed. And he'd paused to take stock. There was the large compound, with its age and its history, and with the poultry in it, that had all belonged to him till then. The small farm, with all its crops and yields, which all belonged to him. So did all the furniture in it, the old photographs – black-and-white daguerreotypes. All the vinyl record albums his father had owned, which almost filled a jute sack, the old radios, bags, kites, and many things. He'd even inherited strange things like the rusting door of his father's first car (the one that had crashed near the Oji River), from 1978. There was his father's hunting rifle, the one with which his father had shot the mother of his gosling; two kerosene stoves; the refrigerator; the small bookshelf near the dining table; the big Oxford dictionary seated on the stool near his father's bed; the ikoro drum that hung on the wall in his father's bedroom; his grandfather's metal briefcase containing the bloodstained Biafran army uniform, with its multiple stitches and missing buttons; the curved knives; his father's box of tools; his sister's remaining clothes, still arranged in her cupboard; dozens of pieces of chinaware; wooden spoons; a cooking mortar and pestle; plastic water jugs; old coffee cans filled with spiders and their eggs; and even the van that bore the name of the farm which, for many years, had been his father's lone car. He'd owned the length and breadth of the land on which he'd grown up. But he'd owned immaterial things, too: the way the leaves on the guava tree created a shower when it rained, dripping in a hundred places; the memory of the thief who once scaled their fence and ran into their compound for safety from the hands of an angry mob threatening to lynch him; the fear of riots; the dreams his father had had for him; the many Christmas celebrations; the memory of numerous holiday travels around the country; the dumbstruck hope that will not speak; the rage that will not unleash itself; the accretion of time; the joy of living; the sorrow of death – all these had all, for a long time, been his.

He looked around, about him, on the fence, at the well, at the guava tree, and everything, and it occurred to him that this compound had been part of him. He would live on from this moment like a living animal of the present whose tail is stretched permanently into the past. It was this thought that broke him the most and which caused him to weep as Elochukwu, who would be handing over the keys of the house to the new owners, locked it all up.

GAGANAOGWU, my host also wept because the young child of a man is born with no knowledge of what he once was in his past life. He is born – reborn, rather – as blank as the surface of the sea. But once he begins to grow, he acquires memories. A person lives because of the accumulation of what he has come to know. This is why, when he is alone, when all else has peeled away from him, a man delves into the world within himself. When he is alone, all of it folds and comes together into this whole. The true state of a man is what he is when he is alone. For when he is alone some of all that has come to constitute his being – the profound emotions, and the profound motives of his heart – rises from deep within him up to the surface of his being. This is why when a man is alone, his face wears a look that is distinct from anything there is. This is a face no one else will ever see or encounter. For when another comes to him, that face retracts like a tentacle and presents the other with something else, something akin to a new face. So thus, alone, throughout the night-time bus journey to Lagos, my host dwelt in memories, with a countenance no one else will ever see.

Although the odour of the man who flanked him on the right troubled him through the night, he fell asleep many times, his head resting against one of the bags that stretched from the booth up to the back of the seat. He had vivid dreams. In one, he and Ndali are walking down the aisle in a church. There are lights everywhere, even above the images of the saints, Jisos Kraist, and Madonna on the wall behind the altar. This was her church which she often told him about. The priest, Father Samson, is standing with his hands clasped together, a rosary dangling from them. The deep-throated bass drums, played by the altar boy with the big scar on his head, are beating near the small office of the priest. He can see, smiling and dancing, as they precede him, her mother, in exquisite dressing. There is her father, too, and Chuka, his beard even longer now, pronounced against his bright, fair skin. Both of them are smiling, too, both dressed in suits. And he looks down on himself with glee now: the suit he is wearing is the same as theirs! All three, plus the one Elochukwu has on. But who's the third man, fat-cheeked, a rounded head, hair the shape of an island – bare skin all around, then hair shaped conically around it? Jamike, it's Jamike, the man who has come to his aid! He, too, is wearing the same blue suit and a black tie. He is dancing, the very last in the procession behind my host's back, sweating to the beat of the wedding song.

> *My wife is given to me by God*
> *My husband is given to me by God*
> *Because God gave to me*
> *It will last till the end of time.*

He woke and saw that the bus was riding on a section of the highway flanked by forests, the headlights and those of the cars and trucks and semis that rushed by them the only illuminations in the darkness. He sat up and thought of the previous night, a night that had been tough for Ndali and whose darkness had slowly thickened, like rainwater slowly trickling into a bottle. He could see how she'd struggled through the day, trying hard to conceal her sadness, and he'd had to tell her repeatedly not to cry. But when night came, although she had taken ill and the smell of her sweat had become malarial, she'd asked him to do it because it was their last day. So slowly he'd slid her underpants down her legs, his heart beating feverishly. Once she was bare again, her place ready, her eyes closed, a pleasured smirk on her face, drops of tears on both eyelids, he unbuttoned his shorts. Then, slowly, gently, holding her hand and she hanging her hands around his neck, he'd made love to her. And she'd held him tightly all through, so tight he'd ejaculated in her and the semen slid down from inside her, down his legs.

When he fell asleep again, I floated out of him, as I often do while he is in slumber. But I saw that the bus was crowded with guardian spirits and vagrant creatures, and the din was deafening. One, a ghost, an akaliogoli, who appeared in so thin a mist that it looked like a small stain in the cloth of darkness, sat by a young woman who was asleep in the front seat, her head on the shoulder of another man beside her. The ghost stood there before her, sobbing and saying, 'Don't marry Okoli, please, don't marry him. He is evil, the one who killed me. He is lying. Don't, don't, Ngozi, or my spirit will never rest. He killed me so he could have you. Ngozi, please don't.' After saying those words, it would wail at the top of its lungs in a shattering, funereal voice. Then it would repeat its entreaties all over again, and again. I watched this creature for a while, and it struck me that it may have been doing this for a long time, probably many moons. I felt sad for it – an onyeuwa abandoned by both its body and its guardian spirit, unable to ascend to Alandiichie, unable to reincarnate. This was a terrible thing!

My host slept through the rest of the journey, and when he woke, it was because the bus had coasted into Ojota Park, and the chaos, the large potholes in the park, had suddenly become a nightmare in daylight. Rain was lightly falling, and the vendors – of bread, oranges, wristwatches, water – were taking cover under a shade, roofed with sheets of zinc and supported by iron pillars, on whose visage the name of the park was engraved in red paint. Some of the women covered their heads with black polythene bags. Braving the rain was a seller of bottled drinks who raced to the bus as it pulled up, squinting. My host disembarked swiftly, worrying about the state of his unwashed mouth. He remembered Ndali had told him to wash it at the airport before his flight. Else he would arrive in Cyprus with bad breath.

Before he could take his two big travelling bags out of the

bus, two men, taxi drivers, hurtled forward to take them from him. He let the first, a short, gaunt man with bulging eyes, take them. The man, who lifted the bag with a swiftness that shocked him, was already well on his way out of the bus park before my host realised what the man was doing. He followed the man, carrying his other bag with both hands against his stomach. The rain dropped down slowly on him as he followed the man across the congested traffic, traipsing between honking cars and buses, the air filled with noise. In the distance, a bridge rose, and beyond it, a body of water. Everywhere there seemed to be birds, many of them. The man stopped in front of an unfinished building with bricks filled with holes and on whose veranda a few men sat. His was one of two taxis, badly run down. It was severely dented at the rear, and one of the side mirrors was gone, with only half of the plastic handle still attached. The man tossed his bag into the boot, then took the one my host had in his hand and dropped it, too, on top of the spare tyre in the dusty trunk. Then, banging the lid till it closed, he signalled my host to get in. 'Airport!' he heard the driver say to one of the men on the veranda. Then he, too, entered the car.

TWO

Second Incantation

DIKENAGHA, EKWUEME—

Please accept my second incantation, the language of Eluigwe, as an offering—

Receive it as an equivalent of *ngborogu-oji*, the four-lobbed kola nut—

I must praise you for the privilege you give us, guardian spirits of mankind, to stand in the luminous court of Bechukwu and testify on behalf of our hosts—

The fathers say that a child who washes his hands clean will eat with the elders—

Egbunu, the hands of my host are clean, let him eat with the elders—

Ezeuwa, let the eagle perch, let the hawk perch, and whichever says the other should not perch, may its wings break!—

Now, as my host departs from the land of his fathers, his story will change because what happens at the shore of a river is never the same as that which transpires in a room—

A burning log put in the hands of a child by his mother will not hurt him—

A tree that would marry a woman must first develop a scrotum—

A snake must give birth to something as long as itself—

May your ears remain on the ground to hear as I testify on behalf of my host, as I plead with you to prevent Ala from punishing him—

Gaganaogwu, if it is in fact true that what I fear has happened, let it be considered a crime of error, deserving of mercy—

May my account convince you of my host's lack of ill will towards the woman he has harmed—

Egbunu, it is night in the land of men, and my host is asleep, a further proof that this, if it is indeed true that it has happened, is a crime of innocence—

For no one fishes in dry lakes or bathes with fire—

Thus, Agujiegbe, I proceed with my account with boldness!

10

THE PLUCKED BIRD

OKAAOME, I have heard from fathers long dead at Alandiichie who wonder why their children have abandoned their ways. I have watched them lament over the current state of things. I have heard ndiichie-nne, the great mothers, bemoan the fact that their daughters no longer carry their bodies in the ways their mothers did. The great majestic mothers ask why the *uli*, which the mothers wore on their bodies with pride, is now almost never worn by their daughters. Why is *nzu*, the pure chalk of the earth, no longer seen on them? Why do cowries blossom and bury themselves in the waters of Osimiri untouched? Why, they cry, is it that the sons of the fathers no longer keep their *ikengas*? From their domain far beyond the reaches of the earth, the loyal fathers gaze around the length and breadth of lands they once dwelt in, from Mbosi to Nkpa, from Nkanu to Igberre, and count the shrines made by men to their guardian spirits and their *ikengas* on the fingers of their hands. Why are the altars of the chis, the shrines of one's *ezi*, now forgotten things? Why have the children embraced the ways of those who do not know their own ways? Why have they poisoned the blood of their ancestral consanguinity and shut out the gods of their fathers in outer dark? Why is Ala starved of her rich feathers of young *okeokpa* and Ozala – Dry-Meat-That-Fills-the-Mouth – without his tortoise? Why, the patient fathers wonder in their solemn indignation, are the altars of Amandioha as dry as the throats of skeletons while ewes graze about unhindered? What they seem not to understand is that the White Man charmed their children with the products of his wizardry. In fact, the venerable fathers and mothers forget that it began in their time.

I inhabited a host more than three hundred years ago, when the White Man brought mirrors to Nnobi, the land of men as valiant and wise as the deities of other places. But they were so enthralled by this, and their women so beholden to it, that that object caused them great anguish. Yet I must say that even then, for more than a hundred years, the people did not abandon the ways of their ancestors. They took these things – mirrors, Dane guns, tobacco – but they did not destroy the shrines of their chis. But their children became convinced that the White Man's magic was more potent. And they sought his powers and wisdom. They began to want what he had, like the flying vehicle into which my host stepped the night he got to Lagos. The children of the old fathers often marvel when they see it. They ask: what is this that men have made? Why is the White Man so powerful? How can men fly in the sky, amongst the firmaments, even higher than birds? These are things I do not understand. Many cycles ago, I embodied a great man who was bound like a sacrificial animal and taken to the land of the White Man. He, his captors and other captives like him then rode on the great Osimiri, that which we see stretch interminably around the world, even from here in Bechukwu. The journey across this ocean had spanned weeks, so long that I tired of watching the waters. But even then I marvelled greatly at how the ship was able to move and not sink, when just a single person could not stand on water.

Imagine, Egbunu, how the children of the fathers must have felt when they encountered this proverb of the wise fathers: *No matter how much a man leaps, he cannot fly.* They should consider why the fathers said this before shaking their heads and thinking of the wise fathers as ignorant. Why? Because a man is not a bird. But the children see something like the plane and they are shocked at how this wisdom has been upended by the White Man's sorcery. Humans fly every day in various shapes. We see them on the road to Eluigwe, filling up the skies in silvered vehicles. Men even make war from the sky! In one of my many cycles on earth, my then host, Ejinkeonye Isigadi, had almost been killed by such a weapon from the air in Umuahia in the year the White Man refers to as 1969. What is more, the old fathers say one cannot converse with another who is in a distant land. Nonsense! Their children must scream because they converse now from afar as though they are lying on the same bed by each other. But this is not even all.

Add to this the attractions of the White Man's religion, his inventions, his weapons (the way, for instance, that he is able to create craters in the earth and blast trees and man to bits), and you understand why the children have abandoned the ways of the illustrious fathers. The children of the fathers do not understand that the ways of the august fathers were simply different from that of the White Man. The old fathers looked to the past to move forward. They relied not on what they could see but on what their fathers had seen. They reckoned that all that needed to be known of the universe had been discovered long ago. It was thus beyond them that a man living in the moment can say, I found this, or I discovered that. It was the greatest arrogance to purport that all who came before a man were slight or careless and that one has happened to see this *now*. So if you asked one of the eminent fathers, why do you plant yam in a mound rather than as seed? He would say, because my father taught me so. If a man told you he could not shake an elder with a left hand, and you ask him why, he'd say, because it is not *omenala*. The civilisation of the fathers was hinged on the preservation of that which already existed, not on the discovery of new things.

Elders of Alandiichie, old fathers of Alaigbo, of the black peoples of the rain forest, custodians of the Black Man's wisdom, hear me: these products of the White Man's sorcery are the reasons you now complain and cry and wail about your children like fowls after a hawk attack. It is the White Man who has trampled on your traditions. It is he who has seduced and slept with your ancestral spirits. It is to him that the gods of your land have submitted their heads, and he has shaved them clean, down to the skin of their scalps. He has flogged the high priests and hanged your rulers. He has tamed the animals of your totems and imprisoned the souls of your tribes. He has spat in the face of your wisdoms, and your valiant mythologies are silent before him.

Ijango-ijango, why have I spoken with such a wet tongue about the ancestors? It is because this object that bore my host and others in the sky was magnificent beyond words. All through the flight, even my host – a lover of birds – wondered how it flew. It seemed to him that the propulsion of the plane was by its wings. It soared through the clouds, and over the interminable expanse of water, which had the colour of the sky at the end of rainy season. This was Osimiri, the great water body that spread around the circumference of the world. It was the water that contained salt, the *osimiri-nnu*. Your sacred tears, Chukwu.

Out of curiosity, I exited the body of my host and soared out of the plane. I was instantly submerged in this wasteland of noises and spirit bodies. All across the horizon, I saw incorporeal creatures – onyeuwas and guardian spirits and others – travelling somewhere, either descending or ascending with magnificent speed. In the distance, a grey mass of creatures crawled over the illuminate orb that was the sun. I tried not to focus on them but to look instead on the plane, whose wings did not flutter as a bird's. I hovered over it, flying at a strange, unearthly speed as the plane raced on. I had never stopped to watch such a thing before, and it terrified me. I returned immediately into the body of my host. He was still examining the plane in fascination, for it had people, televisions, toilets, food, chairs, and all that may be found in the houses of people on land. But much of his thoughts rested on Ndali.

He soon fell asleep, and when he woke, too many things were happening all at once. The people were clapping and cheering even as a voice returned to the sound boxes. The plane itself had thudded and was now speeding down somewhere he could tell was no longer the air, for he could feel the vibrations against the ground. The plane was also now full of light, both daylight and man-made light from the interior. He slid up the window covering and understood the reason for the commotion. Joy erupted in him, too. He thought that if his father and mother had been alive now, how proud they would have been. He thought of Nkiru in Lagos. He asked himself what she was doing now. He wondered, with mild sadness, whether she now had a child from that much older man. When children of men think of things that are unpleasant, their thinking patterns are not the same as they are when they ponder pleasant things. This was why his mind emphasised the age of his sister's husband. He would call her from here, *Instanbull*: maybe it would make a difference. It might restore her faith in him as her brother, her only surviving family. But how could he do it? He did not have her number or her husband's. It was she alone who called him from vendor pay phones on special occasions like Christmas, New Year, sometimes at Easter, and once on the anniversary of their father's death. She'd cried on the phone that day in a way that had shocked him and given him hope that they may yet renew their relationship. But it didn't matter. When she ended the call with the usual 'I just wanted to call to know how you are doing', he knew that she would be swallowed again into the void.

He was thrown out of his thoughts by the sudden eruption of clapping and voices. Their faces filled with smiles, people began extracting their bags from the compartments, slugging on backpacks, propping up the retractable handles of their roller bags. The reason for their joy was varied, but he could tell by the clapping and by the shouts of 'Praise the Lord' and 'Hallelujah' from the back that people were happy the plane had landed safely. He reckoned that it may have been because of the string of recent occurrences regarding planes in Nigeria. For not too long before, a plane carrying dignitaries, including the sultan of Sokoto and the son of a former president, had crashed, killing nearly everyone on board. Only less than a year before that, another plane had crashed, killing a well-known female pastor, Bimbo Odukoya. But he thought even more that these people were happy because they had been lifted from places where they had been suffering into this new country. The plane had lifted out of the land of lack, of man–pass–man, the land in which a man's greatest enemies are members of his household; a land of kidnappers, of ritual killers, of policemen who bully those they encounter on the road and shoot those who don't bribe them, of leaders who treat those they lead with contempt and rob them of the commonwealth, of frequent riots and crisis, of long strikes, of petrol shortages, of joblessness, of clogged gutters, of potholed roads, of bridges that collapse at will, of littered streets and trashy neighbourhoods, and of constant power outages.

OLISABINIGWE, the great fathers say that when a man crosses into an unknown land, he becomes again like a child. He must rely on asking questions and on searching for directions. This is also why when they got off the plane, my host did not know what to do. The place they stepped into from the plane, an airport, was massive and filled to the brim with all kinds of people. At first he thought of his big bags, where he'd folded away most of his belongings that weren't sold or burned or kept with his uncle, but then he remembered he'd been repeatedly told he would pick them up in Cyprus. All he had now was the bag Ndali had given him, in which he kept his admission letters, her letter, photos and all the vital documents which he needed to present to the school in the new country. The other black people from his country stepped into the chaos too, and disappeared into the moving stream of people. Whether left or right or behind, they appeared in flashes, amongst the gathering. He walked up into the centre of the great hall, where a big clock hung from the roof. He stopped behind an old yellow-skinned couple who stood there gazing at the clock as if it were the body of a man hanging on a tree. A small car came behind him and honked. He stepped aside, and it went on, honking at every stop, as it tried to navigate between the innumerable people crowding along the hallways like it was a market in Umuahia, with the intermittent announcement of arrivals and departures echoing through

the expansive hall. He turned and walked in the direction
where he'd seen many of his compatriots go.

He'd walked for nearly half a kilometre, passing many curi-
osities with a load of thoughts in his head, when he came by a
fellow with a long beard and dark glasses. He asked the fellow
what he should do. The fellow asked him for his boarding
card. He took out the slip of paper they had handed him at
the airport.

'Your plane to Cyprus will leave by seven. Now is only
three, so you must wait. Me sef I'm going there. Just relax, er?'

He thanked the man, and the fellow went his way, walking
as if he were slightly dancing. 'Relax,' the man had told him.
It meant wait. It meant too that there are many things that
a man cannot control. There are forces that must assemble,
things that must come together, an agreed measure of time,
and an accepted code which must, in the end, materialise into
something that will occasion movement. This was an example
of that. To leave here, he must assemble with others who also
have paid to get to the same place. When they assemble, they
will board the plane. There will be people waiting for them to
fly the plane. But let's not forget, Egbunu, that it will happen
when the ticking hand of the clock strikes seven. That is what
must summon them – him and all these people. In the days
of the fathers it was the voice of the village or the town crier
and the sound of his gong. As I have spoken about before, the
White Man's civilisation depends on this. Take away the clock
and nothing would be possible in his world.

What must he do while waiting for the hand to strike
seven? Relax. But I, his chi, could not relax, for I could sense
that something had gone wrong in the realm of the spirit, but
I could not tell what it was. Presently, my host found a seat
near a place where people gathered, drinking and smoking

cigarettes. He sat watching the cubicle, the airy image of a bearded man who moved about as if possessed. It reminded him of how his beard had grown after his father died, how he hadn't shaved for weeks, and how one day he looked at himself in the mirror and laughed at himself for a long time – so long that later he wondered if he had become mad.

Beside him, a white woman was asleep, her eyelids twitching like a child's. He watched her for a few minutes, his eyes on the greenish line of veins along her neck and on her long blue fingernails. She reminded him of Miss J, and he wondered if she was still a prostitute. While he sat there, Chukwu, I came out of him briefly. I had been longing to see what the spiritual world of this place was like, but I had not been able to do so because of my host's uncertain state of mind. Now, once I stepped out, I saw that the place was filled with spirits, some so grotesque in shape and form that they were forever imprinted on my mind. One was arrayed in the misty costume of ancient ghosts and discarnate beings, the palest thing my eye had ever seen. It stood behind a withering white man who sat in a wheelchair, staring vacuously forward. A ghost sat by itself on the floor of the airport, unmoved by people who walked in and out through it. A child kicked a ball through its incorporeal torso, but it did not even stir. It kept on shaking its head, gesticulating, and speaking in quick, dribbling speech in a foreign language.

My host had risen from his seat by the time I returned into him. He walked on for a long time before he chanced upon two Nigerian men who'd sat in the row directly in front of him on the plane. They had just emerged from a very brightly lit shop and were carrying the same multi-coloured bag as many of those in the airport. From the bits of the duo's conversation he'd heard while on the plane, and from the way one of the men carried himself, he knew this man had been living in Cyprus for a while. The man he thought had lived in Cyprus was dressed in a plain jacket and jeans, and his ears were plugged. The other, a man of similar height as my host, wore a cardigan. The man looked unkempt, with sleep in the side of one of his eyes. He bore the countenance of someone who was being inwardly tormented. My host hastened towards them, wanting to know from them what he was to do next.

'Excuse me, brothers,' he called after them.

When he came up to them, the man in the jacket moved his bag from one shoulder to the other and stretched out his hand as if he'd been expecting my host.

'Please, are you from Nigeria?' my host said.

'Yes, yes,' the man said.

'Going to Cyprus?'

'Yes,' the man said, and the other nodded.

'You don go there before?' the other man said.

'No, I neva go before,' my host said.

The man looked at the other, who stared at him with a certain curious fixedness as some of those who had been on the same plane walked past.

'I never go, too. In fact, my brother, I wish someone had warned me before I left Nigeria.'

'Why?' my host said.

'Why?' the man said, and pointed to the man in the jacket. 'T.T. has been there before, and he said it is not a good place.'

My host looked up at T.T., who was nodding.

'I no understand,' my host said. 'What you mean the place no good?'

The other man muttered a faint laugh in response, and then continued to shake his head like one who had uttered a common universal truth only to see that his listener was not aware of it.

'Let T.T. tell you himself. I never go there, I just sit with him on the plane from Lagos and he told me many things.'

T.T. told my host about Cyprus. And the things he said were grim. T.T. paused only when my host asked a question – 'You mean no jobs at all?'; 'No, are you serious?'; 'But is it not Europe?'; 'No UK or US embassy?'; 'They put you in prison?'; 'How come?' – but even after he finished telling the story, my host could not believe much of it.

'You know; I am fucked up. Aye mi, oh!' the other man, whom T.T. had identified as Linus during his speech, said. Then he put both hands on his head.

My host turned from these men and muttered to himself that it could not be true, for he was very disturbed. How, he wondered, could there be no jobs in a country *abroad*, where white people live? Maybe the Nigerian students who were going there were lazy. If the place was as bad as T.T. had just told him, why would T.T. go there himself? These things contradicted everything his friend Jamike had told him about the place. Jamike had assured him that his life would change for the better once he arrived in Cyprus. Jamike had assured him that he could easily own a house soon after and that it would be easy to emigrate from there to Europe or elsewhere.

While the man, T.T., continued on about many people who had been deceived into going to Cyprus, my host listened with half his ears, the other battling with the voice of his head. Chukwu, I flashed it in his mind that this was the right decision. Perhaps, he resolved, it was best to call Jamike and talk to him about these things rather than wait until he came to pick him up at the airport in Cyprus. Indeed he recalled just as the last thought dissolved into his mind that Jamike had specifically asked him to call his phone once he reached Istanbul. Although T.T. was still speaking – now about a man who, on reaching

Cyprus, discovered he had been deceived and now walks about the place in tattered clothes like a madman – my host moved his legs to signal that he wanted to leave. Once T.T. paused, he said, 'I wan go call my friend. Make I call am, er.'

The duo shook their heads, T.T. with a slight bemused smile on his face. My host went to the phone booth, determined to confirm from Jamike that all the things T.T. had told him were either untrue or just some effort to terrify the other man. Perhaps he was trying to swindle the other guy, and this false information was part of the plot. He must relate to these men with caution. I was thrilled with this reasoning, for I have lived among mankind long enough to know that any meeting between two persons who do not know each other is often dominated by uncertainty and, to a lesser degree, suspicion. If it is a person one has met at a marketplace and with whom one has engaged in some transaction, then there arises the fear. Is he going to cheat me? Is this grain, this cup of milk, this chain wristwatch worth so much? If it is a man who has just met a woman of interest, he wonders: is she going to like me? Will she, if possible, drink with me?

This was what my host had just done. In that flustered state, with questions rushing into his mind like blood from a severed limb, he tottered off towards the other end of the airport to the phone booths. He stood behind two white men in white frocks for the second of three phone booths. From them came the smell of costly perfumes. They both had two of the same polythene bag nearly everyone in the airport carried – bags bearing the inscription DUTY FREE, the meaning of which he did not know. When the men in the frocks had finished their calls, he climbed into the cubicle. He brought out the foolscap sheet on which he'd scribbled Jamike's number and, following the directions on the side of the phone, dialled it. But what returned was a recurrent burst of static and a voice that sometimes came on to announce that the number was invalid before trailing into some unfamiliar language. He repeated the dial, with the same result.

Ezeuwa, not once since I've been with him had he been this shocked by something. He placed the bag he wore on his shoulder on the floor and dialled the number again, that same number from which Jamike had called him only the previous week. He made to ring it again, but turning, he saw that a queue had formed behind him, their faces eager and impatient. He hung the phone back on the grip and, with his eyes still on the paper, made his way through the crowded airport. When he got to the spot where the two men had been before, there was no trace of them. In their stead sat a heavily bearded white man with rheumy eyes gazing stoically at the world as if someone had set it on fire. Ebubedike, it was here that I first got a glimpse of all that was to come.

OBASIDINELU, at the time, I did not know what I had seen, nor did my host. What I knew – and what he knew, too – was that something had gone wrong, but this was not a cause for panic. This was a world in which things go wrong. Most things. And the fact that things had gone wrong did not always mean that disaster was looming. This is why the old fathers say that the fact that a millipede has more than a hundred legs does not mean that he is a great runner. Things can misalign; darkness can mount and encroach on the light of the day; but it will not always mean that night has come. So I did not raise alarm. I let him walk on in search of the two men until he found them, just an hour before the next flight, by a waterfall, gazing into a computer. He ran up to them with the urgency of one fleeing a leopard. When he got to them, he was breathless.

'We went to eat there,' T.T. said, pointing at the place on whose threshold hung a notice in the White Man's language that said FOOD COURT. 'Have you called your friend?'

My host shook his head. 'I have tried and tried, but it is not going. Not going at all.'

'Why? Let me see the number. Is it correct – the code? It must be eleven.'

He produced the number and T.T. gazed at it in a concentrated manner. 'Is this the number?'

'Yes, it is so, my brother.'

T.T. shook his head. 'But this no be Cyprus number.' He waved the sheet. 'This is not a Cyprus number at all, at all, believe me.'

'I don't understand.'

T.T. came closer, pointing at the figures on the paper.

'Cyprus has Turkish number. TRNC. It is plus nine zero. This one is plus three four. Not Cyprus number at all.'

My host stood still, like a bird transfixed in its thermal.

'But he has called me several times,' he said.

'On this number? It is not a Cyprus number, believe me,' T.T. said. 'Did he give you any address to meet him?'

He shook his head.

'No address. Ah, okay. Did he give you any letter? How you take get your visa?'

'Him send me admission letter,' my host replied. 'I take am to the embassy.'

He opened the small bag, and in haste, he presented a paper to T.T., and he and Linus peered at it.

'Erhen, he contacted the school. I see this na genuine admission letter.' He started to speak in response, but T.T. continued, 'He paid the school fees, too, since this is an unconditional admission letter. I ask because I have seen many occasions where boys just barbed people's heads. They pretend that they are the agents of the school and take their money. But they don't pay the fees at all. They just eat the money.'

Ijango–ijango, my host was stunned. He tried to say something, to thaw up a piece of the thoughts that had congealed into a lump in his mind, but the lump would not thaw. In silence, he took the paper back from T.T.

'Still, I think this Jamike guy is a yahoo boy,' T.T. said, shaking his head. 'My bro, I suspect he has duped you.'

'How?' my host said.

'Did you contact the school directly?'

He wanted to say he did, but he found himself shaking his head instead. In response, a small smile appeared on T.T.'s face.

'So you didn't?'

'That is so,' he said. 'I have the admission letter with the school's stamp and everything. Actually, I even saw his student ID. We browsed the school together from cyber cafe. Jamike is a student there.'

T.T. answered with silence, and beside him Linus stood watching, his mouth slightly ajar. My host gazed at both men, almost trembling.

'Hmm,' T.T. said.

'He paid the school fees because the school only accepts Turkish bank cheques or international money order. They don't accept bank transfers from Nigerian bank here,' my host said. He saw the woman who had been sleeping earlier walking past them, dragging a bag behind her. 'Since he was going back there, I just changed my naira and give him all the money.'

He was continuing, but he saw that T.T.'s mouth had been opened wide in surprise, and even the other man shook his head and said, 'You for no give am all that money.'

T.T. pointed to a gate in the distance, where many of those who had been on the plane from Nigeria had started to line up, and said, 'Ah, we must go board now.' T.T. took up his backpack and hung it up his back. My host watched as Linus picked up his own things. And for no apparent reason, he remembered his gosling, how – in times when it seemed it had remembered its mother and the place of its provenance – it would lift itself and dash for the window, the door, wherever it could find. How once, in a bid to escape, it had assumed the tree it had seen through the window meant it could get outside. So with violent speed it dashed against the window. Concussed, it lay as if dead.

'Are you not coming, too?' T.T. said, and my host looked up, saw the gosling lying there, at the base of the wall, its head bent towards its neck and its wings batting against the ground.

He blinked, closed his eyes, and when he opened them, he saw T.T. encompassed about by a myriad of lights and screens.

He nodded. 'I am coming, too,' he said, and followed them.

'Maybe you go meet Jamike at Ercan. The airport,' T.T. said. 'No fear, er? No fear.'

The other man nodded, too. 'No shaking, nothing dey happen. No fear, fear go fear fear!'

He nodded again and said, as if he believed it, 'I no go fear.'

AKWAAKWURU, the great fathers often say that a toad whose mouth is full of water cannot swallow even an ant. I have seen them apply this to the way in which the mind of a man, when it is occupied by something that threatens its peace, becomes consumed by it. This was the case with my host. For throughout the flight, his mind was hooked to the words of the two men who were now seated at the rear of the plane. He sat close to the front, surrounded by more white people than

were in the previous, bigger plane. They were mostly young
girls and boys who, he assumed, were students, too. Even the
woman who sat by him, with hair that was brown and long,
seemed to be one. And all through the flight she avoided
eye contact with him, gazing in her phone or into a glossy
magazine. But as he sat there, fear, having transformed itself
into a mind-dwelling rat, ferreted about in his head, chewing
through every detail. And when he looked out of the window
as he drew near the country, what he saw seemed to reinforce
the grim words of the duo. For instead of the tall buildings
and the long bridges over the sea he had seen as they landed
in Istanbul, what he saw now were dry patches of desert land,
mountains and the sea. By the time he found himself descending the ladder from the plane into the dim light of the setting
sun alongside the other travellers, the details had blossomed
into genial terrors.

The airport, to his eyes, was small. It looked, in many
ways, like the one in Nigeria except that it was cleaner and
more orderly. But it did not have the beauty or sophistica-
tion of the one in Istanbul. It was cheap, exuding no glow or
pleasantness, conforming in every way and sense with T.T.'s
description of it. Once he saw the men whose words had tormented him through the flight, he went to them. He found
them with another man, who introduced himself as Jay and
who was talking about his time in Germany. They stood at a
place where most of the people had gathered, watching as a
black hole vomited up their bags. His two bags came out with
their padlocks intact, their weight as he last remembered them.
Someone had mentioned how those who loaded bags into
the airplanes at the airport in Nigeria sometimes broke into
people's bags and stole things during the process of transfer-
ring them into the plane. This had not happened to him. He

dragged and pulled the roller bag along, carried the other by its handle, and followed the two men. They were still talking, this time about the attitude of the women in both countries – this one, which T.T. repeatedly referred to as TRNC or 'this island', and Jay's Germany. He listened, his mind still tethered to the phone booth at the airport in Istanbul.

When they stepped out of the airport, darkness had descended with lithe grace, and an unusual smell hung in the air. A pool of cars gathered in front of the airport greeted them. Turkish-speaking men, gesturing towards various black Mercedes-Benz or V-booths, beckoned to him.

'They are taxi drivers,' T.T. said. He'd put on a cap and the gleeful countenance of a person who had returned home. Nothing in him betrayed the dire situation on the island he'd so painstakingly described. Still wearing that curious smile on his face, T.T. spoke with one of the men, an unusual white man, nothing like any my host had ever seen before, even on TV. This one's face was wrinkled beyond normal, and his complexion, although white, seemed to have an unusual dark hue to it. Half the man's head was full of black hair, but the roots at the sides of his head were grey.

'That's our bus there!' T.T. said, breaking off from the taxi driver to point to a big bus, brightly lit on the inside, slowly riding towards them from the other end of the park. On its body was inscribed NEAR EAST UNIVERSITY, its equivalent in Turkish beneath it.

'We go dey go be that,' T.T. said, turning to him. 'That's our bus there.'

My host, gazing up at the bus, nodded.

'No worry, bro. Just wait for your friend here. I am sure him go come.'

'It is so. He will. Thank you, T.T. God bless you.'

'No mention. Just wait here, eh. And if him no come, just take the next CIU bus wey come. Your school bus. E go come same here, probly later. Cyprus International University. Just follow am. Show dem your admission letter – where is it?'

His mind working in distinct haste, he produced the paper from the small bag he carried, but as he did, the foolscap on which Jamike had scribbled the expenses and all it would cost him, as well as his phone number, fell.

'Good,' T.T. was saying as he picked up the paper. 'Best of luck, bro. Maybe we go come see you. Take my number.'

My host took out his phone from his pocket to register the number, but it did not turn on when he flipped it open.

'The battery don die,' he said.

'No problem. We go go now. Bye.'

Gaganaogwu, by this time, my host had begun to believe that the things he'd heard from T.T. were true. Although he started to wait, he thought it was unlikely that Jamike would come. Even though a chi can see into the interior of a host's mind, it is sometimes still difficult to determine where an idea comes from. This was the case with this idea. It was, I think, a collection of things he had been seeing: the quality of the airport here, the behaviour of the drivers, the emptiness of the land, and the problem of communication. These confirmed his worry. I pushed the thought into his mind that it was too early to lose hope. I threw his father's motto into his mind – *Forward ever, backwards never* – but it hit the door his mind had erected around his fears and ricocheted away. Instead he thought of home, of Ndali, what she must be doing at that time. He remembered the anguish of selling his chickens – how, as he dropped the cage of the brown broilers off at one of the buyers', he had nearly choked. He looked now at the two heavy bags in his hands which bore all his remaining possessions – what he did not sell or gift to Ndali or Elochukwu, or charity, or throw away. And these things solidified his fear that something had gone wrong.

He warded off the advances of taxi drivers time and time again. They came at him, speaking in halting language he did not comprehend, their words cadenced with a clicking accent. As night fell, the men continued to call at him, until most of the cars emptied out of the park. But there was still no Jamike. He'd waited for nearly two hours when he remembered that Jamike had told him he would be given free temporary accommodation during the first two nights at the school until he was able to choose a campus apartment. These were Jamike's words, spoken at a time when the waters were calm, and they came to him now in this moment of great roiling waters, of the torment of fear, and of fainting hope.

CHUKWU, the road from the airport to the town seemed as far as the journey from Umuahia to Aba, except that it was smooth, not damaged by erosion or potholes. During the ride, he gazed at the country and its strange and foreign landscape. As he registered every discernible sight, every detail of the things the men had told him worked on him like the hands of a fowler, pulling out feather after feather so that by the time the desert came into view, he'd been completely deplumed. And he, now bald and feeble, hopped about in the plains of fear. The taxi was circling a roundabout when he recalled something Jamike had said about the absence of trees, and it struck him that he had yet to see one tree so far in the journey. He saw the broad attributes of the sierras, one of which was adorned with the lighted outline of a huge flag. It occurred to him that he'd seen the flag before, although he could not recall that it was perhaps at the Turkish embassy in Abuja.

'Okul, burda. School. School,' the man said when they arrived at a place in front of which was a short but long brick wall bearing the name of the school.

He saw the school – a group of unusual buildings linked together, the darkness like a still river around them. Around and about the strange smell he'd perceived at the airport lingered. The man pulled up in front of one of the buildings, a four-storey one in front of which was a table with three people seated. Behind them was a board on which there was a world map – a drawing showing the White Man's knowledge of the world. He paid the driver twenty euros. The man gave him some Turkish lira and coins in return and unloaded the bags. One of the people at the table, a man with shocks of grey hair, came to meet him. The man looked like the people from a place far from the country of the fathers, a place called India. My former host, Ezike Nkeoye, once knew such a man as a teacher. The Indian man introduced himself as Atif.

'Chinonso,' he said, taking the man's offer of a handshake.

'Chi-non-so?' the man said. 'Do you have an English name?'

'Solomon, call me Solomon.'

'Better for me,' the man said, and smiled in a way my host had never seen before, for it seemed as though the man's eyes were completely closed. 'Did you ask to be picked up from the airport?'

'No, I was waiting for my friend, Jamike Nwaorji, your student, here, CIU, to pick me from the airport.'

'Oh, okay. Where is he?'

'He didn't come.'

'Why?'

'I don't know, actually, I don't know. Do you know where he is? Can you find him for me?'

'Find him?' the man said, and turned to reply to something

one of the others at the table, a thin white girl, had said to him in the language of the land. When he turned back, he said, 'I'm sorry, Solomon. What's your friend's name again? I might know him if he is a student here. There are nine students from Africa in this university, and eight of them are from Nigeria.'

'Jamike Nwaorji,' he said. 'He is from Business Administration, from business department.'

'Jamike? Does he have another name?'

'No. You don't know him? Jamike. J–a–m–i–k–e. His surname is Nwaorji: N–w–a–r, no, sorry, N–w–a–o–r–j–i.'

Atif shook his head and turned back to the desk. My host had dropped his big bag on the ground, and his heart pounded as he waited for the Turkish girl to stop talking to the man again. The third person, a stout man with a large beard, snapped open a canned drink. The drink swished and dripped and foamed over his hand to the ground. The man shouted something that sounded like *Olah* and began to laugh. For a moment, they seemed to all forget my host.

'His name is Jamike Nwaorji,' he said softly, making sure he said the surname as clearly as he could.

'Okay,' the girl said now. 'We are looking at the list, but not find this man, your friend.'

'There is no such person here that I know. And now, I have looked at the business department, the only Nigerian there is Patience, Patience Otima.'

'Nobody like Jamike Nwaorji?' my host said. He looked up at the two people on whom, it felt to him at the moment, his life may depend. But he saw in their faces, in the way they gazed at the records, that he would find no succour there. 'Jamike Nwaorji, nobody like him?' he said again, and the words dragged in his mouth this time, inflected by subtle gasps whose origin seemed to be from his bowels. He placed his hands on his belly.

'No,' the man said with something that sounded like a *p* at the end of it. 'Can I see your admission letter?'

Egbunu, his hands were shaking as he brought the paper out of the bag he'd been carrying for all the time he had been away from Umuahia, almost two full days. He watched as the man peered at the roughened paper, conscious of the man's every blink, calculating every change in the man's countenance, terrified by his every move.

'This is real, and I can see that you paid your school fees.' He looked my host in the eye, and then scratched the side of his head. 'Let me ask you a question: Did you pay for on-campus accommodation?'

'Yes,' my host, slightly relieved now, said curtly. Then he explained that he'd sent Jamike money for accommodation for two semesters. He brought out the piece of foolscap on which Jamike had scribbled the breakdown of costs and, pointing at the different figures, said, 'I paid one thousand five hundred euros for one-year accommodation. Then I paid three thousand for one-year school fees, and two thousand euros for maintenance.'

Something in what he'd said surprised the man, Atif. The man flipped open another file and began searching frantically for his name on a list of names. The girl, too, joined in, and even the other man with the drink. They all peered from behind Atif's shoulders. A taxi like the one that had brought him pulled towards them slowly. As it came, Atif raised his head to tell him that even on this list there was no name similar to his. In the next file, too – which was for campus apartments, where most Africans stayed because they didn't always like Turkish food served exclusively in dormitories – his name was not there. In the list of registered apartments subsidised by the university, his name was not there.

When he'd looked everywhere and could not find my host's name, Atif turned to him and said it would be fine. Egbunu, this man said this to a person who – like a fowl – had been deplumed and was now bare before the world. Atif continued to say this as he took him across the campus, up to a four-storey building similar to the one in front of whose facade they had pitched their table, and up into one of the temporary accommodations, where he could stay for five days. Then Atif shook the hand of a man who had been dealt a crushing blow and said, without any shadow of doubt, that all would be well. And, as often happens everywhere among mankind, this man – deplumed, in agony, in despair – nodded and thanked the man who had said these things to him, just as I have seen men do many times. Then the man said to him, 'Just relax and sleep. Good night.' And my host, reckoning that he must do as he had been told, nodded and said, 'Good night, too. See you tomorrow.'

11

THE WAYFARER IN A FOREIGN LAND

EZECHITAOKE, the early fathers say in their peripatetic wisdom that one's own language is never difficult. Thus, because my host arrived in a place I did not know, I must recount everything here, every bit of the next few days, every bit, for my testimony tonight to bear weight. I ask that your ears be patient in hearing me.

AGUJIEGBE, I have spoken already about the poverty of anticipation and the emptiness of hope for the future. Now I would like to ask: what is a person's tomorrow? Is it not to be likened to an endangered animal who, having escaped from a pursuer, arrives at the mouth of a cave whose depth or length it does not know and within which it can see nothing? It does not know whether the ground is filled with thorns. It doesn't know, cannot see, if a more venomous beast is in the cave. Yet it must enter into it; it has no choice. For to not enter is to cease to exist, and for a man to not enter through the door of tomorrow is death. The possible result of entering into the unknown of tomorrow? Numerous possibilities, Chukwu, too numerous to count! A certain man may wake up joyful because he has been told the day before that he will be promoted at work that morning. He embraces his wife and leaves for work. He gets in his car and does not see the schoolboy run into the road in fear. In a second, in the batting of an eyelid, the man has killed a promising child! The world heaps a great burden on him at once. And this burden is not an ordinary one, for it is something he cannot unburden himself of. It will remain with him for the rest of his life. I have seen it many times. But is not this, too, the tomorrow the man has entered?

My host woke up in the new country the next morning after he arrived, knowing only that things were different here, unaware of what awaited him in this new day. He knew that there had been uninterrupted electricity, and he'd plugged in his phone so it could charge all night. And throughout the night, he did not hear a cock crow, even though he'd been awake for most of it. It seemed that in the country from which he'd come, there was noise, constant grinding of some machines, constant shouts of children playing, weeping, the honking of cars and motorcycles, acclamations, church drums and singing, muezzins calling from mosques' megaphones, loud music from some party in full swing – and the source of the constant animated sound is boundless, innumerable. It seemed as if the world of the country abhorred calm. But here, there was calm. Even silence. It was as though everywhere, in every house, at every moment, funerals were going on, the kind in which one could only utter a muffled gasp. Despite this quiet, he slept very little, so little that even now, at day-break, he still felt a need for sleep. During the night, his mind had become a carnival fair in which wanted and unwanted thoughts danced. And as the carnival went on, he could not close his eyes.

When he walked out of the room, the day offered him a

black man, naked to the waist, who stood washing his hands in the kitchen sink.

'My name is Tobe. I am from Enugu. Computer Engineering – doctorate,' the man said, and moved away from the glare of the sun that was shining through the naked windows.

'Chinonso Solomon Olisa. Business Administration,' he said. He shook hands with the man.

'I saw when Atif was bringing you in last night but I didn't want to disturb you. I was at the other apartment with some of the old students. Apartment five.' The man pointed to a building through the window. It had yellow-coloured walls with red brick columns on the sides and wide balconies in front of the four storeys. On the red iron balcony of the one he pointed to, a black man with enormous hair and a big comb tucked into it stood leaning against the wall, smoking. 'There are three Nigerians there, and all of them came last semester. They are the old students.'

My host, stirring, looked in the direction of the place, for a glimmer of hope had sparked within him.

'Do you know their names, all their names?' he said.

'Yes, what happened?'

'Can you—'

'One is – that one is Benji. Benjamin. The other is Dimeji: Dee. He came here before many of them. The third one is John. He is Igbo, too.'

'No one called Jamike. Jamike Nwaorji?'

'Ah, no, no Jamike,' the man said. 'What kind of name is that, sef?'

'I don't know,' he said quietly, beaten back from the door of the apartment where, in that brief moment, his heart had travelled. Yet he kept his eyes on the place and saw that the man, Benji, had gone back in and another man and a black woman were exiting the door.

'Can you come introduce me to them? I want to see if any of them know Jamike.'

'What happened? What do you need? You can tell me.'

He gazed at this shirtless hirsute man whose eyes lay deep in his head behind his large-rimmed glasses trying to decide whether or not to be discreet. But the voice in his head, even before I could stir, nudged him to tell his story; perhaps this man could help him. And with so much care, he told the man the story up to that point. At first he spoke in the language of the White Man, but midway through the story, he asked the man if he spoke Igbo, which the latter affirmed, as if annoyed by the question. Now, given a softer bed to sit on, he spoke in excruciating detail, and by the time he was done, the man told him he was certain he'd been duped. 'I am certain,' Tobe said, and then began describing many scams he'd heard about, comparing the similarities.

'Wait, and when you called him, er, you discovered the number was fake?' Tobe said presently.

'That is so.'

'And he did not come to the airport, I am sure?'

'It is so, my brother.'

'So you see what I tell you? That he must be fake? But look, let's go first, let's try to find him. It is possible he is not what we think. Maybe he drank and forgot to come to the airport – people party a lot on this island! You know this can happen. Let us go buy a phone card so you can call him until he picks up. Let us go.'

The new country presented itself to him outside the apartment with a jolt. The ground was paved with what looked like bricks flattened into the earth. There were flowers in vases, and a host of flowers was placed outside, on the balconies of the houses. The buildings appeared different from the ones in Nigeria, even in Abuja. There seemed to be some finesse to their crafting that he'd never seen before. A building made almost entirely of glass, long and rectangular, caught his attention in the distance. 'The English building,' Tobe said. 'That is where all of us will take our Turkish Language lessons.' While he was still speaking, two white boys, dragging bags, one of them smoking, called at them.

'My friend! *Arkadas.*'

'*Arkadas.* How are you?' Tobe said, then drew near and shook hands with the men.

'No, only English,' the white man said. 'No Turkish.'

'Okay, English, English – English,' Tobe said in an affected accent, his voice altered to mimic the language of these people. As my host watched them, he wondered if this was how one lived here. Did one put on a new voice every time one spoke with one of these people? When Tobe rejoined him, I thought he would ask Tobe questions, to try to find answers to the questions now crowding his mind, but he did not. Agujiegbe, this was a strange trait in this host of mine, something I had seen in few others in my many cycles on the earth.

On the way to the place where they would buy phone cards, Tobe said school was to begin on Monday, and some students were starting to arrive. He said that the campus would be filled by Sunday night, in four days.

They arrived at a building with two glass doors and an assortment of things inside, what he thought was some kind of expanded supermarket. As they entered it, Tobe turned to him. 'This is Lemar, where we will buy the SIM card. You will use it to call Jamike again.'

Ijango-ijango, Tobe spoke with so much authority over my host, as though he were a child who had been handed over to Tobe for guidance. I saw this man as the hand of providence sent to help my host in this time of distress. For this was the way of the universe: when a man has reached the edge of his peace, the universe lends a hand, usually in the form of another person. This is why the enlightened fathers often say that a person can become a chi to another. Tobe, now his human chi, took him where the telephone cards were, and Tobe himself tore open the wrapping of the SIM pack and gazed keenly at it, as if to ensure he had picked out the good apple from a basket before handing it back to the toddler in his care with the words, 'Okay, it is good, it is good. Now scratch the Turksim like MTN or Glo scratch card.'

My host scratched the card outside the supermarket, near an open patch of land covered with wild, clay-coloured earth that had caused Tobe to repeat the word *desert*. He keyed in Jamike's phone number. As it connected, he closed his eyes until the line trailed into the fast-clicking language, after which came the wounding end statement: *The number you have called does not exist. Please check the number and try again.* When he brought the phone down from his ear, he glanced up at Tobe, who'd leaned close and picked up the strange voice in his own ear. Now my host nodded.

He let Tobe decide the next steps, and Tobe said they should head to the 'international office'.

—What is there?

—A woman they call Dehan.

—What would she do?

—She might help us find Jamike.

—How would she do it? His number does not exist?

—Perhaps she knows him. She is the international officer

in charge of all the foreign students. If he was a student here, she must know him.

—Okay, let us go, then.

CHUKWU, with my host growing in desperation and myself increasingly convinced that what he feared had happened to him, he followed Tobe to the office. They went between long trails of beautifully cultivated flowers, and the vegetation of the strange new land opened to his eyes while his heart wept secretly. Here and there young white people swept by, many of them female, but he did not so much as look at them. In the state into which he'd been thrown, Ndali hovered like an unusual shadow, one that shone in the horizons of his darkened mind like something made of steel. At the office, which was located on the ground floor of a three-storey structure with the words ADMINISTRATIVE BUILDING etched on it, Dehan, the international officer, received them with a disarming smile. Her voice sounded like that of a singer whose name he could not immediately recall. In her presence, Tobe looked flustered as he returned to the forced accent. They sat down on the chairs across from her. Dehan swung in her chair while he spoke and then began picking among the papers on her desk. When she found the one she was looking for, she said that indeed my host's admission had been procured by someone on the island. But she had only corresponded with this person by e-mail. She wrote down the e-mail, the same one my host had: Jamike200@yahoo.com. Dehan brought out a file containing his documents and set them on the table. Tobe, seeming certain that he would see things, began looking through the papers and counted the new revelations as he found them:

The school fees he thought had been paid had been only partly paid. Only one semester, not two. One thousand five

hundred euros, not three thousand. In regard to the accommodation he thought he had paid, as Atif rightly observed,
nothing was paid. Nothing. 'Maintenance' – which Jamike
had said the school required you to deposit in a verified bank
account to ensure that you have enough to live on while at
school, so you do not need to work illegally – that, too, was
non-existent.

It seemed that this woman, Dehan, was puzzled by the
term *maintenance*. 'I've never heard it before,' she said, gazing
with perplexity at them. 'Not in this school. He lied to you,
Solomon. Really. He lied to you. I'm very sorry for this.'

Egbunu, he took the news that after all the school did not
have any money in an account for him with a kind of relief,
a mysterious kind. They left the office afterwards carrying
Dehan's comforting words, 'Don't worry', like a banner of
peace. Such words, said to a man in dire need, often soothe
him – even if for a moment. Such a person would thank the
person who had given him the assurance, as my host and his
friend did, and then they would leave with a countenance that
communicates to the person that they have been comforted by
their words. So my host carried with him the file containing
the original copy of his admission letter and unconditional
admission letters as well as the receipt for his school fees, which
was the only document that bore Jamike's name and the date:
6 August 2007.

As they stood resting under the pavilion of a building Tobe
pointed out to him as housing his department, the Ceviz Uraz
Business Admin Building, he remembered the day before that
day – the fifth of August. He could not tell why he remembered this, as he did not always think in dates as the White
Man had framed them but in days and periods, as the old
fathers did. Yet somehow, that date had been burned into his

mind as if by a blacksmith's rod. It was the day he received the full payment for his compound: one million, two hundred thousand naira. The man to whom he sold it had brought it in a black nylon bag. He and Elochukwu, wide-eyed, had counted it, his hands shaking, his voice cracking from the enormity of what he had just done. He remembered, too, that it was just after Elochukwu and the man left that Jamike called to tell him he had paid his school fees and that he should send the money and the accommodation fees as soon as possible.

Oseburuwa, as his guardian spirit, one who watches over him without cease, I'm at once thicketed in regrets whenever I think about his dealings with this man and all that it caused him. I am even more disturbed that I did not suspect anything in the least. In fact, if there had been a shadow of misgiving about Jamike, it was immediately dissolved by his enormous generous act. He – and I, too – thought Jamike was not serious when he promised to pay the school fees with his own money so my host didn't have to rush the sale of the house and poultry and could wait until he found a good bargain. So it was with this unbelief that he drove to the cyber cafe on Jos Street and found the document Jamike had said he needed for the visa, the 'unconditional admission letter', sent to him through this medium that could best be described as an arrangement of calligraphed words on a screen. The letter, he saw, had come from the same woman they had just met, Dehan.

He recalled now, as they walked past a group of white female students playing on a field and a group of white men smoking, how, after the cafe attendant printed the letter for him, he'd gone straight to the bank with the money and requested that the bank send the equivalent of 6500 euros to Jamike Nwaorji – Jamike Nwaorji in Cyprus. He'd waited, and when the deal was completed, he returned home with the receipt showing that the bank had converted his naira into euros at the rate of 127 naira each. He'd gazed at the figure the bank woman had underlined as the total in her slanting hand-writing: ₦901,700, and what was left of the sum for which he'd sold the compound, ₦198,300. He recalled how, at the time, as he drove home from the bank, his mind had been split between gratitude to Jamike on the one hand, anxiety about parting from Ndali on the other hand, and the disquiet that came from the feeling that he may have betrayed his parents.

Although deep within, my host was now cautious and suspicious of the motives of others, he saw in Tobe a genuine desire to help him. So again, Chukwu, he sought to reward this man by letting him lead the way. A man like Tobe is often paid for his pains by the gratification that comes from being in charge, leading his one-man – grievously wounded, disarmed, dispirited – infantry on. I have seen it many times.

Now, Tobe said they should go to TC Ziraat Bankasi, and he knew where it was – at the city centre of Lefkosa, beside the old mosque.

'What will we do there?' my host said.

'We will ask about the money.'

'Which money?'

'The maintenance money Jamike, that stupid thief, was supposed to deposit in an account in your name.'

'Okay, then we should go. Thank you, my brother.'

So they got on the bus that was to take them to the city centre, a bus like the one that had come to the airport the previous day to pick up students while he waited for Jamike. Seated there were several Turkish or Turkish-Cypriot people, as he came to believe most of the people here were. A woman sat with a pink plastic bag on her thighs beside another, a yellow-haired girl in sunglasses to whom, on a different day, he would have given a sustained gaze. Two men in short pants, T-shirts and bathroom slippers stood behind the driver's seat, chatting with him. A black man and woman sat behind Tobe and him. Tobe knew them; they had come on the same plane as he did. The man, who was named Bode, and the woman, Hannah, argued that Lagos was ten times better than Lefkosa. Tobe, a loud talker, engaged them. Tobe disagreed, contending that if nothing else North Cyprus had constant electricity and good roads. Even their currency was better.

'How much is a dollar to their money? One point two TL to a dollar. Our own? One twenty! Can you imagine? One hundred and twenty-something naira! Common dollar, oh. And euro nko, it is one seventy! And you say it is better?'

'But you say that their money be the same as ours?' the other man said. 'They just devalue am ni. If you look well, sef, you go see say if you change hundred naira, or wetin you go buy here for one tele in Naija, na hundred naira. Our money just get more zeros. Na why Turka people still dey call one thousand one million.'

'Yes, it is the same. I agree. Ghana did the same—'

'Ehen!'

'They cancelled zeros and rewrote their currency,' Tobe continued.

Chukwu, my host listened with half his mind, determined to say nothing. He reckoned that only those for whom all was well could engage in such trivial chatter. For him, he was far removed. He now inhabited a new world into which he'd reclined, gaunt and constricted, like an insect in a wet log. So he let his eyes roam the bus, perching like a weak fly on everything from the images on the sides of the bus to its roof to the foreign writings along its door. It was thus he who first noticed the two Turkish girls who'd boarded the bus at the last stop, outside what looked like a car sales park identified by the bold inscription LEVANT OTTO. He'd noticed, too, that the girls were no doubt talking about his compatriots and him because they were looking in their direction, along with others in the bus who knew their language. Then one of them waved at him, and the other pushed herself towards him. My host cursed inwardly, for he did not want to speak to anyone; he did not want to be stirred out of the wet log. But he knew it was too late. The women had assumed he would speak with them, and had come towards him, and stood in the aisle between the empty seats. One of them, waving her painted fingers, said something to him in Turkish.

'No Turkish,' he said, surprised at how husky his voice sounded even though he'd not been speaking much. With his eyes, he directed them to Tobe, who turned presently.

'You speak Turkish?' the girl said.

'Little Turkish.'

The girl laughed. She said something of which Tobe understood not a word.

'Okay, no Turkish. English? *Ingilizce?*' Tobe said.

'Oh, sorry, only my friend, English,' she said, turning to the other, who was hiding behind her.

'Can we, emm, *sac neder mek ya?*'

'Hair,' the other said.

'*Evet!*' the first girl said. 'Can we hair?'

'Touch?' Tobe said.

'*Evet!* Yes, yes, touch. Heh. Can we touch your hair? It is very interesting for we.'

'You want to touch our hair?'

'Yes!'

'Yes!'

Tobe turned to him. It was clear that Tobe was willing to

have these girls feel his hair. He was a dark-skinned man with hair that mimicked the scant vegetation of the desert, which the girls wanted to touch. It didn't matter to Tobe, and my host thought it should not matter to him, either. It should not even matter that he still could not account for the one point five million naira which was what his house and the rest of the money for which he'd sold his poultry had become. It did not matter, either, that while trying to solve a problem, he'd pushed himself into an even greater quandary, one even bigger than what had come before. Now these two women, strangers, white-skinned, speaking in a language he could not understand and in a mangled, tattered version of the language of the White Man, wanted to touch his hair because *they found it interesting*. Agujiegbe, as Tobe bent his head so that the girls grazed their hands over his frizzy, uncombed hair, my host placed his, too, under their hands. And the white hands, thin fingers with painted nails of various colours, ran over the heads of the two children of the old fathers. Giggling, their eyes alight, they asked questions as they touched, and Tobe answered swiftly.

'Yes, the hair can be longer than this. If we don't cut.'

'Why is it curly?'

'It is curly because we comb it, and we cream it, too,' Tobe said.

'Like Bob Marley?'

'Yes, our hair can become like Bob Marley. Dada. Rasta. If we don't cut it,' Tobe said.

Now they turned to Hannah, the girl from the country of the fathers.

'The girl there, is that her hair?'

'No, it is an attachment. Brazilian hair,' Tobe said, and turned to Hannah.

'These Turka people sef, dem no sabi anything oh. Tell am say na so the hair be jare,' Hannah said.

'Is the hair of the black woman, eh, eh long?'

Tobe laughed. 'Yes. It is long.'

'So why you put another hair?'

'Just cosmetic. Because they don't want to plait their hair in African braids.'

'Okay, thank you. It is very interesting for we.'

ONWANAETIRIOHA, I was dwelling in a host who did not live beyond the age of thirteen when the first white men came to Ihembosi. The fathers laughed at them and would go about for days on end mocking the stupidity of the White Man. Ijango–ijango, I recall vividly – for my memory isn't like that of man – that one of the reasons the fathers laughed and thought of these people as mad was because of the idea of 'banking'. They had wondered how a man in his right senses could take his money and sometimes all his livelihood and deposit it with others. This was beyond folly, the wise fathers thought. But now the children of the fathers willingly do this. And in ways that still defy my understanding, when they go, they receive their money back and even sometimes more than they had put in!

This place where my host and his friend arrived was such a place – a bank. Just before they entered, he remembered his gosling; one day he returned from school and found it in its cage, its eyes closed, almost as if swollen. His father was travelling, and he was alone. At first he'd become very afraid, for rarely did he find the bird asleep like this, at least not before feeding on the bag of termites and grains he bought it. But just before he even tapped the cage, the bird rose, raised its head and made a loud call. At the time, he'd kicked himself for becoming afraid too quickly.

So in serenity, he sat in this bank, which looked like the ones in Nigeria – lush and exquisitely decorated. He told himself to wait and see what they would find, to not be afraid too quickly. He waited with Tobe near an aquarium in which gold and yellow and pink fishes swam up and down over the imported pebbles and artificial reefs. When it was their turn, Tobe went up and spoke to the man at the counter. And in words my host would not have been able to find, Tobe explained the situation.

'So if I hear you clearly, you want to know if your friend has an account with us?' The man spoke fluently and in an accent similar to the one Ndali and her brother affected.

'Yes, sir. Also, we want you to check for Jamike Nwaorji, whom my friend gave the money to. See this receipt here? Jamike Nwaorji paid the school fees for him.'

'Sorry, man, but we can only check your friend's account, not another person's account. Can I have his passport?'

Tobe handed him my host's passport. The man keyed in a few details, pausing once to talk and laugh with a woman who peered into his cubicle. Gaganaogwu, this woman looked exactly like Mary Buckless, the woman in the country of the brutal White Man who had desired my host, Yagazie, to lie with her two hundred and thirty-three years before. Mary Buckless's family lived on a plot of land by the farm where Yagazie lived as slave to a master who owned other slaves. Her father had been killed a few years earlier, and she became curiously drawn to my host, Yagazie. She tried to lure him to bed for a long time, entreating him with gifts. But he feared going to bed with her, for death hung over his head if he did, in that land of the brutal White Man. Then one night, she came over the tired mountains, which during the day teemed with the strange, ghastly birds they called ravens. With the other four male captives pretending to be asleep, this strange white woman, unfazed by the crude smell of the lowly slave quarters and driven by a kind of lust I had never seen before, insisted she would kill herself if she did not have him. That night, the young man, birthed by the great fathers and ever dreaming of his homeland, slept with her and basked in the occult richness of her lust.

Now, many years later, it seemed I was seeing her two grey eyes staring at her colleague and biting into the apple, which afterwards bore the shape of her teeth.

'Sir, there is no such account with TC Ziraat,' the man said.

He handed back the passport and turned to the Mary Buckless look-alike to say something.

'But excuse me, can you check the other man?' Tobe said.

'No, sorry. We are a bank, not the police,' the man said with a growl. He tapped his head as the woman, biting into the apple again, vanished from sight. 'Understand me? Here is a bank not a police station.'

As Tobe made to speak, the man turned away and followed after the woman.

My host and his friend walked out of the bank in silence and into the city centre like men who had been served a grim notice about the new country they had come into. Like a desperate maiden, the new country threw itself up at him, flaunting its hollow enchantments. He watched her with the eyes of a noctambulist so that the tall buildings, the old trees, the pigeons that swarmed the streets, the sparkling glass structures all came to him like mirages, blurry images seen through wheezy rain. The people of the country watched them go by: the children pointing, the old men seated on chairs smoking, the women seeming indifferent. His companion, Tobe, was taken by the pigeons, which hopped about the squares. They walked past cafes, banks, phone shops, pharmacies, ancient ruins and old colonial buildings bearing flags similar to the ones in the buildings of the white people who came to the land of the great fathers. My host felt as if part of him had been pricked with a nail and he was bleeding, marking his trail as they went. In front of almost every building, someone stood with a cigarette clasped between their fingers, whipping smoke in the air. They stopped somewhere, and Tobe ordered them food, wrapped in what he said was bread, and Coca-Colas. They were drenched in sweat, and he was hungry. He did not speak. Egbunu, silence is often a fortress into which a broken man retreats, for it is here that he communes with his mind, and his soul, and his chi.

Yet inwardly, he prayed; the voice in his head prayed that Jamike be found. He shifted his thoughts to Ndali. He should not have left her. Tobe and he had, by this time, arrived at a place where shoes were displayed on platters and tabletops, and his eyes caught the inscription on the glass door beside the store: INDIRIM. The thought of the man who now owned his compound crept into his mind again. He imagined the man and his family moving in, unloading their truck, dragging bags and furniture into the now empty place that was his house. He had gazed at his father's room just before he'd left the house: empty, with a wall scarred about with marks and small chinks. The sun had stayed on the wall to the east, where the head of the bed had been, and looking through the louvres, he faced towards the well in the yard. That room where, once, he'd peeped at his parents making love when they forgot to lock the door was now so thoroughly empty that looking at it had given him an eerie sense similar to what he'd felt every time a parent died.

Gaganaogwu, the food came while he was still thinking

about the last time he made love to Ndali, how, after he released her, the semen had seeped down both their legs and she'd begun to sob, saying how cruel he was to want to leave now – 'now that you have become a part of me'. His mind switched to the food, but Chukwu, I describe what had happened afterwards, after that sexual encounter. I had not recollected it because I had not thought it important until now. You know that if we were to collect everything our hosts do in one testimony, it would never end. Hence a testifier must be selective and must render to you that which is relevant, that which must add flesh and bone and blood to the creature he is creating: the story of his host's life. But now, at this point, I think I must recall it. That evening in the empty room his bedroom had become, he'd leaned his head against the wall, her tears running down his shoulder to his chest, and said it was for the best. 'Mommy, believe in me. Believe, it will be good. I don't want to lose you.' 'But you don't have to, Nonso. You don't have to. What can they do to me? Proud people?' He'd held her, his heart beating, planted his mouth on hers and sucked at it as if it were a flute until she, shuddering, said nothing more.

Agujiegbe, the food he was now eating – which Tobe had called 'kebab' – had been served by a slim, tall white man who, as he dropped the food on small trays, green peppers sticking out, said something that had 'Okocha' in it. Tobe enthusiastically said he knew about Jay-Jay Okocha, the Nigerian footballer. My host, although silent, worried that this response would draw more men, all of whom looked like this man. They were white but appeared as if they'd been darkened by the raging sun, for it was hot here, hotter than he could ever remember in Umuahia. He avoided their gazes and ate the food, which, although it tasted good, was strange to him. For he thought that the people of this country did not cook most of their foods. It seemed, my host thought with a sense of mockery, that the people placed a premium on the need for things to be eaten in their raw states, once they had been washed. Onions? Yes, simply cut them up and add them to your food. Tomatoes? Certainly, just get them from your garden, dust off the earth around them, wash them in water, cut them up and put them on the served plate of food. Salt? Same – even condiments and pepper. Cooking is a time-wasting experience, and time must be conserved for something else – smoking, sipping tea from minuscule cups, and watching football.

Although the men spoke with Tobe, my host merely gazed out of the window at the traffic. Cars moved slowly, deliberately stopping for people to cross the road. No one honked. People walked fast, and almost every woman who passed seemed accompanied by a man who held her hand. His mind returned to Ndali. He had not called her since he left Lagos. And it was now two full days and half the third. He had, he reckoned painfully, broken the promise he made at the dawn of his temptation. He imagined where she must be now, what she may be doing, and saw her in the book room where he'd sat before his humiliation at the party. Then it struck him that here, Cyprus, overseas, was a new, sudden dream, the kind of ambition that a child would have – impulsive, instinctive, temporal, with little consideration. A child might, while walking with a parent, see a magician entertaining a crowd on a side street. He might see a man standing on a platform, striking his fist into the air, shouting bogus promises into a megaphone, and being cheered by an enthusiastic, banner-bearing crowd.

—Papa, who is that?

—He is a politician.

—What does he do?

—He is an ordinary man who wants to become the governor of Abia State.

—Papa, I want to be a politician in the future!

It occurred to him that what was happening to him was a mere temptation, that which must come to a man while in the pursuit of any good thing. And it has come to him, with the sole purpose of drawing him back. But he resolved that it would not succeed. He declared this to himself with such vehemence that it had an instant physical effect on him. Clumps of meat from the food he was eating spilled on to the table. 'What time is it in Nigeria now?' he said to deflect attention from the embarrassment.

'Three fifteen here now,' Tobe said, his eyes on the wall clock behind the back of my host. 'Then it must be five fifteen in Nigeria now. They are two hours ahead.'

Even Tobe must have been surprised, he thought. That's all? The time in Nigeria? Tobe did not know that words had become painful now that he was trying to digest what indeed may have happened to him. It was still hard to believe Jamike had planned it all out. How possible was it? Had he not just been on his own when Elochukwu told him that he could find help in the hands of this man to whom he'd given all he had? How did Jamike devise everything so fast? How did Jamike know that he would sell his house and poultry? Why did he expect these things when he'd not wronged Jamike in any way – at least in no way that he could remember?

He'd hardly let this sink in when the voice in his head propped up an example of a wrong he'd done to Jamike. There he was, in 1992, in the classroom standing before desks and chairs, the unvarnished walls covered with old calendars. He was only ten, seated with Romulus and Chinwuba. They were discussing the football match of their street against another, when suddenly, Chinwuba stamped his feet, and clapped his hands and pointed out of the window at the boy walking towards the building, holding something like a folded shirt, his bag hung on his back. 'Nwaagbo, oh, Nwaagbo is coming!' He and the others joined in, calling the boy outside the window a girl while observing with scrutinous gaze the effeminate features of the fellow: the plump flesh at his hips, the big buttocks, his gapped teeth, his bloated chest like small breasts, and his fat body. The boy walked in moments later, and in unison, the three of them shouted, 'Welcome, Nwaagbo!' He remembered now, the way the bespectacled boy had been stunned by their assault and walked with a lumbering gait and a pant in his breath to his seat, one of his hands on his face, over his spectacles, as if to hide his weak tears.

He gazed closely now at the image of young Jamike, weeping from being bullied by him, and he wondered if what Jamike had now done to him was a revenge for this time in the past. Was this a stone thrown from his past to crush him in the present?

'Solomon,' Tobe said suddenly.

'Er?'

'Did you say that a friend brought Jamike Nwaorji to you?'

Agbatta-Alumalu, for a reason that was not immediately evident, my host's heart pounded because of this question. He bent over the table and said, 'That is so, what happened?'

'Nothing, nothing, I just had an idea,' Tobe said. 'Have you called your friend? Do you know if Jamike is in Nigeria? Does he know Jamike's father's house? Does ...'

My host was hit with this idea as if by lightning. He rushed his phone out of his pocket while Tobe was still speaking and began fumbling at it in a frenzy. Tobe paused, but seeing the effect of his wisdom, continued. 'Yes, let's call him, let's find out if this Jamike is here. You are my brother, and I don't know you, but we are not home. We are in foreign land. I can't allow my brother to be stranded. Let us call him.'

'Thank you, Tobe. May almighty God bless you for me,' he said. 'What did you say I need to do to call Nigeria number again?'

'Add zero zero and then plus, then two, three, four, remove the zero, and put the rest of the number.'

'Okay,' he said.

'Oh, sorry, sorry, add only plus. Zero zero is another you can try.'

'Okay.'

Chukwu, he called Elochukwu, and the latter was shocked to hear everything. Elochukwu was near a building running a generator, so my host could barely hear him. But from the little he could hear, Elochukwu assured him that, indeed, Jamike had returned overseas. He knew Jamike's sister's shop, where she sold schoolbags and sandals. He would go there and find out where Jamike was.

He dropped the phone afterwards, relieved somewhat but also surprised that it had not crossed his mind to call Elochukwu until Tobe mentioned it. He did not know in fullness how the mind of a man in despair works. He did not know that it was sometimes better for such a man not to think. For the mind of a man in despair could produce a fruit which, although it may appear shiny on the surface, is filled to bursting with worms. This is because such a mind, wounded beyond reckoning, often begins to dwell mostly in the aftermath.

Egbunu, the aftermath – it is a place of little comfort. In the aftermath there is little movement, but much rumination. The event, having been done and ended, is now lacking in ability and agency. What the mind of such a man strikes leaves no dent on the skin of time. It is in this place that the mind of the man in despair dwells for much of the time, unable to move forward.

Tobe, apparently satisfied at the call my host had just made, nodded in affirmation. 'We will know; we will find out like that. Maybe he is still in Nigeria and lying to you.' My host nodded. 'When you were making the call, I was thinking we should also go to the police station before going back to school. Let us report Jamike so that they can trace him. Maybe he is even in this country, but in another city. They know everybody who is here, so they can be able to find him.'

My host, looking up at this man who had come to his rescue, was moved. 'It is so, Tobe,' he said. 'Let us go.'

12

CONFLICTING SHADOWS

OSIMIRIATAATA, indeed, as the fathers of old said, a fish that has gone bad would be known from the smell of its head. I had begun to suspect by this time that what had befallen my host was what he and I most feared. But there was no way I could know this at that point, as, like our hosts, we cannot see the future. What guardian spirits must do is shield our hosts, guard them even in the face of failure, and we must assure them that it will be well. We must assure them, Egbunu, that that which has been broken will be mended. So what I did was try to help him gather himself, for by this time, he was broken to bits. Elochukwu's return call had done it. Elochukwu had gone to Jamike's sister's shop. He did not tell Jamike's sister what had happened. Instead he lied that there was a contract Jamike had given him, and he wanted to update him on it. But the woman told him that Jamike had travelled. Elochukwu then asked for his new number. 'To my shock,' Elochukwu reported to my host, 'she said Jami informed her not to give anybody, even one person, his new number. I could not belief my ears, Nonso. So I asked her to call him. To my shock, he picked, and said something to her. She looked at me in a suspicious way and then told me that he was busy.' Elochukwu paused as my host breathed deeply into the phone, which was trembling in his hand. 'I am really sorry, Nonso, this is painful. It is like Jamike have duped us.'

Agbatta-Alumalu, just before the police station, Tobe, who had shaken his head several times after hearing Elochukwu speak, asked that they change the euros he still had into Turkish lira. Not all, but a chunk, most of which they would need to rent an apartment in town. Of the 587 still left, he offered 400 to Tobe. Tobe entered a glass building with the word DOVIZ written in illuminated letters on the door and returned with a wad of Turkish lira. They met two African students near the station, one of them in tears. What had happened? The distressed woman was looking for a man who had acted as agent for the other university in Lefkosa, a man whose name was James, who was supposed to have picked her up from the airport but didn't show up. Her friend, a fair-skinned lady who reminded him very much of Ndali's mother, corroborated the information. He wanted to ask them if this James might be Jamike, if he had a foreign name or if it was a fake name, but the women hurried away, in great despair. After the ladies had passed, Tobe gave him a deep, cultivated gaze but said nothing.

He walked into the police station with a slight quickness in his gait and a roiling in his stomach. This was not like the police station in Nigeria, where violent and hungry men with weather-beaten faces and bodies punished by privation showed people little mercy and courtesy. Here, there were three counters, like the bank's. People sat in chairs and waited in lines for their turn at the counters. Policemen, two behind each counter, attended to the people. On a wall behind them, just as he'd seen at the bank, were large portraits of two men, one bald, with his hair on the sides of his head, the other stern. Tobe, unexpectedly, caught the direction of his gaze. 'TRNC prime minister, Talat, and Turkish prime minister, Erdogan.' He nodded.

When it was their turn it was Tobe who spoke. This was another reason he let Tobe lead: because he had a declarative presence, one that seemed to already have affirmed something his mouth had not yet uttered or to have spoken loudly when indeed all he'd done was whisper. Tobe explained everything, in detail. The policeman handed them a paper on a clipboard with a pen, and Tobe wrote everything down.

'Wait here,' the policeman said.

In the intervening period, my host's heart pounded incessantly, and his stomach seemed to bloat in strange rhythms.

'I am sure that devil is on this island, and they will surely find him,' Tobe said, shaking his head. 'Then, ehen, it can't happen like that, just like that. Look at that innocent girl, too, eh? These yahoo boys, so very wicked. This is how they dupe and scam people. We used to think they only did it to white people on the Internet, the *mugus,* but look, see how they destroy their own people, their own brothers and sisters? *E no go better for them!*'

For some reason he could not tell, he wanted Tobe to continue speaking, for there was something in what he was saying that soothed him. But Tobe sighed, hissed, stood up and went to the water dispenser near the entrance, took a plastic cup, fetched himself a cup of cold water and gulped it. My host envied him. This man who had lost nothing, whose money had gone where he wanted it to, and who would study Computer Engineering at a European university. Tobe was lucky; he was worthy of envy, and he had nothing to be sad or angry about. The cross he now bore, he bore for him and would undoubtedly soon relinquish, perhaps by sunset, or at the latest by tomorrow. Tobe reminded him of Simon of Cyrene in the mystical book of the White Man's religion, an innocent man who merely happened to be passing on the same road as the condemned. Like him, Tobe had been placed in the same empty apartment by coincidence. And his conscience, not Roman soldiers, had compelled him to bear my host's cross. But soon he would be relieved of it, and he would bear it on his shoulders, alone. But not yet.

'Just look at how this behaviour, this kind of thing is affecting us,' Tobe said when he returned from the water dispenser. 'Look at our economy; see our cities. No light. No jobs. No clean water. No security. No nothing. Everything, price of everything is double-double. Nothing is working. You go to school suppose take you for four years, you finish after six or seven, if God help you even. Then when you finish you find job so tey you will grow grey hair and even if you find it, you will work-work-workn and still not be paid.'

Again Tobe paused, because the policeman handling their case had appeared at the desk with a piece of paper, but just as soon as he came, he went away again. All Tobe had said was true, my host thought. He wanted him to say more.

'You even know what bothers me most?'

My host shook his head, for Tobe had indeed glanced at him and requested, without words, that he respond.

'All the money they make, these stupid yahoo boys, goes to waste. It never goes well with them. It is the law of karma. See the man in the street of Lagos who used his wife for money rituals? He died a hard death. This Jamike, he will suffer.' Tobe snapped his fingers. My host gazed back into Tobe's eyes and saw in them an impassioned fit that resembled the aggravated politics of a broken soul. 'Just watch, you will see that he won't end well. It will not be better for him.'

It was clear that Tobe had stopped speaking because he'd risen to go back to the water dispenser. My host felt alive in the aftermath of all that Tobe had said. There are certain situations in which, long after one has stopped speaking, words remain in the air, palpable, as if some invisible genie were repeating them. These were such words. *This Jamike, he will suffer. Just watch, you will see that he won't end well.* In the ambient silence that followed, my host pondered these words. Is it he who would see Jamike suffer? How would he, when he did not even know where Jamike was and how to even reach him? Was it that he would be somewhere at a given time in the future to see this same Jamike suffer and pay for the way he humiliated him? He wished it to be so. He would take what Tobe had said to be a prayer – this Tobe who, after all, wore a rosary under his shirt and who had said he would have been a priest had his parents not wanted him to procreate, since he was the only male child of the family. This priest-that-did-not-come-to-be had in fact prayed for him who could not pray for himself. And so, in the secret of his mind, he said a loud *Amen.*

When they left the station, the sun was slanting down towards the mountain whose ridges could be seen from everywhere in the city. Tobe said, 'You see, there is hope. They can still find him. At least now they have found his records, they know who he is. They will be looking for him. And once that idiot returns to this island, they will lock him up. And he will – I swear to God who made me – return your money. All.' My host nodded in agreement. At least some connection had been made with Jamike. A question had been answered, even if with an incomprehensible babble. For now, that was enough. A fetid pool, in the time of drought, becomes living water.

He gazed again at the small note on which Tobe had scribbled the information he received from the police – six details:

1.   Jamike Nwaorji
2.   27 years old
3.   Student at Near East University since 2006
4.   Not registered for class this semester
5.   Last came into TRNC on 3rd August
6.   Left TRNC on 9th August

These six details, Tobe had assured him, would suffice for now. The details had been fetched from a hard source. He'd watched as Tobe asked the questions and the policeman answered them.

—Where did he go?

The police, the state, had no record.

—When will he return?

They did not know that, either.

—Do the police know anyone, a friend or anything, who would know precisely where he went?

The police did not keep a record of such things.

—What will they do if he returns?

They will detain and question him.

—What if he does not return, will they look for him?

No, they are only North Cyprus police, not the police of the whole world.

Then Tobe and he had run out of questions. So those details, which Tobe had jotted down legibly on a clean sheet of paper and handed to him, would do. He let Tobe decide what they would do next, and because it was now a few minutes past five, they would have to return to the temporary lodging. They would have to go to Near East University tomorrow, Tobe suggested, after he finishes his own registration for his courses and gets to know his course adviser. They had seen the school from a distance on the way to the city centre earlier. They would ask at Near East if anyone was Jamike's friend and might have information about his whereabouts. Then, after they had gathered their findings, they would go and look for an apartment together in the town because, although my host had only been there one night, Tobe had been there for four, and a new student was only allowed one week of stay in the temporary apartments. They should, Tobe suggested further, share a room until his financial problems were over because – Tobe emphasised – he would do everything to make sure that evil did not prevail, that his brother did not get stranded in a strange land.

My host felt he had no choice in this but to acquiesce. Even more, it would be a form of reward to share the cost of board with Tobe, who had said that it was expensive for a single student to rent an entire apartment all by himself. He felt obliged to this man who had done so much for him. He agreed to share the rent, and he thanked Tobe.

'Don't mention,' Tobe said. 'We are brothers.'

Egbunu, as the old fathers say: the fact that one has seen the shadow of his lost goat nearby does not mean that he will catch it and bring it back alive. The fact that a man has been given some hope does not mean that what was broken has been mended. So it was understandable that, before they boarded the bus back, he had the impulse to stop at an off-licence near the bus station. He bought two bottles of strong drinks and put them in his bag. The look on Tobe's face had been one of so much bewilderment that he felt a need to rationalise his purchase.

'I'm not an alcoholic. It is just for peace of mind. Because of what happened.'

Tobe nodded more than he should have. 'I understand, Solomon.'

'Thank you, my brother.'

OSEBURUWA, I would naturally simply tell you what my host did and said after they got back that day, but a spectacle they saw while on the bus on their way back and its impact on him afterwards merits this digression. For my host, at the beginning of his despair, was thinking about his compound, the small farm, the okro Ndali planted two weeks before, which must soon begin to bloom, his poultry. He was thinking of her asleep on his old bed, and of him watching her one afternoon, surrounded by the books she was studying. He thought again how it had happened that she chose him and that she gave herself to him. He was abruptly drafted into these pleasanter plains, when Tobe tapped him and said, 'Solomon, look, look.' And looking, he saw through the window of the bus a black man, swarthy beyond normal, a moving, animated sculpture coated with tar. The man Tobe had been talking with said the strange man had been on the island for a long time and had become so famous that he had been profiled in a Turkish-Cypriot newspaper, *Afrika*, whose logo, the student emphasised, was the face of a monkey. No one knew this man's real name. But they held that he was from Nigeria. He was a great wanderer who trekked the length of the city carrying the single briefcase that seemed to be all he had and which over time had become worn. The man spoke to no one. No one knew how he ate or how he lived from day to day. It struck my host that it might be the same man T.T. had told him about at the airport. Egbunu, he watched this strange man until the man faded into the distance, greatly shaken by the spectacle. For he feared that it might be that the man had suffered a fate

similar to his, and he had lost his mind. And he feared that, in
the end, he might become like this strange man.

When they arrived at the apartment on campus, he retired
to his room. The room was empty except for his bags on the
floor, the shirt he'd travelled in on one of the two chairs, and
the towel he'd used that morning, hung on one of the two
wooden bunk beds. He reckoned that the room was to be
occupied by two people. He sat on the other chair and opened
one of the drinks. It struck him that he did not know why he'd
bought the drinks, only that he must drink these drinks whose
white colour made them appear like palm wines – the drink
of the pious fathers. They'd cost fifteen lira, which amounted
to one thousand five hundred naira. He stood on the chair and
looked on the top of the cupboard, where he could place his
luggage. There was nothing there except for dust and an old
toothbrush that clung weakly to a loose, thin cobweb, its bris-
tles gaunt and hardened with disuse. He was doing things that
no longer made sense, he reckoned. Once, he'd been told – by
whom he could not recall – that the worst thing adversity can
do to someone is to make them become who they are not.
This, the person had warned, was the ultimate defeat.

Having been warned afresh by this long-ago-received
advice, he set the white bottles down and climbed up the
bunk into the bed. It was bare, sheetless. He tried to wade
through the thick crowd of thoughts in his head, but he could
not. They were speaking all at once, their voices deafening.
He climbed down, picked up one of the bottles. 'Vodka,' he
whispered to himself, and wiped his hand against the wet
label. He gulped it again, then again, until his eyes revolted
with hot tears, and he burped. He set the bottle down and sat
in the chair. He listened to Tobe walking about the empty
apartment. A tap turned on. The thudding of his feet on the

floor. Another tap, followed by the sound of urine in the toilet. The plop of saliva in the sink. Coughing. A tune from a church song. The footfalls again. The door of a room opening; the gentle creak of bunk. When Tobe was out of earshot, or was silent, my host shifted his thoughts to where he'd wanted them to be: on the man, Jamike.

Ebubedike, he brooded so much on this man that by late evening, when the native darkness had almost completely covered the horizon, the transformation the unremembered voice had warned him against had been completed. He lay then, half naked, on the bare floor, his mind warped, fully changed into who he was not. He saw himself turned into a lion, grazing in a wild forest, searching for a zebra whose name was Jamike – the animal that had vanished with all he, his father and his family had owned. With much struggle, he captured a picture of Jamike in his mind and gazed at it with jealous curiosity. A cough caught in his throat, and he spat tittles of the drink across the room.

He recalled the incident he remembered earlier, which had occurred in the year the White Man calls 1992, and how later that week Jamike avenged the wrong my host and his friends had done to him. Jamike included their names on a list of 'noise makers' when in fact my host had not spoken at all. But on the strength of Jamike's false account, my host and his friends were flogged by the discipline teacher. My host was bruised by the punishment, so angry that he waylaid Jamike after school and tried to fight him. But Jamike had refused to engage. It was not the custom among boys to fight one who refused to fight or hit a person who did not hit back. So at the time, all my host had been able to do was claim victory for the unfought fight. 'Girl, you refuse to fight because you know I will beat you,' he'd shouted. And at the time, everyone there agreed that he'd won. But now, lying on the floor of the room in this strange country, he wished badly that they had fought back then, and even if he'd inflicted only a slight injury on Jamike at the time, that would have been a consolation, even if small. He would have beaten Jamike, scissored his legs with his own, and rolled him in dust.

Egbunu, angered, he wished the fight would happen now, here in this country, and he'd break these vodka bottles on Jamike's head and watch the alcohol seep into the wounds. He closed his eyes to suppress the growing palpitation of his heart and as if some unsought deity had heard his request, a vision of Jamike covered in blood appeared before him and stood there. Pieces of broken bottles stuck in the skin of Jamike's head right above his eyes, his neck, his chest, and even on his stomach, where a thick lump of blood clung like a patch of extra skin. He blinked, but the image stood firm. In it, Jamike was tearful from the apparent excruciating pain, and words dribbled from his quivering lips.

This vision had come to him with such vividness that he shuddered into a jerk. The bottle tumbled out of his hand and spilled on to the rug. A strong sudden wish for Jamike to not bleed to death seized him. He stretched his hands and pleaded with the suffering man, as if he were there, to stop bleeding. 'Look, I don't actually want to injure you like this, er,' he said, shading his eyes from the ghastly image of the bloodied man before him. 'My one point five million naira, please, Jamike, please. Just give it to me back and I will go back home, I swear to God who made me. Just give to me back!'

He looked up again at his hearer, and as if in response, the shimmering figure trembled even more. He looked down in horror and saw blood gathering into a puddle between the feet of the wounded man. He sat up and pulled himself away from the sight, which, although in his vision, he assumed was in the room.

'Look, I don't want you to die,' he said. 'I don't—'

'Are you all right, Solomon?' This was Tobe, in the real world of objects and flesh and time, rapping on the door.

'Yes, Tobe,' my host said, astonished that he'd been loud enough for Tobe to hear.

'Are you on the phone?'

'Yes, yes, on the phone.'

'Okay. I heard your voice, so I wondered. Please make sure you try to sleep to rest your mind.'

'Thank you, my brother.'

When Tobe had gone, he said aloud, 'Yes, I will call you again tomorrow.' He paused, to feign listening, and then said, 'Yes, you too. Good night.'

He gazed about now, and there was no Jamike. He wiped his eyes, in which tears had gathered, while he'd begged the phantom. Ijango-ijango, in a memorable moment of life which I cannot forget, my host searched about him, looking up on the bed, behind the red curtain, on the ceiling, tapping the floor, whispering and looking for the conflicting shadow of Jamike. Where was the man who had been bleeding? Where was the man on whom he'd struck the death blow? But he did not find him.

The image of the mad black man came to him now and, in fear, he climbed into the bed. But he could not sleep. Every time he closed his eyes, he leapt at once like an enraged cat into the wastelands of this burned-out day, in which all he'd achieved was to gather more convincing evidence that he'd indeed become undone. He rummaged through the rich dirt of the wasteland, prancing in the choke of refuse, digging, scrounging up detail after detail – about the bank, the girls who had touched his hair, the inquiry at the police station, the meeting with Dehan, the unearthed memory of what he did to Jamike many years before, which he believed may have caused this great hatred, this genuine malice to be sustained through the ages. He would pounce, dig and scrounge on until he had brought up everything, until the surface of his mind had become strewn with the debris. Only then would he fall asleep. But not for long. For he would soon wake again, and the cycle would repeat itself without mercy, time and time again.

AKATAKA, so disturbed was I with the state of my host, and so afraid for the future, that for the short time he was asleep, close to midnight, I shot out of his body. I waited, and seeing no spirit in the room, I made my way into the ether and flew into the plains of Ezinmuo, through the concourse of spirits. In time, I was in the Ngodo cave, in the dwelling of many thousand guardian spirits. The moment my feet touched the luminous ground, I saw a guardian spirit I knew from many years ago. It had been a chi to the father of a former host. I asked it if it knew the chi of a living person by the name of Jamike Nwaorji, but it did not. I left the spirit, who sat alone, playing with a silver jar by the side of the waterfall. I asked a cluster of guardian spirits, one of whom had not had a host in twenty human years, and it told me it would be difficult to find a chi who might know the current location of a living host or the host's chi. Indeed, I looked around at the multitude of guardian spirits, who were simply a tiny fraction of the innumerable guardian spirits on the earth, and I realised the futility of my mission. I knew that I would not be able to find Jamike or his chi if I did not know where they were. Sad, defeated, I ascended with preternatural force towards the skies and soon found myself in that single esoteric path of descent known only to you, Chukwu, and me. For it is the single route by which I can return to my living host, as if drawn by a magnetic force, from anywhere in the universe.

13

METAMORPHOSIS

OBASIDINELU, the great fathers in their naturalist wisdom say that a mouse cannot knowingly enter into a trap set for it. A dog cannot know for certain that there is a deep miry pool at the end of the path and knowingly plunge into it to drown. No one sees fire and throws himself in it. But such a man may walk into a pit of fire if he did not see that it is there. Why? Because a human being is limited in sight; he cannot see beyond the boundaries of what his eyes can reach. For if one comes to a man in his house sharing a meal with his household, he may say, 'Dianyi, I just came back from the big north, Ugwu-hausa, with two cows and they are worth so much money.' He may garnish it by saying, 'I have come to you because my cattle are special breeds, rich in good milk, their flesh as edible as that of *nchi* caught from Ogbuti forest.' The man of the house might be convinced. He may thus think of the seller as one of goodwill and believe all the man says, even though he did not himself witness it. But he does not know that the cows are poorly fed and afflicted or that they are inferior breeds. And because he does not know, he buys the cows for so much. I have seen it many times.

Chukwu, why does a thing like this happen? Because man cannot see what is not revealed to him, nor can he see that which is concealed. A word spoken stands as truth, firm, unless it is revealed to be a lie. Truth is a fixed, unchangeable state. It is that which resists any touching, any fiddling. It cannot be adorned, nor can it be garnished. It cannot be bent, or rearranged, or moved about. One may not say: 'May we make this account clearer by adding such-and-such detail, perhaps the listener will understand better.' No! To do so would be to corrupt the truth. One may not say, 'My friend, if they ask me at the court if my father committed the crime, because I do not want my father to go to prison, do I say he did not commit the crime?' No, foolish man! That would be a lie. Speak only what you know. If a fact is thin, do not feed it to make it fat. If a fact is rich, do not take from it to make it lowly. If a fact is short, do not stretch it to make it long. Truth resists the hand that creates it, so that it is not bound by that hand. It must exist in the state in which it was first created. This is why, when a man comes to another with a lie, he has cloaked the fact. He may be offering a rattlesnake in a calabash of food. He may dress destruction in the garments of compassion until he who is targeted is trapped, until such a one is deceived, until such a one is stripped of his possessions, until such a one is destroyed! I have seen it many times.

Oseburuwa, I say this not just because of what had happened to my host but also because when he woke in the deep throat of night, soon after I returned from the cave of guardian spirits, the first thing that occurred to him was that he had not yet called Ndali as he'd said he would. She had made him promise her that he would never lie to her. It was a few days before he was to leave for Lagos, and they were seated in the backyard, watching one of the broilers who'd just had chicks preening and making perfunctory stabs into the plumage around its neck. Turning to him as if she had suddenly remembered something, she said, 'Nonso, you promise?'

'Yes,' he'd said. 'I promise.'

'You know, lying is one evil thing. How can I know what I don't know if it is not told me, if something else is said instead of it?'

'It is so, Mommy.'

'Obim, then, that means you will never ever lie to me?'

'Ye—'

'Never ever. I mean, no matter what? Ever?'

'I will not, Mommy.'

'Promise?'

'With all my heart.' She then opened her eyes, but when she saw his, she snapped them closed again. 'No, no, Nonso. Really, listen.' He waited for her to speak, but she would not speak for a long time. Even now, he could not tell what it was that had stopped her. A thought, perhaps, so large that it had distracted her for that long? Or was it fear big enough to cause her to weigh her words with a caution similar to that of a person about to identify whether the mangled body about to be uncovered is that of a loved one?

'You will never lie to me, Nonso?' she said, finally.

'I will never lie to you, Mommy.'

ONYEKERUUWA, my host rose that morning as if awoken by a shout from an unseen person. When he opened his eyes, he heard the sound of a distant vehicle, something like a crane or a heavy truck screeching. For a while he listened to this vehicle to keep afloat the fear that settled on the surface of his mind like a drop of oil. He sustained it with thoughts of things he could do by himself to find Jamike. Garbed in the light that fell through the curtains, he sat up and tried to locate Jamike in the tangled thickets of his thoughts. Once the rest of the night was broomed away, he would rise and walk into the new country. He would go wherever he could to find anyone who might know where Jamike had gone or how to contact him. Somewhere there must be a friend who might have information about Jamike's whereabouts. No longer would he let Tobe carry his cross; he must now bear it alone.

He washed himself, picked up the bag containing the documents, and stepped out before he could hear Tobe's movement. He walked into the school as the sun rose, past the places where Tobe and he had walked. He sat at a bench beside a pool where the sculpture of a frog stood overlooking the ringed pond, brackish with a dredge-black underbelly. At the tip of the bench sat a light-skinned couple speaking in Turkish. The two rose as soon as he settled into the bench, glancing back again and again as they walked away in a manner that convinced him they were speaking about him.

He sat there until the time on his charged phone said it was 8.14. He rose, and behind him, the 8.15 bus had pulled up. In the space between him and the bus, someone had created a fountain in the ground – certain unfamiliar materials rigged into the ground like strange plants – from which water sprayed about. My host paused before the sprinklers to determine the water's direction, then, when it turned away from him, he made a safe passage and rushed up to catch the bus.

As he made to climb into the bus, the driver said something to him.

'No Turkish,' he said.

'*No Turkish*,' the driver said.

'Yes, English but no Turkish.'

'You, Nijerya?'

'Yes. I am from Nigeria.'

He said the last words distractedly before sitting down. The bus passed between two pavements, on one of which two Nigerians were carrying nylon bags from Lemar, the supermarket where Tobe and he had bought telephone SIM cards. He did not know why he lifted himself from his seat at the sight of one of them, then caught himself and sat back. Something he could not explain had made him think for one sharp moment that the man was Jamike. He sat, aware of the startled gaze of the people on the bus, perhaps wondering if he had gone mad.

When he saw that the bus was approaching the stop where he was to disembark, he stepped forward, out of the spot on which he'd stood and out of the untamed thickets of his thoughts. Staggering, he walked to the front and held on to one of the support poles. The driver caught sight of him in the mirror that hung in front of him and grinned. 'Nijerya, very goodt, futball. Very very goodt. Jay-Jay Okocha, Amokachi, Kanu – very goodt, Nijerya, wallahi!'

Once out of the bus, he fell back into the memory of that evening in the yard as if knocked back in there by an invisible club. And Ndali had sat back on the bench and the hen had crouched on its belly, gazing at them in silence.

'*Mommy*,' she said, then laughed. 'You are one unusual man, Nonso. Will you always call me this thing?'

'It is so, Mommy.'

She laughed again.

'Do you like it?'

'Yes, but it is strange. I have never heard any person call their girlfriend Mommy before. They say "baby" or "darling" or "sweetheart". You know. But "Mommy"? It is different.'

'I under—

Ehen, I remember, I remember, Nonso! Today, during our service in the church, we sang a song that reminded me very much of you, Nonso. I don't know why, I don't know why, but no, I think I know why. It is the wordings of the song, about coming to me. *And you come to me.* It so reminds me of you, of how, suddenly, out of nowhere, you came to me.'

'You should sing it, Mommy.'

'Oh God! Nonso, I should?' She gave him a slight blow on the arm.

'Ah! Ah! You will kill me, oh.'

She laughed. 'I know my blows feel like feathers to you. But you say it is heavy? Ah, *this is a lie.* But, see, it's a song to God. So I don't want to use it for you as if it is love song.'

'I am sorry, Mommy. I know. I just want you to sing it. I want to hear you sing and also to know why it remember you of me.'

She opened her eyes now after he'd stopped speaking.

'"Remind", not "remember". "Remind you of me".'

'Oh, Mommy, that is true. Sorry.'

'Well, okay, but I am shy. *Ama'im ka e si a gu egwu.*'

'Good Igbo,' he said, and laughed.

'Stupid!' She hit him again. He squirmed and wrinkled his face into a tuft of pain. She stuck out her tongue, pulled down the flesh beneath her eyelids so that the full balls of her eyes were exposed down to the constellation of veins coated in red flesh. 'That's what you deserve for laughing at me.'

'Will you sing now?'

'Okay, Obim.'

He watched her raise her eyes to the ceiling, fold her fingers into each other, and begin singing the song. Her voice moved and swayed, softly, tenderly, as the words came out. Egbunu, the power of music on the consciousness of man cannot be lightly observed. The old fathers knew this. It was why they often said that the voice of a great singer could be heard by the ears of the deaf, and even of the dead. How true, Oseburuwa! For a man may be in a state of profound sadness – that uterine, entombed state. For days he may be still, in tears, perhaps not even eating. Neighbours have come and gone; relatives have streamed in and out of his house, saying, 'Take heart! It is well, my brother.' Yet, after all has been said, he has returned into the dark place again. Then let him hear good music, whether sung by a gifted voice or on the radio. You'll see his soul rise, slowly, from the dark place past the threshold into light. I have seen it many times.

My host, whose fear of losing Ndali had been growing in those days, was gripped by the strong hands of the last lines:

> *You are my king*
> *You are my king*
> *And you come to me*
> *Jesus, you come to me*
> *And you come to me*
> *And you come to me*

When she finished, he grabbed her hand and kissed her so fervently that, later, they'd made love, and she asked him if it was the song that'd made it so good.

The song was material in his head as he alighted from the bus on to the paved terrace that branched towards a long road leading to Near East University. It remained with him even afterwards, like a persistent din caught in the ear of the universe. *And you come to me*. Before and around him, everywhere his eyes could see, he found evidence of the things the man he'd met at the airport, T.T., had said to him about the country, how it was mostly deserts and mountains and seas where nothing consumable grew. The only thing in sight was a large stretch of empty land. Sometimes, a big rolled-up bunch of dry tares, which looked like what the people across the great ocean called hay, lay on the land. And by the shoulder of the road, big billboards stood. Just before the bus stop, he saw a field of wrecked vehicles and all kinds of scrap metal. A lorry that had been stripped to its frame sat on the brush, staring with empty sockets where its headlamps had been. Beside this was a white sports car, upturned and held in place by the burned-out remains of what must have been a truck. Beside this sat a reticulated lorry, twisted into a ring, one of its cabs crushed beyond repair.

He thought to call T.T., since he was going to his school, the same one Tobe had written in his note as Jamike's school. He'd begun to search his phone when I put the thought into his head that he'd not taken T.T.'s number. His phone had been dead when they met at the airport. He gazed at the phone in anger, rubbing his hand over its edges. It crossed his mind to throw it somewhere and never see it again. But he found himself slipping it into his pocket. He had by now reached a place that looked something like a racetrack. In front of its gate was a group of people waiting, a black girl among them. Her ankara dress reminded him of a dress his sister used to wear. The woman's ears were plugged, he saw, and she was bobbing her head every now and then to the music that was being received through the device plugged to her ears, which my host rendered to his mind as 'earphone'. He went to her.

'Please, my sister, is this Near East?'

'No. Near East is still far,' the lady said.

'Err, oh far?'

'Yes, but this bus coming will take us there. Oh, here it

is. We take it and it will drop you where on campus you are going.'

'Thank you, my sister.'

The bus was neater and newer and fuller than the one from his own school, with many Turkish youth speaking their language. The black girl recessed into the back, where, finding no seat, she stood and held on to a rubber handle that extended from an overhead pole. Its interior was covered with posters of every kind. Not one of them was in a language he could understand. In one of the posters, a black male student stood beside a white male student, both pointing at a building as tall as some of the ones he'd seen near the city centre the previous day. He thought now about how much things were different in this country. Back in the land of the great fathers, beggars and people who sold different products mobbed buses, hawking their wares and trying to command the attention of the passengers. He recalled the congestion at the bus park in Lagos, how he'd tried to haggle about a cheap bottle of perfume with a seller who had persistently bothered him. It occurred to him that had he come in a good situation, he probably would have loved it here – at least for its orderliness.

He exited at the first bus stop at the school. Two male students, carrying books, had also got off. The bus coasted on with a loud whine as it slid between two fields of what seemed to me to be artificial grass, not like anything in the land of the great fathers. A building lay beside a massive roadway, across from a small hill. He had not thought it deeply through, where to go. I could not do anything to help him, as nothing here was like I have known, not even like when my enslaved host was taken to a place across the mighty ocean, your powerful vast waters that cover much of the surface of the earth. In that place, Virginia, my former host, Yagazie, found himself living among others captured from the nations of black people, many of whom did not speak the language of the great fathers. That place was very sparsely populated. There were mighty buildings, two of which he participated in building, around where his captors lived. The rest were fields and mountains, fields as thick as the forests of Ogbuti-ukwu. There was none of the magnificence he saw now, no bright lights on the streets at night, no equipment that made various sounds. So I was silent as he thought of what to do. Egbunu, at this moment when my host's mind could not come up with a problem-solving thought, and I, his guardian spirit, could not help him either, the universe lent him a hand. For as he started walking again towards the nearest building, his phone rang. He opened it in a rush and picked up the call.

Tobe's voice on the other side of the phone was sullen, bearing seedlings of concern. My host replied, 'I am at Near East, my brother. I didn't want to continue to bother you with my problems.'

'I understand. Have you found him?'

'No. I just arrived at the school. I don't even know what I should do.'

'Have you gone to their international office, like the one of Dehan here in CIU?'

'Jesus Christ! That is so, my brother. That must be where I should go.'

'Yes, yes,' Tobe said. 'Go there first.'

'*Chai, da'alu nu,*' he said, almost breaking into tears, for he wondered again how this potent idea had escaped his thoughts.

'Will you come back so we can go to the house agent? Dee gave me an address. Today is my fifth day in this apartment, two more days.'

'It is so, Nwannem. I will come back soon. Once I finish.'

Up till now he'd walked with warm courage, propelled by his own determination that he should bear his cross alone. But now his courage left him, whether it was because he had heard Tobe's voice or because he'd arrived at a place in this country where he was certain Jamike had been and did not know how to proceed I do not know. What became clear was that something changed in him after the call ended. He began walking with the gait of a cricket forced out of its hole until he found a man whose face was round – the kind his people referred to as 'Chinese'. 'Ah!' the man gasped in response to my host's enquiry, and said he had just left the international office himself. This man took him close to the building, which had a facade like nothing he'd ever seen before. Beside it, flags hung from innumerable poles, amongst which he spotted the green–white–green flag of the nation from which he'd come.

Egbunu, before he entered through the door, my host, in fear, sought spiritual help. In this he acted like the faithful fathers. But where the fathers would have offered prayers to their *ikenga*, or their chi, or their agwu, or even another deity, my host prayed to the White Man's alusi for help in finding Jamike here – his first time praying in many years. For here, he feared, might be his last source of hope.

'God Jesus, have mercy on me. Forgive me all my sins as I forgive all those who have trespassed against me. If you help me get all my money back, if you don't allow this to happen to me, I will serve you for the rest of my life. In Jesus's name I pray. Amen. Amen.'

AKATAKA, you must forgive me. You designed us in such a way that we are one with our hosts. So that in time we begin to suffer their pains. What ails them ails us. It is thus why I am loath to describe his experience at that office but would rather give you an account of its effect on him, of the aftermath. For I do not want to stand here much longer, seeing these many guardian spirits who are seeking your audience, too. I will therefore say what he found here about the man he sought was that, as the policeman had said, Jamike was indeed a student there and was well-known among the foreign students. He found, too, that Jamike had been a student for only one semester, even though he had been in the country for two years. He stopped attending classes after three weeks. One of the workers at the school's international office who gave his name as Aiyetoro and who was from the same country as my host drew him aside into an empty hall after he'd finished with the chief international officer.

'Omo, you may be in serious trouble, oh,' the man said.

'I know,' said my host.

'You do? Wait, did you know Jami before, in Nigeria?'

My host nodded. 'We went to primary school together, my brother.'

'What, Umuahia?'

'That is so.'

'So, after, did you know him? Did you know that he is an original yahoo boy?'

My host shook his head. 'No.'

'Ah. He is a serious scammer, oh – professional yahoo boy. How much did he take from you?'

My host gazed at this man, and for a moment, he thought of his gosling, the bird he loved very much, the first thing to which his heart had clung. The image in his mind was a still one, but Egbunu, it was much bigger than that. It was an event. It was after he had read books about falconers and begun calling himself a falconer and thought of flying his bird around the town. He had decided to buy a very long twine, sturdy but long. And he had had his father buy him jesses, something that he tied around the bird like an anklet when he released it into the air. At first, the gosling refused to lift itself. It would rather call and mourn. But one day, it flew so high, so far beyond the guava tree, to the limit the twine could go, even with my host raising his hand high and only twisting the twine around his wrist in one fold. At the time, the joy of the gosling flying had been so overwhelming he'd cried.

'You no want tell me?' the man asked. 'I want to know so I know how I can help you, er?'

'Very much, my brother. Almost seven thousand euros.'

'*Ye paripa!* Jisos! Okay, you know what? No shaking, eh? Just relax. I go help you. That guy has duped plenty of people. I haven't seen him since last year, but I know some guys he shares apartment with who has seen him.'

Gaganaogwu, what this man had given my host was hope. A man in need will hang on to whatever he can get to survive. I have seen it many times. A drowning man will not request a rope when a rod is presented to him or the branch of a tree instead of a raft. That which comes within reach is that which he clings to. And so, at the outskirts of the school, right back where he'd questioned the dark-skinned girl earlier, Aiyetoro flagged a taxi for him and gave the driver an address in a place he called Girne. My host thanked Aiyetoro, shook his hand with sweating palms, and the man said, 'It is well, bro.'

My host then left for Girne a broken man. For a long time, the drive took him through empty desert plains flanked by mountains. He got a closer view of the painted flag on the sierra, which he'd seen in lights on his first night. He gazed at its patterns: the crimson crescent and a star placed on a sea of white. It was, he reckoned, much like the Turkish flag: a white crescent moon on a sea of crimson. In the peace that the car provided him, Ndali returned to his mind through the song he'd remembered earlier. It brought him to the verge of tears. He knew that if she had this new telephone number, she would have tried to call or send him a message. In a jolt he keyed in her number after a plus sign and dialled it, but he could not bring himself to go through with it. Yet he feared that she must be very worried, wondering what had happened to him. He dialled it again and waited, his heart pounding, until she picked on the third ring. Egbunu, I find it difficult to describe the emotion he felt when he heard her voice. He shifted, rubbed his hand against the seat, as she said, 'Hello, hello – who is this? Can you hear me? Hello? Hello, can you hear me?' He suspended his breath, making sure no identifiable sound escaped him. He heard her sigh. 'Maybe it is network,' she said, and sighed again. 'Maybe it is even Nonso, er.' Then she ended the call.

He gazed at the phone, her voice still in his head as if trapped in it. 'I should ...' he began saying, but stopped to look at the phone again.

'I should not have come here,' he said in the language of the fathers. 'I should not have come. I should not have come.'

'Pardon?' the driver said.

My host, astonished, realised that he hadn't thought this but spoken it aloud.

'Sorry, not you,' he said.

The man waved his hand. 'Not problem. Not problem for me, *arkadas*.'

Again, my fear was inflamed, for one of the first signs of a man in despair is that he is no longer able to distinguish between reality and imagination. Throughout the rest of the journey, he carried himself delicately, like a liquid-holding glass bottle cracked in many places, which was nevertheless held together by what seemed like a miracle. As the journey progressed, and in a brief period of reprieve, he became drawn to the natural beauty of the island. For once they came close to Girne, the landscape became like one he'd never seen before – very different from the land of the opulent fathers. Castles and houses, some bearing Turkish flags, sat on top of mountains and granitic outcroppings. It shocked him that people could build houses on mountains and hills. The last section of the highway lifted off, out of something that looked like a valley – a long, solid rock on one side and a sparsely shrubbed field, tenanted with pieces of rocks and stones, on the other side. And slowly, they seemed to be approaching the ascending road from where the entire city spread out before his eyes: houses big and small, some towering and others with spires. And in the distance beyond them all, he saw a bowl of the Mediterranean Sea's blue water, visible between the dense streets. As they drew closer, the sea seemed to expand, so that by the time they arrived at the great bridge at the entrance to Girne, it seemed the entire city was held back by some invisible fence which, if removed, would plunge it into the sea.

Later, in front of a three-storey building, the driver pointed and said, 'There, *arkadas*.' My host dipped into his pocket and gave the man thirty-two lira. Then he walked through the metal door, struggling to retain in his head the name of the man who had sent him there – Aiyeoto, Aiyetoo.

He knocked on the first apartment, marked with the inscription APT 1. A poster hung on the door with an inscription in Turkish, below which was the translated version: WELCOME. A Turkish woman appeared, and behind her a young girl, holding a wild-haired doll.

'Sorry,' he said.

'Not a problem. Looking for the Nigerians?' the woman said in clear English that surprised him.

'Yes, the Nigerians. Where are they?'

'Apartment five.' The woman pointed upwards.

'Thank you.'

With thoughts flourishing in his mind, he hurried up, his heart pounding, a single bud of hope rooted in his mind like the mushroom he'd once seen growing on the seat of an old abandoned car. Perhaps he would find Jamike here, hiding, perhaps secretly returned through the porous borders from South Cyprus to evade the police. Perhaps this was why the state record showed that he had left the country. This hope, wild as it was and growing without soil or water on the gnarled and ramshackle fixtures of that car, remained alive as he reached a level from which he began to perceive the aroma of Nigerian food and hear loud male voices arguing in the language of the White Man and its broken version. He waited at the door, his hand on his chest, as it seemed that he could hear Jamike's distinct voice among them, shouting in his swaggering tone with the prominent echo of 'mehn'. Then he knocked.

AKWAAKWURU, the job of a guardian spirit is often made more difficult when the spirit of our host, his ageless onyeuwa, which exists in the host's body only as an expression of his mind, is broken. When it is broken, the host slips into despair. And despair is the death of the soul. It is therefore very difficult to hold up one's host against this, to keep him, as long as one can, from falling. This was why, when he left the house of the people who knew Jamike's whereabouts, I threw thoughts into his mind to amuse him. I reminded him of that day when he'd eaten the *ugba* and shitted endlessly. He saw himself spattering shit into the creepers. This should have made him laugh, but it didn't. I made him remember one of the things that used to fascinate him the most: the way the gosling yawned. How it opened its mouth and its grey tongue shivered with a nacre-like substance that bloomed into a globule under its tongue. Its mouth, wider by double than any human's, dragged a good portion of the sheet of its skin into a strained exertion that wrinkled its face. In an ordinary time, he would have laughed. But now he didn't; he couldn't. Why? Because all the world becomes dead to a man like him in such a time as this, and therefore all the pleasant memories, all the images that would have brought him pleasure, mean nothing in this moment. Even if they had been gathered in his mind in their multitudes, they would merely accumulate in abysmal futility, like a stack of gold in the mouth of a dead man.

So he stepped back out into the city, carrying, like a gift on a platter, the conviction his talk with the men had birthed in him: that it was all over; that that which has been done has been done. They had told him in clear words that the plan had been elaborate. Jamike had let his friends in on the intricacies of it all. He'd told them that he was on to a major big deal, after which he would cross into the south.

What did they mean by that? My host, with a trembling voice, had asked them.

Simple, they answered. North Cyprus and South Cyprus were once one country, until they fought a war and Turkey split the island in 1974. This Turkish part is a rogue state, and the Greek part is the real Cyprus. The two countries are separated by barbed wire. If you go to Girne Kapisi, the city centre in Lefkosa, inside it you will see the border and Europeans coming into this part of the island from the other side. They are in the EU. Many Nigerians pay to be smuggled there, and some try to cross into the territory themselves by jumping the wire and claiming asylum. Jamike, too, had paid to cross.

'Is he never coming back?' he asked next, and although he'd spoken with the kind of menacing panic that would have drawn even the sympathy of an executioner, one of them said, 'He isn't. Him don go be that.'

Egbunu, my host accepted this revelation with a grim firmness, like a man who'd run into an enclosed space sealed behind him, out of which there was no escape. If he turned to the left, he met an impenetrable stone wall. If he turned to the right, he met a granitic door against which the strength of a hundred stout men would be fruitless. Forward? Same. Backwards? Sealed, too.

So he asked the men, what might he do?

'I don't know, bros,' the man who had identified himself as Jamike's 'best friend' said. 'We tell people for Nigeria may them shine their eyes, make you no dull yourself, because people – er, broda – are bad. But some of you just no dey listen. Look at how that boy don gbaab you.'

'Try and stay, mehn,' another said. 'You are a man. Endure it. What have happen have happened. Many people are here like you. And they survive. Even me, someone lied to me, an agent, that this is America. I pay, pay, pay to come here and then what did I discover? Africa in Europe.'

They all laughed.

'No *rope*, no *E-u*,' the first man said. 'Na so! What did I do? Did I kill myself? I found a menial job. I do construction.' He showed my host his palms. They were firm, as hard as concrete, the insides rough like the surface of sawed timber. 'I don work with Turka people tire, but see me, I am still in school. In fact, to worsen the matter, their women no like us. Kanji don kill boys finish!'

The men laughed loudly at this, in the presence of a man on fire who watched them with empty eyes. 'Or just go back home,' one of those who'd spoken before said to my host now. 'Some have done that. It can even be better for you. Just buy ticket with wetin remain, and go back home.'

Chukwu, were I not his chi, one who has been with him even before he came into the world, before he was conceived, I would not have believed it was he who left that place that evening and walked into the sun. For he'd metamorphosed, turned in the blink of an eye from a solid thing into a mass of weak clay and was now unrecognisable. I have seen much: I have seen a host enslaved, bound in chains, starved, flogged. I have seen hosts die violently, suddenly. I have seen hosts suffer diseases: Nnadi Ochereome, many, many years ago, who – whenever he went to stool – passed blood and had a swelling from his anus that was so excruciatingly painful he could not walk sometimes. But none of these times can I recall witnessing this great shattering of a man's soul. And I know him well. As you know, Egbunu, that in truth, every man is a mystery to the world. Even in his most extroverted moment, a man is concealed from others. For he cannot be fully known. He cannot be fully seen by those who look at him, nor can he be fully touched by those who embrace him. The true being of a man is hidden behind the wall of flesh and blood from the eyes of everyone else, including his own. Only his onyeuwa and his chi – if a good chi and not an *efulefu* – can truly know him.

Gaganaogwu, this man he had become in the batting of an eyelid left the apartment, walked across the road and entered a shop he had seen similar to the one from which he'd bought the last strong drink. He picked the same bottle from the fridge and paid the quiet man with rheumy eyes who watched him curiously, as if he were some alien emerged from a craven hole in the earth, drenched in soil and mud. The world around him, this strange land, this frightful awakening, felt sharp and alive, like tempered steel. For over across the road was a white man who was walking with his child. On the other side was a woman pushing a thing with wheels packed full of supplies and a pigeon that dabbled at pavement dirt. He thought of himself, and that he was hungry. It was almost noon, and he had not eaten a thing. It surprised him that he had not considered it, had not thought how quickly things could change.

He left the spot, sipping the drink, a lilt in his gait. He stamped his feet on the ground and pressed it, as if by so doing he'd firm it against a fall. He put the drink in his small bag and hailed a taxi. When he sat down, he noticed that he had not zipped his pants after using the toilet at the Nigerian students' apartment. He zipped, and as the car began to race back to Lefkosa, he closed his eyes. In his head, thoughts competed for supremacy. They argued, their voices raucous, until it turned into a shouting match. He pushed his way out of their midst and into a secluded space where only Jamike resided, and began to think about the day he met Jamike. Until then, he had been on his own, going about his business. For much of his life he'd been a withdrawn man, one who did not gaze at the world as if he could divine and understand it but rather peeped at it as if it were something he should not be looking at. He had not asked too much of the world. What he had asked recently was simple: just to be with the woman he loved. That was certainly not too much. Yes, her family had presented him with a hurdle, but wasn't that what he'd been taught? That a hurdle meant an opportunity to advance and grow? Had he not gone to buy the university entrance forms for Nigerian schools before he ran into Jamike? What had he done to deserve this fate?

He gulped the drink and belched noisily. He shifted in the taxi and bent his head sideways as the car returned over the road on which he had come, as if retracing its steps, except that this time a lorry full of building materials slowed down traffic on the one-lane road. Then the taxi overtook the lorry, crawling behind a red pickup from which a white dog stuck its head out of the window. He watched. He gazed at the dog carefully, at the way its head shook mechanically, as if it were being controlled by the wind, surprised at how such a banal sight as a dog sticking its head out of a window could help a man forget his present state of burning.

As they approached Lefkosa, passing a stretch of painted rocks on the side of the road, the dog vanished and Jamike returned to him as if forced by the energy of the car. He sipped the drink again and belched.

'What, no, no, my friend! What is doingk? What is doingk, *yani*?'

He could not understand.

'Alcohol, no alcohol in my taxi, my friend. *Haram! Anadim mi?*'

'You say I can't drink? I can't drink? Why?'

'Yes, yes, no alcohol. Because *haram*, my friend. Problem. *Cok* problem.' The man banged his hand on the dashboard and then snapped his fingers.

'Why?' he said, a foreign kind of anger in his mind. 'I can do what I want. Just drive your car.'

'No, my friend. Me, Muslim. Okay? You drink alcohol, problem. Big problem. I don't take you Lefkosa.'

The man pulled up at the side of the road on the highway close to Lefkosa.

'You must leave my taxi now, *arkadas*.'

'What? You drop me here?'

'Yes, you must go out my taxi now. I say you no alcohol, you say me no. You must go.'

'Okay, but I won't pay you!'

'Yes, no pay me, no pay!'

The man spoke in rapid Turkish as my host stepped out of the car into the road. Then the man sped off towards the city, leaving my host behind in the wild plain surrounded by desert and road and air and nothing, like a head severed from its body, rolling into a field – as I have once seen before.

AKATAKA, in this state of anguish, he walked towards the city, its expanse, its world, opened before him like a great cosmic secret. Desert, desert, he'd heard again and again – from T.T., Linus, Tobe, and even Jamike – as the one word that adequately described this landscape. But what is a desert? It is a place of abundant but loose earth. In the land of the fathers, it is hard to scoop earth from the ground. Something firmed it to the ground, perhaps the frequent rain, and made it difficult for it to come off easily. One has to scratch or dig to scoop earth. But here, not so. The very stepping of one's feet worried the ground and whipped up dust. No sooner has one walked a distance than one's shoes become covered in this darkish clay. And it spreads and runs about everywhere, accommodating little vegetation and resisting most of what seeks to plant its roots, to become, to vegetate here. Thus that which grows in it is tough and resilient. The olive tree, for instance – a tree that does not need water to grow, except whatever it can obtain from deep beneath the soil, for the country sits on water. Every other thing that inhabits this land must first subdue it. There must be a struggle, a hemispheric battle in which huge stones (hills, mountains, rocks) find their way here or emerge from some immensity beyond all knowledge and crush the enemies of earth and dust and insist that here, on this place, I must stand. And so shall it be. I must say, though, that in this it shares affinity with the land of the great fathers, where the earth – in its fecundity – exhibits an exuberance that mocks the desert.

He walked on for what must have been half an hour more, with the strides of the slightly drunk, until he arrived at an alley of houses. The longing to reach the city was in his mind like the thirst for water in the desert. He wanted to reach there and find the nearest bus station where he could wait to be picked up. Presently he sauntered into the half-closed mouth of a street which wound down inwards, away from the long main road, as if in fear. It seemed to be a poor neighbourhood, for the houses were low-roofed and old, their facades strewn with flower-bearing plants firmed to the clay-coloured earth. An uprooted gate leaned against a wall in front of one of the houses. A man stood on a ladder stretched against the walls, nailing something into it. Across, on the other side of the road, overlooking a bridge, was a deep crater that stretched for kilometres, the earth rising in sinuous rows towards what seemed to be a more developed part of the city.

He followed the trail, tired, half-mad, walking against the will of his heart past empty houses that sat like shadows in the sun, the sweat-soaked fabric he wore sticking to his skin. He heard itinerant voices of people he could not see. Birds he'd never seen before plunged across the plains and sailed at an unhurried pace. Egbunu, as soon as he advanced around a bend where the road turned back right towards the main one, he was jolted by a shout and the sound of rushing feet behind him, followed closely by the sound of approaching voices. He turned, and a group of children, having burst out of a gate from a compound – for he saw the small gate swinging – came rushing towards him, shouting what sounded like 'Ahbi! Ahbi!' and then 'Ronaldinho! Ronaldinho!' Chukwu, in the moment between the closing of an eye and its reopening, he was in the midst of a thronging mob full of noise and push that was speaking in an unfamiliar language. A hand tugged at his faded sports shirt from behind, and before he could turn in that direction, another pulled its hem. Someone shouted in his ear, and before he could make sense of what this voice had said, he was submerged in a well of words.

Agujiegbe, he stamped his feet on the ground, waved his arms about to free himself from the grabbing hands, and in the dim reprieve, he realised that he was thicketed in a mob of curious boys. The recognition shocked him, and in that instant he yelled that they desist. He clutched his bag with one hand and raised the other hand, swung himself from a grip, and staggered. The boys behind him stepped back from him like scared flies. He clenched his teeth, raised his hand and landed it on the first head he could reach. He stepped back as quickly as he could, and, in a quick moment, he was free.

The children, what are they? From where had they come? Could they not see that he bore no resemblance to Ronaldinho? Did they not know also that Ronaldinho could not possibly be here, like him, eviscerated – a walking shell of what he'd been only a week before? One of the children stepped forward and motioned the others to back off. He was dressed in shorts and a singlet, taller than the rest. This boy started saying something and gestured to a small boy who was carrying a ball. Then he demonstrated that they wanted signatures. Another brought a pen and a book. They all gestured, and it became clear to him that their hectoring would cease quickly if he heeded their request.

As he took the ball to sign it, an image he'd once seen at the back of his father's house in the village came into his mind to insult him: a shell that must have belonged to a big snail, now empty, dried, calcified, moving slowly away. At first it seemed a miracle, but when he examined it, he saw it was being ferried by a team of ants. He felt that the same thing was happening to him now, in this poor neighbourhood of this strange country, where these children had mistaken him for the best footballer in the world. They did not know that he was a man of great poverty, a man whose poverty extended beyond the diameter of time. In the past, what he owned he lost. In the present, he owned nothing. And in the prospected future, nothing. And here he was, with the pen one of them had offered him, signing a ball, books, shirts, even their palms. At the time, he'd screamed at the sight of the moving shell carried by the borrowed legs of an army of ants. In wonder, he'd called for his mother to come and see it. But now, at the lifting of himself before the eyes of these strange boys, he broke down and wept.

The impact of his tears was immediate. When the children noticed that he, 'Ronaldinho' and 'Ahbi', was crying, they stopped dead. Here was the great footballer doing what children were prone to do. It was a dead giveaway. One after the other, the small hands withdrew, the voices went silent, the cheerful eyes were replaced with perplexity, and the feet that had encircled him like a silent subterranean army withdrew. He turned from them and continued on his way, sobbing as he went.

14

THE EMPTY SHELL

AGBATTA-ALUMALU, in the land of the fathers, if a man is weeping in broad daylight like this, in public, people would come to him and hold him up. They would look and see that the light in his eyes was that of a man who had danced through life's theatre of fire and now bore the scars of his partial incineration like a trophy. They would ask what was wrong. Had he lost something – a parent, a sibling, or a friend? If such a one said yes, then they would shake their heads in pity. They would put their hands on the man's shoulders and say, *Take heart, God has given, God has taken. You must stop weeping.* If it is that he has lost something else, money or property, then they may tell him, *God who provided will replenish. Do not grieve.* For the Igbo society is not one in which sorrow is allowed to thrive. It is treated like a dangerous thief whom the entire community must gather and chase out with clubs, and sticks, and machetes. Thus, once a person incurs a loss, his friends and family and neighbours gather with the sole aim of preventing such a one from grieving. They plead, they charge, and if the sorrow persists, a person amongst the comforters – all shaking their heads, gnashing their teeth – will order, with feigned anger, that the bereaved one cease at once. The sorrowful one may break away from his grief in that moment like the lobe of an old kola nut. The comforters may begin to talk about the weather, or the state of crops in that season, or the rains. This may continue for as long as possible, but in the end, once there is a lull, the bereaved will often break down again, and the cycle will begin all over.

I have seen it many times.

But here, Oseburuwa, in this strange country of desert and mountains and white-skinned people, he received no response. The women who walked past him as he approached a busy area looked past him as though he were invisible. The men seated on chairs under awnings outside restaurants, on balconies sucking at pipes, or standing outside some building smoking, looked at him with bald indifference, as they would a street beggar to whom – although he sings and dances better than the celebrated musician who fills the auditorium with a crowd – no one pays attention. The children who saw him, an adult whose face was soaked in tears, gazed at him in hollow bemusement. So he walked on, carrying on his back the burden of anguish like a damp sack of decayed things. So broken was he, Egbunu, that I, his guardian spirit, could not recognise him. His movements were not ordered by a sense of direction but rather by despair. Like the man Tobe had shown him, the world had suddenly become to him a field on which he must walk, outside of which nothing existed.

—What place is worth going to?

—Nowhere.

—What is worth doing?

—Nothing.

Everywhere he turned, he saw his problems. Yes, indeed, he was walking by fancy shops and beautiful buildings, but

they were meaningless to him. Was that small crowd gathered
there around a truck from which music was blaring watching a
concert? Were those young white people dressed in uniforms
of orange and red dancing? They meant nothing. How about
this man, in front of whom he now passes? Are these some of
the Turkish soldiers T.T. had said make up 30 per cent of the
country's population? The sandbags piled in front of them, the
tanks and big vehicles behind. Yes, it is they, but he does not
care. How about the small birds that tail each other and dive
around that shapeless tree covered with the dusts of the street?
On another day, he – an avowed lover of winged things –
would have wondered strongly and tried to determine what
kind of birds they were. Are they found here in Cyprus alone?
Are they birds of prey or friendly ones? But now, a man of deep
sorrow, he does not care. In another circumstance, he would
have loved this country, as he had hoped to when Jamike first
told him about the possibility of it. Joy had burst forth from
within him like confetti, filling his dark places with shiny
things. But now it struck him that that unguarded burst of joy
had been the aetiology of his undoing.

Gaganaogwu, I watched all this astonished, tongue-tied
by my own impotence, by my inability to help him. He was
now walking down a street whose name, he saw from a blue-
coloured signpost, was Dereboyu, and as he passed by the shops
built of glass, he remembered his flock. He remembered the
day he sold the last of them – the last nine of his treasured coop
of yellow chickens. They had borne witness to the quietness
of the mornings, the lack of cocks crowing, which had – to
his surprise – affected Ndali. She had said it made the place
seem deserted and that it made her fear even more that she
would not be able to withstand his leaving. Only the hens
were left. Together they took them out of the coop slowly and

dropped them in one of the raffia basket-plaited cages. The anxiety in the coop, he could tell, was palpable. For every time he dropped a bird in the cage, so loud were their cries that he paused a few times. Even Ndali could tell that something was wrong.

'What is this they are doing?' she said.

'They know, Mommy. They know what is happening.'

'Oh God! Nonso, they do?'

He nodded. 'Look, they have seen many going inside that same basket. So, they can know.'

'My God!' She shrugged her shoulders. 'This must be their crying.' She closed her eyes, and he saw tears gather at the corners. 'It is heartbreaking, Nonso. I feel for them.'

He nodded and bit his lip.

'We imprison them and kill them when we want because they are not as powerful.' The rage in her voice cut deep into him. 'They are making the same sound, Nonso. Listen, listen, it is the same sound they made when the hawk attacked them.'

He looked up at her as he sealed the cage with its lid. He moved his head in a way that feigned listening.

'Did you hear it?' she said even louder.

'It is so, Mommy,' he said, and nodded.

'Even when hawks steal their children, what do they do? Nothing, Nonso. Nothing. How do they defend themselves? They have no sharp fingers, no poisonous tongue like snakes, no sharp teeth, no claws!' She stood up then and walked slowly away to a distance. 'So when hawks attack them, what do they do? They only cry and wail, Nonso. Cry and wail, finish.' She slapped her palms together in a sliding gesture, as if she were dusting one palm with the other.

He raised his head again and saw that her eyes were closed. 'Like even now. You see? Why? Because they are *umu-obere-ihe*, minorities. See what the powerful have done to us in this country. See what they have done to you. And weak things.'

She took a deep breath, and he wanted to speak but did not know what to say. He could hear the sound of her breath even though it was a cool day and the air was stifling. And he could tell that what she was saying was coming from deep within her, as if she were drawing water from a dried-up well, bringing up dregs, scrap metal, dead ferns and whatever lay in its bed.

'See what the powerful have done to us, Nonso?' she said again, stepping back as if to leave, and then turning to him again. 'Why? Because you're not rich like them. And isn't it true?'

'It is so, Mommy,' he said, as if in shame.

But it seemed she did not hear any of it, for while he was speaking, she'd started to say, 'Listen, listen, Nonso. Can you see that their crying follows a pattern like they are talking to each other?'

Indeed, as though they could hear her, the fowls had raised their voices. He gazed at the cage, then at her. 'It is so, Mommy,' he said.

She came over again to the pen, nudged him slightly aside, and bent her ears towards the crying birds. When she turned to him again, tears stood in hanging drops on the lids of her eyes.

'Oh God! Nonso, they are! It is like a coordinated song, the kind they sing during burial ceremonies. Like a choir. And what they are singing is a song of sorrow. Just listen, Nonso.' She stood silent for a moment, then she stepped back a bit and snapped her fingers. 'It is true what your father said. It is an orchestra of minorities.'

She snapped her fingers again. 'I feel for them, Nonso, for

what we are doing to them, and it is a song of sorrow that they are singing.'

Egbunu, at the time, he had listened, listened the way someone listens to a tune he has heard countless times but which, in every new iteration, moves him and opens his eyes to new vistas of meaning. He was watching the cage with all the concentration he could muster when he heard the sound of a sob. He went and held her to himself.

'Obim, why are you crying?'

She hugged him and placed her head on his chest, against his beating heart.

'Because I am sad for them, Nonso. And I am sad for us, also. Like them I am crying inside because we don't have power against those who are against us. Mostly, against you. You are nothing to them. Now you will leave me and go somewhere I don't even know. I don't even know what will happen to you. You see? I am sad, Nonso, I am very sad.'

Chukwu, it struck him now, in this distant country of sky and dust and strange men, that what she feared that day had now happened to him. A poultry farmer named Jamike Nwaorji, having groomed him for some time, having plucked excess feathers from his body, having fed him with mash and millet, having let him graze about gaily, having probably staunched a leg wounded by a stray nail, had now sealed him up in a cage. And all he could do now, all there was to do now, was cry and wail. He had now joined many others, all the people Tobe had listed who have been defrauded of their belongings – the Nigerian girl near the police station, the man at the airport, all those who have been captured against their will to do what they did not want to do either in the past or the present, all who have been forced into joining an entity they do not wish to belong to, and countless others. All who have been chained and beaten, whose lands have been plundered, whose civilisations have been destroyed, who have been silenced, raped, shamed and killed. With all these people, he'd come to share a common fate. They were the minorities of this world whose only recourse was to join this universal orchestra in which all there was to do was cry and wail.

AKWAAKWURU, the fathers say that a smouldering fire can easily be mistaken for one that has been extinguished. My host had walked aimlessly for nearly one more hour, hungry, thirsty, drenched in tears, when he found himself at a crossroads. One headed northwards into a road that appeared interminable, another forked into a dead end, another led back the way he'd come, and all of them were channelled in these directions by a roundabout he could see from a distance, almost a kilometre away. The ferocity of the sun that shone here was something he'd never encountered before. People have talked about the hotness of Ugwu-hausa, the north of Nigeria – even his father, who'd once lived in Zaria. His father had told him that further north, in the Saharan desert, the sun made the living appear like they were dead.

He had now been walking for close to two hours since the taxi dropped him, covered in sweat and slightly drunk. Moments after he stepped out of the taxi, he'd dropped the drink gently by the side of the road, between a clot of dry grass, as if hoping that someone like himself would find it and finish it. And now he reached a large tract of land covered in low grass on which was a house under construction. Two black people stood amongst the dust-coloured workers, sweating in the flesh-killing sun. He trod on, his tears now dried, the freedom of stagnancy, of not knowing what to do next or what would happen next, offering him unaccustomed peace.

He was again thinking of Ndali and the chickens and of his last day in Umuahia, and of the sound of her voice when he'd called her earlier, when from the road near the roundabout he heard a loud sound like something exploding. He looked on and about him but saw nothing. He walked on between two big buildings and came into a clearing, at the edge of which was a main road. He saw then from the distance the source of the sound he'd heard: about two stone throws from him was a car, upturned, covered in smoke. He heard rushed voices behind him, from the way he'd come, and saw the construction workers from the big building he'd passed earlier running towards him.

He gazed now at the field, his face painted with dust like the *uli* patterns worn on the faces of the dibias amongst the old fathers, and saw that up the field, the dust had settled. He saw more clearly, and the damaged car was now surrounded by people in various states of distress. Up close now, he saw the fate of the other car in the accident. It was a minivan, now facing the roundabout, pressed almost in half. When he came to the car on the field, one of the black construction workers, whom my host reckoned was a son of the affluent fathers by virtue of his accent, turned to him.

'Terrible, terrible,' the man said. 'In that other car, no one survived. In this one, two girls in the back of the car, eh. *Chai!* They are the ones screaming.'

My host, too, had heard the screams. His compatriot stepped back, as did others in front of him. A police car had arrived, and a policeman was ordering them to turn back. In the distance, an ambulance was speeding towards the scene. My host, afraid because of the presence of the police, stopped short of reaching the scene. For in Alaigbo, this mysterious office of men who have the power to punish others is feared. He

reached for his phone to see what the time was, but his pocket
was empty. He patted down his trousers. He retraced his steps
with hurried feet and found it a few metres back, the way he
had come. He blew dust off its face and saw three missed calls
from Tobe. He remembered that they were to go and find a
place together and it was now long past noon – 2.15. Egbunu,
so much had happened since the last time they'd spoken. He'd
called Ndali but did not speak to her. He had been chased out
of a taxi by an angry driver. He had drunk and thrown away
some drink. Yet even more things had happened. He had been
mobbed by street children. He had cried. He had been almost
killed by a car. His misery had deepened. The hope that in
the previous night still crawled, despite being gravely wounded
and covered in blood, had now been struck a death blow, and
in falling, expired. These things were excuses enough for his
failure to return to Tobe. In fact, they were too strong.

He could see, as he walked, that one of the doors of the
upturned car had been opened and the screaming and shouting had increased. Everywhere, on the adjoining roads, cars
were lined up. I wanted to come out of my host, to see if the
passengers had all died and to commune with their chis and
find out if this tragic fate that had befallen their people could
be avoided for mine. What had these people done to have died
this way? What answers could their guardian spirits give? We
often ask this, too, after things have happened. Was there a
way, for instance, that I could have engaged Jamike's chi and
found out the intents of its host's heart? Even if I'd found his
location and gone there, I may not have got it to come out,
for it is difficult to persuade a chi out of the body of its host. I
did not, however, leave my host this time, because I was afraid
of leaving him while in a broken state. As he drew close to
the scene, pulled only by curiosity to witness a tragedy in this

strange land, a feral epiphany jumped out of the smoke towards
him: that he was not meant to come to this country, that if he
stayed here much longer he might die.

When he reached the spot, men in white coveralls were
loading a bloodied man into the back of an ambulance. On the
ground, the body of a girl lay bleeding from the side, where
there was a deep gash, her blonde hair coloured with blood.
People were gathered around her, and a man was pushing
others back. He saw on the sparsely leafed part of the clearing near the accident scene a patina of flesh lying on a tray
of flattened grass where the hospital people had lifted a man
who'd been thrown from one of the cars. And the grass about
this spectacle was stained with thick blood, so that it appeared
as if it were covered with red phlegm. As he watched, one
of the nurses broke from the group and walked frantically
from person to person, saying something in the language of
the country. In what seemed like a response to the words of
this woman, a man wearing a blue visor stepped up. Another,
an elderly woman. The nurse nodded, wagged her fingers as
if to say the woman could not do this. As the white woman
talked, his stomach rumbled. He turned back to go, to find
some water at least.

'Mister, mister,' the nurse called after him.

As she made to speak, someone called at her in the strange
language. She turned to say a word to the man. Then she faced
my host again, moving swiftly towards him with the dispo-
sition of extreme anguish. 'Excuse me, can you please donate
blood? We need blood for the victims. Please!'

'Er?' he said, and slammed his hand on his leg to free it from
shaking. He was trembling slightly.

'Blood. Can you donate blood? We need blood for the
victims, please.'

He turned as if to ask someone behind him for an answer, then looked back at the woman. 'Yes,' he said.

'Okay, thank you, mister. Come with me.'

AGUJIEGBE, among the old fathers, it was said that in wrestling bouts, rarely was a man thrown because of inferior strength. Men of weak or small bodies did not attempt *egwu-ngba*. So how did they throw men – the great wrestler of Nkpa, Emekoha Mlenwechi, the sleek snake; Nosike, the cat; Okadigbo, the Iroko tree? It was either by a trick or resilience. In the latter case, the opponent slugs it out with the great wrestler for so long that his muscles become weak, his limbs tired. He caves, relaxes his grip, and in a flash, he is lifted like an empty drum and thrown in defeat.

This can apply in any situation beyond the field of wrestling. If a man has contended for too long with an unrelenting enemy, he may cave in submission and say to the trouble that had come to him: 'Here, did you ask for my cloak? Take my turnip, too.' If such a man has been asked to go a mile, he may say, 'Did you say you want me to go a mile with you? Okay, here, let us go two miles.' And if such a man, after just escaping death, has been asked to donate blood, he would not reject the request. He would follow the nurse who has made such a request of him – a stranger, a man of black and foreign skin – to the hospital and do just as he has been asked. And after such a man has donated blood to one victim, he would say to the nurse – who has drawn his blood and dabbed a wool, the like of which the old mothers made into fabric, on the spot to staunch the bleeding pore – that he wanted to donate to a second victim.

'No, mister, one is enough. Believe me.'

But the man would insist. 'No, take more for the victims. Take more, please, ma.'

He would insist despite his chi speaking into his mind that he should desist from this, because blood is life itself, and it is the thing that leaves the body in protest against an injury done to it. He would insist despite his chi saying that suicide is an abomination to Ala, and that there was nothing broken at this point that could not be repaired, and that there was nothing the eyes can see that can cause them to shed blood in place of tears. But the host, a man broken, defeated, possessed by the silent tyranny of despair, would pay no heed. The woman, visibly astonished, would stop in her tracks.

'Are you sure about this?' the woman would say, and he would say, 'It is so, ma. I am very very sure. I want to give blood for them. I have enough blood. Enough.'

Still staring at him, as one would regard a madman on a pulpit, the woman would take up another syringe, tap it three times, and then, wiping his left arm with a piece of wet cotton wool, draw his blood again.

Afterwards, he rose, weak and tired, hungry and thirsty, and in his mind was the question: what was to be done next? The past three days had upended any philosophy he had about life, and he now resolved that it was better not to plan anything. No, how foolish to think that a man who leaves his house and says to his friend, or even to himself, 'I am going to school,' that such a man would in fact get to his destination. Such a foolish man might find himself in a hospital instead, giving blood to people he does not know. How foolish to think that because one has boarded a taxi and given the driver the right address, one would end up at the right place. Such a fool might find himself walking only a few moments later towards an unfamiliar destination very far away from the school, thronged and hectored by a mob of boys.

So no need to plan. What he could do was thank the

woman who had drawn his blood, then go his way. He must step into the day, into the sun, and go — perhaps to the temporary accommodation. And this, Egbunu, was what he did. For after he'd said, 'Thank you, ma,' he walked out, both his hands curved up to hold the moist cotton to the needle spots.

He'd walked past the long aisle of people, past the offices, and out into the car park when he heard, 'Mr Solomon.'

He turned.

'You forgot your bag.'

'Oh,' he said.

The woman came up to him.

'Mr Solomon, I am worried. Are you all right? You are a kind man.'

Before he could think, his mouth said, 'No, I am not fine, ma.'

'I can see that. Can you talk? I'm a nurse, I can help you.'

He gazed past her at the sun, now in the sky, peering at him.

'Leave the sun,' she said, pulling him back under the awning attached to the hospital's facade.

'You tell me, I can help you.'

15

ALL THE TREES IN THE LAND HAVE BEEN REMOVED

BAABADUUDU, I have spoken at length about the longest day in the life of my host – a day of rain, and hail, and pestilence. But I must tell you also that it ended with a drop of hope. I must therefore hasten to say that he returned to the temporary apartment he shared with the man who had been his companion the previous day. He was climbing the stairs up to the apartment, holding the bottle of drink the nurse had bought him, when it struck him to call Ndali again. The idea came to him as a whiplash on his mind, and with true surprise, he wondered why he'd dithered for so long. He began to key in her number, then he remembered he had not added a plus. So he erased it and began again. When it started to ring, he turned off the phone so frantically that it made the sound of a clap. He must approach her with the utmost geniality and great care, he told himself. He must tell it from the beginning, from how much he had missed her and how much he loves her. This would disarm her.

So, standing with one leg on the stairs and one hand on the banister, he dialled again.

'Mommy! My mommy!' he shouted into the phone. '*Nwanyioma.*'

'Oh God! Nonso, Obim, I have nearly gone mad from worrying about you.'

'Oh, it is network. Bad network. It is—'

'But, Nonso, not even a call, not even an ordinary text message? Er? I have been worried. In fact, someone called me and I was speaking, shouting hello, hello, but the person could not hear me, and my spirit told me it was you, Nonso. Did you call me today?'

Egbunu, he was trapped for a moment between the truth and falsity, for he feared that she would suspect something had happened to him. In his hesitation, her voice came again – 'Nonso, are you still there? Can you hear—'

'Yes, yes, Mommy, I can hear you,' he said.

'Did you call me?'

'Oh, no no. I wanted to call you when everything is fine so you don't worry.'

'Hmm, I see . . .'

She was still speaking when a Turkish voice came over the line followed by another speaking in the language of the White Man, informing him that his credit was exhausted, and his call terminated.

'Oh-ooh! Which kind of nonsense is this? Er? The credit I just bought.' It surprised him, after he uttered those words, that he had bothered about something as trivial as a phone credit. For the first time in days, he was not gazing at the battered image of himself before the mirror in his head and gasping at the gashes, the swollen eyes, the pulp on the lips and the masks of his great defeat.

He rang the bell at the door of the apartment and heard the sound of feet in the house.

'Solomon, wa!'

'My brother, my brother,' he said, and embraced Tobe.

'What, where have you been—'

'Mehn, thank you for yesterday,' he said as he sat down on one of the couches in the living room.

'What happened?'

'Many things, my brother. Many things.'

In the same mood of joy, he told Tobe about all he'd done that day, the accident, and the nurse, up to the point I have just testified to you and the hosts of Eluigwe and beyond.

Egbunu, it would have been futile, even stupid to have planned anything after his blood was drawn. If he had planned to go back to the campus, for instance, reality would have again shown its wrinkled face on the screen of his consciousness, laughing at him with its toothless mouth, as it had been doing relentlessly for the past four days. So he had done the wise thing and allowed himself to float, be carried by time wherever it willed. An hour after his blood had been drawn, he remained with the nurse, having told her his whole story, and was seated in the passenger seat of a small grey car, riding back to Girne! Yes, Girne, where he'd been told a few hours before that he would never find Jamike by those who would have been with the man. But how could he know he'd return here, where his hope had been struck with a death blow the same day?

'It will take about forty minutes, so you can sleep, okay, lie down maybe, and sleep, if you want.'

'Thanks, ma,' he said.

So relieved was he that he wanted to cry. He threw his head back against the seat and closed his eyes, hugging his bag closer to his body. Some of the vegetables from the kebab she'd bought him were still stuck between his teeth.

He pushed them to the top of his tongue and spat them out noiselessly.

'I think I must tell you about my troubles, too, Solomon,' the nurse said.

'Okay, ma.'

'I have already told you, please call me Fiona.'

'Okay.'

He heard her laugh – a laugh between everything she said.

'When I moved here from Germany, and married my husband, I gave up everything, too, except my German citizenship. The government said I could keep both because Cyprus is not a real country. One year, two years, it was good. Whatever. Then, everything, everything, began to explode. Now, we live together like two strangers. Total strangers.' He heard a laugh, her voice cracking slightly. 'I don't see him; he doesn't see me. But we are husband and wife. Very weird, right?'

He did not know what to say, and he did not know what the word *weird* meant. Even though I, his chi, knew, it would have been an overreach to tell him, so I didn't. All he thought was that the people here – like him and his people back in Nigeria – have problems, too.

'You can imagine I haven't seen him in three days. Once, last night, I heard his voice as he came in the middle of the night. Then, his footsteps as he went to the bathroom, then, to bed. That was it! *Genau*.'

'Why is he behaving like this?' he said.

'I don't know; I don't know at all. It's complicated.'

They drove to a place where she said she would help him get a job, a well-paid 'under-the-table job'. He could earn one thousand five hundred lira every month, enough to help make up all he had lost and even pay his way through school. The employer – she said his name – was her close friend. The place was a casino attached to a hotel also owned by this friend.

They enquired at the casino, but the man was not there.

'He has gone to Guzelyurt,' said the secretary, a woman dressed in a white blouse and black skirt.

'I can't reach him on his number.'

'Yes,' the other woman said, then trailed into a long speech in the language of the land.

'*Tamam*,' Fiona said. 'I understand. I'll bring him another time, then.'

She told him they would come back again soon to see Ismail. So they returned to Lefkosa, and for most of the time they did not speak. She put on the radio, and it played music like he'd never heard before. It reminded him of Indian movies – the intermittent bass drums that would stop, then rise again with fervour, as in the movie *Jamina*. 'It doesn't matter. It is a casino. They are always open.'

She drove past the place where the accident had happened earlier. There was now, only three hours or so later, almost no trace of it, except for the broken brick on the surface of the roundabout and shards of glass in the field where the car had fallen. She shook her head as they passed it and talked about how people drove recklessly in Cyprus and caused many accidents. By the time she pulled up at the school, he'd started to doze.

'I'll call you as soon as I've spoken with him. We'll go to my house, and I'll make you a home-cooked meal.'

'Thank you so much, Fiona. Thank you.'

'*Genau*,' she said. 'Take care and talk to you soon.'

He told Tobe about how he had watched this woman drive away, every word she had said alive within him. A total stranger had shown so much compassion for him that as he told the story of his great defeat, her eyes clouded in tears – perhaps because of the way he told it, the way he described all that had been taken away from him and the catalogue of losses that was his life. She asked question after question – 'Was this man, Jamike, not your friend?'; 'He did that?'; 'So, even the money in the bank was not true?' – until, by the time he came to the accident scene, her eyes were red from crying, her face pink from the withering emotion, and she was blowing her nose into the tissue she'd extracted from a polythene pack. Her sympathy had been genuine.

'I can't believe it!' Tobe said when my host finished. Tobe cocked his head sideways and snapped his fingers. 'Have you seen it? Have you seen our God in action?'

'That is so, my brother,' my host said, elated and grateful for this man's generosity and wanting to share even more with him. 'Look at me.' He spread his hands. 'This morning, I thought my life had finished, that I have fallen into a deep pit. *Echerem ma ndayere na olulu.*'

They both laughed.

'It is God,' Tobe said, pointing towards the ceiling. 'God. That woman is an angel sent from God. Have you not heard the adage: "It is God that swats flies from the bottom of a tailless cow and from the food of the blind man"?'

'That is so! And he gives voice to the insects, the birds, the mute, the poor, the chickens and all the creatures that cannot sing, and to the orchestra of minorities!'

Tobe nodded and stamped his feet on the floor. 'Even on the side of accommodation, I just returned from the agent's office,' Tobe said. 'I have found a cheap, nice place for eight hundred telc a month. That is, two hundred euros for each of us if we take one room.'

'Ha, very good, my brother. Very good.'

'Yes, they take deposits here. So I paid the deposit already.'

'Ah, my brother, *da'alu.*'

While he was still speaking, his phone rang. He rushed up to his feet to see who was calling.

'My fiancée,' he said. 'Please excuse me, Tobe.'

Agujiegbe, it was with drunken excitement that he raced into his room and closed the door. I could still see that the effect of the alcohol had not completely eased from him and that he was still in a slightly dazed state. When he punched the Accept key, her familiar voice came crashing into his ears, antiseptically clear.

'Nonso, Nonso?'

'Yes, Mommy!'

'Oh, and so it is network?'

'I know, Mommy. I know. Look, I miss you. Mommy, I love you so much.'

'Ha, you say this but why didn't you call me? You said it wasn't you that called earlier? It is almost five days.'

'Mommy, it is because of the stress, when we did not arrive on time, and when we came here, I discovered many things like school registration, getting a place — all taking, taking my time.'

'I don't like it, Nonso. I don't think I like at all.'

He imagined that she'd closed her eyes, and the beauty of that eccentric demeanour lit him up with desire.

'I am sorry, Mommy. I will never do it again. Never. I swear to God who made me.'

She laughed. 'Silly man. Okay, I miss you, too.'

'*Gwoo gwoo?*'

She laughed. 'Yes, Igbo man, *gwoo gwoo.* Really, very much. Tell me, what is the place like?'

Now that he was relaxed, laughing, he let himself take in

the room with his eyes, and he saw something he had not noticed before. On the screen windows, close to the ceiling, was a wooden valance on which some paper image had been pasted, half scratched out and now only bearing the image of the legs of a white person in an outstretched position on a couch.

'Are you there, Nonso?'

'Oh, yes, Mommy, say again?' he said.

'You are not listening to me? I said tell me what it's like in Cyprus.'

'I am,' he said, even though he'd moved closer to the window, wondering what the full portrait must have been like. 'Mommy, it is a barren, stupid island. It doesn't even have any trees, just desert, desert.'

'Oh God, Nonso! How do you know?' she said, stifling laughter. 'Have you gone round?'

'Er, Mommy, I am telling you the truth. It is like all the trees in this land have been removed. I'm telling you, all of them. Not even wan single tree. I am telling you.'

'What, no trees at all?'

'None, Mommy. And the people, they don't hear English.'

'My God!'

'Yes, Mommy. Most of them don't hear English at all. Even come-go they don't hear. I am telling you, it is not a good place, and Turka people' – he shook his head, Egbunu, as if she could see him, for he'd remembered what the driver had done to him a few hours before, and the children, and the people who'd watched him cry as he walked in the burning shadow of the sun – 'they are bad. I don't like them, *cha-cha*.'

'Ah, Nonso! What about your friend Jamike? Is he happy there?'

Ezeuwa, at the mention of this name, he felt his heart sink.

He paused to gather himself, for he did not want Ndali to know what he'd been passing through. He'd resolved within himself that he would only tell her after he had solved his problems. And Egbunu, I encouraged him by flashing affirmations in his thoughts that this was the right thing to do. 'Have you written the second quiz?' he said instead.

'Yes, yesterday. It was simple.'

'And have you—'

'Obim, they are telling me my credit will soon finish. And I bought two hundred naira. So please talk quickly, I miss you, Obim.'

'Okay, Mommy. I will call you tomorrow.'

'You promise?'

'It is so.'

'Have you read my letter? In your bag?'

'Er, Mommy, letter.'

'Read it anyway, there is something I want to tell you, but I want you to settle down first,' she said in haste. 'It is big, big news, even me, I am surprised. But I'm very happy!'

'You will—' he said, but the line had gone dead.

Agbatta-Alumalu, because he had finally spoken to her, because he had heard the one voice that could soothe his broken spirit, he felt a peace that was far deeper than the relief that hope had brought him. He laughed to himself, a laughter of satisfaction that things were mending quickly, at the pace at which they had been broken. For even Ndali, whom he thought he had offended gravely, had forgiven him. So happy was he that he teared up. He lay in the bed, and sleep came quickly to his tired, haunted, but tranquil body.

I had been wanting to leave his body to see what the spiritual world in this country of strange people looked like, but because of his anguish, I had been unable to, with the exception of going in search of Jamike's chi at Ngodo. For when a host is in trouble, we must watch, we must keep alert, open our eyes as wide as those of fish, until there is reprieve. So now that he slept soundly, I left his body and soared with unearthly energy into the spiritual realm. What I saw – Egbunu! – surprised me. I saw none of the things one sees when the veil of consciousness is parted: the patterned darkness of the night, the keening sound of the voices of revenants and various spirits, the noiseless footsteps of guardian spirits. Rather, here, in the stratus that formed at night, I saw oneiric forms ambling about like weary noctambulists. But what was most shocking for me was the paucity of these creatures here. For it seemed empty. I soon saw why: once I looked around, I saw unearthly temples, with ancient majesties and numinous architectural structures, at almost every corner. It seemed that in their Ezinmuo, the spirits sought dwellings like those of men, and most of them were inside these dwellings. There were even some parts that were so empty that they were filled only with the golden leaves of the luminous trees and the lucent footprints of all who'd trod them in the night. A soft, hollow tune remained, too, as if made by an instrument unknown to the fathers, which I have come to understand is called a piano. Its sound was different from *uja*, the flute of the eminent fathers and the spirits in their lands. I had wandered the length and breadth of this place on a slow pilgrimage not unlike the one my host had himself had in the land of the men until, fearing my host might wake up from some dream, I returned to find him peacefully asleep.

CHUKWU, the venerable fathers of old say that tomorrow is pregnant, and no one knows what it will birth. As what was in a woman's womb was concealed from the eyes of the old fathers (except for the initiated among them, whose eyes are able to pry into the world beyond men), so was the pregnancy of tomorrow. No one can know what it will bring. A man rests at night with the vaults of his mind full of plans and ideas for tomorrow, but nothing in those plans might be fulfilled. The great fathers understood a mystery lost on the children of the fathers now: that every new day, a man's chi is renewed. This is why the fathers conceive every new day as a birthing, an emanation of something new from something else – *chi ofufo*. Which means that what the chi may have conferred or negotiated on behalf of his host the previous day is done with, and a fresh action must be taken in the new day. Egbunu, this is the mystery of tomorrow.

My host, though, being human, woke with the joy of the hope that had been given to him the previous day and of his reconnection with his lover. When he came out of his room, Tobe was there, staring at his computer through his glasses. 'Good morning, bro. You know that Saturday is orientation?'

My host shook his head, for he did not know what the word meant.

'I really say you should go. It is very good. They say it make a person understand the island, and see many many beautiful places and history.'

'Uhm,' my host said. 'Have you go before?'

'No, it happens every Saturday. I came on Sunday and you came on Wednesday.'

'No, I came on Tuesday. *Ngwanu*, I will go.'

'Good, good. Once we come back, we will pack our things and call a taxi to move us to our new house. It is a very good thing that when you start your work, by God's grace, you will already have a place to stay. This is very good.'

My host agreed. He thanked Tobe again for everything,

for how the man had been helpful to him. 'I will never never forget what you have done for me, a person you don't know before.'

'No, no mention. You are my brother. If you see an Igbo brother in another man's land like this, how will you let them suffer?'

'It is so, my brother,' my host said, shaking his head.

His spirit lifted, he washed his socks, which he'd worn all through the journey down to Cyprus, and hung them on a wooden chair beside the parted curtains so the sun could dry them. He'd not worn this thing called a sock since primary school. But Ndali had bought them for him and insisted that his feet would get cold on the plane if he did not wear them. Outside the window, on the balcony, he saw pigeons on railings, cooing. He'd seen them the previous day but had paid no attention because while in a state of misery, a man is not himself. For instance, during the long walk the previous day, he'd remembered something that often made him laugh. One of his father's friends and his wife had visited them. The woman then went into the bathroom, although it was almost dark and there had been a power outage. They did not know that one of the chicks had found its way there. Not seeing it crouched at the back of the water drum, the woman removed her underpants and was about to start urinating when the chick hopped up to the sink. The woman screamed and ran out into the sitting room, where his father and the woman's husband were seated. The man, ashamed that my host's father had seen his wife's private parts, would end their friendship. Whenever he recalled this event, it often made him laugh. But that day, in that time, his mind merely swatted the memory away like an errant fly.

On this new day, though, as Tobe and he ate bread and

custard, he laughed and joked about the ways of the people of this land, about his own naïveté, and about how – never having been on a plane before – he'd appeared like a fool. Then, after Tobe went to school to see his teachers, he lay down and slept so long, so soundly, that he did not wake up until sunset. When he woke, he saw that Ndali had tried to call him. He rang her, but the voice of the operator reminded him that he'd exhausted his credit. With Tobe he went to the restaurant in the school, and they sat eating and watching the people of the country, his mind filling up, his spirit mending. That night I saw, as my host slept, the guardian spirit of Tobe loitering around the place. I thanked it for the help its host had rendered to mine, and we sat down talking about the Ezinmuo of the strange country and all that our hosts had been through until, close to dawn, it insisted it must return into its host.

Early Saturday morning they set off towards the bus park. As they walked past the block of apartments, Tobe pointed at an apartment in the distance on which was a Turkish flag. 'They are putting up their flags on the front of their houses and windows because of the soldier they have killed.' He gazed at my host to see if he had awakened some curiosity in him, as is often the case in such situations. And if he sees that his companion is now curious, he will go ahead and feed him more. 'Turkey is fighting with Kurdish people. PKK. The first day I came, some of their soldiers died.'

My host nodded, not knowing what his friend was talking about. When they arrived at the bus stop, many foreign students were already there, mostly those who, like my host and Tobe, had come from the nations of black people. As they waited to get on the bus, my host, watchful, noted the difference between the people of this strange country and those who had come from his. The voices of the latter seemed loud while the former seemed muted, or calm. Presently, for instance, near the back of the bus, three men and a woman from the nations of black people were talking at the top of their voices, stamping their feet and gesturing. While around and about them, the white people of this country stood in clusters of twos and threes, whispering or silent, as if gathered at a funeral.

The woman from the international office, Dehan, and a white man who spoke English with an accent similar to Ndali's welcomed everyone. The man said they were about to see the 'great beauties of this beautiful island. We will visit a lot of places – a museum, the sea, another museum, a house, and my favourite, Varosha: the deserted city. I have been living on this island for a long time now, but I'm still amazed. It's one of the wonders of the world.'

'So nobody is living there?' one of the black students from around the land of the fathers said.

'Yes, yes, my friends. Nobody. Of course, Turkish soldiers live around the place, but only them. Only the soldiers. We cannot enter, my friends.'

The students started to speak amongst themselves, intrigued about the idea of an abandoned city where no one has lived for more than thirty years.

'Okay, everybody listen,' Dehan said, raising her hand and smiling at the chattering crowd. 'We must go now. We will eat at the beach later. Now, let's go.'

As they entered the buses, the woman came to my host and his friend and asked what had happened. Had he seen Jamike?

'Not yet, ma,' he said. 'But we have reported him to the police station, and they are looking for him.' He saw that the woman was looking around, anxious to leave, and for closure and to assure her, he said, 'I know that I will find him.'

'Good, fingers crossed,' she said, and walked to the front of the group.

Egbunu, I was happy, glad indeed that my host had found reprieve from his troubles. In just a few days, a dream had almost been dashed. He watched about him, observing things now that his mind could allow him to do so. On the bus, he and Tobe sat beside two white-looking people Tobe said were Iranians. And about the others, brownish men dressed in thin fabrics, he said, 'Pakistanis.' My host nodded, and Tobe added, 'Or maybe Indians.'

While Tobe gave him the history of India and Pakistan, he noted that at the front of the bus were two chairs on either side, with a raised platform on which the driver and Dehan sat. He watched the desert pass before his eyes as if on a sprint. He noted that the landscape, although dry and sandy, was interspersed here with some faint promise of vegetation. Awkward-looking plants, brown, skeletal, naked, firmed to the soil, filled the plain. He saw, in spatial distribution, trees grafted to the dry earth like elements from some other world. Trees, he whispered to himself, as he used to do when he was a child. He gazed back to see that his loud thought had not leaked into the ears of the others seated around him. Then it struck him that he'd seen a few trees around, but they were mostly on the edges of the roads. He thought how different the highway in Nigeria was from this one. Most of the land between cities in Nigeria was not inhabited. By contrast, the land between cities here was filled with casinos, hotels, houses and sometimes nature – mountains and hills. At a place where the land was flat and cleared, and one could see for kilometres on end, Dehan pointed and said, 'That is South Cyprus. The Greek side.'

He stared in the direction where, indeed, even though the distance limited his vision, he could see tall buildings like the ones in American movies. The people he had visited in that city called Girne a few days ago had told him that that was the real Europe, where Jamike was. He wished that by some extraordinary means he could find himself in that place, among those giant buildings, crossing the street to see Jamike. He wished he'd catch Jamike in his house and take back his money and then bring him to the police here to be imprisoned. He thought of the German lady and the promise of his deliverance. As it often happened, when something is only a promise, a thing of hope, its anticipation is shadowed by fear. And as he thought of it now, he wished that he would get the job. I intervened and put it in his thoughts that the kind woman had been moved by him. *Perhaps she has never seen a man become so broken that he was willing to give his blood twice. She will do everything within her means to help you.*

Chukwu, I achieved success again. For my host heard me, and my words brought him succour. His thoughts shifted at once to the resolve that he would not tell Ndali any of the things that had happened to him until he was fine again. He would shield her from them, but after he'd got the job and recovered his money and things were going well at school, he would tell her everything, about how he was almost destroyed by this move. He was thinking about how much she'd cried and how he wanted, badly, to be with her again when they entered a city. 'Gazimagusa,' Dehan announced. 'Bigger, much much bigger than Lefkosa. But we are going to the old ancient part, surrounded by walls. I live here.' She stuck out her tongue, and the students laughed. She said something to the driver, and the man trailed off in a rushed, high-pitched response, and the students answered ecstatically.

From that moment onwards, the views changed. Giant walls rose high, and, carved into a fortress of high stone and concrete, bricks which he'd never seen before. It seemed like they had not been made with cement and water – a material with which the children of the old fathers now built – but with something solid yet earthen-looking, resembling the colour of clay. Even though I have lived through many cycles, have followed and acquired knowledge from numerous hosts across times, I had never seen anything like these before. The stones had beams that were big and deeply cast, as if baked by the hands of the minions of Amandioha.

The bus drove under an arch formed with these bricks which had small dents and holes, as if a thousand men had stood below them pelting them with small stones for a hundred years. Egbunu, I could dwell on this endlessly, for I was greatly fascinated by these structures. But I'm here to testify about my host and his acts and to make the case that what he has done – if it is in fact true that what I fear has happened – was done in error.

The bus stopped just after this, and Dehan signalled that they alight. The other bus had arrived ahead of them, the guide with them. And when the people in my host's bus had all alighted, the man raised his voice and proclaimed: 'Ladies and gentlemen, welcome to the walled city of Gazimagusa, as we say in Turkish, or Famagusta, as we say in English. What you see around you now, here, is the Venetian walls. They were built in the fifteenth century.'

Like the others, my host turned around and saw the gradations of the massive structure, and again, these were so mighty and immense that I had the urge to leave his body and wander amongst these massive stones. Even though I had done so once, I feared that spirits in lands outside of Alaigbo, where the people have a reverence for the great goddess, are often violent and aggressive. I had heard that in these places roam a

great many akaliogolis, agwus of all kinds, spirits of the hem-
isphere, creatures long extinct, and demons. I'd heard stories
from sentinel spirits at the caves at Ogbunike and Ngodo about
how violent spirits even forced a chi out of the body of its host
and possessed him, something unheard-of even amongst the
weakest of guardian spirits! So I stayed back. I sought instead
to see everything through the eyes of the man with whom
you, Chukwu, had made me one.

While most of the people seemed to dwell on the structures, my host observed the trees scattered among buildings.
He thought they were trees similar to palms, as in the land of
the fathers, but without fruits. Other kinds existed, too – one
whose leaves covered it like tangled hair on the head of an
unkempt person. At every step, the guide spoke of history,
trailed by the crowd of students, who fed their eyes while listening to him. They stopped again at the centre of a skeletal
structure with five-columned spaces between its crumbled
white walls. A great mass of stones that must have once stood
as part of the building was now scattered about the space, some
sinking into the rich earth of its ancient floor.

'Church of Saint George,' the man said, his eyes raised
towards the top of the immense ruins. 'It was constructed
during the early time of the Church, maybe only a hundred
years after the death of Christ.'

Chukwu, as they walked on, he recalled suddenly how,
once, he'd slept during the day and woke to find the gosling
standing at the threshold of the sitting room's door. Outside,
the day had aged – its subdued light cast the gosling as a silhouette. He'd almost never remembered that, for it didn't
mean much until the days before he left for Lagos: he'd slept
by Ndali, only to wake and find her standing in the same spot
as the gosling, made into a silhouette by the dusk light.

He was deep in thoughts when he felt his phone buzzing in his trouser pocket. He took it out and saw that it was the nurse. He broke off from the group, but fearing that if he picked up, he'd call attention to himself and disrupt the guide's speech, he let it die. He'd barely rejoined them when it buzzed again. He saw that it was a message, so he opened it in a hurry.

My friend, hope all is going well? I am hoping you will fill your day with the good sun. nice man. Don't worry, my friend says we can come on Monday. Don't worry. Fiona.

EZEUWA, he followed the tour conscientiously, as if he were not the same man as the day before. He stood breathless as he and the other students lingered near the shores of the great Mediterranean Sea, where I struggled to contain the urge to get out of him and observe this curious place the guide had referred to as 'the ghost city of Varosha'. He listened, as if to lifesaving instructions, while the man talked. 'Hollywood stars, presidents of many many countries, many many people, have come here.' He marvelled at the damaged structures – multi-storey buildings pocked with holes, their bricks fallen out, some riddled with bullet holes, images that reminded me of the towns and villages in the land of the fathers at the heat of the Biafran War. He gazed intently at one which must have been a great hotel, with massive corridors, but which now stood empty and abandoned. Beside it was a grey-coloured building, its paint worn out and fallen away like pieces of soot. He tried to decipher the name of the hotel, but only part of it was still standing, and most of the cursive lettering had become detached from the wall. Holes adorned this building and gave it a peculiar look. He fell behind the group as he looked intently at the houses in the inner parts of the town, barricaded away by barbed wire and thin fences, buildings whose doors had fallen out. In one, the door knelt as if in plea at the threshold and leaned against the balcony with the rest of its body. Down below this building, sturdy plants threaded themselves through the streets in patches and stretched, as if through soft clothing, through the old faces of the walls.

The town opened a window in his mind which, throughout the rest of the trip, he could not shut. He was moved by The Blue House, which the former Greek leader with the strange name – who the guide had said was the one who caused the war between the Turkish and Greek Cypriots – had built for his children. But he kept thinking about the other abandoned places the guide said existed – an airport with planes, restaurants, schools, all vacant now. The place where they came to now the guide called the war museum. He was reminded at once of the Biafran War museum in Umuahia, which he had visited when he was a child with his father. Of that incident, I could not bear much witness, Egbunu. This is because no sooner had he and his father entered the place than they saw a tank which had been driven by one of my past hosts, Ejinkeonye, who had fought in the Biafran War and driven that selfsame tank. I was immediately overcome by the kind of crippling nostalgia that sometimes comes upon a guardian spirit who encounters the memorial of a past host or his grave. So I had left my young new host and gone into the tank, which I had been in many times in 1968, when Ejinkeonye drove it. The past is a strange thing to us guardian spirits, for we are not humans. Once I sat in the tank, I re-enacted many of the bloody scenes of battle – how once the tank had raced into a forest to escape air bombs and had felled trees and trampled over the bodies of people as it went, my host weeping within it. It had been a sobering moment, and I had stayed in it while my current host and the other visitors inspected it, looking in it but not seeing a creature seated on its shrivelled seat, a creature which, even these many decades later, still recognised the dried-blood smell of its interior.

From the war museum in this new country, they went to the 'green-line zone', back in Lefkosa, and he saw the other Cyprus, a different country, separated merely by barbed wire. He marvelled. It reminded him of the stories his father had told him about Biafra. He was moved by the sight of the Museum of Barbarism, of which the guide said, 'Don't come in with us if you don't like horror movies.' Then they had gone in with him, almost everyone. In the crowded doorway, he'd see the bathtub in which a woman and her children had been shot dead, their blood left smeared on the wall and the bathtub, just as it had been in the year the White Man calls 1963. 'The blood on that wall is older than all of us here,' the man said as they looked at the gruesome sight.

This he remembered, and those last words remained with him long after the tour had ended and he and Tobe had returned to the campus. But none of these touched him like the ghost town. It troubled him so much that later that evening, when he fell asleep on the couch in the living room, he dreamt of Varosha. He saw himself chasing his gosling as it leapt and raced into the abandoned houses. He chased it past the Turkish soldiers mounted on top of the buildings, watching. The bird ran, enfeebled by the twine on its left leg. It entered one of the buildings, the one whose door leaned against its balcony. He followed the bird, his heart palpitating. The house smelt of rust and decay, and dirt and dust had festered on the floor. Colloids of wall paint had massed about, as if waiting for something that would never come. Past this, he saw the gosling mount the stairs, its colour turning dark as it came in contact with the dirt and dust in the house. The railings had cracked and, beneath them, clasped to the feet of the wall as by talons, were beds of moss. A shirt hung on a broken door, and he peeped in to see chairs and waste and upturned furniture, all bound with a monstrous network of impenetrable cobwebs. He was sweating and panting, and the gosling, rattling, kept ascending, mostly flying in leaps, turning in the gyre of stairs, as if its path had been mapped for it and its travel was deliberate. At last he found himself on the top of the building. He did not know why, but he cried to the gosling to stop, to not go, and it turned to him. But the bird leapt into the air and descended towards the shore. In panic, he followed it headlong, forgetting in the heat of the moment where he was. He was falling and screaming, headed for certain destruction, when he woke up.

The sun had almost gone down, and its vast endless shadows had dimmed. He opened his eyes and saw Tobe standing in the room, looking at his wristwatch. He would have been thinking on about that ghastly dream, but Tobe said, 'I didn't want to wake you. But we better go move into our house before Atif brings the new students here.'

He nodded and picked up his phone. There had been three missed calls from Ndali, none of which he had heard because the phone was still set to the mode that rendered even the longest ring silent. He found that there was a text, and he opened it at once: Obim, are you OK? Pls dnt forget 2 call me, OK? He wanted to ask Tobe how one sent text messages to Nigeria. One needed to add symbols and additional numbers in order to call, but what of messaging? Instead, he hurried to his room to prepare. While he packed, it occurred to him that he had not yet read her letter. He decided that once they got to the new place, he would read it.

*

AGUJIEGBE, after they arrived at the new apartment and moved their belongings into their rooms, he reached into his bag and searched until he found her letter, hidden in one of the pen pockets, folded many times. He wondered when she had written it. Was it the last night, when she had cried for most of the time and insisted they sit on the bench under the tree in the yard? They had sat there, a soft wind blowing, listening to the sound of the streets.

His hands shook as he unfolded the piece of paper, taken from one of her lined jotters, some of which he'd once flipped through. He put it down, lay flat on his back, and took it up again to read as she'd told him was best – reading aloud to himself:

When you read, especially the Bible, say it to yourself. Speak it, because Nonso I tell you words are living things. I don't know how to explain it but I know it. That everything we say, everything, lives. I just am sure.

He looked up and then about at his bags before reading the next line, which stood alone.

Obim, I am sad. I am very sad.

Egbunu, he put it down, for his heart raced. He heard the sound of music starting up, perhaps from Tobe's laptop. He felt something – a thought – flash in his mind, but he could not tell what it was. He was certain that he had not merely forgotten it, for it had not fully materialised in his mind but rather flashed in and fled.

I have come to confess that many times I have wanted to leave. While in Lagos I planned to text you and say that I

*am not doing again. In fact, I typed everything out but my
heart did not allow me. It is because I love you. Sometimes
I feel I want to leave because of my family but it is like
something stopped me. It is like you captured me, like our
chickens. It is like I cannot get out. I cannot leave at all,
Nonso. Even 1*

Ijango–ijango, as the heart of a troubled man often leads
him on tangents at such a moment as this (many instances of
which I have seen), his eyes pored over a dab of ink that spread
across the paper from the last word so that it seemed as if the
last letter, *1*, was an upturned number 7.

*night they asked me why I love you. For a longtime I did not
know it myself Nonso. Yes, I wanted to find the good man
who helped me at the bridge that night, but I cannot explain
why I became intimate with you after we saw again. I liked
you but I didn't know why I did it. But the day you pursue
the hawk, I knew that day that you can do anything to protect
somebody you love. I knew that if I give my heart to this
man, he will never disappoint me. When I see the love you
show to ordinary animals, I knew you will show me greater
love, greater care, greater help, greater everything. This is why
I love you Nonso. See it now? Is it not true? Who can do
this? How many men in Nigeria or even all over the world
can sell everything they have for the sake of a woman? AM I
CORRECT NOW OR NOT?*

She had written the last question in capital letters, and
the perceived tone, the force of how she may have felt while
conceiving it, caused him to drop the paper, for his heart was
beating faster now. He could not tell exactly why at first, but

out of the emptiness of his mind, he saw his father and his mother and him during an environmental sanitation day in the year the White Man calls 1988. They were cleaning the front of their compound. His parents were both watching him and clapping for him because his mother had mocked his father for not being able to sweep thoroughly. And his father had complained that the broom was too lean. As he swept, many of its bamboo sticks had fallen off. His mother, having taken the broom from him, had given the broom to my host and said to his father, 'You will see that he would sweep it better than you.' And taking the broom, he, a mere six-year-old, swept as his parents cheered him on.

It struck him now that it was that same compound that he had sold. He reread the passage about how he was the only man in the world who could have done it. An idea came to him. What if he called the man who had bought the compound and told him to hold off, that he would send the money for the place with interest? He could pay every month, every month, until all was paid plus 10 per cent. He nearly jumped up at this thought. He would call Elochukwu the following day, and then Ndali, so they could go to the man at once and ask him to hold off ownership of the house.

Ijango-ijango, I, too, was overjoyed at this idea. It was not in the custom of the old fathers to sell a land. For lands were sacred. It was given to them by Ala herself and was not the possession of the man who came to own it but that of his lineage. Although Ala never punishes one who sells his land out of his own will, it angers her. With the enormous relief he felt at this decision, he picked up the letter again, its edges now wet from the sweat on his palms, and finished reading it.

*I know myself. From the first day, I knew you were genuine.
I knew you were the man God has prepared for me. And I
want you to know that I love you and will wait for you. So
please be happy.*

Your love,
Ndali

16

VISIONS OF WHITE BIRDS

EBUBEDIKE, the great fathers speak of a man who is anxious and afraid as being in a fettered state. They say this because anxiety and fear rob a man of his peace. And a man without peace? Such a man, they say, is inwardly dead. But when he rids himself of the shackles, and the chains rattle and tumble away into outer dark, he becomes free again. Reborn. To prevent himself from falling again into bondage, he tries to build defences around himself. So what does he do? He allows in yet another fear. This time, it is not the fear that he is undone because of his present circumstances but that in a yet uncreated and unknown time, something else will go wrong and he will be broken again. Thus he lives in a cycle in which the past is rehearsed, time and time again. He becomes enslaved by what has not yet come. I have seen it many times.

Although my host's promise of salvation was still firmly in place – the nurse had texted him twice since they met and the second time had added a yellow image of a laughing face and repeated that he was a 'good man' – the fear came after he read Ndali's letter. It held him bound for the last portion of the night, dangling flashing images of other men having

romance with her in his mind. He was released from this state
in the early hours of the morning when Tobe knocked and
asked from behind the door if he would go to church. 'If you
come,' Tobe continued, 'you will meet a lot of Naija people
there. And I tell you, you will like it. You can thank God for
everything, and also, we can buy some things to cook from
the market there. We should start to cook before school starts
tomorrow.' My host said he would join.

Later, they were walking along a road that appeared like one
he'd passed on Thursday, just after he left the taxi. The streets
were compact, and the buildings seemed to have no partition
between them. A barbershop constructed in glass sat by the
pavement. A man smoking in front of it, blowing billows of
smoke into the air, yelled '*Arap!*' at them as they passed.

'Your papa *arap!*' Tobe yelled back.

'Your father, mother, everybody *arap!*' my host said, for
Tobe had told him that whenever he heard that, it meant he
was being called a slave.

'Don't mind them, they are idiots. Look at that dirty-
looking man calling us slaves. That's the thing. They are
so foolish.'

They crossed into a lone street whose houses had gates like
the ones in Nigeria. Big green metal boxes filled with earth sat
at every corner. But on one street they passed, Tobe pointed
to one of the buildings and said that the white people from
Europe loved to come and see it. It was a building of rich clay,
like nothing my host or I had ever seen before. He was enrap-
tured by the sight. The building was roofless, with mighty
pillars. A temple to a Greek or Roman god, Tobe suggested
aloud, perhaps so the old European man taking photos of it
could hear him. An ancient temple destroyed by age, its old
beauty trapped beneath the skin of its ruins. Yet in some way,

it still was beautiful, for this is what turned it into a spectacle, why people travelled from afar to see it. A beauty out of ruins: this was a strange thing.

When they turned on to a street Tobe said was near the church, they saw other people who had the colour of the great fathers, a group of four men, two of them wearing visors, walking towards the church. With this group, they entered the church. It was full, and one of the men they had seen at the apartment with Nigerians on campus, John, was directing people and offering chairs to those who did not have seats. The place was full of black students as well as some white people. A different kind of white man, one who looked not like the Turkish people but like the ones who ruled the land of the old fathers for many years, stood at an altar in front, speaking in the same accent as Ndali, and he knew at once that he was British. The man spoke about the need to sing with all their hearts. He and Tobe sat in the very back, behind two people who looked somewhat familiar to him.

He thought of the church of his childhood, which he had stopped attending. His father had stopped after the death of his mother, angry with God for letting his wife die in childbirth. My host had continued, sparingly, until an incident with the gosling had changed his mind. The gosling had become ill, refusing to eat and falling whenever it walked. The idea came that he take it to a church where he'd heard of faith healings – of a blind man seeing again. So he took his gosling to the church, carrying it close to his chest. He was stopped at the door by uniformed ushers who thought him mad for bringing an animal to the church. That incident killed his faith in the religion of the White Man. Why would God not care for a sick animal if he cares for human beings? At the time, he found it hard to under-stand why one could not love a bird just as one loved people.

Hoping that he would turn to the religion of the pious fathers, I had encouraged his decision, adding to his thoughts that if he went to an odinani shrine with his animal, Ala or Njokwu or any number of deities would not have cast him away. But like many of his generation, such a thought was verboten.

Now he listened even harder as the preacher began speaking of resurrection and life. The man talked about Jisos Kraist and how he had died and risen. Sleep came upon his eyes as the man, whose voice careened in the air and shifted between high and low, spoke of how only true Christianity could lead to possessing a life of resurrection, of rising again after a fall. He opened his eyes, for the man had spoken to him. He was a witness to how, when lost, a man could descend into the abyss and still be raised up and restored.

When the preacher finished his sermon, they sang, and the church was dismissed. Once the people began to leave their seats, a man tapped him on the shoulder.

'Jesus Christ, T.T.!'

'Oh boy! Happy to see you here.'

'Yes, my brother.'

'How are you, how far, did you later see your friend?'

'No,' he said, and told T.T. everything that had happened. By the time he finished, they were standing outside the gate of the church, and Tobe, who'd greeted a few people, had come to stand by his side.

'Mehn, casino pays very well for here,' T.T. said. 'God sent that woman to you true, true oh. Some of the Turka people are good. There's a woman like that who really helps a lot of people. She gave a Naija boy scholarship, sef. The boy was working for her, doing everything, and instead of just paying him, he said make she kuku pay his school fees.'

'Hmm, good people.'

'Yes, yes, but be careful eh. Sometimes, the people just get kanji.'

T.T. laughed and said, 'Take my number.'

ONWANAETIRIOHA, when he returned home with Tobe, it was already dark. He reached for his phone, and a text message was on it. He read the message from Ndali. Nonso, call me tomorrow pls. He shook his head. He dialled her number, but only a long-drawn static noise came back to him. He resolved to call her after he'd confirmed the job, after he knew for certain that he would recover that which he'd lost. And when he called her, he would tell her everything – everything from the airport to his meeting Fiona.

He sat back in his chair in his room and thought of the days, of all his being in a new country. He reached in his bag and brought out the photos of Ndali naked. As he watched them, his body caught sensual fire. He brought out his penis. Then he rushed and bolted the door so Tobe could not come in at will. He pushed his ear against it for any sound of Tobe, and when he did not hear, he looked at the naked photos of Ndali and began touching himself, gasping, moaning until he fell into a limp state.

AKATAKA, amongst the people of the world, anywhere, there is a common thread of compassion for a man who is wounded, or poor, or lowly. This kind of man earns their pity. Many would desire to help such a man if they believe he has been wronged. I have seen this many times. This is why a white woman in a foreign land can see a man from the land of the fathers, tattered, broken, and offer help, and in offering, create a pleasant expectation in him.

He woke the following morning, having slept for a full

night for the second time since he arrived in the strange country. So full of expectation was he that he called Elochukwu and told him to go at once to the man to whom he'd sold the land and ask him to not do anything, that he would refund the money. 'But how is this possible when you don't give him the money immediately?' Elochukwu said.

'Tell him I will give him double. We should sign agreement; I will pay double within six months. Then I can have my house back.'

Elochukwu promised to meet the man and talk to him. Assured, my host washed himself and joined Tobe, who had cooked fried eggs.

Tobe talked about how difficult it had been to find good bread that morning.

'All of the bread they have are like stone,' he said, and my host laughed. 'I don't even understand this people at all. Not wan single bread in the whole shop.'

'You have watched *Osuofia in London*?' my host said.

'Heh, the one he went to that place and asked for Agege bread and the Oyibo people were jus looking like mumu?'

They ate in sudden silence, he thinking of how mornings were different here. He'd not heard any cock crow, not even a call to prayer from a muezzin. The image he'd remembered the previous day returned and he saw Ndali almost naked, standing at the threshold of the sitting room's door. She was standing there looking away, her back turned to him like a thing to be feared. He did not remember what he had done – had he called to her? Had he turned away? He could not tell.

'This people, they stick to time,' Tobe said again. 'If they tell you ten o'clock, it is ten o'clock. If they tell you it is one, it is one. So we should go quickly to the letting agent's office, collect your own keys and go wait for the woman.'

He nodded. 'It should be so, my friend.'

'I called Atif yesterday, and told him we have found a place. He asked about you. When I go, after my registration and class, I will go to his office.'

'Thank you, my brother,' he said, for he was paying little attention, his mind fixed on the errand he'd delegated to Elochukwu and the job Fiona would soon take him to.

They cleared the table and left the house, Tobe carrying a bag with his computer inside, and books. The bag resembled the schoolbags children wore on their backs, as Tobe himself wore his. My host carried the bag Ndali had given him, which contained his documents, her letter and her photos, as he'd been doing since he came to the country.

They found the agent's office in the interior of the city centre, tucked into an area full of clothing and jewellery outlets. It was on a street behind the centre, compact and full of shops, a cyber cafe, restaurants and a small mosque. Pigeons hopped about, feeding on something or other. Here they found a lot of white people different from the Turkish people. Tobe said they were Europeans or Americans.

'They are different,' Tobe insisted. 'These ones, the Turkish people, they are not real whites. They look more like Arabs. You know how – have you seen Sudan people before? They are different from our black – that *kain* difference.'

A group of the kind of white people they were speaking about was walking along. Two young women, almost naked, in half shorts, brassieres and slippers, passed by. One of them carried a towel. 'My God, see Omo!' Tobe said.

He laughed. 'I thought you were a born again,' he said.

'Yes. But see, these girls fine. But Turkish woman beat them. But Naija still remain number one.'

Egbunu, when they entered the office, the air was filled

with cigarette smoke. A stout white woman in a chair was smoking. I noted that at the threshold of the door was a round amulet, the colour of Osimiri, with a white inner sphere within which looked like a human eye. Because it appeared so much like an amulet, I came out of my host to see if it posed a danger to him. And at once I saw a strange spirit in the shape of a snake curling around the object. This creature was a fearful sight even for me, a guardian spirit, who journeys regularly into the plains of the ethereal. I fled in haste.

When I rejoined my host, the woman was counting the money Tobe had given her. Later, when they stepped out with the keys, he felt an overwhelming relief. When they came out, it was nearly ten. So they walked to the bus stop. They stood there for only a few minutes when Fiona arrived in her car, dressed in a white frock with a necklace that sparkled around her neck. He shook Tobe's hand and ran towards the car.

'You're looking happy,' Fiona said once he entered.

'Yes, Fiona. Thank you. It is because of you.'

'Oh, no, come on! I haven't done anything. You were in big trouble.'

He nodded.

'I got an apartment with my friend.'

'Ah, that's very good. Very good. It helps your psyche, you know, to have a house.'

He said yes.

'My friend Ismail is in the office. He is waiting for you.'

As soon as he sat, I noticed that the woman wore – around her wrist in the form of a band – the same kind of amulet I had seen earlier. I flashed the image of the one at the agent's office in my host's mind and pointed him to the woman's wrist, for I was curious to know what it was. Unexpectedly, Chukwu, it worked.

'*Es ma*,' he said.

'Yes?'

'What is this blue thing that resemble eyes everywhere here——?'

'Oh, oh,' the woman said, and thrust her hand into the air. 'Evil eye. It's like, you know, a good-luck charm. Very big deal to Turkish people.'

My host nodded, even though he could not fully comprehend what the object was. But I was relieved to know it was merely a personal fetish, not something that could harm my host.

They drove, a tune playing from the stereo. She asked him what music he liked, but when he listed them, she didn't know any. It struck him, once he'd finished speaking, that he did not mention Oliver De Coque. The thought of the singer annoyed him, as if De Coque had done something to hurt him. But he knew that he'd come to associate the memory of the day he was humiliated at Ndali's family's house with De Coque, who was playing his music that day. And he now resented the musician for it.

'This is Emre Aydin, a very good Turkish singer. I like him very much.' She laughed and glanced at my host. 'By the way, Solomon, I've been thinking about your story. It's very painful.'

He nodded.

'It reminded me of a book I read recently about a man who was asked by his wife to join the army during the war, and when he did, she became very disturbed by the actions, you know, of the army. Hitler's Nazi army. She left him. It is a very difficult book. You do something great because of a woman you love, and then you lose her. I am not saying it will happen to you, don't get me wrong.' She waved her hand. 'You will be fine and your fiancée will be there for you – I'm sure. I am speaking of the sacrifice. *Genau?*'

He looked up at her, for her words had shot into his heart and pierced it.

'Yes, ma, I—' He stopped himself and said instead, 'Yes, Fiona.'

They passed the strange road again and climbed a mighty bridge, then went down a small ramp made of interlocking bricks. As the car approached what seemed like the limits of a village, giving way to densely vegetated lands, the sun seemed to drop lower, and its heat, visible in the illusory wave, made it appear as if the car had suddenly plunged into a river. But soon the deception was busted, and they entered into the town's small streets. The car made a grinding sound as it raced past others, jerking so much that even the thought of Ndali leaving him, a thought which had lain like a child in the cot of his mind, shifted violently from one end to the other. He struggled to still it. But he could not.

OSIMIRIATAATA, the peace that concrete hope brings to a man who has suffered cruel defeat is difficult to describe. It is the sublime incantation of the soul. It is the unseen hand that lifts a man off a cliff over a pit of fire and returns him to the road from which he has veered. It is the rope that pulls a drowning man out of the deep sea and hauls him on to the deck of a boat to the breath of fresh air. This was what the nurse had given him. But what I have seen many times before is that the hands that feed the chicken are the same ones that kill it. This is a mystery of the world, one which, in this strange country, my host and I would come to experience. But I must render it all in as much detail as I can, Egbunu, for this is what you desire of us when we come before you here in the luminous court of Beigwe.

When they arrived in the city from which he'd emerged four days before with a bleeding spirit, his heart was so warm and his joy so grand that he wanted to take a photo of the place. So before they entered, he asked Fiona if she had a camera phone.

'Yes, yes,' she said. 'It's a BlackBerry.'

'Okay,' he said.

'You want a photo?'

He nodded and smiled.

'Ha!' she said, and blew air out of her mouth. 'You can't even tell me you want a photo? You are a shy man.'

She snapped a photo of him folding his hands across his chest, then pointing at the light-box sign on the facade of the white marble building, then with his hands spread out, both ways. He looked through these images of himself looking happy, and they pleased him.

'I will send them to your e-mail.'

He agreed. As they walked into the place, part of his mind was thinking of Ndali, how she would like the photos. The other half was in awe of the magnificence of the building – the blood-red rug with tiger prints, the ornamental light-bulbs, the machines and TV screens. He stopped thinking of all these when he started walking behind Fiona through a narrow hallway. It must have been because of the kind of shoes Ndali called 'heels', but her buttocks danced in a shapely way. And through the white frock, he saw the outline of her underpants.

Ebubedike, it surprised him, the strange sudden beat of his heart at the sight and the quick fist-punch of lust on his mind. It came at him like a burst of flame, so quick and unnatural that he was taken aback by it.

As if she suspected what had happened, she turned. 'Solomon, I have told you what he will pay, yes?'

'That is so, Fiona.'

'Okay, take it for now. We can increase later. *Genau?*'

He nodded. He walked by her side now as they arrived at the entrance to the manager's office. But the desire remained, even against his will. He wondered how old she must be. Her body looked young, like that of a woman in her thirties, but her neck showed skin gradations that suggested otherwise. And he'd seen traces of wrinkles on her legs too. But still he could not determine such things about white people, about whom he knew little.

Through a glass door they came into a room where a man sat across a desk, his face intent on a computer screen. The computer, Chukwu – an instrument that is able to do so much. It can gather information, serve as a device for communicating with those afar, and much more! When it becomes common among the children of the precious fathers, it will further alienate them from their ancestors. Fathers of the hills and lands, dwellers of Alandiichie, do you weep that the altars of the *ikenga* have been abandoned? What you have seen is nothing. Do you worry that your children do not observe *omenala*? This thing, this box of light into which this white man is staring, will cause you greater grief in the fullness of time.

The man rose once my host and his companion entered the room. He shook the man's hand but understood little of what the man said. He thought the man spoke the language of the White Man well but seemed to prefer the language of the country. What he noticed more was how the man hugged Fiona and touched her shoulder and patted her on the arm. For a while they spoke the language, and he gazed at colourful images on the four walls of the room – images of the great sea, the swimming turtle, and of some of the ruins he'd seen on the tour – all the while praying that the man would give him the job. So folded away was he that he gave a start when the man stretched his hand towards him and said, 'So you can start from tomorrow, Tuesday, if you want.'

'Thank you very much, sir,' he said, shaking the man's hand and bowing slightly.

'Don't mention. Okay, see you, my friend. Congratulations.'

The man walked back into the hallway and made to leave but turned hurriedly and took Fiona's hand again, and they embraced. The man seemed to kiss her cheeks, the way Ndali would sometimes ask him to do to her. It was a strange thing, Chukwu. A man kissing another woman who was not his wife in plain sight? The man lit a cigarette and began speaking to Fiona again in the language of the country.

When they came out of the building, Fiona said she had baked a cake for my host. She would bring it from the oven, wrap it up for him, and they would go to a restaurant. And while at her house, she would show him her garden, for she, too, was a farmer, like him. He agreed and thanked her even more. By the time they got on the road again, his lust had fizzled out, suppressed by an infant rage which stood in the midst of his joy like a stranger among a crowd of friends. An Igbo man like him, one he could call a brother, an old classmate, had cheated him and almost destroyed him. But here, among a people he did not know, people of a different country and race, a woman had come to save him. This woman and her friend had even gone further than Tobe, who for a long time had borne his cross with him. They'd taken his cross and set it on fire, Fiona and this man. And by the time she arrived at her house, his cross — all that it was, and all that was within it — had burned to ashes.

EGBUNU, I have spoken about the primal weakness of man and his chi: their inability to see the future. Should they have possessed this ability, a great many disasters would have been easily prevented! Many, many. But I know that you require me to testify in the sequence that things happened, to give a full account of my host's actions, and thus I must not stray from the path of my story. I must thus proceed by saying that my host followed this woman to her house.

The house was big. Outside it, a garden, water hoses, and flowers arranged in neat beddings. She said her mother, who sometimes visited from Germany, was a farmer. A dry pool filled with leaves lay near the low wall on one side beside a shovel and a wheelbarrow. She did not plant anything that could be eaten, except for tomatoes. But she hadn't planted in a long time. The garden, he realised, was a storage area for things she wanted to keep possessing. She said that the old paraffin lamp that hung on the branch of a low, lean tree from which a fine laundry rope stretched out to the house was her cat's. Miguel. He did not know that people could keep cats as pets, let alone that they could be named.

This thing that looked like the engine of a car seated on the ground was from the truck in which her husband's father had died. She paused at the sight of this one and dropped both hands to her sides. Then, without looking at him, she said, 'It was the beginning of the trouble. From then, he always says: "Why did I let him drive? If he didn't drive at seventy-two, he'd still be here today." That's why he drinks himself to stupor and turns his back to the world.' Then an unexpected thing happened. For when she turned to him, this woman whom all the while had been full of life was now almost in tears. 'He turned his back to the world,' she said again. 'The whole world.'

Thinking of the job, of the casino, of the charge he'd given to Elochukwu, how it would turn out, he barely heard the

things she was saying. That long walk he had thought of as
the most unbearable time of his life, he reckoned, had in the
end become the thing that had brought him great hope. He
followed her into the house, curious to see what white people's
houses looked like. They went through the back door into a
kitchen that was nothing like what my host had seen before.
It was marbled (although he did not know the word, Egbunu)
and covered with paintings.

'They are my drawings,' Fiona said to him as he gazed at
one which was different from the rest. It was not the image of
a cat, or dog, or flowers, but a bird.

'They are very nice,' he said.

'Thank you, my dear.'

He walked with her into the sitting room, and he was
struck by the enormity of Ndali's father's wealth. Their house
was lusher than that of a white family. He gazed about at the
piano by the yellow wall, a big television and a speaker. There
was only one couch, long and black, made of some kind of
leather. The walls, from beginning to end, were covered with
paintings and photographs. Near the television and a shelf of
books stood what looked like the dry white sculpture of a
human skeleton. The sculpture wore a necklace with the evil
eye image on it.

'So I will change. It's hot. I'll put on some pants and a shirt,
and we will have the cake and go. *Genau?*'

He nodded. He watched her climb the stairs, the thighs
under her frock visible. Desire erupted in him again. To shove
off this urge, he looked up to the image on the wall above the
piano in which sat the man he believed might be her husband.
His eyes in the picture were happy. Yet there was a sternness to
them that gave him the appearance of a man of tough temperament, something close to what Fiona described as 'turning his

back to the world'. Beside that lone portrait was one of the man and Fiona, years younger, with fuller hair that was fixed into the shape of a hanging tail behind her back. They were seated, Fiona in front of him, he behind her, half of him concealed so that only his chest was revealed. The picture was taken, it seemed, at a function, for there were people in the background, some prominent, others faded out by distance. The trunk of a green car – rear pointing downwards – stretched into the picture, its other half lost to visual oblivion.

Egbunu, at this point, I can tell you that there was nothing in his mind about this man other than that he was curious about what grief had done to him. He was searching the picture of the man to see if he could find any sign of the darkness Fiona had described. He'd also noticed a kind of quiet fear in Fiona since they arrived at the house, as if she was afraid of something which she was unwilling to confront. Chukwu, I know that it is quite possible that our recollections are not always accurate because hindsight can influence them. But I am giving you the unfiltered account when I say that my host gazed at this man's photo closely and introspectively, as if he were aware, even vaguely, of what would come next. He turned from it to the small recess in the wall containing wood and dry ash – what he thought of as firewood inside a sitting room but which I knew from the days of Yagazie as a fireplace, where white people sunned themselves when it was cold. There was such a place in every house where my host went in Virginia, in the country of the brutal White Man. Without it, the cold – something unthinkable in the land of the great fathers – would kill them. He was examining this when Fiona began descending down the stairs. She had changed into short pants and a shirt with the image of a half-sliced apple on it.

'Okay, let me get the cake, and let us go.'

'Okay, Fiona.'

He watched her open the oven and bring out something wrapped in a white paper-like material; neither I nor my host knew what it was. She put the thing in a polythene bag.

'What kind of food do you like?' she said.

He had begun to speak when she cut off his speech with a wave of her hand. He turned in the direction where her eyes were looking and saw the reason why. The main door was opening, and an older, much more worn-looking version of the man in the portrait stepped into the house. His shirt was unbuttoned, a wrinkled blue shirt whose sleeves had been rolled up, revealing a white skin so hirsute it appeared as if his hands were black. He walked a few paces into the living room and stopped where he was, gazing at them.

'Ahmed, wow, welcome,' Fiona said in a voice that betrayed restlessness, fear. 'Where are you coming from?'

The man did not speak. He stood with eyes roving from my host to his wife and back again with an intensity that was familiar to me. It was a gaze whose import may be understood more in effect than in contemplation, like the understanding of the full enormity of life in the moment before death. The man's mouth was poised for speech, but instead, he laid down the bag he carried on the floor gently. Fiona moved towards him, calling his name, but the man stepped towards the bookshelf.

'Ahmed,' she said again, and spoke in the foreign language. The man responded with a countenance that frightened my host. As the man spoke, saliva splashed from his mouth. He pointed to Fiona, clenched his fist and pounded it into his palm. Fiona, gasping, her hand over her mouth, spoke in rapid gusts in what seemed like protests, to which the man paid no heed. He spoke even louder, in a high-pitched tone. He snapped his fingers, thumped his chest and stamped his feet. Fiona fidgeted as the man spoke and stepped backwards in increments, turning back and forth from her husband to my host and back again, her eyes filling with tears. She was talking when the man faced him.

'Who are you?' the man said. 'Do you hear me? Who in hell are you?'

'Ahmed, Ahmed, *lutfen*,' Fiona said, and tried to grab him. But the man wrenched himself away with a cruel force and struck her across the face. She fell down with a scream. Her husband followed her to the floor, beating her with his fists.

Gaganaogwu, my host was terrified by what was unfolding before him, and I, his chi, was too. He stood where he was and said in a quivering voice, 'Sorry, sir, sorry, sir!' He glanced at the door, whose path he could reach without much trouble if he hastened, but he stood still. Go! I cried into the ears of his mind, but he merely stepped forward an inch. Then he turned again to Fiona. He lunged forward and punched the man on the back and pushed him away. The man rose, picked up the bag and rushed at him with it. The man slung the bag at my host's face with a brutal force that sent him across the room. The bag bounced off his face to the floor, and from the sound it made, and from the frothing liquid that poured across the floor, I knew at once that it contained a bottle.

My host lay where he had fallen now, dazed, his body in a state of frugal peace. When he opened his eyes, a fast-moving figure rushed into his field of vision, and before he could tell what it was, his eyes had closed again. Slowly and continuously, he felt cold liquid run down his shoulder, chest and arms. Ebubedike, although I was greatly shaken by this, I was mightily relieved that my host was alive. If this man had killed him, what would his ancestors have said of me? Would they have said that I, his chi, was asleep? Or that I was an ajoo-chi or an *efulefu*? This is how, sometimes, the life of a person ends – suddenly. I have seen it many times. One moment they are singing; the next, they are gone. One moment they are saying to a friend or a relative, I will go to that shop across the road, buy bread, and come back. I will be back in five minutes. But they never return alive. A woman and her husband may be talking. She is in the kitchen, he is in the sitting room. He asks a question, and while she is answering – while she is answering, Egbunu! – he is gone. When she does not hear from him for a while, she calls out, 'My husband, have you been listening? Are you there?' And when he does not respond, she steps in and finds him slumped, one hand clutching his chest. This, too, I have witnessed.

My host lay, alive but in sublime pain, his face and mouth covered in blood. He wanted to keep his eyes closed, but Fiona's screaming and pleading prevented him. When he opened his eyes again, he saw the man and, in the man's hand, what had hit him: a big white bottle whose bottom half had broken off, leaving it in the shape of half-formed fingers, its edges red with blood that slowly dripped to the floor. The man was standing with the object over Fiona. Then he saw the man bend over her, shouting and moving the bottle about so that drops of blood and wine spattered on her face. From the dim vision of his closing eyes, he saw the man throw the bottle away and sink down and begin to reach for her throat again, unmoved by her screaming and pleading. Slowly, he crawled towards them, stopping to gather strength as Fiona's screaming grew louder with each step, for the man had now succeeded in reaching her throat. In this memorable moment of life, Egbunu, my host, bleeding profusely, reached up, lifted a stool, and tried to keep his eyes open to prevent the blood from clouding his vision.

The stool in his hand felt heavy. He had been weakened by the blood he had lost, not just now but a few days before, at the hospital. Yet Fiona's screaming propelled him forward. He rose up and lifted one foot, then the other, until he reached the place where they were. With every bit of strength he could summon, he hauled himself forward like a sack of grain and brought the stool down on the man's head.

The man fell over backwards against him and lay still. From his head, an aureole of blood formed. My host staggered, wiped his face and batted his eyelids. Then he fell back to the wet floor and lay down on the black veranda between consciousness and unconsciousness. In the meaningless space that the world suddenly became, he saw Fiona turn into a strange creature, at once a bird and at once a white woman dressed in white. From the margins of his anguished vision, he saw her stretch and rise slowly like a snake unfurling from a rigid coil and then begin to scream and shout. He saw her perch on the corner of the room beside her husband, her plumage rich and almost immaculately white. Then she materialised again into a human, trying to waken her slumped husband, who did not stir. He heard her say, 'He is not breathing! He is not breathing! My God! My God!' Then her wings spread, and she flew out of the range of his vision.

He lay there with a still vision in his mind of Ndali seated on the bench under the tree in his compound, looking straight ahead. He could not see what she was looking at. Whether this was from memory or from his imagination, he could not tell, nor could I, his chi. But it continued as he watched Fiona, wings still splayed, return to the place with a majestic stride. He saw her enlarged sternum, with the sparkling necklace around it, and a beak that seemed to carry something indistinct clamped in it. Then she moved again, now with her human feet, and he heard the sound of her feet on the floor. He heard the sound of her dim cries.

He heard the white woman speaking on the phone, her voice frantic, helpless. He opened his eyes to see her, but he was blinking so rapidly that the muscle below his eyes had begun to ache. In the all-encompassing darkness into which his body was thrown, a sudden chill came upon him and he became aware of a presence. Chukwu, he became still: for he could tell that yet again, it had come. From the backstage of life, it had come. That creature which has a red mother and whose complexion is the colour of blood. *Again, it had come.* It had come again – to steal everything that had been given to him and to destroy the joy he had found. What is this thing? he wondered. Is it a man or a beast? A spirit or a god? Ijango-ijango, he did not know. And I, his chi, did not know, either. The great fathers often say that one cannot, by looking at the shape of the belly of a goat, tell what kind of grass it has eaten.

He heard Fiona crying, but he did not open his eyes. She said something to him which at first he did not hear, then to her husband, who lay still, like a plank. It was then that he heard what she had said, loud and clear: 'You've killed him. You've killed him.' She broke down into a loud sound. She had barely begun to cry when, in the distance, a siren began to wail. But he lay still there, his mind fixed on the curious vision of Ndali staring into the unknown, as if in a mysterious way she had broken the barrier of thousands of kilometres and was looking at him.

17

ALANDIICHIE

EBUBEDIKE, the old fathers in their cautionary wisdom say that the same place one visits and returns to is often the place where one goes and becomes trapped. My host had found succour in the white woman, but this same place where he'd found succour is where he now lay, wounded and bleeding, blinded by his own blood. Frantic, unable to do anything, and wary as to how I would explain this tragic end to you, Chukwu, and to his ancestors, I left his body to see if help might be found in the spirit realm. Once out, I saw that spirits of all kinds had gathered in the room like dark auxiliaries marching upon the entire army of mankind itself. They hung everywhere, near the arch of the ceiling, suspended over the body of my host and the other man, some hanging like curtains made of shadows. Among them was an unsightly creature who gazed at me with an ugly frown on its face. I noticed that it was an incorporeal replica of the man on the floor. It pointed its finger at me and spoke in the strange language of the country. It was speaking when the door opened and police officers stormed in with people in white frocks like the one Ndali wore, and the white woman, too. She was crying and speaking to them, pointing at her husband and then at my host, who lay there, slowly slipping into unconsciousness from loss of blood.

Three of the police officers and nurses carried away the man who had attacked my host, Fiona following behind them. Then they returned and took him, their shoes soaked in his blood, red footprints marking their trail. Chukwu, by the time they got into the vehicle that resembled my host's van (called an 'ambulance' among the children of the great fathers), he fainted.

I followed them through the streets of the strange land, seeing what my host could not see – a car loaded with watermelon, the kind found in the land of the fathers, and a boy on horseback followed by a procession of people beating drums, blowing trumpets and dancing. All these gave way for the ambulance to pass, its siren blaring. I was besotted with fear and a great regret that I had allowed him to come to this place, this country, just because of a woman, when he could easily just have got another. I repeat, Egbunu, regret is the disease of the guardian spirit.

The veil of consciousness that occludes my vision of the ethereal world now torn away, I beheld for a second time the living phantasmagoria of the spiritual world here. I saw a thousand spirits nestled at every breadth of the land, hanging on trees, flowing in mid-air, gathered on the mountains and in places too numerous to name. Near the Museum of Barbarism, where my host had been only two days earlier, I saw the three children whose blood was in the bathtub displayed inside the house. They were standing outside the house, dressed in the exact same shirts they'd been wearing at the time of the attack, torn, ripped by gunfire, blackened with blood. Because they were standing alone, unattended by other spirits, it occurred to me that they must be perpetually standing there, perhaps because their blood – their life – remains on the wall and on the bathtub, on display for the world to see.

At the hospital, they wheeled my host into a room, and when I saw that he was secure, I ascended immediately to Alandiichie, the hills of the ancestors, to meet his kindred amongst the great fathers to report what had happened – after which, if indeed he had killed the man, I would come to you, Chukwu, to testify of it, as you require us to do if our host takes the life of another person.

IJANGO-IJANGO, the road to Alandiichie is one I know well, but on this night, it was more winding than usual. The hills that border the road were dark beyond all imagining, speckled only here and there by the savage light from mystical fires. The waters of Omambala-ukwu, whose sibling is situated on earth, flowed with a muffled roar in the blackened distance. I crossed its luminous bridge, over which multitudes of humans from the four corners of the earth travel in a violent rush towards the land of the ancestral spirits. From the river I heard a stream of voices singing. Although the voices were in accord, one was at its heart. This distinct voice was loud but thin and resilient, swift in its tone, and as sharp as the blade of a new machete. They sang a familiar lullaby, one as ancient as the world in its conception. It wasn't long before I realised it was the voice of Owunmiri Ezenwanyi, attended by her numerous maids of unmatched beauty. Together they sang in an ancient mystical language which, no matter how many times I heard it, I could not decipher. They sang for the children who died at childbirth and whose spirits traverse the plains of the heavens without direction – for a child, even in death, does not know his left from his right. It must be shown its way towards the realms of tranquillity, where the mothers dwell, their breasts filled with pure, ageless milk, their arms as supple as the warmest rivers.

They call us *nwa-na-enweghi-nku* – 'wingless' because we are spirits and can travel in the air without wings and 'children' because we dwell inside the bodies of living men. So I knew it was for me they were singing. I paused to wave and to acknowledge their song. But Chukwu, as I listened to it, I wondered how you created voices so enchanting. How did you equip these creatures with such powers? Isn't it tempting for one who hears such a song to halt in his tracks? Isn't it tempting to even completely stop the journey to Alandiichie? Isn't it why many dead people remain hanging between the heavens and the earth? The spirits of the dead sitting by the warm shore, aren't they those who, although dead, have not found rest and whose ghosts roam the earth? I have seen many of them – walking about unseen, unable to be seen, belonging neither there nor here, permanently in a state of *odindu-onwukanma*. Aren't some of them in this condition because they are trapped by the enchanting music of Owunmiri and her troupe?

The fathers of old say that a man whose house is on fire does not go about chasing rats. So although I was thrilled by the tune, I was not charmed. I walked on until the music died away and any sight of the habitation of man was completely gone. No longer could I see the shiny *kpakpando* whose numbers are so vast that a duality was ascribed to them in the language of the fathers. They pair with the sands of the earth to form the single word: stars-and-earth. As I walked, the stars and all that was connected to the earth rolled away like a blanket of darkness into an empty abyss whose expanse is beyond measure. Across the hills was a long winding path lit in every corner by torches, their flames as bright as the light of the sun. It is here that one begins to encounter ndiichie-nna and ndiichie-nne from all over Alaigbo and beyond, gathered in pockets as they walk towards the great hills yonder. The path is decorated on both sides by strands of the sacred *omu* leaves, fastened to the trees like strange ribbons. Attached to the fresh palm leaves are also molluscs, cowries, tortoise shells and precious stones of all kinds.

From here, as one ascends the hills, the number of travellers increases. The recently dead throng towards the hills, still bearing the agony of death with them and the marks of life – men, women, children; the old and the young, the strong and the feeble, the rich and the poor, the tall and the short. They tread, their feet soundless against the fine earth of the road, which sparkles in the bright lights. But the hills, Egbunu, the hills are filled with light – an arrangement of shimmering radiance that seems almost to flow like an invisible river into the eye that beholds it and then dissipates into a misty whorl of glow. I have often thought how close the living came to capturing Alandiichie in the moonlight song the old mothers (and their living daughters) sang:

Alandiichie
A place where the dead are alive
A place where there are no tears
A place where there is no hunger
A place I will go in the end.

Indeed, Alandiichie is a carnival, a living world away from the earth. It is like the great Ariaria market of Aba, or the Oreorji in Nkpa the time before the coming of the White Man. Voices! Voices! People, all dressed in spotless shawls, walking about or gathered in *omu*-ringed circles around a big earthen pot of fire. I located the one in which the Okeoha's kindred had gathered. And it was not hard to find. The eminent fathers were there. The ones who had died at a ripe old age, a long, long, long time ago. Too numerous to mention. There was, for example, Chukwumeruije, and his brother, Mmereole, the great Onye-nka, sculptor of the face of ancestral spirits. His sculptures and masks of the deities; the faces of many arunsi, *ikengas* and agwus; and pottery have been displayed as some of the great arts of the Igbo people. This man left the earth more than six hundred years ago.

The great mothers dwell here, too. Too numerous to mention. Most notable, for instance, was Oyadinma Oyiridiya, the great dancer, who was synonymous with the saying *At the pleasure of gazing at her waist, we slaughter a goat*. Among many others, there were Uloaku and Obianuju, the head of one of the greatest umuadas in history, one whom Ala herself, the supreme deity, had pomaded with her honey-coated lotion and who poisoned the waters of the Ngwa clan many centuries ago.

Anyone who saw this group would know at once that my host belongs to a family of illustrious people. They will know that he belongs to the genealogy of people who have been in the world for as long as man has existed. He is not of the class of those who fell from trees like mere fruits! It was thus with utmost reverence and humility that I stood before them, my voice like a child's but my mind like an elder's:

—Nde bi na' Alandiichie, ekene'm unu.

'Ibia wo!' they chorused.

—Nde na eche ezi na'ulo Okeoha na Omenkara, ekene mu unu.

'Ibia wo!'

I was silenced by the stately voice of Nne Agbaso, which was as shrill as that of a caged bird. She began singing the usual welcome song, 'Le o Bia Wo,' her voice as enchanting and serenading as that of Owunmiri Ezenwanyi and her crew. Her song rose and scattered solemnly through the air and surrounded the gathering, crawling up and encircling every man. And so silent did they become that I was made acutely aware again of the absolute distinction between the living and the dead. Afterwards, she rattled a string of cowries and performed the ritual of authentication to ensure I was not an evil spirit pretending to be a chi: 'What are the seven keys to the throne room of Chukwu?' she said.

—Seven shells of a young snail, seven cowries from the Omambala river, seven feathers of a bald vulture, seven leaves from an anunuebe tree, the shell of a seven-year-old tortoise, seven lobes of kola nuts and seven white hens.

'Welcome, spirit one,' she said. 'You may proceed.' I thanked her and bowed.

—I'm the chi of your descendant Chinonso Solomon Olisa. I have been with him from the earliest emergence of his being, when Chukwu called me forth from the Ogbunike cave where guardian spirits wait to be called into service and told me to guide his foot in daylight and to shine the torch on to his path at night. On that day, I had just gone to Ogbunike from the mortuary in Isolo General Hospital in Lagos, a land far from Alaigbo but a place where many of the children of the fathers now live. Ezike Nkeoye, who now sits over at the gathering of the kin of my host's mother, had just died, and I had been his chi. He was just twenty-two. The day before, this bright student of the White Man's education had gone to bed after studying. I had stayed in him, watching as he slept, the way guardian spirits are called to do. And indeed he was asleep. Then he woke suddenly, clutched his chest, and fell out of bed and on to his neck so that it snapped. The agreement with onwu, the spirit of death, was swift because he, like the rest of your children, does not have an *ikenga*. In a moment after the fall, he was dead.

—Even though I had lived among mortal men many times before, I was shocked by this. So quickly had it happened, and with such intensity, that I was left without a word in my mouth. Death had come to him swiftly, with the violence of a young leopard. Only the previous day, he had been kissing a woman, but he was now gone. So strange was it that I did not go at once to report to Chukwu in Beigwe, as we guardian spirits are required to do. I did not immediately escort his spirit to Alandiichie, either. But at the time, I went with his body in the ambulance to the place where it would be kept at the mortuary. It was then I became satisfied he was dead and brought his onyeuwa with me to here, to the compound of the Ekemezie kindred of Amaorji village. After I left here, I hastened to Ogbunike, to rest and wash in its cataract, in water so warm and ancient it still carried the peculiar smell of the world at creation. I was lying in the stream when I heard Oseburuwa's voice summoning me and asking me to ascend forthwith to Alandiichie, as Yee Nkpotu, the ancestor whose incarnate my host is, was ready to be reborn. As you know, a man and a woman can sleep together for eternity. If one of you here has not decided to return to the earth, conception is impossible. Thus knowing that conception was about to happen, I swiftly heeded his call.

—So on the night my host was born, I brought his ancestral spirit from here in Alandiichie, and you all were distant witnesses as I took his onyeuwa away to Eluigwe, where it was received with wondrous celebration. Then I led it from the Eluigwe fanfare to accompany him to Obi-Chiokike, where the great fusion between spirit and body to form *mmadu* – the ultimate bodily expression of creation – happens. That was a glorious day. The white sands of Eluigwe, glistening with pebbles that bore in them the very essence of purity, was the ground on which we marched. We were followed in the distance by a group of the adaigwes, the spotless, luminously beautiful maidens of Eluigwe who sang of the joy of living on earth, of the innumerable cravings of man, of the duty of the mind, of the desires of the eyes, of the virtues of living, of the sorrows of loss, of the pain of violence, and of the many things that make up the life of a human being.

—The family and household of Okeoha and Omenkara, you all have been there and know that the journey to the earth is far but not tiring. In your oracular wisdom, you liken this journey to the proverbial sturdy egg that falls from the nest of the raven, tumbles down through the black branches of the ogirisi tree, and lands on the ground unbroken. The road is beautiful beyond words. The trees that stand in the distance on both sides of the inner road not only provide deep vegetation, they are also transparent, like the silvery calico veils weaved by Awka women. The trees bear golden fruits, and on them, within them and outside of them stand a chattering of emerald birds. They glide around the procession, swinging their wings in the thermal, diving and playing as if they, too, were dancing to the song of the procession. As I walked, they shone in the pure light that filled the road. I could not tell when we reached the great bridge that serves as the crossing between Beigwe and the earth. But just before we reached it, the women stopped in their tracks and raised their voices in a strange, spectral song. Their lovely tunes turned, suddenly, into a threnody, and they sang with trembling voices. Their cries rose as they sang about the suffering in the world, the evils of man-pass-man, the shame of disgrace, the affliction of infirmities, the wounds of betrayal, the suffering of loss and the grief of death. They were joined by the onyeuwa and I had bonded with them and with the dwellers of Eluigwe, who stopped every time we passed by to say, 'May he who is going to uwa have peace and joy!' and even with the flock of white hornbills, the sacred birds of Eluigwe, who hovered around us, beating their wings in obeisance.

—Afterwards, as if signalled by an unseen banner, the singers separated from us and waved at us from a distance. They waved. The birds did, too, as they hung suspended above the bridge as if there was a line they could not cross which neither I nor the reincarnating spirit could see. We waved back, and once we stepped on the bridge, I found myself in a place I seemed to have been before. The place was filled with a bright light similar to that of Eluigwe, but this was man-made. The source of light was thronged by moths and apterous insects. A gecko stood beside one of the lightbulbs at the arc of a wall, its mouth full of the insects. On a bed under the bulb of light, a man screamed, trembled and collapsed against a sweating woman. The onyeuwa entered into the woman and merged with the semen. The woman did not know or realise that the great alchemy of conception had happened within her. I joined the onyeuwa and became one with the man's seed, and in joining we became a *divisible* one.

—Ndiichie na ndiokpu, *unu ga di*.

'Iseeh!' the eternal bodies chorused.

—From that moment on, I have watched over him with my eyes as wide as a cow's and as sleepless as a fish's. In fact, were it not for my intervention, or were I a bad chi, he would not have been born in the first place.

To this, a cold murmur echoed through the gathering of this deathless throng.

—It is true, blessed ones. It was in his eighth month, while in his mother's womb. She was seated on a stool sandwiched between two buckets, one containing clean water, with a transparent film lying over it, a spill from suds, and the other containing muddied water, in which clothes are soaked. A packet of Omo detergent lay on the pile of unwashed clothes. She had not seen, nor had her chi warned her, that a poisonous snake, sniffing the wet earth around her and the dewy smell of the tree leaves and shrubs around the place, had crept under the pile of clothes and begun to suffocate. But I stood out of my host and his mother, as I frequently do until my hosts possess their bodies in fullness. I could see it – the black snake slithered into one of the legs of a pair of trousers, and as she made to pick it up, the snake bit her.

—The strike had an immediate impact. From the dazed look on her face, I could tell that it was a terrible sting. On the spot where she'd been bitten, a deep-coloured bead of blood appeared. She screamed so loudly that the world around rushed to her aid. Once the snake bit her, I became aware that the poison could travel and kill my host in his abode in the womb. So I intervened. I saw it moving towards my host, who was then only a foetus asleep in the sac of the womb. The venom was full and hot and powerful, instant and destructive, and violent in its movement through her blood. I asked her chi to force her to cry so loudly that neighbours would immediately gather. A man quickly fastened a rag around her arm, a little above her elbow, stopping the venom from travelling further up and causing the arms to swell. The other neighbours attacked the snake and dashed it into a paste with stones, their human ears deaf to its pleas for mercy.

—You all know that it is my duty to know, to probe the mysteries around the existence of my host. And truly, even a goat and a hen can assert that I have seen and that I have heard many things. But I have come here mostly because my host is in serious trouble – the kind that can cause the eyes to bleed instead of shed tears.

'You speak well!' they said.

—The men of your kin say that even a man who stands on the highest hill cannot see the whole world.

They murmured in agreement, 'Ezi okwu.'

—The men of your kin say that if a person desires to scratch his hands or an itch on most other parts of his body, he does not need help. But if he must scratch his back, he must ask others to help him.

'You speak well!'

—This is why I have come: to seek an answer, to seek your help. Dwellers of the land of the living dead, I fear that a violent storm has petitioned for the closure of the only road to the utopian village of Okosisi, and it has been granted its request.

'*Tufia!*' they spat in unison. To which one of them, Eze Omenkara himself, the great hunter who in his lifetime travelled as far as Odunji and brought home a great deal of game, stood to speak.

'Ndi ibem, I greet you. We cannot wave our hands to swat away a snake threatening to bite us as we do mosquitoes. They are not the same.'

'You speak well!' they said.

'Ndi ibem, kwenu,' he said.

'Iyaah!' they said.

'Kwe zueenu.'

'Iyaah!'

'Guardian Spirit, you have spoken like one of us. You have spoken like one whose tongue is matured, and indeed your words stand on their feet, they stand – even now – amongst us. Yet we must not forget that if one begins bathing from the knees up, the water may be finished by the time one gets to the head.'

They shouted, 'You speak well!'

'So tell us about this storm that threatens our son Chinonso.'

AGBATTA-ALUMALU, I told them everything as my eyes had seen it, and as my ears had heard it, and as I have now conferred to you. I told them about Ndali, his meeting at the bridge, and his love for her. I told them about his sacrifices, how he sold his home. I told them about Jamike, how he swindled my host, and how my host, thinking he had been saved by the white woman, now lay unconscious, having possibly killed another man.

'You speak well!' they chorused.

Then there was silence amongst them, a silence like one that is impossible on earth. Even Ichiie Olisa, anguished that his son had sold the land, merely gazed into the hearth with empty eyes, as silent as a dead log. A group of them, about five, rose and went to a corner to confer. When they returned, Ichiie-nne, Ada Omenkara, my host's grandmother, said, 'Do you know anything about the laws of the people of this new country?'

—I do not, great mother.

'Has he killed a man before?' Ichiie Eze Omenkara, the great-great-grandfather of my host, said.

—No, he has not, Ichiie.

'Spirit one,' Eze Omenkara said now, 'perhaps the man he hit with a chair will survive. We bid you return to watch over him. Do not proceed to Beigwe to report to Chukwu until you know for sure that he has killed this man. We hope – if he was hit by a chair alone – that he would not die. Make your eyes as those of a fish and return here when you have another word for us.' Then, turning to the others, he said, 'Ndi ibem, have I spoken your minds?'

'Gbam!' they chorused.

'A chi who falls asleep or leaves its host to go on journeys – except when necessary, as this one is – is an *efulefu*, a weak chi, whose host is already a lamb bound with twine to the slaughter pole,' he continued.

'You speak well!'

—I hear you, Dwellers of Alandiichie. I will go back now, then.

'Yes, you may!' They cried, 'Go well the way you have come.'

—Iseeh!

'May the light not quench on your way out.'

—Iseeh!

I turned to leave them, they who are no longer susceptible to death, relieved that at least I had found some respite from my panic. And as I travelled, not turning back, I wondered: what was that beautiful voice that rose again in a song to bid me onwards?

CHUKWU, thus was my journey completed. I flew through a long stretch of the flaming night, past white mountains of the furthest realms of Benmuo, on which black-winged spirits stood, speaking in sepulchral voices. As I neared the sublime borders of the earth, I saw Ekwensu, the trickster deity, standing in his unmistakable garb of many colours, with his head carried on his long neck, which stretched about like a tentacle. He stood on a limb above the moon's disc, gazing at the earth with his wild eyes and laughing to himself, perhaps devising some evil trick. I had seen him in the same spot twice before, the last time seventy-four years ago. As in the past, I avoided him and proceeded towards the earth. And then, with the alchemic precision with which a chi finds its host no matter where in the universe he may be, I arrived at the place where my host lay and fused with him. I saw at once by the clock on the wall that I had been gone for nearly three hours, in the White Man's measure of time. He had been revived, Egbunu. Stitches laddered down on his face, and a big bloody piece of cotton wool was sticking out from his mouth where his teeth had been broken. There was no one else in the room, but by his bed a thing with a screen like a computer sat, as if keeping him company, and from his arm stretched a small bag that hung on a pole, and in it was blood. His eyes were closed, and in his blurred vision, the image of Ndali looking at him had stood, as if bound to his mind with an unbreakable cord.

THREE

Third Incantation

GAGANAOGWU, may your ears not strain—

Even as I stand here, I can hear the singing, the joy, the sweet tune of the flutes. I have been to this palace where you dwell, many times. I know that the guardian spirits and their hosts will come to you here for your final approval of their rebirth, for a reincarnation into a fresh body, and live on earth again as a newborn—

The fathers say that a man does not stand on burning coals barefoot because his feet are wet—

One does not dance near the pit of venomous snakes because one's *obi* is too small—

The wingless bird said I should spit into a calabash with holes, but I say to it, my saliva is not meant to be wasted—

The head that stirs the wasp's nest bears its sting—

The one-eyed serpent of shame shelters near my door. May I? it asks. No, I say. I don't want your terrors in my abode—

Destruction says to me, 'Shall I come under your roof and pitch my tent?' I say, 'No. Go and tell whoever sent you that I am not at home. Tell them you did not see me'—

Egbe beru, ugo ebekwaru, onye si ibe ya ebela nku kwaaya—

May the words I shall continue to speak hasten to the conclusion of my account—

May my tongue, as wet as a mangrove, not dry of words—

And may your ears, Chukwu, not tire from hearing me—

May this incantation usher in a fruitful end to my testimony tonight, after which I will leave the halls of Beigwe and return to the waiting body of my host—

Iseeh!

18

THE RETURN

AKANAGBAJIIGWE, the universe does not dwell on the past, gathering around the miasma of burned-out fires like a pack of crows. Rather, it forges ahead, always on the winding path of the future, stopping only briefly at the present to rest its feet like a weary traveller. Then, as soon as it is rested, it moves onwards, it does not turn back. Its eyes are the eyes of time, cast perpetually forward and never looking back. The universe travels on no matter what happens to its inhabitants. It proceeds, crosses the footbridges, scales the ponds, circles the craters, and continues. Has a conflagration destroyed a nation? No matter. If such a thing has happened in the morning, it does not matter because the sun will rise, as it has done for as long as the world has been, and in that selfsame city, the sun will set and night will descend. Has an earthquake devastated a land? It does not matter; it will not interrupt the seasons at all. And the life of the universe is reflected in the lives of those who live in it. Has the patriarch of the family been killed? The children must sleep this night and wake up tomorrow. Everyone continues, carried forward like old leaves on the river of time.

But although the universe continues its journey, carrying all the living with it, there is a place where a man can remain still, as if his personal universe has halted. This place is one humans dread because it is a place where they do nothing. They do not so much as stir. They are locked in like captured animals in a circumscribed space. One who is here has his diameter marked out as if by an invisible ink that says, 'From this wall to this wall, from this length to that length, is all there is for you in the world.' But I must establish, Agujiegbe, that a man whose movement is limited – that man is not truly alive. The passage of time mocks him. And this is what happens in confinement.

For in this place, almost no new memory can form. The man wakes in the morning, eats, excretes in the small hole which he covers with a lid after he has washed it down with water that he fetches in a small bucket from the tap in his room. Then he sleeps. When he wakes up again, if it is night, it is night; if it is morning, it is morning. Only a shadow of light rears its feeble head into the cell like the head of an infant snake. If it is daylight, the light comes in a single rod through the window at the top of the high wall near the old ceiling. The window is closed off with strong iron bars.

A man sits here all day, merely alive, the enamels of life peeling away from him and withering into flecks at his feet. The world conceals itself from such a man. It conceals its deepest and most shallow secrets and even its non-secrets. He knows nothing of what is happening, sees nothing, and hears nothing. The bridge he'd crossed to get here, like one constructed by a retreating army, has been destroyed behind him, and all the links with the known world with it. And now he is confined to this space – for however long he must stay. It does not matter. What matters is that his life is stagnant. He spends the day gazing at the walls or the bars that lead out to the other cells until his eyes grow weary from looking. Every now and then he sees something move about in the field of his vision, but soon it is lost to his eyes. No new memory is made of it, for such things, occurring as they do, appear like weak animals who pound their fists against the sealed door of his noiseless humanity and then retreat. Or the vacuous insects that rush to a lightbulb and perform a withering ritualistic dance that only results in their own death. I have seen it many times, Egbunu.

As soon as my host was taken from the hospital, where he had been for two weeks, to the cell where he would stay in solitary confinement, he could make no new memories. If in a rare case a man makes new memories while in prison, they are often the things he does not wish for but which are done to him. They are not wilful history. Because a man has no control over this kind of thing, it lodges in him without recourse to his will. For once he has witnessed a thing, it slips as if through a crack into the mind and stays there. It does not go away.

My host stayed in this state for four years. To chronicle these four years, to labour over the monotony of living, the anguish of still life, is comparable only to the pain of a slave, as I saw in my past host, Yagazie. For a prisoner, too, is a slave, a captive of the government in this strange country. For many cycles, I have known the darkness of youthful hearts, wallowed in the mud of the ambitions of many men, and peeked into the graves of their failures. But I have never seen anything like this.

Now he has returned back to the land of the living and to his own land. The process that led to his return to the land of the fathers happened very quickly. For in the early morning of his troubles, I had tried to save him. Once the police took him to the hospital and he was alone in a room, unconscious, I had no choice but to do that which a chi must do as a last resort, when all the strength of man has failed: I went to Alandiichie to seek the intervention of his ancestors, an account of which I have now rendered to you.

One morning, in the fifth month of his fourth year in prison, his release happened suddenly, without warning. Nothing had prepared him for it. He was seated, his back resting against the wall whose paint had peeled from his resting against it for so long. He was in that moment thinking about some inconsequential things – of the choreography of ants on a hill, then of maggots in a decayed can of milk, and then of small birds congregating on a wild tree – when the bars of his cell began to be unlocked. A guard and a man dressed in a suit stood on the threshold, and the man told him in the language of the White Man that he was being released.

He followed them to an interrogation room, and later, the interpreter would tell him that his case had been reviewed. The primary witness falsified her initial testimony. He had not gone in to rob or rape her, as had been reported, but she had taken him to her house of her own will. It was her husband who had become jealous and in a fit of rage descended on her and him. My host had merely tried to save her by attacking the man. This, the woman now reported, was the truth about what happened. Gaganaogwu, this was not what was told to the police at all! Quite the opposite. The woman and her husband had conspired against my host, an innocent man, and had said that he tried to rape her. They'd said that it was in the process of doing it that her husband had found her struggling with him and intervened by knocking him, the assailant, unconscious.

After he heard these things, he said nothing to the guard and the interpreter. He merely sat there staring at the well-dressed man with the files and the interpreter but not seeing them. His eyes had now grown accustomed to registering an image, then immediately disregarding it, and moving on. He kept his gaze unbroken on a great blank wall, a magnificent nothing which, however, had occupied his vision and his mind.

'Mr Ginoso, do you have anything to say?'

When he did not respond, the interpreter bent his mouth towards the ear of the other as if to kiss him, and the two came forth nodding. It was a strange thing, even to my host. One of the men spoke in haste, and the other nodded effusively.

'My friend Ms Fiona Aydinoglu wants to offer her apologies. She is very sorry for what happened. Again, this is her lawyer. And she has asked us to give you this money. She wants us to do all we can to help you regain your life.'

He said nothing, and his eyes remained where he had cast them – on a fly that was droning between the window and the netting located behind the table where the two men were seated.

'Mr Ginoso.' It was the non-English-speaking lawyer who spoke now, perhaps worried that his interpreter had not delivered his message in a clear enough way and that it was better for the originator of the message to deliver it, no matter how battered the language. Surely it would mean more. Surely it would be respected. 'I say truth now, my client only truth. We are very very sorry, your sufferingk. Very sorry. For many—' He turned to his friend and asked something. 'Years, *yani*, years. For many years Fiona is sad because this. She sorry, very sorry, my friend. Please, Mr Ginoso, you must accept her sorry.'

He said nothing to this man, either. For four years, all that needed to be said and discussed with these people had been said. And afterwards, words had lost their usefulness and had evolved into something else, something without form, amorphous, worthless. In their place, contempt had rooted and blossomed. A man of little rage, he'd become vandalised by a spiritual politics into which he had been unwillingly conscripted. And now so strong was the contempt he felt that while the men spoke, his mind came alive with vivid conjurations of violence. The man in the police jacket he saw lying on the floor, his throat slit with a knife in my host's hand from which blood trickled on to the lifeless body. The lawyer he saw gasping, the man's tongue hanging out of his mouth as my host strangled him against the wall.

Even if faintly, my host realised that this was the person he had become. Without knowing it, something in him had changed. For the spirit of a man may long endure pitiless circumstances, but eventually it will stand erect, unable to take any more. I have seen it many times. In place of submission, rebellion will erect itself. And in the place of endurance, resistance. He will rise with the vengeance of a black lion and execute his cause with a clenched fist. And what he will do, what he will not do, even he will not expect.

Egbunu, the man of rage – he is one whom life has dealt a heavy hand. A man who, like others, had simply found a woman he loved. He'd courted her like others do, nurtured her, only to find that all he'd done had been in vain. He wakes up one day to find himself incarcerated. He has been wronged by man and history, and it is the consciousness of this wrong that births the change in him. In the moment the change begins, a great darkness enters him through the chink in his soul. For my host, it was a crawly, multi-legged darkness shaped like a rapidly procreating millipede that burrowed into his life in the first years of his incarceration. The millipede then yielded a number of progeny, which soon began eating him up, so that by the third year, the darkness had snuffed out all the light in his life. And where there was darkness, light could no longer encroach.

For most of the time, the man of rage is consumed with one passion: justice. If he has been stuck, to strike back at those who had stuck him. If he has lost someone, to regain it from those who had stolen it. This is important because that recovery is the only way he can become himself again.

In my host's case, the meeting with the lawyer and his interpreter was the first time he had to act on his emotions in a long time. In confinement, what he felt at any time was meaningless because he could not act on it. What use, for instance, was it to feel anger? There was nothing he could do about it. To feel love? Nothing. Everything he felt he swallowed back down into the belly of his incapacitation.

He would realise that 'Mrs Fiona', whom he never saw again after her last appearance in court, had insisted that the money be put in his bags if he refused to take it and returned to Nigeria with him on the flight. 'Not deportation,' a very young black woman who'd identified herself as a Nigerian, one of the many people who'd spoken to him, had said. 'They have asked you – your university offered to give you a free scholarship as compensation if you still want to attend and remain in TRNC, but you have refused to say anything at all to any one of them. Because you refuse to talk, even to me, they are returning you to Nigeria, with everything you brought here.'

Even to that woman, although he had given her his attentive gaze, he did not speak. This was why those who sought to do something about him or for him had refrained and merely resorted to parsing out meaning from his little gestures – side glances, shakes of the head, even non-communicative actions like coughs. So they had concluded, or decided, that his not speaking meant that the only thing he wanted was to return home. They looked on his university admission forms and contacted his next of kin, his uncle. Then they drove him two days after his first release to the airport. They gave him tickets and put him on the plane and told him that they had contacted his uncle and that he would be waiting for him at the airport in Abuja. Then, wishing him good luck, the lawyers, the Turkish-Cypriot government officials, one of the officials of the school he had been admitted to, and the Nigerian woman waved him goodbye. Even to this he did not respond.

He did not utter a word until the plane took off. At once dead events opened their eyes, and long-forgotten images began to rise from the graves of time. As the country in which his story had been rewritten became reduced to only a speck, he found himself struggling again to retrace the trajectory of his journey. How had he come to this place where such unheard-of things were done to him? He waited for a moment as the answer stirred in ripples from beneath the tundra, then floated to the surface of his mind: he had come to be able to be with Ndali, whom he'd thought about for most of these years until, tormented by persistent fears and imaginations and dreams that she had left him, he stopped letting himself think of her. He recalled the party at her father's house and his humiliation. He remembered Chuka, who had tormented him. The plane was landing in Istanbul when memories of his poultry emerged, wet and shimmering. He watched the coops and himself feeding them, as he'd done hundreds of times these past four years. He gazed at himself marking the wall of the coops with the dates of the last general cleaning, which he did every two weeks. He saw himself harvesting eggs from the coops, blowing away earth and feathers and putting them in a bag. Then, in an undefined time in the past, he saw himself registering the birth of the newborn chicks into the big six-hundred-leaf foolscap record book whose cover had fallen away, which, in its first seventy-something pages, still bore his father's handwriting. Then he was out in the big Ariaria market, selling a cage full of the yellow broilers and an albino cockerel whose comb had been torn in half during a fight with another cockerel. Chukwu, the memory of these things, even after these many years, broke his heart again.

AGUJIEGBE, as the plane neared the country of the children of the great fathers, I left the body of my host, hungry to see again the beautiful rain forests of Alaigbo, this land where the velvety green shades of the morning become a shuddering veil at night. The trees, unhindered in their growth, stand in their multitudes, drinking from the restless rain. When one soars over them, looking down into the forests as a thing with wings, the forests appear as dense as the viscera of an antelope. Within the forests are rivers, streams, ponds and the sacred waters of the gods (Omambala, Iyi-ocha, Ozala, amongst others). One does not walk for too long outside the limits of the forests before one comes into the boundary of a village. What one first sees are more trees with edible fruit – bananas, pawpaw, green mangoes, the kinds that are rare in the deep of the forests. In the time of the fathers, the huts gathered in a nest. And an accumulation of these, stretching merely a few stone throws, would make a village. In this time, villages have expanded into towns, and the forests have encroached upon the habitation of man. But the beauty of the land remains; the quiet peaks of the hills and valleys, magnificent to those who walk to see them. This is what I have missed in the time my host has been away, and this was the first thing I went to see – when my host and his uncle who'd picked him up at the airport arrived in the land of the great fathers.

He and his uncle did not speak about anything concerning his situation until they reached Aba, where only two years before, the older man retired from civil service. All through the journey, whether in the taxi that brought them from the airport or the bus that took them on the eight-hour trip from Abuja to Aba, they'd been in the company of strangers. But now, at the entrance into Aba, with the bus stopped at the shoulder of the highway for passengers to ease themselves in the bushes, his uncle, while urinating, asked him if anything bad had happened to him in the prison. At first, he did not speak. He was standing a little ahead of his uncle, urinating into an old beer bottle which stood among the creepers, half filled with what must be rainwater. He released his urine into it until the bottle, filled, fell and emptied into the bush. The old man spoke on, saying he'd heard accounts and speculations about how Africans in prisons abroad are treated 'li-like dogs'. At this he stared at his uncle, who had finished and was now waiting for him to zip up. It seemed his eyes betrayed that which his mouth could not say, for his uncle caught his eyes, and then shook his head in agonising pity.

'You m-ust th-th-than-k God for your lai-life,' his uncle said. 'Of co-co-urse you ma-made a bi-bi-g mistake by go-ing there. Bi-g-big mis-take. But you m-m-ust t-han-k God.'

When they arrived at his uncle's house, at the sight of his aunt, whom he had not seen since his father's funeral and who was now much older, with a shock of grey hair, he broke down. Later, when his uncle returned to the room they had given him, which belonged to their son, who had gone on the NYSC service in Ibadan, he still could not speak of the things the older man had asked of him.

Gaganaogwu, you made all things, and you know that what our hosts cannot say, we – their chis – cannot say. For it is a universal truth that *onye kwe, chi ya e kwe*. Hence, what he has not affirmed to, I cannot affirm. And thus if he is silent over something, I must be silent, too. What he does not want to remember, I do not remember, either. Yet even though my host could not speak of these things, he constantly thought about them. They lodged like secret blood in the veins of every passing day. At every bend in the day, they emerged and ambushed him. And sometimes when he lay down in his bed and stared at the lightbulb or the kerosene lamp, as he'd become accustomed to doing since his release from prison, the memories emerged in vivid colours, as if they'd been imprisoned in the bulb or lamp and had broken free.

He embarked on the task of rebuilding himself with these things a constant torment on his mind. But as days passed, he found that they little occupied his mind. What dwelt more with him was the enormous riddle life had placed before him, which he wanted badly to solve. At first, he stayed away, far away from this riddle, and tried not to solve it, for his uncle would have deemed him crazy for even harbouring such thoughts. The older man had said in unequivocal terms that anything that brings such pain and suffering on a person is not worth having. His uncle, a man supple with the oratory of the old fathers, whose tongue dripped with the oil of convincing imagery and proverbs, had asked him, in the soft, tender way he spoke, what use it would be for a man to pick up a scorpion because of the beauty of its skin and put it in his pocket. When my host did not offer an answer – for such a question as this was not meant to be answered – the older man continued, 'No, n-no, that would be foo-fo-foolishness.'

But once he left his uncle's house, with the five thousand euros the German woman had paid him as *damages* – as part of the punitive measures against her – he returned to Umuahia and rented a flat. He opened a feed-and-mash store on Niger Road, and with what was left of it he bought a motorcycle.

In the weeks that followed, brick by brick by brick, he reconstructed his life. Akwaakwuru, if a tortoise has been upturned, even if it takes a long time, it will slowly try to return to its feet. It might be that the tortoise cannot at first because a stone has hedged it in, so it must turn the other way. This might be the only way it can rise again. Egbunu, he must continue, for to be still is death. So by the end of the month, when his uncle and aunt visited him and said he had 'risen', he believed them. For when he stood at a remove from the once broken things which had now been rebuilt, he agreed that at least the beginning of his life's reckoning had been initiated. This was a soothing feeling. It gave him courage, and it was only after that that he turned again to the riddle and began to advance towards solving it.

The effort took him one evening, two months after he returned to the land of the fathers, to a mansion on Aguiyi Ironsi Layout, which, with much difficulty, he located. It was older, and the sculpture of Jisos Kraist on the gate had been removed, peeled off, leaving the imprint of its presence like a scar. In front of the gate, between the fence and a new culvert, a sedge with brittle stems had sprouted, and a young tree had risen from the sewage at the end of the road. He'd reached this gate with his heart pounding, and so he could not stop, could not give the place – where Ndali had been living before he left Nigeria – more than a passing glance. For suddenly, he'd felt overwhelmed by the memories triggered by the sight. And in haste, he rode past the mansion into the darkening streets.

I stayed back, Oseburuwa, for one of the most difficult missions of my existence in the nearly seven hundred human years since you created me had happened in front of that gate. Not long after my host began his prison sentence, I could not bear the sight of his suffering. An innocent man, *onye-aka-ya-kwuoto*, punished for a crime he did not commit. I was as shattered as he was. He'd done all this to be able to marry Ndali, and now he'd destroyed himself. For her sake. I wanted her to know about it, but saw that there was no way for him to contact her, and I, a mere spirit, incorporeal, cannot write a letter or make a call. So, Egbunu, I resorted to *nnukwu-ekili*, in order to deliver a message to her through the dream space. I had been told that we can use this highly esoteric process to reach a non-host at Ngodo cave more than a hundred years ago by a guardian spirit who had done it, but who had stated that it was rarely attempted. So while my host sobbed in the prison, I embarked on the astral flight and arrived at her house. I projected in and, after moving from room to room, I found Ndali crouched in a corner of her bed, the sheets crumpled, holding on to a pillow while asleep. By her head was one of the photos she'd taken of my host, holding one of the fowls and smiling into the camera. I was about to begin incantations, the first process of *nnukwu-ekili* by which I would have gained access into her dream space, when a presence materialised at the other end of the room. It was her chi.

—Son of the dawn light, you have come to trespass, to anger a spirit who has done you no wrong.

Egbunu, you must understand that I was taken aback by this accusation. I know this guardian spirit will soon come to tell you its version of this encounter, should what I fear has happened to its host actually come to pass, so please remember my account. For in response to its question, I had begun to speak.

—No, no, I merely—

—You must leave! the chi said with vehemence and authority. Look at my host: she has suffered much already, wounded

by Chinonso's decision to leave. Look at how she has been sad,
waiting for him. I hate your host.

—Daughter of Ala, I said, but the chi would not hear.

—This is trespass. Go and let nature take its due course. Do
not interfere in this way or it will backfire. If you insist, I will
take a report to Chukwu.

At this, it was gone. Without hesitation, I left the room and
returned to my host in the far country.

OKAAOME, he could barely sleep that night. He sat in his
one-bedroom flat, the table fan oscillating and droning, and
under the light of the bulb that hung from the ceiling by gaunt
wires taped together, he tried to bring his phone back to life.
The phone had not been turned on since he first took it out
of the bag that held the clothes and shoes he had been wearing
the day he was taken into the hospital, his admission letter and
receipts, and all he'd brought into the prison. He'd fitted its
parts together, but it did not work. One of the policemen had
picked it up from the bloodied floor of the German woman's
house in Girne, and it had not worked since.

He rode his motorcycle the following day, under the cover
of darkness, to the mansion. There was light within it from
some generator buzzing. Everywhere, darkness stood, almost
unblemished, only the light of oncoming vehicles relieving
the streets as they cut their paths through the ample flesh of
gloom. He stopped the motorcycle and dismounted, then he
walked to the gate, and with a courage that came quickly – as
if it had leapt from a clandestine position on to its target –
he knocked on the gate. When the metal began rattling, he
had the temptation to flee. For it occurred to him, now that
he was at the threshold of what he'd been seeking all along,
that he was not prepared to confront it after all. He realised

that despite all that had happened to him, despite the time
that had passed, nothing had changed. He was still an *Otobo*.
He had not acquired higher education; his status had not
changed. In fact, the epiphany deepened with the voice of
rage: things had worsened for him. He had become much
poorer. If he owned a house before, now he did not. If his
heart was once without hatred, now he carried within him a
mighty sack of hate in which many people were trapped. If
he had good looks before, now he wore a battered face, one
from which doctors had to remove a bottle that had stuck in
his forehead, a jaw that had been stitched so that he could not
shave the area for fear of loosening the stitches, and a mouth
from which no fewer than three teeth had been knocked out.
If in the past, his pain and grief had stemmed merely from
things done physically to those he loved, now it came with
a vengeance from things done to him in other ways, too.
For not only had he been physically damaged, he had also
been inwardly broken. He had been penetrated from behind
by another man, violated beyond redemption, flogged out
of his body.

Standing in front of this gate, he became aware of his true
condition. It shocked him, for he had not considered his
wretched state in its completeness this way before. He stepped
back as the gate opened.

'What can we do for you, sir?' the person who emerged
from the gate in the uniform he had once worn said. He was
much younger, perhaps in his late teens.

'Ah, I am looking for, ehm, my friend, Miss Ndali Obialor.
Is this her house?'

'Yes, this is the home of Chief Obialor. But his daughter is
not here now.'

His heart raced. 'Oh? When is she coming back?'

'Madam Ndali? She doesn't live here. She lives in Lagos. Didn't you say you are her friend?'

'Yes, but I have not been in town, many years. Since two o o seven.'

'Okay, I understand, sir. Madam Ndali lives in Lagos since – since two thousand and eight.'

The man had started turning back.

'Good night, Oga.'

'Wait, my brother,' he said.

'Oga, I can't wait anything. I can't answer your question again. Madam Ndali is not here; she is in Lagos, period. Good night.'

The gate shut as it had opened, and he heard the bar fold into its lock. Where he was, darkness returned, along with the sporadic noise of the street. He stood there, his hand on his chest, feeling his heart. For he was relieved that after four years, he'd finally heard something about Ndali, even if it was only a tiny detail. As he rode back to his flat, he wondered what would have happened if he had seen her. Would she have changed as much as he and everything else in Umuahia had? He had almost not recognised parts of the city. Here and there, new markets had been cleared out and pushed from inside the city limits to its outskirts. A telephone communications revolution whose beginning he'd witnessed had been concluded, and now, the city was living in its aftermath. Now everyone owned a mobile phone. Towers of telecommunications companies with acronyms such as MTN, Glo and Airtel were everywhere. On both sides of the street, yellow or green umbrellas stood with tables and chairs under which a man or a woman sat. On the tables were phone cards and SIM cards and a mobile phone operator who charged people to make calls on her phone. Around the streets, new lamps had sprouted with flat panels behind them, which people often simply referred to as 'solar'. A new attitude seemed to have spread amongst the people like a harmless germ, a new bleak humour that trivialised the horrifying, and a litany of lingos which he did not comprehend.

He paid little attention to these changes because his mind was occupied with thoughts of Ndali. When the unforgiving blow of his undoing struck him, at the German nurse's home, he had tried to contact her. As he lay on that floor, in a pool of his own blood, fearing he would die, thoughts of her had stood unshaken in his mind like a guard. He'd relived all the moments when she offered any kind of resistance to his leaving Nigeria, like when she had told him about the dream whose details she did not disclose. Even before he was taken away by the police, he'd seen her watching him, as if merely sitting at the other end of the bloody room. And after they took him away, he'd tried to reach her by phone, but his phone had died. He tried to get a phone, repeatedly begging the nurses, but they told him every time that he could not be helped. The police had given them instructions that he not be allowed access to anything aside from food and treatment. None of the nurses shared any information with him, either. Only one of them could speak the language of the White Man, and even this one struggled to understand him when he spoke. As the days passed, he'd grown frantic, angry and delirious. For he had come to firmly believe that Jamike and the evil spirit seeking to destroy him had been persistent and relentless to the end. And now it had paid off. He'd fought hard, but he'd fought against a foe whose weapons were unsurpassable. Just when he thought he had escaped and was off the hook, he had swum right into another, sharper hook.

The finishing off happened over several weeks, during

which everyone he knew abandoned him. Not even Tobe, who had slowed his journey and bore his cross part of the way, appeared within an inch of the territory of his renewed suffering. Only a representative of the school, one of the old students, together with the vice rector, came to the court during the first day of the trial. They'd secured his property and kept everything for him. If he was freed, it was likely he would be deported, so they would just send his things to the airport. They'd called to inform his uncle. In the frenzy of the moment, he'd begged the Nigerian student Dimeji to help him reach Ndali. With his hands shaking, he'd written down her number.

'What should I tell her?' Dimeji had said.

'What?'

'Yes, what should I tell her?'

'That I love her.'

'Is that all?'

'That is so. I love her. I will *return*. I am sorry for leaving, and I'm sorry for everything.' He'd paused to push the words into Dimeji by the force of his eyes. When Dimeji nodded, he continued, 'But I will return. I will find her. Tell her that I promise. I promise.'

That was it, all they had time for. He never saw Dimeji again. No one whom he'd known prior to the events that led him to trial in a foreign country appeared within sight in the ensuing four years. The only one, the German woman, was his prime accuser. The other, her husband, who had been unconscious in the hospital bed for sixteen days, was his second accuser, corroborating his wife's testimony. This man had maintained that he'd found the black man on top of his wife, struggling. So on that day, the judge had turned to Fiona's husband and spoken to him in English.

'So, Mr Aydinoglu, did you know before that your wife would be seeing this man?'

'Yes, sir. She is a nurse. Good woman who likes to help people. So she wanted to help this poor rapist from Africa. *Walahi yaa!*'

'May we ask you to watch your language before this court, Mr Aydinoglu?'

'Am sorry, Your Lordship.'

'Comport yourself. Now, so you let her bring him into your home?'

'No, she always help people. It is normal for her, *yani*. When I came to my house, he was tryingk to rape her.'

'Can you tell this court what you saw?'

'My wife, *yani*, was on the floor, near to the dining table, and this man was on top of her, and his hand was holdingk her on the neck, one hand. Pardon – the other hand. One, he was tryingk to force himself into her. It was very disgustingk, my lord. Very disgustingk.'

'Go on—'

'I immediately threw myself for him and we began to fight, before I ask my wife to call the police. I had a bottle, so I injured him with it, then went to check my wife, who was still lying on the floor, weeping, breathing very loud. Then, this man came very low behind my back and hit me on the centre of my head here – on this spot, my Lord – with a stool. I fell, sir. That is all I remember.'

Agbatta-Alumalu, the fathers say that the switch that broke the head of a dog must be called something else. There was no more my host could do in his defence. After that second court session, judgment was passed. It was already late by then, five weeks late. The judgment passed by the words of a man's mouth, couched in words – first in the language of the land, then in the language of the White Man – meant nothing because a greater judgement, one passed by actions so powerful they'd imprinted themselves for ever on his mind, had happened to him. So the pronouncement that he was to be sentenced to a combined twenty-six years in prison for attempted rape and attempted murder meant nothing. By that time, already, his life as he once knew it had separated from him like an ill-fated shadow hewn from its bearer and thrown over the cliff into a bottomless pit of oblivion, and even through all these years, he could still hear its dark voice screaming as it continued its fall.

19

SEEDLINGS

GAGANAOGWU, I must here argue that to prove my host's motive in the action I am claiming he is innocent of, you should consider that he has suffered because of his love for this woman. The early fathers say that it was in the hunt for a worthy cause that Orjinta, the mighty hunter of yore, was torn to pieces. Although even amongst the old fathers this was told as a proverbial tale, you know that it happened at a time when Alaigbo was at its prime, when everything was almost as you had intended it to be. Even I had not been created then. The people constructed rectangular houses made from mud bricks, kept their shrines in their *obis*, consulted their ancestors and fed them constantly, and no one trampled on the personal liberty of his neighbour because he believed in the primal law of coexistence. (*Let the eagle perch, let the hawk perch, and if either says the other should not perch, may his wings be broken.*) Orjinta, a young man who had made a habit of calling his betrothed before she grew the age of a clear moon, would crouch behind her father's compound at night and whistle until she would come out, jump out through the window, and follow him into the brush. Orjinta knew it was forbidden to whistle at night, as it bothered the spirits of the living dead in the Ogbuti forest. But a man in love would crawl into a viper's hole to find his lover. He ignored the creatures of the night, who are terrified of human cries and whistles. As he whistled one night, an angered spirit possessed a leopard and drove the beast through the forest, howling, trampling young saplings underfoot, scratching up rows of yams, driven by a hellish fury that was not beholden to even the most basic statute of civilisation. Orjinta whistled on as his woman listened for her parents, for any sound in the house, waiting for the best time to jump out unseen for the night's rendezvous. The beast continued its journey towards him, its track mapped by a devilish magnetic pull towards its prey and its violent strides echoing in the dark terrain of the night, until it found the exact spot at the very moment when Orjinta, raising his head, saw his lover coming. The beast fell on him, and with an anger originating from a time beyond history, before the inception of love and romance, and of flesh and blood, tore him to pieces and dragged his corpse away into the forest.

Egbunu, what are stories like this for? They are meant to warn us about the dangers of such actions as Orjinta took. This was why, starting from my host's second year in prison and after my second encounter with Ndali's chi, I had begun to try to make him forget her. But I have come to understand that such efforts often are futile. Love is a thing that cannot be lightly destroyed in a heart in which it has found habitation. I have seen it many times. And there is an extent to which a chi can make suggestions and it becomes coercion. A chi cannot coerce its host, even in the face of the most violent dangers. Insanity is the result of an irreconcilable difference between a man and his chi. Even among the fathers, consensus was the mode in which they operated. They began every discourse with the bellowing of '*Kwenu*' – an invitation to agree, for if a man in a group refuses to respond '*Yaa*' and says, '*Ekwe ro mu*,' then the discussion cannot continue until the dissenters have given consent.

How, then, can a chi disagree with his host? How can it say to him, 'Leave this pursuit, for it may lead you to dark places,' when his host is determined to continue on this path? Had I not seen that all these years, in the midst of anguish and torment, in the midst of prayers that the nurse would tell the truth and he would be free, the one thing he longed for most of all was to return to her? As unbelievable as it may sound, almost daily, he wept for her. He longed for her. He begged for pen and paper and wrote the letter, but where would he send it? He did not know the address of her house. And even if he could guess, how to send the letter? For the first two years, he lived in terror of the guards. They seemed to have a certain contempt for him, and this was early on, even long before the great evil that happened to him while in the prison. The guards called him *arap* or *zengin* and would often comment on his rape of a Turkish woman. To these men he asked for help in sending his letter, but none paid any heed to him. In his second year, a certain Mahmut, in love with a football player from the country of my host, Jay-Jay Okocha, would agree to post his letter. But only if it was within Cyprus. '*Nijerya, cok para*,' the man would often say. '*Parhali, cok, cok*, big, big, Mr Ginoso.' 'Sorry, my friend.' What about the money he had in the pocket of the clothes he wore on the day he was arrested? 'Sorry, Mr Ginoso, we cannot take. The court lock money. Nobody take money. Sorry. Understand me, Mr Ginoso?' After this man, too, declined, he gave up. He did not know that even I, his chi, had tried to reach her.

So Agujiegbe, I let him lie in bed after he returned from

searching for Ndali that night, and he continued to ponder the possibility of reconciliation with her. But then, as the night deepened, he allowed himself – with a certain back-to-the-wall bravery – to consider that which he'd refused to consider: that he may never have her again. Into the fragile ear of his mind was delivered the thought that enough time had passed. She could have married and had kids by now. She could have forgotten about him, or she could have died. Whom did she know to contact to find out anything about him? There was nobody. He thought with bitter regret that he should have given her his uncle's phone number. Or even Elochukwu's. He resolved that he should not think it was possible that she could still be waiting for him all these years. Enough years have passed, the voice in his head repeated with finality. *She is gone for ever.*

The impact of this realisation struck him with despair. Chukwu, it has always perplexed me how a man's mind sometimes becomes the source of his own confrontation and inner defeat. So floored did he become that night that he considered himself foolish for all those years he'd wasted thinking of her, clinging to pieces of the memory of their time together. Perhaps she was in the arms of another man all those nights when, sleepless, he'd restage a moment of sexual experience with her as vividly as he could, so much that he'd touch himself with the lather of his saliva.

He rose with a sudden cry and smacked the kerosene lamp across the room. Its bulb broke and threw the room into instant darkness, and the sound of glass shattering was trapped in his head. He stood fuming in the dark, his chest heaving, the air filled with the smell of kerosene. But none of this could stop him from wallowing in the fitful thought that a man he does not know has been sucking Ndali's breasts.

He slept very little that night, and over the following days he attended to life with a feeling of having failed in everything. It threatened his existence. Even I, his chi, feared for him. For so lost was he in the new meaninglessness of all things that he veered into oncoming traffic. Twice, he had close brushes with death in accidents that could have killed him. Once, after a car had knocked him and his bike into a ditch, the driver of the car said, 'How come you survived this?' The man and the onlookers who had immediately gathered were astounded. 'Your chi is truly awake!' one said. A third person insisted he must have been saved by an angel, a messenger of the White Man's alusi.

Many times, when tormenting thoughts of his loss of Ndali came to his mind, I would push a counterthought in. *Think of the girl at the mash store who was kind to you and called you a good man*, I would suggest. *Think of your uncle. Think of your sister. The football match. Think of the good future you can have.* Sometimes, when all these failed, I'd try to go with him in the direction he had chosen. I'd try to give him hope that he could still find her. *Think of it this way: love never dies. You see, in that film you saw,* The Odyssey, *in which the man returned after ten years to find his wife still waiting for him, the wife knew that her husband loved her and was just being kept away from her because of the circumstances of life. So she remained faithful through the years, refusing, no matter how much she was pressured, to betray him. Is this not the same situation with you? Is it not, simply, only four years? Only four years.*

It was during one of these moments, on the very day when I reminded him of that movie, that I stumbled by serendipity on to something neither he nor I had given any serious thought to in all those years. I acknowledge that once or twice he'd replayed the experience in his mind, but in none of those times did he consider its possible outcome. They had started making love in the yard in full view of the fowls when, suddenly, she pulled away from him and said it was not good for the birds to witness it. He then carried her into the house, her legs wrapped around his body, her arms clasped around his neck. They'd made love with such intensity that when he started to pull out, she grabbed him so tightly he squirmed.

'Do you love me, Solomon?'

Although all of it – the grip, her apparent unconcern as to whether or not he was about to ejaculate, and the fact that she'd called him by his Christian name, Solomon, which she rarely did – shocked him, he answered, 'Yes—'

'Do you love me?' she asked again, more fiercely, as if she had not heard him.

'That is so, Mommy. I love you. I am about to release.'

'I don't care. Just answer my question! Do you love me?'

'Yes, I love you.'

He'd started to let himself loose, trembling through his speech, and when he'd emptied himself, he collapsed against her.

'Do you know we are now one flesh, Nonso?'

'That is so, Mommy,' he said breathlessly. 'I – I know.'

'No, look at me,' she said, reaching for his face. 'Look at me.'

He swerved to her side and turned to face her.

'Do you know we are now one flesh?'

'Yes, Mommy.'

'Do you know we are now one? No more you or me any more?' She paused, her voice rising, tears running from her eyes. Thinking she'd finished, he started to speak. She said, 'Do you know we are just one now? Us?'

'Yes, Mommy. It is so.'

She opened her eyes, and through the glob of tears, she smiled.

My host sat with this piece of tranquillising memory as if it were a sudden, strange gift from a divine messenger come to help him. It was one of the cherished events of his life, and what she had done was monumental. She had allowed him to ejaculate into her. Yet she'd done it so offhandedly, as if it were a trivial thing. That time, he'd been too shocked to comment on it. But when they made love again later that night, and she held him stiff, forcing him to ejaculate into her as before, he asked why she was doing it. She said she did it to show him she loved him and was ready to marry him at all costs. But what if she got pregnant, then? he'd wondered. In response, she inclined her head, thought about it, perhaps considered how her parents would have taken it, and said, 'So what? Are they my god? You want me to take Postinor?'

'What is that?' he'd said.

'God! Village boy!' she'd said with a laugh. 'So you don't know? It's after morning. A drug women take so they don't get pregnant after sex.'

'Ah, Mommy,' he'd said. 'I did not know.'

As these vivid events revisited him, his slumped hopes opened their weak eyes. Through the days that followed, ideas came to him, possibilities. If she still believed what she'd told him that day – that they were one and the same – she indeed must be waiting for him. She could not have given up after only four years. He began to devise his next moves. Daily, in between measuring out cups of feed, millet, brown seeds and clumps of loam, he would leap into the hole of ideas and rummage within its crevices. It was on the fourth day after the hope-bringing remembrance that he finally dug up something convincing enough for him to consider: whether or not he should return to her house and try to speak with the gateman again. Perhaps the man was poorly paid and he could bribe him to give him some information. Perhaps he could give him the letter he'd written to her in his first weeks in prison. Yes, even that would be enough. The letter contained everything, everything he wanted her to know about his disappearance and his failure to keep his own side of the promise never to leave her.

OBASIDINELU, the great fathers, in their esoteric wisdom, say that whatever a man desires to see in the universe, that he will see. How true, Egbunu! A man who hates another will see evil in whatever that individual does, no matter how well-intentioned. The fathers also say that if a man wants something, if he does not desist from pursuing it, he will eventually find it. I have seen it many times.

It did not cross my host's mind that the universe was about to grant him that which he'd been seeking for many years that day; it was simply the resolve to go to the gateman that formed strongly in his mind and caused him to stop the task he was doing – grinding melon seeds on the manual grinder clamped to the other end of a small bench. He removed his apron, locked his store, and set off for Ndali's family house. As he removed the stone wedge holding the door open, thoughts of what he would miss if he did not commit to his business that day trickled into his mind. In one hour, the agriculture professor who was coming to buy a bag of broiler feed for her poultry would arrive. He would miss the opportunity to sell in one transaction what he sold in a week. But even this did not deter him.

He mounted his motorcycle and raced on to the road towards a roundabout. On the side of the road was a construction site a few square metres long, cordoned off with a zinc roofing sheet held in place by bricks. A man carrying a slab of wood crossed the road dangerously, forcing the traffic to pause until he was on the side of the road, where everywhere sheds were erected. A house with a sun-scorched roof towered above, painted in dim red, with 0802 inscribed on it in white letters. From here he entered Danfodio Road, meandering between a water tanker and a white car whose boot was open, pressed down by the weight of the overload of grain sacks held in place only by strong, tight ropes. On the shoulder of the road, beneath a high billboard, stood a man speaking into a megaphone, surrounded in a half circle by others who carried Bibles, guitars and flyers.

He'd halted because a semi turning in front had temporarily paused traffic. He would have driven on, but that pause – just a few hundred metres from the billboard – allowed him to hear the distinct voice blare from the megaphone. Despite the many years that had passed, he recognised the voice right away. He pulled on to the shoulder of the road, and once he came within view of the man, it became clear to him and me that something extraordinary had happened in the universe. I felt indeed that some great argument had been settled in the realm of the spirits, one which not even I, his chi, had participated in. And now, after my host had given up all hope, after he'd resolved to simply swallow whatever life like an unhinged mother had put in his infant mouth, the universe had heard his pleas and come to his aid.

He'd spent nights pleading with whosoever could hear him to give him only one chance, just one, so that he might find the bearer of this voice again. That he may make the fellow pay for what he'd done to him. He'd made these requests to deities big and small, sometimes to 'God', sometimes to 'Jesus', even once to 'Ala', and once – unexpectedly – to me, his chi. When the prayers went unanswered, or when he thought that was the case, he would recline into himself and spend the time conjuring up images of a confrontation with this man, some more violent than others. One very prominent one was that he would be eating at the restaurant where the man and he had eaten the day he first met him in 2007, and the man – now wealthy from the money he'd stolen from him and others – would walk in with a good-looking woman. The man would walk in with majesty, booming with grace and attended by a chorus of praise from those seated in the restaurant. He would order them all drinks and settle the tab, happy with himself that he was impressing the woman he brought with him. The man must have come on short visits to Nigeria, perhaps thinking his victim might still be in prison. And was thus completely at ease. He would not realise that fate had planted his comeuppance in the form of my host, a vandalised man waiting for him to arrive.

My host would bend his head towards the table to conceal his face so the man could settle into his chosen seat, then he would rise quickly, break the bottle of beer he'd been served, and launch his attack. In attacking, he would be a person he never imagined he could ever be. He would have grown the heart of an executioner – merciless, quick, collateral, brutal. Within the span of a few eye blinks, he'd break the bottle and sink it deep into the belly of his enemy. But that would not be all. He would pull it out and stab it again into the man's chest. He would not be deterred by the inflorescence of blood or its affluent spattering all across the room. He would keep stabbing – at the man's neck, hands, chest – until people would wrest him off the body. But by then, it would all have been done. There would have been a reckoning, as has been known amongst men for thousands of years. He who had come the hard way would have fallen hard. Egbunu, this is the image which, for a long time, had stood in his mind as the truest portrait of the day that he has stumbled into by serendipity.

My host pulled his motorcycle up towards the gathering and had barely dismounted when the man of guilt recognised him, too. The man halted his speech and in haste handed the mega-phone to another who stood by his side, dressed, like him, in the way of the White Man: a shirt, a tie and plain trousers. Then the man ran forward, crying 'Chinonso-Solomon!'

Ijango-ijango, this is one of the instances when I often wish that we, guardian spirits, are able to see what other humans, not our hosts, are thinking. Yes, clearly he looked afraid, but was he truly afraid? Was he as afraid as he should have been? I do not know. All I could see then was that although he hastened towards my host, there was caution in his expression. For he stopped a few steps away from my host. As his enemy drew near, my host realised that things would not be as he'd imagined. For where he had found the man was an open place where he could do nothing. Now stopped in the presence of my host, this man broke down in tears. 'Solomon,' the man said, and inched forward, turned his eyes back to the gathering, and then stretched his hand towards my host, who stepped back slightly. The man's hand came down slowly, trembling as it did. 'Solomon,' the man said again, and turned to face the crowd. 'Brethren, it is him. It is Solomon. Hallelujah! Hallelujah!' He threw his hands into the air and jumped.

Then, without warning, this man for whose death my host had prayed for so long jumped forward and embraced him. In the moment when he should have gripped the man by the neck and started strangling him, the man turned back to the crowd, took the megaphone, and said with genial vehemence,

'God, the God of heaven has answered my prayers! He has heard me! Praise the Lord!' And the crowd cried in response, 'Hallelujah!'

'You don't know, you don't know, brothers and sisters, what the Lord has just done for me,' the man said, and stamped his feet so hard that dust swelled around them.

'You don't know!'

The man brought out a handkerchief and wiped his eyes, for indeed, Egbunu, he was crying. My host looked about now and saw that the crowd was growing. A man and his wife had parked a lorry on the corner and moved closer to witness the evolving scene. An elderly woman had come out of a house on the other side of the street and now leaned on the balcony, watching. Round and about, faces, eyes, encircled him as if with an invisible chain that completely becalmed him.

'This man here is the reason I'm saved. I was a thief. I stole from him and others. But the Lord used him to touch me. The Lord used him to save me. Praise the Lord!'

The people responded, 'Hallelujah!'

Now, was there anything my host could have done with these people surrounding him? No, Chukwu. They were the weapons of finality that neutralised all his vivid conjurations and elaborate plans. What was happening was incomprehensible to him, for now, this creator of all his sorrows took his hand. What could he do but let the man have it? Then he watched, amazed, as the man knelt before him and held his hand.

'Brother Chinonso-Solomon, I kneel here before you, in the name of God who made you and, I and the whole world and … forgiveness, forgiveness. Please forgive me in Jesus's name.'

Although some of the words were lost in the eruption of

static from the megaphone, nearly everyone there seemed to understand. A murmur rose amongst the crowd. A young man in a red shirt and brown tie on which there was an image of a church and cross began to pray, shaking a tambourine whose metal clippings, when knocked against the palm of his hand, released a jingling sound similar to that produced by iron staffs carried by priests and dibias. Even though my host could not hear him, he could sense what this individual was saying. But I, his chi, heard every word of it: 'Lord help him. Lord help him. Let him forgive. Touch his heart. For you made it possible for such a time as this. Lord help him! Lord help him!'

IJANGO-IJANGO, my host stood there, helpless, transfixed, surprised at how his hand trembled as his enemy, who had stood up again, thrust the megaphone into his hands. Once he held it, the crowd erupted. His enemy wept even more vocally, like one mourning a parent. The tambourine attended with a ringing acclamation, and the crowd cheered even louder. My host knew they were waiting for him to speak.

'I ... I,' he said, and brought the megaphone down.

'Help him, Lord! Help him!' the man of guilt said, his words attended by the ritual jiggle of the tambourine.

'Yes! Yes!' the crowd chorused.

'I ... I for—' my host said, and his hands began to shake. For he remembered now, as if an apparition had appeared before his face, the white men gathering as he walked towards his cell. He saw the one with the ugly scar on his face, and another, coming at him with their fists, saying, 'You rape Turkish woman, you rape Turkish woman,' with a flurry of Turkish words he could not understand. He saw himself trying to open the cell and run into it, catching the eye of a black man watching from the distance, while the men kicked him on the back. He saw himself falling against the bars of the cell and gripping them as the men tried to wrest him off.

'Touch him, Lord! Jesus, touch him!' the man in the tie and suit said again, and the strange instrument that produced the jiggling attended.

'Yes! Forgive! Amen!'

'I will forgive,' my host let out.

The eruption of the crowd this time was wild. In the heat of it, reality insulted him even more. Without warning, he whom he should have killed lifted my host's hand like a referee who raises the arm of a victorious wrestler to the cheers of onlookers. My host had, however, just been defeated. For this man was Jamike: the man he'd sought for so long, one of the things that had kept him alive all along. And now, after all those years, he had found Jamike, and what did he do? He'd simply announced that he would forgive.

'Some people say there is no God!' Jamike shouted presently, and the crowd responded with an acclamation. 'They say it is not true what we say we believe. I say shame on them!'

'Shame!' the crowd yelled.

'Who else could save me so? Who else?'

'*Onwero!*'

Agbatta-Alumalu, his anger grew as Jamike – now slim, bespectacled, possessing an innocent gaze, and exuding an unexpected warmth – gave a brief testimony of how he stole everything from 'Brother Chinonso-Solomon' four years ago and how 'Brother Chinonso-Solomon' came to the Turkish Republic of Northern Cyprus but he, the thief, fled south to the Republic of Cyprus. How, two years later, after he had been involved in an accident, he started to rethink his life. So he reached out to people in North Cyprus and was told about the fate of the three people he had duped – one lady at Near East

University had become a prostitute and 'Brother Chinonso-Solomon here, who was sent to prison, and brother, brother Jay'.

Jamike struggled with the last name, and when he finally uttered it, he fell into a caesura of despondency, during which he wiped his eyes with the hem of his shirt.

'Do you know what happened to him because of me?'

'No,' the people replied.

'I heard he committed suicide! He jumped from the top of a building and killed himself.'

The crowd gasped. My host, fearing that he would not be able to restrain himself, detached his hand softly from the man's and put it to his chest as if stifling a cough.

'When I heard that and another story of what I had done, I gave my life to Christ. My brothers and sisters, I began to pray that God would let me see him again to ask for forgiveness. Glory to God!'

'Amen!' the people cried.

'I say glory to God!' Jamike said now, in the language of the White Man, as if the language of the fathers were no longer sufficient.

'Amen!' they repeated.

'*Otito di ri Jesu!*'

'*Na ndu ebebe!*' the crowd shouted.

Jamike turned back to him with eyes that were filled with tears and a face that bore the visible stigmata of his own suffering. My host had not expected this: before him was Jamike, in tears, with a weather-beaten face, cracked lips – a face that bore the insignia of shame. It was not the face of one who has conquered another but of one who has been subdued. The face disarmed him.

Chukwu, the things he was feeling at that moment were in

fact strangely common. I have seen it many times. The face is, beyond all else, naked — a thing of great poverty. It does not conceal itself from anyone, not even strangers. It is that which bears no secret. That which communicates continually, unrestrainedly with the world. Warriors of old amongst the great fathers often told of how, in wars, when confronted with the face of the enemy, they found their resolve to violence weakened. Almost instantly, their drive to kill for the sake of killing became a drive to kill simply in order not to be killed. It becomes as if the warrior, in the presence of his enemy's revealed face, strips himself of all enmity. Egbunu, it is a thing that is hard to understand. Even the wise fathers grappled with it. Their tongue wove many proverbs to explain this phenomenon, but nowhere was it more pronounced than in their articulation of what that powerful emotion is which a man develops for a woman or a mother for her child. They referred to it as *Ihu-na-anya*. For truly, they understood that only when a man is without malice towards the other can he look him in the eye. So when a person says, *I can look you in the eye*, he has expressed affection. And in reverse, a man who is masked, or who is distant — that man can be easily harmed.

I am certain that it was for this reason that my host allowed Jamike to embrace him again and to weep on his shoulder while the gathered crowd shouted 'Hallelujah' and clapped for them. It must have been why — although my host did not know this — he gave this man who had caused him irreparable damage his phone number and nodded in response to his adversary's request to meet the following day at Mr Biggs, down the street.

'At five o'clock?'

'Yes, at five o'clock,' he said.

'I shall be there, Brother Chinonso-Solomon.'

I am certain that it was the confrontation with Jamike's face that made him turn afterwards and make his way through the cheerful crowd that had gathered there. It was why he mounted his motorcycle and raced away from the scene without so much as looking back – not onwards to the place where he had been heading initially, but back to his flat.

20

RECKONING

IKUKUAMANAONYA, anticipation is one of the most curious habits of the human mind. It is a drop of vicious blood in the vein of time. It controls all that is within it and renders a person incapable of doing anything but beg for time to pass. An action delayed by the natural agency of time or human intervention comes to perpetually dominate an individual's thoughts. It bears down against the present until a view of the present is lost. It is why the old fathers say that when a child's food is cooking, the child's eyes are unblinkingly fastened to the top of the hearth. When a person is anxious, he attempts to peek into the unformed time, to try to gain knowledge of an event that has not yet happened. He may see himself already in a country he has not yet travelled to. He may find himself dancing with the people of the place, eating their local cuisine, and walking along the country's scenic parts. This is the alchemy of anxiety, for it is hinged on the promise of something, an event, a meeting, for which a participant cannot wait. I have seen it many times.

In the meantime, though, the man may dwell in much thinking and agony, as my host did after the encounter with

Jamike. He returned full of spite and lunged about his room, kicking at the shelf, the bed, a rubber cup, cursing, raging. He blamed the heavens, the conspiratorial entities, for what had happened to him. He blamed *his* god. Why, he said, did he have to meet Jamike after all these years in such a public place? And why, of all things, was Jamike preaching, a situation that had fettered him? It would have been nearly impossible to assault one who was preaching the gospel. People in Alaigbo and in the world of the Black Man in general revered the kind of man Jamike had become so much that he would not have been able to do anything. He blamed himself for not contacting Elochukwu since he returned. He should not have blamed Elochukwu for the many failures while he was in Cyprus – like failure to help get back his house and get Jamike's location from Jamike's sister. Had my host made contact upon returning, Elochukwu would have told him that Jamike was in Umuahia. He would have simply invited Jamike somewhere secluded and exacted his revenge.

Agujiegbe, I had never before seen my host like he became that night. So angry was he that he cursed, punched the wall, took a knife and threatened himself. In a moment of great uncertainty, when I could not tell if truly this was my host or an agwu who had possessed him, he stood before the mirror, brandishing a knife and saying, 'I will cut myself, kill myself!' He brought the knife close to his chest, and with his hand trembling, his eyes closed, he wagged it so that it touched his flesh. I rushed thoughts into his mind, reminding him first of his uncle, then of the possibility of reunion with Ndali. And I must say, humbly – Chukwu – that I may have helped save my host's life! For my words – *What if she still loves you like Odysseus's wife?* – filled him with sudden hope. He unclenched his fist and the knife fell into the sink, did a mild dance, and settled there. Then he burst into tears. So hard was his pain and so great his grief that I feared he might not recover from it. I put it in his thoughts that it was only the first time he'd met this man since the events had happened. And that they would be meeting the following day, this time in private. His enemy would come to him as he had always wished, and he could do with him what he willed, even show the man the letter he'd written for Ndali, chronicling what had happened to him, so the man could know the gravity of what he had done. He should not think that the wasted opportunity was all he would have. No.

Again, he listened to my voice. I had affirmed a thing, and he'd followed. He washed his face and drained his nose into the sink and wiped his face on the towel that hung by a nail on the wall. He returned to the living room and removed the letter containing the story of his life, which he'd now decided he would show to Jamike the following day. He examined it carefully, trying to make sure the changes he'd made to it two days earlier had not altered its message. In fact, it struck him now that fate, or whatever it was that initiated events, had foreseen this meeting with Jamike. For only two days earlier, he'd woken from sleep in the middle of the night and could not fall back. This had become part of his life since he returned from prison. He had formed the habit of turning on the radio and then listening to it to help him sleep. He'd started to fade out when the voice of a preacher came on. And what was the man talking about? Hell. The same topic he had sometimes thought so deeply about during his years in prison. A place from which no one can escape. From everything the preacher described, as he listened, he realised that if he asked any questions about hell, the speaker's speech would contain all the answers: in hell, there is no redemption. It is a place of perpetual suffering where man is held up like a prisoner and where, the preacher emphasised again and again, 'the worm never dies'.

He turned off the radio and sat to ponder what he'd heard, menaced by his own mind. Then he rose and read the letter he'd written for Ndali. He'd not read it since he returned to the land of the great fathers because he'd felt that all he'd needed to tell her was there. He took a pen now and crossed out the title and wrote under it a new one:

~~My Story: How I Suffered in Cypros~~

My Story: How I Went to Hell in Cypros

When he finished reading through the letter, he was satisfied that nothing had been fundamentally altered. Tomorrow, he would give the letter to the man who had helped him construct it. And he could not wait for that to happen.

CHUKWU, the brave fathers say that a man who has been bitten by a snake becomes afraid of earthworms. For years, time and space had hidden this enemy from him, but that day, he would be alone with the man. He woke the following morning, from a night in which he'd slept little, with a kind of peace. He sat in the bed and let his plans play out till the imagined end, in which Jamike would lie on the floor in a pool of his own blood. He did not yet know of the importunity of hatred, how, even when one resists it and tries to push it away, it merely hoards itself for a moment like a tide, then comes flooding through until the mind is again drowned in it.

Egbunu, I have seen it many times, what men have done from hearts filled with hatred. I cannot describe it all, for time would fail me. But not wanting to stir up further emotion in my host, I watched in silence as his mind ran its bloody errand until, tired, he fell asleep.

It rained for most of that morning. Since he returned to

Alaigbo, he felt the most at home when it poured. This was because most of the earliest memories he formed in Umuahia were shadowed by the presence of storms. The clouds were a constant image in his mind as a child. Claps of thunder, the shrapnel of lightning, these gave this world a beating heart and a memory as vivid as that of war. In some nations, like Ugwu-hausa, other elements might dominate, but rain reigned supreme here. Amongst the Igbo people, the sun was considered a weakling.

He did not go to the store that day, for the rain continued till almost the time when, having run its course, it yielded to sunlight. For the rain is the master of all other elements. The previous day, when he'd encountered Jamike, the sun had emerged early, effulgent against the morning sky. Then slowly, clouds swarmed up and contested its right to stay.

A weak sun was rolling slowly through the pool of wet clouds like a ball through sloam when he stepped out of the house. He peeled the tarpaulin from over his motorcycle and mounted the bike. For the first time since he returned, he carried the bag Ndali had given him. The white print on its leather face was still apparent: CONFERENCE OF AFRICAN AND CARIBBEAN POLITICAL SCHOLARS, APRIL 2002. All its contents were still intact, except for the two photographs of Ndali and her letter. He recalled then how, after he was released from the hospital and taken to the police station, one of the officers brought out the photos while searching the bag. He'd have tried to grab them, but he was handcuffed. The men had passed the photos between them, laughing and saying something, making gestures – the hand slapped against the palm – which, he would later come to understand, meant sex. One of them had spoken to him in halting English: 'You, you like pussy many-many. Black pussy, good? Yes? Good?' It was a moment he would

never forget – one in which his punishment had been extended
to the most innocent of people: Ndali. At the time, many thousands of miles from the land of the fathers, he was witnessing
her being violated by the eyes of strangers. Later, one of the
men, visibly angry at the actions of the others, would take the
photos, put them in the bag, and say to my host, 'I am sorry,
my friend.' Then the man would leave with the bag. He would
not see the bag until his release. When it was handed back to
him, the first thing he looked for were the photos. Her letter
had been removed from his bloodied trousers after he arrived
at the hospital, badly damaged.

Now he carried a knife in the bag, hidden between the
pages of a book. He'd planned it all out. He would get to the
restaurant and sit down calmly at a table by the door for easy
exit once the deed had been done. He would place the book on
the table and eat quickly, for once Jamike came, he would be
too angry to eat. He would try to disarm his enemy by making
him feel at ease, even believing that he'd been forgiven. Then
he would invite Jamike to his flat. He would not use the knife
in a public space. But if the man refused out of suspicion, he
would have no choice but to use the knife right there at the
restaurant. He would stab the man dead and run away to the
bus station and take a bus to Lagos. He would try to locate his
sister or go to his father's village and stay in his father's empty
house there.

Chukwu, I was afraid that this plan, if fulfilled, would
bring him even greater troubles. So I flashed the thought in
his head that if he did all these things he had planned to do
he would lose Ndali for ever. And, I added – although with
great hesitation – that such an act would return him to prison
and deprive him of ever finding her again. He considered this
for a while with fear. He even took out the knife from the bag

and placed it on the table. But then a monstrous rage gripped him again, and he slipped it back into the bag. I will do it, I will kill Jamike and find her, the voice in his head said. I will kill Jamike, I don't care!

Egbunu, often a man, even while knowing that he cannot see the future, plans nevertheless. You see people like that every day, couples dressed up visiting families, telling them their wedding is five months from now. Along the road near the end of the street, there are numerous projects. A man has bought a house, laid the foundation, and hopes to build on it in the future. Even though he can die one minute after laying the foundation, it matters little. In fact, human life revolves around preparations for the future, of which he has little control! This was why, despite all his planning, when my host entered the restaurant, he heard, 'Brother Chinonso-Solomon.' He was startled, as if thrown off horseback. The man he'd seen the previous day stood now, almost alone with him. Across from them was a counter from which a woman watched. Behind her braided head were posted items for sale with their prices.

'My brother, my brother,' Jamike said, coming towards him.

'I want us to just sit down,' he said quickly, in the language of the fathers, although when with this man he primarily spoke the White Man's language.

Jamike, his hands still afloat in the air, stopped. 'Okay, brother,' he said.

My host pointed to the chair near the door and began walking towards it. Jamike followed with a weak smile on his face.

As he sat, he realised that something had happened yet again and had caused him to calm in the presence of this much-hated man. But he could not tell what it was. Suddenly his great, maddening anger was gone, and he sat down slowly in the chair, surprised at himself. Jamike stretched out his hand, and he shook it.

'Madam! Madam!' Jamike cried.

The woman at the counter reappeared from the kitchen, where she'd gone.

'Please bring us two bottles of soft drinks. Cokes.'

'Okay, sir,' the woman said.

He could see, now, that part of what disarmed him was the change he'd seen in Jamike. The man had slimmed down so much that instead of a big, fleshy head, he now had a lean face with protruding cheekbones. His eyes had retreated inwards so that the eyelids hung like small awnings. His thinness was pronounced in the long-sleeved shirt he wore, which was much larger than his diminutive frame. His lips were cracked, with a spit of blood on the ridge between them. His whole constitution was that of an emaciated, suffering man, malarial and gaunt. And in his eyes, there were signs of tears. On the side of the table, he'd set the big Bible he'd brought with him, and now he placed his hand on it and said, 'Brother, I have been looking for you. I have been waiting for you. Many years, my brother. I did not know you had returned. I even asked Elochukwu, but he did not know.'

Egbunu, my host wanted to speak, but it seemed as if the words had been bound with chains within him, and they could not get out.

'Ever – oh God – ever since I heard about your prison. I have been looking for you, Solo. I have been looking for you everywhere.' Jamike shook his head. 'I have been in a very bad state. I have been very very sorry. I have not been myself. I have not – how do I say it? – been alive. God help me. Help your son!'

Then Jamike began to cry. The woman arrived with the

drinks and set them down, her eyes on the weeping man. Then, with an opener, she uncapped both drinks.

'Do you want to order?' she said.

'The drinks are enough,' my host said. 'Thank you.'

'Ah, only drinks?' she said. 'Oga sorry, er.'

'That is so,' he said, without looking at Jamike.

'Thank you, madam,' Jamike said.

When the woman was gone, he said, 'Jamike, can we go to the house? I need to tell you my story.'

He'd spoken quickly because his hatred had returned, and he was afraid it would go back into wherever it had come from. He wanted it to stay, to be ever present with him while he was with this man. Without it, he feared that he would never be well again.

'Oh, you don't want to eat?' Jamike said. 'I am buying the food.'

'No, we can eat after.'

Jamike paid the woman for the drinks and they walked out of the restaurant, my host carrying his bag, and his heart beating loudly for fear he may have betrayed his intentions through his tone. Although he listened for the sound of someone following him, he did not look back.

'It is not far. We can ride on my motorcycle to the place,' he said aloud.

'I want to come,' Jamike said.

He turned and looked, for the first time that day, at Jamike's face. 'Let us take my machine,' he said.

He realised he had not fully considered his request until Jamike mounted behind him and their bodies touched. It sent a shiver through him, as if he had been poked with a sharp rod. He lost his grip on his keys, and the bunch fell on the ground. Jamike rushed to pick them up.

'Brother Solo, are you fine?' he said.

He did not speak. He merely pointed to the street ahead and started the motorcycle.

GAGANAOGWU, revenge is a debris field. It is a situation in which a man who was once defeated in a fight drags his enemy back to a cleared field after the battle has been won and lost, hoping to revive a dead fight. He returns to pick up the rusty weapons, to scrape clean the blood-encrusted swords, and to light again the violent fire of hatred against his foe. For him, the fight was never over. But for his foe, so much time may have passed that the enemy, if he had felt himself the victor, may have forgotten about the old battle. Thus he may be astonished when he who was smeared in the mud, whose bones were broken, who was vanquished, seizes him again by the throat and begins to drag him back to the battleground.

The broken man may himself be surprised by the force with which he has now seized his enemy. But this may be the beginning of his surprises. What if he seizes his enemy by the throat, wrestles him to the ground, and begins to strangle him without any resistance? What if his enemy simply lies there, closes his eyes and simply says, 'Please, brother, go ahead'? What if the other's face, red and bursting with veins, continues to entreat him? 'I am in Christ. Praise the Lord. To die in him, I am willing to do ... Argh ... I love you, Chinonso-Solomon. I love you, my brother.'

What would the broken man do? What would he say when the man he was about to kill speaks of love for him? What would he say when his heart had been further broken by all the misreckonings of life, by all the false calculus of time and the dubious permutations of fate? What would he do when he had done no wrong to warrant the trouble that came to him?

He had fallen in love with a woman, just like any other man. He'd tried to marry that woman, the way every good man should. Indeed, her parents had tried to obstruct it, but he tried to scale the obstacle, the way people do when wanting to achieve a goal. Now, certainly that had led him into even greater trouble, but what did he do? He plotted his revenge and sought it as if his life depended on it. It had taken him a long time to find his enemy, but he'd finally found him. And now, he is strangling the man, trying to kill him and discard his body in the Imo River, as people would do to someone who had destroyed their lives. So you see, Egbunu, he has done nothing out of the ordinary. Yet nothing he has done has yielded a common result!

If he headed north just as every other traveller did, he found himself in the south. If he put his hand into a bowl of water, it burned him as if it were fire. If he trod on land, he drowned as if he'd stepped in water. If he looked, he did not see. If he prayed, what is heard was a curse. And now, when he engaged a wicked man in a fight he'd rehearsed for many years, what he finds instead is a saint who prays for him; instead of protestations, he finds a singing man.

So he resigned. He unclasped his hands from the throat of his enemy, who had begun to cough frantically, trying to gather air into his lungs. He sank to his knees and began weeping, while the man whom he had tried to kill whispered prayers through his aching throat: *God forgive him, please. Put all his sins on my head. You know what I have done. Please, Lord, help him. Heal him, heal him, Lord.*

On his knees, my host wept aloud, for everything. He wept for that which had been lost and would not again be found. He wept for the time which would not replenish itself. He wept for the sickness which ate out the interiors of his world and left it as a cracked shell of its old self. He wept for the dreams washed down the pit of life. He wept for all that would come, all that he could not yet see or know. He wept, even more, for the man he had become. And his weeping was attended by the words dripping like poisoned rain from the mouth of his enemy who lay beside him: *Yes, Lord, you are merciful. Merciful father. King of kings. Heal him. Heal my brother. Heal him, Lord.*

CHUKWU, they stayed this way for some time – he kneeling and sobbing, the man praying quietly while lying on his back on the floor. Into their ears came the world from the outside. A neighbour was chopping firewood at the back of the house, a dog was barking somewhere not too far away, and on the long road that led to the big market, cars were honking and streaming about interminably. The sun outside had started to set, and the last light of the day lay outside the window as if too afraid to enter the room. In his mind, the great anguish had subsided like a receding storm. Now he sat empty, watching the shadow on the wall forged from him and his enemy by the subdued light of the evening sun.

In the small serenity of his mind, a vision of the gosling materialised. It was one of those times when it seemed to have suddenly forgotten that it was on the leash, for it sometimes forgot about it, and was enraged by it and wanted out. It would rouse itself and make a rustling, held back by the leash, bound to the leg of a chair or a table. When it had tired, the bird would smear down, its wings spread out as if in surrender. Then it would orient its head downwards and peer at him, its yellow eyes on the sides of its small face bulging as if they would pop out of their sockets. But then the thin sheets of skin that formed its lids would cover them and open again, revealing pupils now dilated. It would sit that way for a while, and then a sudden epiphany would strike it and it would leap up again, seeking the familiar pool of the Ogbuti forest – its true home.

My host rose afterwards and sat on the lone chair in the room. Then he pulled one of the two stools forward so that it faced him, and called to Jamike to rise.

'Come and sit here,' he said, tapping the stool in front of him.

Jamike stood and moved towards the stool, planted himself on it, and folded his hands across his chest. My host examined him, as if to assure himself that this was truly the man who had dominated his thoughts for four years. He was again surprised by what he saw. The man before him was nothing like the one he'd stored in his head for all those years and who sometimes visited him in vivid dreams. What sat before him now was a shadowy creature from an inchoate dream, one who, in some indefinable way, seemed to have suffered a fate similar to his.

He took up the bag Ndali had given him and brought out the letter.

'I want you to read this,' he said. 'It contains my story. I want you to read it loud to me. I want to hear it, together with you. I want us both to read my testimony. So go ahead, read!'

The man passed his eyes around the four pages stapled together and folded into columns. Then, raising his head to look at my host, he said, 'Everything?'

'Yes, everything.'

'Okay.'

MY STORY: HOW I WENT TO HELL IN CYPROS

Dear Mommy,

I am writing you from my second year in prison in cypros. You will not believe my story but everything I am saying here

will be truth. Just belif me in the name of Almighty God I beg
you. Please Obim. you know I love you. Do you remember?

Jamike raised his head to look at him.

'Read on!' he said. 'I want you to read what I went through
because of you.'

After you saw me to the bus garage, I said to myself, I will see
you again soon. I said I will return to you and I will marry
you. my mommy. I was happy. I beliefed that what I was
doing was—

'What is this?'

He bent forward to see the titled page. 'For you, I believed
that what I was doing was for you.'

'Okay.'

For you I beliefed that what I was doing was for you. I fly to
Istanbul thinking of you. not even a single time did you leave
my mind. Actually I even dreamt of you, many dreams, both
of the future, and past time. Then, in the plane, I began to
listen to tow Nigerians. They were talking of this country I
was going. They were talking how bad cypros was. They said
it was like Nigeria, that agents who ask people to come there
lie to them. It is false what they say. All telling serious lies.
cypros is not like europe. They said if you go there, it is like
a pit. You can come back to Nigeria or you can stay there.
And if you stay you will not get a better job. You will always
work bad job. So I become afraid. I ask the men when we got
to Istanbul if there were true, and they said yes, yes. It is so.
So I become afraid again. I said to them, but my old classmate
Jamike Nwaorji say it is a good place. He lied to me.

'Look, I said you should not stop. Read on! *Gu ba!*'

My host, becoming desperate, did not want to harm this man but rather to threaten him so he would read the letter in its entirety. He brought out the knife from the bag and held it. Ijango–ijango, I must emphasise that my host was merely desperate to make Jamike read the letter in its entirety and was not intent on doing harm. I, his chi, who would not want him to shed blood and incur your wrath and Ala's, would have attempted to stop him. But I could see that he would not use it, so I did not interfere. Brandishing the knife, he said, 'I will kill you here, and nobody will know, if you don't read on now.'

It worked. For Jamike, slightly shaken, continued.

I tried to call him. The phone never go. I was very surprised because I called the number many times before. So I ask the men and they say it was not cypros number. I try many times. So when we reached cypros naw, the man was no where to be found. Actually no where at all. I can't by then reach his number also. Please God, help me I was praying. I was very afraid. But my spirit told me, if you are afraid that is not good. It means this man will win. You must be strong. So I went to the airport in cypros. I wait, wait, wait. He didn't come at all. His number did not go through still. Even in cypros. What can I do now, I ask myself then. This is everything I have. So I decided to wait. For three hours, he did not come to the airport, after all of his promises. So I took a taxi . . .

Chukwu, at this point, Jamike shook his head gravely. I have cycled the habitation of man for so long like a falcon, but I have never seen anything like this before: a man stripped naked of all dignity and forced to gaze at his unpleasant self in the dark mirror of his own past malevolence.

Turkish people don't hear English. They don't hear at all.
If you speak even 'come' they don't hear. Only few of them
hear. So the taxi man who took me did not hear English.
When we got to the school I was very afraid. I prayed to God,
let it not be true, let it not be true. So but they cannot see my
name. I find out only one semester school fees is what Jamike
paid for me, even though I gave him equivalent of 4500 euros
for both two semester school fees and accommodation. The
money I gave him to open a bank account for me also. He ran
away with. So out of 6500 euro, he use only 1500 for me.
He ran away with all the rest. Everything mommy. All of the
money they paid me for the house and the fowls.

'Read, I say, read or I will cut your throat!' my host said, brandishing the knife.

'Can I stop, please, my brother?'

'If you don't read on now I will smash your head!' He threw the knife away across the room and with all his might struck Jamike on the cheek. The man fell off the stool to the ground with a scream, his hands on his mouth.

He'd struck Jamike with so much force that his knuckles hurt. Now he held that hand in the other and began to blow at it to ease the pain. He could tell that his hand had broken something in Jamike's face, and even though he did not know what it was, it gave him relief.

'I swear to God who made me,' he said between deep pants, his chest heaving, 'I will kill you if you don't finish reading this thing. I swear to God who made me. You must know everything that happened.'

Indeed, Agujiegbe, the murderous rage had returned, and my host – in one flash – had become unrecognisable even to me, his faithful chi. He paced from one end of the room to the other while the man on the floor lay still, his eyes closed, blood running down the side of his mouth. The sun had dropped and sunk away from the habitation of living men. Light from its retreating shadow held everything in a dim receptacle.

He stopped before the single wall mirror in the room and saw himself in it. He saw how far fury could take him. He saw, as if portrayed in the mirror, the potential of a wounded man to do damage if he did not bring himself under control. It was this that calmed him so that he returned to the chair.

EBUBEDIKE, it is not for nothing that the world is as old as it is. Perhaps every day, in every nation, amongst every people, through time, people are coming face-to-face with their tormentors. What a man carves with his hands, that shall he bear on his head. Again, as the great fathers say, the head that stirs the wasp's nest bears its sting. Guardian spirits of mankind, we must all take this to heart. Children of men must listen to us, to this, to *this* story, to the stories of their neighbours, and take notice: there is a comeuppance for everything, every action, every careless word, every unfair transaction, every injustice. For every wrong, there will be reckoning.

Man, do you take your neighbour's property and say, 'Oh, he does not know?' Well, beware! Some day he might catch you in the act and demand justice. Man, do you eat that which you did not plant? Beware! Someday it might purge you. Every person must hear this. Tell it in the village squares, in the town halls, along the corridors of the big cities. Tell it in the schools, at the gatherings of the elders. Tell it to the daughters of the great mothers, so they may tell it to their children. Tell, O world, tell! Tell them this: in the end, there will be reckoning. They must recite it like an anthem. They must tell it from the tops of the trees, on the tops of the mountains, on the pinnacle of the hills, along the river shores, at the market-places, in the town squares. They must say it again and again: in the end, it does not matter how long it takes. There. Will. Be. Reckoning.

Guardian spirits of mankind, all you who stand in the court of Bechukwu to testify, tell! And if they doubt you, then tell them to look at my host: he had cried for justice so much, so loudly, all these years, that it had now been given to him. And now, his enemy was on the floor, and he was on the chair. The evening bore an uncanny resemblance to the day in Cyprus when the scars on his jaw and face were inflicted on him. But this time, the equation had been reversed. The contention was now between my host, a man with a weapon and an impregnable will, and Jamike, a man who, if he had any power at all, seemed determined not to claim it. This man had no weapon and did nothing against his foe. The man, after a long period of praying, began waving one hand in the air, the other placed on his bloodied mouth, chanting, 'Thank you, Lord. Thank you, Lord. Amen. Amen. Amen.'

Jamike sat up, and blood spattered on his neck and shirt. My host gave him a rag to clean himself, but Jamike would not take it. It seemed, Egbunu, that Jamike had come to understand that reckoning had come. It must have been this awareness that caused him to open his mouth to speak. He closed it again without speaking, shook his head, and snapped his fingers.

'Brother Chinonso-Solomon, I am sorry for everything,' he said. 'The Lord has forgiven me. Would you forgive me, too?'

'I want you to read this all first,' my host said. 'You have to know what happened to me, what you caused me, for you to ask for forgiveness and for me to consider it. You must read, first. You must read. You must finish it.'

'Okay,' the man said.

My host took up the letter and pointed to a part of it, on the second page, and said, 'Continue from here.' Jamike nodded and held the paper with the hand not stained with blood, put it close to his face, and began to read.

The nurse was very sorry for me when I told her all that happened. She even cried for me. Her eyes were very read. She took me to a restaurant and buy me food, and assorted things like biscuit and coke. Then she said tomorrow she will come and take me to another city in cypros there, The name of the city is Grine. So we can go and look for job. In fact, very long time. She can speak Turkish also, this woman. In fact very well also. This woman gave me hope very much hope. That was why I called you that day if you still remember. I didn't call you for long because I was afraid of what to say to you. but I finally called you because of this. I told you everything will be alright because of the woman. I also tell you about the island, that all the trees in it have been removed. Mommy the following day she come. OK, this was after my friend and me go get a place to stay in the town, Lefkoshia. The nurse took me to the city girine where she intronduce me to the manager of the casino. The man say he will employ me. Actually he said I can start the following day also. I was very glad mommy. In fact I was so glad I was thanking and thanking this woman. I really believed she was godsent. Really, god sent.

At this point my host saw that darkness had arrived and that the man before him, who was now almost entirely turned into a silhouette, was struggling to see. There was a power outage. So he motioned for Jamike to stop and went out of the house to an open area where there was a kitchen – a half-covered place with old cupboards, almost black with soot. One of the people in the other flats who shared the kitchen with him was bent over a stove in a corner of the room, peering into a bubbling pot with a torchlight. He did not speak to the man, who had previously sparred with him over the cleanliness of the shared kitchen two days before when he'd rushed back from his store hungry. Then, he went to the shop near the house, he bought Indomie and eggs, cooked the noodles and fried the eggs. In haste, he'd left the eggshells near the stove. The neighbour would find flies congregating in the shells, the air thick with odour from what remained of the eggs. Enraged, the man would knock on his door and admonish him, threatening to report him to the landlord.

He swept past the man presently, took a box of matches, and hastened back to his flat. For it came into his thought just then that Jamike could leave before he returned. He found Jamike still seated, hugging himself in the near darkness, only the sound of his breathing and the rumble of his intestines audible. He was touched by Jamike's demeanour, the way in which he'd submitted himself to my host's wrath. The voice of his head told him to consider this as the ultimate act of remorse. But he could not bring himself to stop. He was determined, Chukwu, that Jamike would have to hear everything that had happened to him – from beginning to end. He raised the lever of the kerosene lantern on the table and lit it.

Ezeuwa, later he would regret forcing Jamike to continue reading the letter. For Jamike began reading from the parts my host often refrained from going to. Whenever his mind tried to drag him close to these places – dark beyond all things – he would fight, like a mortally wounded beast, with defiant violence to be spared the torture of such recollections. But now, he'd plunged himself into its pit by asking that it be read to him. A supreme act of self-flagellation. For as Jamike read to him about the incidents in the house of the nurse, he began to weep. And as Jamike read on, he saw the inadequacy of his own words to express what he had experienced. When Jamike read about how he'd passed the days in prison, portions of which had been too heavy for him to write down (. . . *about some of these things, please don't ask me to tell you, Mommy. And please don't ask also* . . .), my host became possessed with a desperate urge to correct the insufficiency in the narration. He wanted to add, for instance, that there had been times when he did not just see 'visions' but had completely lost his mind.

For how might he explain the times when, while drifting to sleep at midday, he'd be roused by the sound of an imagined rifle? Or how might one explain times when, half asleep, he'd feel a hand on his back trying to pull up his clothes and he'd scream? One could call these things hallucinations, but they felt real to him. What about those times when, in the veranda between sleep and wakening, the man he could have been would appear in the vision of his mind? The uncreated man would conjure up peace and sublunary bliss. And, by turns, he'd see himself helping what would appear to be their kids – a fine-looking boy and a beautiful girl with long braided hair – with their schoolwork. He'd see Ndali and him marching together at what was a vision of their wedding, often leaving him with a crushing envy for a version of himself that never was. This and many more were the things that he had not been able to express in the narrative because of the inadequacy of his words.

When Jamike was almost done, when he'd read the part about his hopelessness in prison, his incarceration for a crime he did not commit, the horde of unwanted memories rushed into his head. At once the violent rage came upon him again. In terror, he seized the man and began to hit him. But the memory did not abate at all. It was as if the images held his two hands and forced him to see what he did not want to see, and hear what he did not want to hear. The same way the men, now alive again and clear in his mind as daylight, had held him down, one pressing his neck to the wall that stank of rank sweat while the other slid his penis into his anus.

He struck at Jamike, everywhere he could find, but the images in his head remained, for the mind, Egbunu, is like blood. It cannot be easily staunched when a wound is deep. It will bleed at its own pace, at its own will. Only something powerful can staunch it. I have seen it many times. But now, no such thing was near. So he felt the man's palm becoming sweaty on his back and buttocks. He felt the forbidden thrusts. His onyeuwa felt it. His chi felt it. What was happening in that moment was transformative, life-altering. The moaning man's words – 'You rape Turkish woman! You, *ibne, orospu-cocugu*, you rape Turkish woman! We rape you too' – was not the voice of a human being but of something unfamiliar to any man. It sounded like something beyond time, beyond man: perhaps the voice of a prehistoric beast whose name no one alive or in living memory knew. And the man's smell, which he could recall now in striking vividness, was the odour of ancient animals.

He knelt on the floor beside his enemy, weeping. But, Ijango-ijango, this particular memory, when it begins, often bleeds till the body is emptied and the bloodless body falls and expires. So he would recall how the man's semen splashed around his buttocks and streamed down the back of his thigh. So although completely undesirous of it, he remembered even how he'd felt in the aftermath, after the world had scourged him with this severest of flagella. How he'd lain there for days that did not seem to cease, everything else alive but him.

Beside him, Jamike, having been beaten into a human pulp, lay still again, curved into the shape of a foetus. A slow, drawn-out moan of pain emitted from him, and his bloodstained hands trembled. It seemed that a revulsion of feeling seized him and he began to stitch words together, his teeth clattering, blood dripping from his mouth until, at last, words burst out of him in a voice slightly above a whisper:

'Heal him, Lord.'

21

MAN OF GOD

GAGANAOGWU, the magnanimous fathers often say that if one keeps a record of all the wrongs done to him by his kinsmen, he will have none left. This is because they know that you did not create the human heart to be capable of accommodating hatred. To harbour hatred in the heart is to keep an unfed tiger in a house filled with children and the feeble, for it cannot afford communion with a human being, nor can it be tamed. No sooner has it rested enough and woken up in need of food again than it falls upon the man who has nurtured it and devours him. Indeed, hatred is a vandalism of the human heart. A man seeking justice with his own hands must dispense it as quickly as possible, or he risks being destroyed by his own dark desire. I have seen it many times.

As is common with men, they often realise this truth long after the hatred has driven them into retributive acts. That night, my host realised these things. He helped the man up and took him to the clinic down the street. There was healing in this realisation. But he'd been moved even more by Jamike's reaction. Jamike had thanked him after the nurses attended to his wounds and cleaned them up and refused to tell the nurses what happened to him. The nurses had gazed at my host as if to demand the truth from him. 'He was attacked by armed robbers,' he said. One of the nurses nodded and sighed. He stood there, expecting Jamike to deny it. But Jamike said nothing, merely keeping his eyes firmly closed. Later, on their way out of the clinic, with his head bandaged and a plaster on the bridge of his nose, he said, in the language of the White Man, 'Brother Chinonso-Solomon, please do not tell lies any more. God says, Thou shalt not lie. Revelations twenty-one verse eight says that all liars shall inherit the kingdom of hell. I don't want you to go there.'

Jamike, who walked with a limp in his gait, put a hand on my host's shoulder as he spoke. My host said nothing. He could not understand it at all. He could not understand how, despite all he'd done to this man, all that seemed to matter was that he'd lied. When they came to the place where he'd parked his motorcycle, Jamike asked if he had forgiven him.

'You can cut off my hand if you want, or my leg. But all I want is that you forgive me. I have five thousand euro at home. Your money. The money I took from you. I have kept it for more than two years waiting to find you.'

'Is this true?' he said.

'Yes. Now the value has increased. When you change it now, it must be as much as your seven thousand.'

'Ah, Jamike, how is it possible? Why didn't you tell me you had this money before – before all I did to you?'

Jamike looked away and shook his head. 'I wanted you to forgive me from your heart, not because I repaid you.'

Oseburuwa, it is difficult to fully describe how this gesture made my host feel. It brought him the first touch of healing. It was a resurrection, a revival of something long dead. He was so shaken by it that when he got home that night, he could not sleep. He thought at first that Jamike was faking it all – the transformation, the docility he now exuded, must be false, the mask of a wicked man seeking to evade justice. He would have attacked Jamike that very first day if they had been in private. But now, that gesture of restitution convinced him that Jamike was indeed a transformed man. That night, in between struggling to breathe through a stuffed nose, he wrestled with the thought of forgiveness. If indeed the Jamike who damaged his life was dead, why punish the new one for the sins of the other? He considered: was it not what Jamike did to him that had caused him to change? If this was indeed so, then was it not a good thing? Was it not a thing to celebrate?

Chukwu, these were questions that I would have asked him, but the voice in his head asked them instead. And I flashed thoughts in his mind, accentuating them. The following day, early in the morning, while he brushed his teeth, Jamike arrived with an old envelope containing the money. Not once in all these years had he imagined even remotely that he would get his money back. And now, not only had the German woman paid him, so, too, had Jamike. It offered him renewed hope that he could regain all the things he once owned. This thought opened up slowly like a frontier in his mind. As he counted the money in disbelief, Jamike sank to his knees again.

'I want you to forgive me all the wrongs I have done, so that I may be forgiven by my father in heaven.'

He looked upon the man whose death he once sought with an all-consuming zeal. As he made to speak, his phone rang. The screen showed the name of Unoka, a trader who had been lately trying to persuade him to add turkey feed to his stock. But he ignored the call. And when it had rung out, he said in a shattered, speckled voice, 'I forgive you from now on, Jamike. My friend.'

Ebubedike, that was the beginning of his clemency – when the soul of the afflicted embraces the soul of the afflicter, with his paralysed limbs, both of them become forever marked by that embrace.

CHUKWU, I will again take you to the deeds that are necessary to explain and defend the actions of my host and to plead that, should it be the case that he's harmed the woman in the way I fear he has, he would have done it in error. So I must say, simply, that my host was transformed by the embrace I spoke of. His healing, Egbunu, had begun. He bought a car the following week with part of the money Jamike returned to him – his money! I need not waste time trying to describe the joy, the relief my host felt at this touch of redemption. For when a man has dwelt in misery for long, he becomes blind to the life that surrounds him like the ocean surrounds the shrunken earth. I, his chi, was delighted, for he'd become again a man of peace, even if part of his soul was still black with sorrow. For now, it was enough.

It restored his confidence so much that he and Jamike drove in his new car to his old house, the property his father had left him. A few days after he received the money, he decided to reach out to Elochukwu. Elochukwu was shocked to hear from him. And when he saw my host, he wept, saying that if he knew it was going to go the way it did go, he would not have encouraged him to travel to the foreign country. The thing was, Elochukwu kept saying, that you loved Ndali so much. 'I saw it, Nonso. I saw it so much that I just thought you would never be happy if you did not try to resolve the problem with her parents.' My host agreed. He would not have been happy if he had not tried all he could to be with her. Together, they attempted to reach the man who had bought the property, but the phone yielded no result. The number had gone into disuse, and the man, unreachable.

The next day, he went to the property with Jamike. This was one of the things Jamike had promised to help him do. It was on the list of the three important things he had said that Jamike must do to help him heal and be whole again, so his forgiveness could be complete. 'One,' he'd said to Jamike, with whom he now perpetually spoke in the language of the fathers, 'you must help me find Ndali, and restore her to me. I love her and have lived for her. You took her away from me and you must restore her to me with your own hands.' Two: 'You must help me get back all that I lost. My compound and my poultry. I want to get back my father's land and rebuild my poultry farm on it. You must help me do this.' Three: 'You must help me forget about the things the prison men did to me. I don't know how you will do it. Pray for me, counsel me – anything, just make sure I don't remember them any more.'

The first thing they did was go back to Ndali's father's house. He told Jamike about wanting to send the letter to Ndali through the gateman, and Jamike agreed that he should. So they drove at night, one week after their reconciliation, to Ndali's family house. Then he went up to the gate while Jamike stayed back in the car. He knocked, deeply afraid. The small gate opened, and another man, one of those with whom he'd served at Ndali's father's party four years earlier, appeared. To his great relief, the man did not recognise him.

'Oga, wetin I fit do for you?' the man asked. 'You wan see Oga Obialor?'

'No, no,' my host said, his heart leaping at the thought of seeing Ndali's father again. He looked about him, up at the two black plastic septic tanks towering above the gates, then at the man. Then he brought out a wad of cash, twenty thousand naira. He stretched it out to the man.

'Er, Oga, what is this?' the man said, stepping back rapidly.

'Money,' my host said, his breath catching.

'For wetin?'

'Erm, I want you to, erm—'

'Oga, you wan do bad thing for my Oga house?'

'No, no,' he said. 'I want you to give this letter to Ndali for me.'

'Oh, you want Madam Ndali?'

'No, I want to give her a letter,' he said.

'Okay, bring am. I go give im mother and them go give am to am for Lagos. Bring am.'

Chukwu, at first he gave the man the letter and the money. The fellow thanked him and returned back in. But when he told Jamike, the latter said, 'What if her mother opens it?' My host was stunned. 'Did you write your name on the envelope?'

'Yes!' he cried.

'Then they will open it, even try to make sure it doesn't get to her. The man should just give you her address, or give to her by himself.'

He ran back to the gate and asked the man to bring it back.

'Why, Oga you no wan send am again?'

'No, no, I go come back with am,' he said. 'Do you have her address?'

'Amdress? For Lagos?' the man said.

'Yes, for Lagos.'

'No-oh. I be omdinary gateman.'

'Do you know when she go come?'

'No, they no dey tell me that kain thing.'

'Okay, thank you,' he told the man. 'Keep the money.'

He left, despondent but thankful that he had saved himself

from the possible outcome of Ndali's parents seeing his letter. Jamike counselled him not to despair and assured him that they would eventually find her. It was early March, he said, and she would most likely return for Easter if they are big Catholics. Jamike advised that they try to recover his house in the meantime. In a moment that reminded me of Tobe, the man who'd helped my host in the strange country, Jamike and he drove to his old compound. He parked his car outside what used to be his garden and sat waiting in the car for Jamike to return. The garden had been cleared, and in its place was a pile of unused gravel and a few cement blocks. A wheelbarrow lay tumbled over the gravel, a red rag tied to one of its handles. There was a big signboard with the inscription: LITTLE MERCY NURSERY AND PRIMARY SCHOOL, P.M.B. 10229, UMUAHIA, ABIA STATE. He looked about him. What of the house of the neighbours? They were still there, only now what he believed was a telephone pole stretched out from beside their compound. On the long cable, a few birds – sparrows – sat, gazing emptily into the distance.

To soothe his anxiety, he focused on the toy bird he'd bought from a crafts shop and hung from the rearview mirror of his car. The toy bird swung back and forth when the car was in motion, reminding him of a hen he once had which he'd named Chinyere. He tapped the toy's beak and stirred it into a whirl. He watched the rope twist at the top and knot together until it reached its limit, then begin to unwind, the bird swirling quickly as the centrifuge that was the rope propelled it. He found meaning here, Chukwu, the way a desperate man, if he looks close enough, finds meaning in just about anything – a grain of sand, a quiet river, an empty boat rocking on the shore. The twirling rope that held the bird, that hand-like object, like a sailor's, directing its course, that cord that binds two things, each of which moves when the other moves, shifts when the other shifts.

He'd been seated for what he thought was close to thirty minutes, and Jamike had still not come out. Although he'd rolled down the windows, it was suffocating. The rain had stopped for a week, and now the days were hot and humid. A bell tolled from the premises of what had been his home, and now the voices of children rose in an enthusiastic chorus. As if nudged by something he could not see, he got out of the car and began circling the big fence that had been erected around the property, stopping only in the front near a pile of gravel and blocks. He saw as he walked that only a little of what his family had built of the fence remained. Most of it was now fresh unvarnished bricks held together by rough ligaments of cement. Lizards tailgated each other across the wall in rudimentary choreographic movements. The chickens had loved them, and even though the lizards were fast and too slippery for them to hold firmly, the roosters would frequently catch them and eat them. Once, a white hen chased a weak gecko who had ambled into the yard and nipped it against the base of the wall, causing a chap in its beak. For days, even weeks, the striking image of the hen with the live gecko in its mouth remained in his mind. When the chicken had turned from the wall, the gecko's tail curled up its face, stretched up into the space between its eyes, so that it seemed the bird wore a Roman centurion's helmet, complete with the cock's red comb.

He stopped behind the school, separated only by the fence from the place where his poultry once was, and he could not move any further. For in the place where, years ago, his fowls would have gathered, their voices melding in squawks, was now a little crowd of children who were jointly reciting a poem. This opened a sudden hole in the shield of his spirit, large enough for the dart of hatred to again penetrate and shatter the peace that had held him together beyond all comforting. It broke him, Agujiegbe. He bent, one hand on his thigh, one elbow against the wall, and wept.

When he emerged again from behind the school fence, his enemy was waiting for him. The same man whom, for more than one week, he'd loved with half his heart – the only part capable of such a feat. For the other half was dead, a permanently tranquillised flesh. The man came with a frown on his face, but when he saw my host, his countenance slumped even deeper.

'What is it, brother?'

'Tell me what they said,' he said, without so much as a glance at the man's face.

'Okay. The person who now runs the school says there was no way they can move from this land. The man they bought the land from has moved to Abuja. The school is doing well here and the government recognises it. The land is not open for negotiation. What took so long was because I was waiting for him to finish a meeting. A long meeting, my brother.'

He did not say anything but drove in silence until they reached his flat. Rather, he communicated with the voice of his conscience, that reticent being in the other compartment that was his soul. Chukwu, whenever I'm in a host and the voice of his conscience dialogues with the voice of his mind, I listen closely because I have come to know that the best decisions a man makes come when both voices agree.

—You are full of hatred again, Nonso. Remember he has done nothing to you now.

—Nonsense! How can a reasonable person even say that? Look at the land, my compound, the house of my father!

—Put your voice low. Calm yourself. A man who whispers too loudly will be heard from a distance.

—I don't care!

—You promised never to hold anything against him any more. You said you have forgiven him. He asked if you wanted to be his friend, and you said yes. After he gave you your money back, you could have said no and he would have left and let you alone. You even prayed to his God and went to his church with him. Now you hate him again. Now you are plotting to harm him again. Look, just look: a knife lies on the floor of your imagination, stained with his blood. Is this good? Is it?

—You don't understand how much evil this man has done to me. Keep quiet! You don't understand a single thing!

—That's not true, Nonso. It is not me but you who is weak and in need of understanding. What has he done? For the past two weeks he has helped you, done everything you have asked him, as if he were your slave. He has spent most of the time with you, done everything for you. How much did you get from the 6500 euros he gave you? 1.4 million naira. One hundred thousand more than he took from you four years ago. Yet he has nothing. Look at him – are these not the same clothes that he wears every day? You have been to his flat, a face-me-I-face-you flat. It has one window, and it is an old one made of wood. Sometimes, when he sleeps at night, he can hear termites scavenging within its walls. If he were not a truly changed man, would he have this kind of money and endure near poverty so that he could mend that which was broken?

The voice in his head did not respond now.

—Answer me. Do you keep silent now?

He said nothing. Instead, with a sigh, he steered the car into the compound and parked it.

—I will say no more to you. Count your teeth with your tongue. Count your teeth with your tongue, Chinonso!

The dialogue with his conscience seemed to have borne fruit, for it seemed that his anger had dimmed by the time they entered his flat. While his enemy waited in the sitting room, whispering to himself, he went through the back door to the kitchen in the yard. He took the knife from the cupboard, the image of the fated stabbing still in his mind, but then he put it down again. He stamped his feet into the earthen floor and bunched his fist. 'My house, my house,' he said. He threw his fist into the air as if his assailant had appeared before him and fell on his knee. 'No,' he said, 'I will not suffer alone. I will not. I don't care what anyone thinks.'

—*Ngwa nu, ka o di zie,* the voice returned to him in a whisper. You may do as you like; I will not say any more to you.

He went back into the flat, the anguish visible on his face.

'My brother, what is it?' Jamike asked.

He merely gave the man a look. From the crate of Fanta under the bed, he brought out two bottles.

'I am getting us something to drink. Wait here.'

He went to the kitchen and set both drinks on the table. Then he closed the kitchen door. He threw a portion of the first uncapped bottle into an empty bucket on the floor and unzipped himself. He held the bottle over the bucket and urinated until it frothed over. Then he let the rest into the bucket. When he was done, he put back the cap on the Fanta and, with a tip of his finger on the cap, shook the drink to mix it together. He then placed the bottle on the table beside the other one.

Egbunu, I was horrified, even before the act began, for I had seen the intent of his heart. But I could do nothing at this point. I have come to understand that the most persuasive voice of caution a man can hear before any action is that of his conscience. Should he not be persuaded by that, not even a gathering of all his ancestors living in Alandiichie can change his mind. For the conscience is your voice, Chukwu – the voice of God in the heart of a man. Compared to the conscience of a man, the voice of his chi, of fellow man, of an agwu, or even of an ancestor is nothing.

When he stepped out to drain the bucket into the gutter behind the kitchen, it occurred to him that the bottle might carry the smell of urine. So he turned to the sink and washed it with water from another container, his finger firmly on the cap. Then he wiped the bottle with a rag and took it into the living room. He placed the bottle on the centre of the table before him and said to this man, 'Take and drink.' And the man to whom he had offered the drink took it, gave him thanks, and drank. The hated man drank it with a light twitch on his face, and then a bemused gaze. My host watched him drink without a word and he drank until the bottle emptied. Then he set it down by his feet and said to the man who hated him, 'Thank you, brother.'

IJANGO-IJANGO, that night, Jamike's chi projected through the ceiling as through a rip in the aperture of time, into the room.

—Son of the morning light, it said to me. My host has atoned for what he has done.

But, Chukwu, I was displeased. I told it about the full extent of my host's suffering and how I had not done much to prevent it. I told about how I had gone to the caves to look for it or any word but failed. The chi listened with a silence and sobriety that struck me with awe.

—The great fathers say that when a child who does not know his left from his right tells a damaging lie, he can be forgiven by both the living and the dead. But when an elder tells such a lie, even his ancestors will curse him. Your host is receiving what he deserves.

—The great fathers say that an old woman often feels uncomfortable when she hears a proverb in which dry bones are mentioned. I'm guilty of all that you have said. But still I ask that you recall that a man who insists on breaking the bones of those who offend him in the slightest way will become crippled before long. With these words, it went on to plead with me to restrain my host. I will not relate all that it said, but I will emphasise that it exhibited the new character of its host and assured me of its host's repentance. But there was also something it said that moved me: Jamike was not a bad person at first. He was made so by people, including my host. The chi related the incident even my host had recalled in Cyprus in which, while in primary school, my host and his friends had repeatedly mocked and shamed Jamike, calling him Nwaagbo for having big breasts. It was these things, the chi said, that had caused him to begin trying to control others, to assert himself, in hopes that he would heal himself by so doing. I believed it and resolved to persuade my host even more strongly to forgive Jamike.

OSEBURUWA, if a man dwells in the debris field of revenge for too long, he might step on something – the blade of some weapon, anything – that could injure him. For the field is a wasteland filled with an assortment of things, and one cannot always know what he will find in it. Indeed, I must say that my host had stepped on something in the wasteland that bruised his feet. He became ashamed of what he had done to Jamike. He was convinced that Jamike had known what was in the bottle but went ahead and drank it anyway. Why he could not tell. Was it out of fear? Was it out of reverence? But it disturbed him greatly that a man would knowingly drink another man's urine – no matter what the man had done. He resolved that this was the furthest he would go with his revenge. That thing Jamike had done was the ultimate act of atonement, enough to pay for the loss of the woman he loved, the penis that violated him, the loss of his father's house. He swore to never again lift a finger against Jamike.

So rather than do harm to Jamike, he would not see him any more. Agujiegbe, if, for instance, he remembered the event in the prison or the beating at Fiona's house or any of the things that sent him into a murderous rage, and Jamike was not nearby, he would vent and the anger would leave him. He could wail, he could hit his wall, or his furniture, or threaten to harm himself, but at least he would no longer lay his hand on a man who was contrite, who was truly sorry for what he had done – a transformed man who had returned that which he had stolen from him.

So when he told Jamike he no longer wanted to see him, he did not give these reasons for why, only that he did not want to.

'I will respect your desire,' the other, visibly troubled, said. 'But, my brother, son of the living God, I want to be your friend. I will miss you. But I will not do what you don't want me to do. Believe me. No longer will I come to your flat, or to your shop. I will not call you as you have requested, unless it is urgent. And even then I will text you first, I promise. But oh my brother, Chinonso-Solomon, my bosom friend, I pray for you. I pray for you. But I will do as you have requested. Yes, indeed, no longer will I look for you! No longer will I knock on your door! God bless you, my brother, God bless you!'

That was it – a protest, an acclamation, an acceptance, a prayer, a lamentation, an argument, a plea, a plea yet again, another protestation, a plea, an acceptance, and then submission. And no longer did Jamike contact him. For nearly three weeks, Egbunu, my host lived by himself, in his improved state, enticed by the things he had abandoned. He came to understand how much his life had changed in the time he'd spent with this man whom he now sometimes called by his nickname: M.O.G., or Man of God, a man so unlike his former self that he sometimes wondered if the previous version had existed. Even the way Jamike now spoke, refusing to call him by the childhood nickname Bobo Solo and never using the word 'mehn', was different. Were he not a living witness of the old Jamike's atrocities, he would not have believed them to be true.

He missed Jamike's friendship and came very close, several times, to breaking the embargo in the third week, when he'd taken ill. Oseburuwa, the sick man – he is one whose body has been overpowered by some malady. The change in his body begins with the feeling of something out of the ordinary happening. As pain spreads through the body, of the fever toll in one's skull, emotions erupt – a nervousness first. One becomes nervous about the day, about its course, and about life itself. Then some form of anxiety sets its inchoate machinery in motion. Has the day broken? Will it get worse? Will the world continue without me? How long, how far, to what extent will this illness persist? The anxiety overcomes one. But these are not the only things. Afterwards comes the astonishment that sickness brings, the way it takes ownership of the body and dictates which parts of one's body one must pay to caress or heal. But of the utmost significance is how it initiates the belief in the sick man that he may have caused the illness by himself. Something he has done is the reason why this fever torments his head. If he coughs or sneezes, it must be because of that time when he stayed out in the rain. If he defecates frequently, it must be that bad food he ate the previous night. Sickness, then, becomes the quiet snake that, dislodged from its peaceful abode, is filled with spite and fury. And the sickness it inflicts on a person, now, is its sanctified revenge.

My host had started to recover and was seated in his room when his phone rang on the fourth market day of that third week, which the White Man refers to as Thursday. Ijango-ijango, my host was in his flat, cleaning a bucket in which he would keep feed at his store, when his phone rang. He picked it up and saw that it was Jamike. He ignored it at first, fearing that he had not yet completely forgiven the man and that if he saw him the rage would possess him again, and he would do things he did not want to do. He went on cleaning congealed mash from the bucket and whistling to the soft song Ndali had taught him. Jamike called again, and again, and then sent a text: Brother pick the call. It is gud news! Parise God!

His heart skipped. He sat down on the bed and pressed the key.

'Hello, my brother Solomon,' the other man said, his voice bearing a certain haste to it. 'I have found her!'

He sprang up to his feet. 'What? What?' he said, but the other did not seem to hear him.

'Praise God, brother,' Jamike kept saying. 'I have found her!'

'M.O.G., who, what have you found?'

'Who else, my brother? Who else? The one you have been looking for. Ndali!'

He stared at the phone, unable to speak. Again, it has come: that which silences him and deprives him of words, the freest of all human gifts. It has come, its feet assured, as it always has.

'I cannot thank God enough, Nwannem. God is indeed God. He is helping me fulfil my promises to you, all the things on your list. Now you will finally experience the peace I have experienced. You will get forgiveness from her from whom you must get and give it. And ye will be healed.'

Indeed, he would be healed.

'Where is she?' was all he managed to say.

'I saw her at Cameroon Street. You know the new pharmacy and laboratory they are building there? The two-storey?'

He knew.

'It is there. She is the owner of the place. She has returned to establish it. This is answers to our prayers, Brother Solomon!'

Jamike had gone on, thanking the alusi of the White Man, quoting the books of Corinthians, James, Isaiah and Romans while the firmament of my host's thoughts constellated with fire. He told his friend to let him rest a bit and return the call later, and the other obliged. He put away the phone, entranced in the new knowledge. A great silence came upon him, one so overpowering that he could not hear the faintest breath. But it was a deceptive silence, for he knew that in that moment an army was approaching, the sound of their marching feet thundering through the land. And that soon they – the thousands of thoughts, imaginations, memories, visions of her – would arrive, illimitably vast across the wrinkled face of time. So he lay down as one merely waiting, as still as a dead hen stiffened by rigor mortis.

22

OBLIVION

MMALITENAOGWUGWU, the old fathers say that if a secret is kept for too long, even the deaf will come to hear of it. It is true, also, what the wisest amongst the great fathers, the dibias, those who are second to you, Chukwu, say that if one seeks something one does not have, no matter how elusive that thing is, if his feet do not restrain him from chasing it, he will eventually have it. I have seen it many times.

My host's feet had chased after this great, elusive thing, this thing which had escaped from the leash he had bound to his heart, for more than four years. And that evening, an hour or so after Jamike rushed to his house, he became certain he had found it.

'So it is true that it is her you saw?'

'It is true, my brother. Why would I lie? Remember I promised that I would do everything I could to make sure you recover everything – everything. Er, my brother, one day it came to my mind to check Facebook. Because of my past life I had stopped using my own. So I decided to open it again.'

'Is it e-mail?' my host said.

'No, Facebook. I will show you when next we go to the cyber cafe. But I went there and searched for her, and *lo and behold*, I found her.'

'Ha, is this so?'

'Yes, my brother Solomon. Ndali Obialor. I saw her face – she is fair in complexion with a very beautiful face. She had a black weave on her head. I sent her a friend request and she accepted just today.'

At this, Jamike clapped his hands. My host, at a loss as to what he was hearing, nodded and said, 'Go on.'

'Immediately when I went to the cyber cafe, I opened it and saw she had posted a photo of the new pharmacy near the big supermarket on Cameroon Street.'

'Is it true,' he said, as if the other had not spoken at all, 'that you found her?'

'It is true, Solomon. She is the one I saw. It is her I saw. She in that photo whose half you covered and showed me.'

'What if it is someone who looks like her?'

'No, it is not. After I left the cyber cafe, I went up to the chemist and asked one of the workers there. And the woman said that indeed it was Ndali.'

'Are you sure she is the one you saw? I will show you the photo again ... here, I have covered the chest with a paper. Look in her face, look at it very well.'

'I have looked, my brother.'

'And you say she is the same person you saw?'

'Yes, she is.'

'Same nose ... look, Jamike, look very well: is it the same eyes?'

'Indeed, my brother. Why will I lie to you, my brother?'

'Then it must be her,' he said with resignation.

Ijango–ijango, for two days they had this kind of discussion in his flat. And at the end of each turn, my host would pace about the room with an exuberant heartbeat. He would halt, bend briefly, peer into the face of the world, close his eyes, and shake his head at the displeasure of what he'd seen. He was still sick, his spirit humbled within his flesh. But he was a man who had heard too much. And this too much was enough to shatter a man. Too much was the fact that he knew Ndali was now certainly in Umuahia. Too much was also the fact that he knew he must go to her.

'I don't understand what is happening to you, my brother,' Jamike said one evening. 'You have been wanting to see this woman for many years, you have lived for this. And now you shut your door to it? You do not want to see her?'

They were seated on stools outside Jamike's room for fresh air. The vicinity was quiet, except for the voice of a transistor radio in one of the rooms and the sound of crickets.

'You don't have to understand,' he said. 'The elders say it is not everything the palm-wine tapper sees on the tree that he speaks about.'

'True, but don't forget that the same elders who say that also say that no matter how long a mangrove branch lies beneath the water, it cannot become a crocodile.'

Agbatta-Alumalu, Jamike was right. My host had been confused. It was as if he had been waiting for this thing, and now that it had come, he realises he has no power, no strength to confront it. So he did not respond to the wise words of his friend. He moved the toothpick between his teeth, up to the ridge above his two upper front teeth, and spat specks of meat on to the ground before him.

'I know how you feel,' Jamike said. 'You are afraid, my brother. You are afraid about what you will find out about her.' He shook his head. 'You are afraid of what you will find, that you may have been wasting everything loving a woman who can never be yours again.'

My host glanced up at Jamike and was, in that instant, filled with rage. But he fought it.

'I know I caused all this, but please, brother, you need to face her, no matter what. It is the only way you will heal and move on with your life and find another woman.' Jamike moved his chair to face him, and as if feeling that my host did not understand what he'd said, he turned briefly to the language of the White Man. 'It is the only way.'

He looked at Jamike, for the very thought of another woman hurt him.

'At least you should let me deliver the letter to her, or I could go and tell her everything that happened – what I did, what you did – and ask for forgiveness. It is the only way. You must see it.'

'What if I discover she is married and no longer loves me?' he said. 'Will it not be worse than not knowing? In fact, I don't like that she has returned. It would have been better if she had not returned.'

'Why, Brother Solomon?'

'Because,' he said, and then paused to let his thoughts fully form. 'Because I cannot accept to lose her.' Then, as an afterthought, taking advantage of the perplexed silence of his friend, he added, 'After all I have suffered for her sake.'

It was those words, out of everything they said that day, that lingered in his mind after he drove his car back to his flat and lay on his bed, which still had the malarial smell of his sick days. Chukwu, in my many cycles of existence, I have come to understand that there are times when, although one might have thought about something many times before, hearing it said again imbues it with new meanings strong enough to lend it the appearance of novelty. I have seen it many times. In all those years, he had not thought the way it struck him that night – that all he'd been through had been because of her. He considered it, his story, in wilting chronology: he had been mourning the death of his father when he met her on the bridge. It was from there that his life began to fall in the direction it now was going. It was for her sake that he sold all he had, went to Cyprus, and ended up in prison.

He sat up, near midnight, weighed down by heavy thoughts. He reckoned that without her, none of this would have happened to him. 'It doesn't matter,' he said aloud to himself. Ndali now had no choice but to return to him. He let his inflated chest settle so he could breathe easy. 'I have paid enough price to deserve her, enough. And, no one, I repeat, no one can take her away from me!'

He would go to her in the morning. Nothing would stop him. He picked up his phone and texted his friend, then sat back, panting, as if exhausted by what he had decided to do.

IKEDIORA, the brave fathers were at their most instinctive when they said that a person often becomes the chi of another. It is true. I have seen it many times. A man may be in grave danger, and there might be nothing his chi can do to help him. But he may meet a person who, having seen the danger ahead, tells him about it, saving his life. I once met a chi in Ngodo who was chattering endlessly with bitterness about the evil on the earth and the unworthiness of humans to exist. There were a lot of guardian spirits in the cave, most of them silent, lying in a corner of the great granite chamber or washing by the pool or conversing in low tones. But this guardian spirit kept shouting about how his deceased host had tipped off a potential victim about the plot to kill him. Later, the person whose life he saved sent people to murder him. Oh, man is disgusting beyond grave worms! Oh, man is terrible beyond a dirge! I don't want to return to the earth of man! It had been a perplexing thing to watch this rebellious spirit speak such profane things. I left it there by Ngodo but heard from another guardian spirit that it had refused to return to the earth and that you cursed it and turned it into an ajoonmuo. And now it crawls interminably down the length and breadth of Benmuo with three heads and the torso of a vile beast. But what Jamike had done for my host was the reverse of what this chi had described. For Jamike had become my host's second chi and had led him to what he had been looking for for so many years.

He went with Jamike to look for Ndali, carrying a jar of fear in his heart, wearing a cap over his head and dark eyeglasses covering most of his face. When they arrived, he found the pharmacy to be a new building he had seen nestled between the Saint Paul Anglican church and the new MTN office. It was a two-storey building that bore the sign HOPE LABORATORY AND PHARMACY. The lettering was bold against the background of a white woman in a white medical frock, peering into a microscope. In front of the building, on one side of its fence, was a pile of sand and pebbles, relics from the construction of the building. He parked the car on the other side of the street, in front of a barbershop from which deafening music blared, mixed with the constant buzz of a power generator.

'You are afraid, brother,' Jamike said, shaking his head. 'You really love this woman.'

He looked at his friend but did not speak. He knew he was acting irrationally but could not tell why this was so. Something in him was preventing him from what he'd sought so desperately.

'The Bible says, *Let not your heart be troubled. Casting all your care upon him; for he careth for you.* Do you believe God that it is possible that she may still love you and be unmarried?'

He gazed at his friend, taken aback by the latter's switch to the White Man's language, the language in which Jamike discussed the Bible. Frightened by the possibility of what the other had spoken about, my host closed his eyes. 'I believe.'

'Then let us go. Don't fear.'

He nodded. '*O di nma.*'

They stepped out of the car with his heart fastened into a knot and crossed the crowded street. There were shops everywhere. A shoe shop covered with shoes that hung from the awning, strung together with ropes like beads. A shop in which pots and cooking wares were sold, GOD'S HANDS COOKING SUPPLYS. As they walked, he tried to anchor his thoughts on the people, on how the streets were different from the ones he'd seen in Cyprus. Jamike went ahead of him, the lilt in his gait from a wound on one of his toes. When they set to cross the road, my host tilted his cap lower to cover his face and balanced the glasses over his eyes. A taxi honked at them in reaction to what the driver may have perceived as a daring crossing. Jamike jumped the litter-filled gutter that separated the pharmacy from the road. Were Ndali to gaze in that moment from one of the shiny new screened windows of the pharmacy, she might have seen them. My host tilted his cap even lower, and grabbed his friend's arm.

'I can't, I can't go in,' he said.

'But why?'

Again he adjusted his cap and sunglasses.

'Ah, what are you doing?' Jamike said.

'I am changed a lot,' he whispered back. 'See my face. See the long scar on it. See my mouth: three teeth missing, the long scar around my jaw from where it has been stitched. Look at the permanent swelling on my upper lip. I am too ugly now, Jamike, I look like a baboon. I want to cover them.'

His friend was about to speak, but he held him more tightly.

'She won't recognise me. She won't.'

'But my brother, I don't agree,' Jamike said with what may have sounded like agitation. He looked at the pharmacy, then at his friend.

'Why not? How can she recognise me looking like this?'

'No, brother. She cannot dislike you because of your wounds.'

'Are you sure?'

'Yes. Love doesn't work like that.'

'So you think she will still be attracted to me, with my face like this?'

'Yes. All she needs to know is why you left and disappeared.'

He was slightly fidgeting, looking up about him as he spoke. Egbunu, this was my host: a man who, when afraid of uncertainty, often propels himself towards internal defeat. And when this happens, when his spirit has been thrown on the ground in the wrestling bout, his defeat begins to manifest in the physical. It is a strange thing, but I have seen it many times.

Jamike wiped the sweat from his brow and started to speak again but stopped abruptly and tapped my host, wanting him to look in the direction of the pharmacy.

It is difficult to describe this moment: the one in which my host, who had suffered so much, beheld the woman for whom he would have done all that again. She had come out of the door of the clinic. She was slightly changed, weightier than the slender woman whose image he carried in his head all these years. She was dressed in a long white cloth that reminded him of the nurse in Cyprus. From her breast pocket, a pen stuck out, and on her upper chest, visible in the opening of the collar, was a necklace. He stood watching her, taking an inventory of everything around her. She was talking to a woman with two kids – one strapped to her back, the other stretching its hand towards Ndali, then taking it back. She would stop to try to catch the child's hand, but it would retract it, laugh, and turn to its mother.

'I told you it was her,' Jamike said as the other woman turned back and began walking past the parked cars, out to the street, and Ndali returned into the pharmacy.

'It is true,' he said. 'It is her.' His heart was beating now, as if to the moves of ogene music. 'It is true, Jamike, it is her.'

It was indeed her, Egbunu. Ndali – the same woman whose chi had confronted me when I went to entreat it on behalf of my host. It struck me then, in a way I had not considered all these years, that it might be that her chi may have carried out its threat to cut its host away from my host for ever.

'Then let us go in. I am not returning without seeing her, brother. I want you to heal, to be well, and to be filled with the joy of the Holy Spirit. You must do this. You must take courage. If you don't, I will go alone into that pharmacy and see her. And talk to her for you.'

'Wait! My God, Jamike!'

He held Jamike again and saw in the man's eyes something that gave him hope.

'All right, I will come,' he said. 'But see, let us take it slowly. I can just look at her now. Then, maybe another time, I will talk to her?'

Jamike considered the suggestion with a slanting, informed smile that made his forehead bow against the lower side of his face.

'Okay, let us go then, Nwannem.'

He walked with trepidation, slowed by the wealth of his anxiety, until, Jamike leading, they entered the pharmacy. It was a big room with many glass windows, so the place was showered with light. Ceiling fans, loud in their swinging, supplied extra air. He sat quickly in one of the six plastic chairs facing the counter, a big wooden structure that concealed half the pharmacists. It was on this that he placed his eyes after exchanging muffled greetings with the man who sat next to him in one of the chairs, shaking his legs.

Ndali was attending to someone when they entered. Although it was the other woman who called to them, 'Next customer,' he heard her voice.

Jamike did not respond immediately but stood by his chair, his eyes on the counter. My host beckoned to Jamike, and the latter bent to hear him.

'You know, you know – I just came to look at her,' he whispered into Jamike's ear.

His friend nodded uncomfortably, gesturing at the pharmacist to wait a moment.

'Just tell her you want a drug for malaria for me.'

Jamike nodded.

He watched Ndali from where he sat, his cap pulled over his face and his eyes hidden behind the sunglasses. She seemed to him more beautiful than she had been before. How old was she now? Twenty-seven? Twenty-nine? Thirty? He could not recall exactly what year she was born. Now she looked like a woman who had entered her prime. Her hair was permed, slick, and serenaded down her shoulders. There seemed to be a change to every part of her body, down to even the very shape of her face. Her lips were fuller, this time wearing a deeper pink colour than he could ever recall. He'd gazed for hours that morning at the images of her, the images that now increasingly supplied him with pleasure. Yet the face before him was slightly changed. What he could best say was that it seemed she'd been sent back to her creator for renovation and returned even better.

The other woman was starting to put the drugs in a small polythene bag when Ndali opened the small door and stepped out from behind the counter. He noticed that her breasts seemed bigger, although he could not see their full size behind her clothing. He had the chance to see her posterior, almost as he could remember it. He stared at it with all his powers of concentration until she disappeared into an office whose door, closing behind her, bore the inscription NDALI ENOKA, MSC. PHARMACY. He did not see her for the rest of the time they spent there. The nurse attended to Jamike, and they left with the malaria drugs.

AGUJIEGBE, when a man cultivates a great and ambitious expectation, and when that expectation comes to fruition, it usually confounds him. A man may have told his friends, 'Look, look, my brother's home in the far city is big. He is a rich man.' But that selfsame man soon goes to the city and discovers that his brother is nothing but a street sweeper, scraping to get by. But so great had been his expectation, so long had it been sustained, that at first he will doubt reality's uncontestable truth, shattered though he may be. I have seen it many times. This was the case with my host. The reality of Ndali's marriage, signified by her change of name and the ring Jamike was convinced he'd seen on her left finger, confounded him. It put out the light from his universe and left him in a world of unblemished darkness. He stood afterwards at the entrance to Jamike's church, so deeply rattled that the sound of his heartbeat came to him as whiplash.

'I believe that she still loves me, despite all.'

'My brother, I understand thee,' Jamike said in the language of the White Man, in the way he always did when they went to church or soon after they had been to church, as if the language of the fathers was too unholy to be spoken on such grounds.

'Please speak Igbo, this is serious issue,' my host said in the language of the great fathers.

'Sorry, Nnam, sorry o. But it is what it is now. As I have been saying, just give the letter into her hand; put it on the centre of her hand. That is all. Then you can go, and God will see you have done your part.'

He shook his head, not because he believed it but because Jamike did not understand it all. He wanted Jamike to go inside for his service and leave him to ponder things, so he said, 'I understand. I will wait for you here.'

Jamike went in to see the two others with whom he was setting up the special gospel event that evening: a screening of a Christian movie about Jisos Kraist. My host sat on a lone block, one of the remnants of the construction of the church building, only a year ago. A soft wind was blowing, and the banner, a piece of cloth fastened to two wooden poles rigged into the ground, was flapping in the travelling wind. He gazed at the congested street, where men and their wares struggled with motor vehicles and wheelbarrows for space. As he looked, he thought about all the things he had seen and those hidden from him. Did she have children? How long ago did she marry? Was it yesterday or a year ago? Could it have been the same month – or even week – that he arrived in Nigeria a damaged man? It could even be, if things were to follow the usual pattern of life mocking him, the same day. The thought ignited: he stepping down from the plane on to the tarmac of the ramshackle airport in Abuja, she stepping up to the altar with her groom. He imagined the priest looking at her and her husband, asking them if they would be together in sickness and in health, till death. At the same moment the shell of what he once was was falling at the feet of his waiting uncle at the airport.

He considered the things he had seen: Ndali, alive, well, and a more beautiful woman. Had Jamike not appeared in his life, sent like a stone from an unseen enemy to crush him, he would have married her. They would have continued to live on his compound, alive in the midst of his birds, harvesting eggs in the mornings and waking up to the orchestral song of roosters and winged things at dawn. His joy would have been abundant. But he'd been robbed of it all. As mosquitoes buzzed around him, and the voices inside the church reached him in whispers, anger welled within him.

He stamped to his feet and began searching about for a weapon. He found a stick lying near the church's generator and picked it up. He moved towards the church like a madman, and he'd almost reached the door when he stopped. Egbunu, his conscience had reacted, and a stream of light had pierced the sudden darkness into which his mind had precipitously plunged. He dropped the stick and sat back on the block. He put his hands on his face, gnashing his teeth. Moments later, as he allowed himself to calm down, he felt something on his face moving around down his cheek. It was an ant that had crawled from the stick to his hand, and then from his hand to his face. He slapped it away.

'My brother, my brother. What happened?' Jamike called to him just then from the threshold.

He rose. 'I will go home and be alone,' he said.

'Oh, Brother Solomon. I really want you to see this film, *Passion of the Christ*. It will touch your heart. It will touch your soul.'

He wanted to speak, to tell this man that only a moment

before he'd been filled with hatred towards him. But he did not, for he'd been disarmed again by Jamike's face.

'I will watch,' he found himself saying.

'Praise God!'

He sat in the back of the church, torn into shards within, as Jamike and his church members set up the screen for the movie. He sat until the service started. The pastor mounted the stage and talked about salvation, how a man suffered to give his life for others. As the man spoke, he rose up and left the church.

Chukwu, he returned home, struggling to stop himself from falling into fresh despair. He realised, deep in the night, that his point of distress came wholly from his desire to regain that which he had lost. It was not healing and forgiveness that he wanted, not the things Jamike spoke of. Instead, he wanted his life back. He wanted to pick up the coconut that had fallen into the latrine and wash it clean. For he believed it was possible that it could be clean. He sat up, resolved that this was what he wanted, that it could be done. To do anything else was to capitulate.

This incantation of thoughts, having flourished in his mind for so long, formed into a firm decision – that he would fight for her, married or not.

I will not give up, no! he told himself. I have travelled too far to give up. Yes, I repeat it: people's wives are taken from them; so, too, are people's husbands. A man is robbed of his child, and a woman is robbed of her baby. A goose is robbed of its gosling. *Onweghi ihe no na uwa mmadu ji na aka.* Again, I repeat it: nothing in this world belongs firmly to anyone. We own whatever we have because we hold it firmly, because we refuse to let it go. In being here, in standing here, under a roof, I am holding on to my life. If I let it go, it will be taken from me.

In gesturing, his hand clung to his chest. He put on the bulb in his room and went to the mirror.

Tell me, he said, squinting at the image of the changed man who now stood pointing back at him, his face a catalogue of scars. Tell me, was my own future not taken from me? Was it not wrested out of my hands by Jamike, Chuka, Mazi Obialor, Fiona, her husband, Cyprus police – and everyone?

He turned away from the mirror and pointed his finger at the wall and gestured like one confronted with something – a thing to be feared.

Did I not try to hold it, my life, but it was taken from me? What of my body? Did I give it to them? Did I? Tell me! Did I say, 'Take my buttocks, put your penis in them?' He reached for the stool beside his feet and smashed it to the floor.

Tell me!

He stood now, in the wake of the dismembered furniture, panting, aware of his sudden slip into insanity and that he had shouted at midnight. It shocked him. Shaken, he switched off the bulb in haste and settled himself slowly on to the bed and lay there fearing that he may have woken the people in the other flats. He waited for someone to knock on his door, his eyes on the space below it, where he could see shadows of light. For a good while, he lay there as if bound to the bed, both arms held together to his belly, his head thrust histrionically sideways. But no one came. From somewhere, he heard what seemed to be a church service in full swing and the distant sound of drumming and music. In the serenity, it settled on him that he must return to that place where half of him never once left. It is in returning that he would regain his peace, and it would be there that he would fight his greatest battle.

23

THE ANCIENT TALE

ECHETAOBIESIKE, I have said already that man is limited in his capabilities. I say this because, as I will now tell you, my host would have done things differently if he had more capabilities. But this is not to say that his strength is unlike every man's – no. You have not denied him anything that you have given to others. I went with him into Afiaoke and the garden of Chiokike to pick talents and gifts which, in your generosity, you had sought to bestow on him, as you do on every human being. But still, he remained limited. Like everyone else, he is constrained by nature and time. Therefore, there are things that, once one has done them, cannot be undone. All one can do, if one cannot change a circumstance, is give up and move forward, in another direction.

Ebubedike, this wisdom came back to my host six weeks after he saw Ndali again. Because I do not want to take much more time in this luminous court, and because I must render only the details that can in some way lead to the conclusion of the matter about which I've come before you, I must let this man, Jamike, speak. For he'd seen that, from the day my host saw the woman he loved again, he fell into a turmoil.

He was no longer himself. He was unable to move forward or backwards.

'Brother, you have done what you could do. You have gone over and beyond and must now stop. I tell you because I love you with the love of Christ, Ezinwannem, that you must put all of this behind you and move forward. I am telling you, this is the best thing you can do for yourself.'

They had by this time been best friends for the past two months. They sat now in my host's poultry-feed store. In the months since my host opened it, the store had grown to accommodate bags of feed, fertilisers and other agricultural products. Rows of wood had been nailed to the wall, and arranged on them were cans of items related to poultry. A calendar from the Abia State Ministry of Agriculture hung on the wall, open to the page on which 'the Last Pioneer', my host, stood in front of his store squinting into the camera. It is the first picture of him that had been taken since his face was reshaped by the violence in Cyprus – the deep scars on his forehead and on his jaw, his missing teeth.

But Chukwu, I must let his friend speak:

'Let me remind you what you have done, that you have done a lot. After I found her for you, you and I went in search for her. At first, for a long time after we saw her, you went without wanting to reveal yourself to her. As a man whose heart was still filled with love, you did not want to have it destroyed by finding out that the one for whom you'd stored up this vast wealth of love no longer has an ounce of reciprocity left in her.

'Yet even though you had these fears, you did not give up. One day, five weeks ago, you took your chance. I was there with you, Nwannem Solomon. I saw every moment of it. You appeared before her undisguised, at her pharmacy.

You took your chance. It was well planned. We went when we thought there was just she and one of her staff there. Of course, we did not know that two of her friends were seated in her office, whose door was opened. Perhaps, as I have said to you so many times already, it must have been because of these people that she reacted that way. When she saw you, the man she truly loved, whom she had vowed she would never leave nor forsake, she was afraid. It was not told to me in a story, nor did I dream these things. I saw it with my two eyes. With my eyes, I saw her hands tremble. The small rubber bottle she had in her hand, on the body of which she was scribbling something, fell as she gasped "Argh!" then clutched at her heart.

'I saw it, Solomon my brother. It was as if she had seen a ghost in daylight. You could tell that she thought you were either dead or never coming back to Nigeria. You stood there, my brother, calling her name, saying it was you who had returned. Your hands were opened in front of the counter. But she gasped and screamed in terror, and her friends rushed out of the office to see what had happened, and her staff who was cleaning the medicine-filled shelf turned to her. I am sure it was because of nothing else but these people that she changed, turned from a mouse to a bird in the bat of an eyelid and began to shout at you, "Who are you? Who are you?" and without waiting for you to even answer, again began shouting, "I don't know you! I don't know this man!" I am certain that she had recognised you that day.'

He stopped because my host was shaking his head and gnashing his teeth.

'You saw it, too. First, there was that unquestioning spark of recognition. If she didn't recognise you, why would she gasp? Why would she tremble? Does one react that way when they suddenly meet someone they do not know? Do you gasp and tremble?'

My host's heart lit with quiet fire. He shook his head even more and said, 'M.O.G., I agree. I completely agree with all you have said. This is how it transpired. But I wonder, why did she claim she did not know me? Was it not because of my face?'

At this, his friend put on a countenance whose expression I could not decipher.

'Maybe, Nwannem Solomon,' he said. 'What you fear might indeed be true, and it may not only be because of those who were there at that time. Her actions were extreme. She was shouting, screaming louder, as you tried to explain yourself to her. At the mention of your name she screamed in English, "No, no, I don't know you! Leave my office! Leave!" Indeed, such a reaction has more to it. There was undoubtedly a snake hidden in the brush. But you should also know that she may have been afraid. This is a woman who is married. Who—' Perhaps because Jamike knew that these details oppressed his listener, and that what he was about to say would sting him even more, he paused. Then, with eyes out of the store's window, where a dazed fly droned up and down the netting behind the louvres, he said, 'Has a husband.'

In truth, it stung his friend.

'It could be that she is afraid that the man she loved before would destroy her new life. She must have been afraid of you.'

He nodded in acceptance, in defeat.

'But you did not stop there. Yes, after we left the pharmacy in disgrace, hectored out by her friends, she ran out of the pharmacy in tears through a back door. And for some time it weighed you down, my friend. You were ashamed, humiliated, knocked down by this. It wasn't told to me in a story, my brother. I was there. I saw it with my two eyes. If she was rejecting you because of your scarred face, why would she be so moved?'

Ebubedike, his friend had spoken with the frankness of the old fathers and left my host confounded by what he'd heard. He gazed out of the window, and his eyes fell on a peddler hawking CDs on a wheelbarrow. The peddler had been stopped by a woman who was running her eyes over a record.

'But one must add, too, that it may also be because she is angry with you,' Jamike said suddenly, and again gave his friend that warning look that says, *Steel yourself.* 'She may have hated you then because she does not yet know your story. *She is ignorant.*'

This, said not in the language of the fathers, was meant to stand out, to punch everything else into the listening ear whose bearer again nodded desperately.

'She does not know what you went through, how you spent one week in hell on arrival in Cyprus because of what I did to you. She didn't know of your anguish. She did not yet know how lost you were because you gave up everything for the sake of love.'

He listened to these heavy words that bit at his heart with sharp teeth, nodding sporadically.

'She did not know, as yet, how you paid for it dearly. She did not know how you were humiliated, stripped bare, robbed of everything you ever owned. She did not yet know the pain of such self-sacrifice. Then after, as if all that was not enough, they threw you in prison.' Again, Egbunu, he gave my host the searing gaze. 'I will not say more, Nwannem, for there are no words one might use to describe what you went through there that will not scald one's tongue. None. But this is what I mean: she had not yet any knowledge of these things. She had not yet read the letter.'

His eyes were fixed on Jamike, who pulled a handkerchief from the pocket of his plain trousers. He tucked the pocket, which had turned itself out along with the kerchief, back inside and wiped his forehead.

'Yes, she did not know these things before, but then after you gave her the letter and it was only a few days after you made yourself known to her. I remember that day. We had come up with a plan. So we found a man to act as a courier who delivered the letter, with unmarked stamps, to her address with her full name. It was successful. Tokunbo said he went out of the pharmacy after handing her the letter, and then through the window, he saw her open the letter and begin reading it. You and I had rejoiced. For me, that was enough. You got her to understand you were not the kind of man she assumed you were, to realise that you fought hard to have her back. You did not merely go abroad and vanish. You did not even merely give in to oppression but were valiant in the face of it. You proved there that you loved her, and that not once in all those years – despite all that you faced – did you forget her. You woke every morning and imagined her in the same room as you, and said to her, often, "I will return to you. I will return to you." These were the words that gave you life in those painful years. You said there what you said every day to that conjured-up presence of hers you felt in your cell. For. Four. Good. Years. Four good years, blessed Brother Solomon.'

My host was nodding, his eyes vacant, as if the other were speaking words strong enough to overpower all his senses.

'In your letter, which you had delivered to her, you described how this happened to you, how you survived those years. You said it was like a battle—'

The word *battle* hung on his friend's tongue like a fish on a hook, because two men dressed in blue aprons entered the store at that moment. On their clothes was the inscription MICHAEL OKPARA UNIVERSITY OF AGRICULTURE, UMUDIKE.

He knew them.

'Oga Falconer abi na fowler,' one of the men said, removing his cap.

'Ah, university people, una don come?' he said.

'Yes, oh, Na professor send us come.'

He shook hands with them. They shook hands with his friend.

'Wetin him want?' he said.

'Layers,' one of the men said. 'Half bag. Also, him say make you add one bowl of boiler.'

'La-yers, ah layers,' he said, a finger on his lips as he glanced around the store. 'E be like say we no get am again. Wait.'

He pushed open a door to the other room, a small storage area that stank from the silos and bags of poultry feed stored in it. He looked amongst the silos, which were full of corn and placed on wooden slabs, their mouths opened to let in air, and the jute bags of millet, which were stacked one on the other.

'We no get am. E don finish,' he said when he returned back into the store, his hands white from turning over sacks and bags.

'Ah!' one of the men said.

'But broilers dey yan-fun yan- fun. Him no wan millet?'

'No, we over get am,' the man said. 'Okay, just bring the boilers.' And upon consulting in whispers with his colleague, said, 'Two mudus.'

'Okay, sir,' he shouted from inside the storage room.

He came back into the store with a metal bowl and a black polythene bag which he unfurled to open widely so that its inside swelled in expectation. Counting, one, he scooped a handful of the grey-coloured mash into the bag. He found something that looked like a raffia broom in it and, removing it, threw it out of the door. He scooped another bowlful and poured it into the bag. Then, looking up at the men, he scooped a handful with his hand and threw it into the bag.

'Na jara be that,' he said.

'You do well,' the men said.

He shook their hands and thanked them.

GAGANAOGWU, after the men had paid and left the store, my host sat down with Jamike and asked him to continue what he was saying. The other, who had started to gaze into his big Bible while my host served the feed buyers, closed the book and put it on the upturned megaphone on the floor. Then Jamike bent over so that his elbows rested on his thighs and continued.

'I was saying that if she has indeed read your letter she must have seen all this by now.'

Although Jamike had spoken without the oratory of the fathers, his words carried the hypnotic power of their tongue. For my host had received his words the way an ancient story slowly crowds the mind, like embers from dying coals. Afterwards, while Jamike left to do some evangelism, carrying his Bible and megaphone, he sat digesting the things Jamike had said, trying to let them soothe his spirit. He regained all the confidence he had lost. He went to Mr Biggs, the restaurant she had introduced him to, and had a meal. He sat in the far corner of the restaurant, where he had sat with her, only now on a new chair and table. Then he went to an electronics shop down the street and bought a used television set while Jamike went to his church. He was prepared for the time when they eventually would begin to meet again, so she would not mock him for not owning a television.

Although my host sought it, from that day onwards, Jamike did not talk about Ndali. He was convinced that she would either call the number scribbled at the end of the letter or post a letter to the address on the envelope. My host, too, believed this. It consumed him. He went about his life unbalanced, thinking perpetually about what she would do or what she would not do. He would sometimes seek desperately to be free for a moment, to think about the stampede at the Ascension Crusade rally or the impending activities of MASSOB which Elochukwu – with whom he was no longer close – had told him about and which could flare into a riot in the city. He would thrust out all these and imagine, instead, that Ndali had read his letter and wanted to meet him or that she read it and did not believe a word of it. Perhaps she simply thought it was impossible that all that could have happened; perhaps he was making it all up. Or maybe she read a bit of it and tore it up, never seeing the rest. Or perhaps she may not have read it at all. Maybe she tore it up and the courier saw her reading something else and mistook it for his letter. Let us even say she read it. Really, let us assume beyond reason that she read it and thought it was all true, but that it was now too late. She was now married, inseparable from that man. They had become one, nothing can put them asunder. Nothing. The man has slept with her for years, *every day*, far more than he ever had. It was too late, too late, too late.

These uncertainties, these fears strained his mind so much that he became sick from pondering what she may have done with the letter. On the night of the fourth day after Jamike's long speech, he became so sick and weak that he did not rise from his bed. The rain did not help, either; it had rained so hard, rapping continuously against the roof of his flat, that it kept him awake far into the morning. Thunder clapped a few times and I rushed out to see it. It was the young kind, the kind Amandioha used as a weapon. In its aftermath, lightning struck the face of the horizon, shaped like thin branches of phosphorescent trees. The rumbling in the bowel of the sky was so loud that it morphed from sound into invisible object: a spark of teeth-white light. By morning, the volume of rain had become so enormous that it seemed there was some kind of movement in the land, as if the world had become reduced to an ark in which everything – man, beast, birds, trees, buildings – was crammed and was floating towards some shore.

He did not leave the house for most of the day but lay in bed tormented by the thought of the loss of Ndali. Between thinking and imagining, vivid things emerged in his head. He would rise and walk about his room. He would gaze at himself, his face, his mouth, in the mirror. He would nurse a certain memory of Ndali, now blurred, dulled by time, of them making love. Then he would think of the new man in the same position. And it would kill him. An image of wishful violence would jump out into his field of vision like a beast and howl into his rankled head.

Oseburuwa, I did not know what to say to him in this time. In the years before he saw her again, I always told him to have faith like the white man of ancient times, Odysseus, in the tale he loved as a kid. In that tale, the man had been stopped from returning to his wife by an angry god. I would have kept mentioning this story to him, if the man did not eventually reunite with his wife. I could not remind him because his woman had yielded to another man. I feared that to remind him now would instead fill him with a sense of failure. I did not know how, at all, to help him. I knew it was futile to try to discourage him from loving her, and I could only give suggestions. His will was sealed. There was more to what he now felt. It was not only love, it was not only that he wanted her back, it was also that her rejection of him made him feel his suffering had been futile. He wanted her to acknowledge, to make a concession towards him, a man who has been damaged for her sake.

The hands of the small wall clock without a glass covering on the wall of his room were pointing at 4 p.m. when he rose, brushed his teeth, and spat into the gutter that flowed out of the compound. One of his neighbours was in the shared bathroom, the sound of splashing water reaching him, and suds washing up and down the drain. He chewed what was left of the bread he'd bought the previous day, finishing it in two bites. He dressed and walked out of the house.

He saw that the rain had created a fjord outside the compound. Egbunu, although since his prison days I have cut down very drastically on the frequency with which I left the body of my host, I went out that night to see the rain as I had done of the thunder, to wash in it while he was fast asleep. I had spent much of the night there, with a thousand other spirits of all kinds, taking in the empyreal smell of Benmuo. I was confident that because of the storm, no spirit would be going around looking for bodies to inhabit or harm. And now that my host had left his flat, I had the chance to see the impact of the rain for myself. The clay earth had been softened, so that as he walked his shoes made small ruts on the earth. A house across from the block of flats in which he lived, made of unvarnished adobe bricks, now stood precariously on a shelf of earth.

With the hems of his trousers stained with mud water, he arrived near the pharmacy, his face concealed behind his sunglasses. Across the road from the big shoe shop, he saw Elochukwu and a group of men dressed mostly in black vests carrying Biafran flags as they walked towards the other side.

The MASSOB. They were not protesting, simply walking, some of them with sticks, redirecting traffic. He saw Elochukwu among them, consumed with this agitation. My host shook his head and walked on to the pharmacy.

When he reached a short distance away, he saw that the car he'd identified as Ndali's – the same one she used to drive to his house – was there. As he looked at the car, at the small poster on the back window, he lost all confidence again and began to wonder why he had come. He did not know what to do next. I put in his mind caution – Jamike's words that he should no longer try to meet her on his own. 'Don't do it, cha-cha, please, I beg you in the name of Jesus, the son of God. If she is married and says she doesn't want you, then once you have sought forgiveness from her, let her go.'

But he could not. Even when he tried to let himself do it, to give it all up, something drew him back. One time, a crushing desire to be reunited with her. And next time, a desire to have his suffering, his sacrifice acknowledged.

He walked on towards the other side of the street, past a group of small fruit hawkers lined up with their wares balanced on rickety tables. Two boys in school uniforms, talking about a pig, walked by him. The bag of one of them was open, dangling from his back. My host stopped at the GSM table a few metres away and sat with the lady on one of the plastic chairs.

'I wan make call,' he said.

'Oh,' the woman said. 'Glo, MTN, Airtel?'

'Emm, Glo.'

He dialled Jamike's number with the woman's phone, whose keypads had been cleaned off. Jamike answered in a husky voice. 'My brother, we have just finished counselling. Have you closed for the day?'

'Yes,' he said. 'Can you come? There is something I want to talk to you about.'

'Okay, I will come in the evening.'

He walked back all the way, stopping to buy a cup of garri and a bag of peeled oranges. While he waited for Jamike to arrive, he rehearsed the idea that had come to him while standing across from Ndali's car. Chukwu, I will let you in on this later. He put it through various iterations until he was confident of its final form, so that when Jamike arrived, he did not mince words.

'You leave in two days for this long prayer, and I will not see you for – how long?'

'Forty days and forty nights. That is the number of days our Lord Jesus Christ fasted and prayed—'

'Okay, forty days,' he said bitterly. He glanced around his one room, looking to find traces of the torment he'd been in the past two days. He'd wanted to tell Jamike about it but decided not to.

'Tell me whatever you want, my brother Solomon, and I will do it. You know you have a friend in me.'

'*Da'alu*,' he said, and adjusted himself on the bed, on which he sat to face Jamike, who sat on the lone wooden chair in the room. 'I want us to urinate together so we can generate more foam than when one of us does it alone.'

'Okay, my brother,' his friend said.

Indeed, Ijango-ijango, it was not very common for the children of the old fathers, now sold in the ways of the White Man, to speak with the oratory of the wise great fathers. But it came often in the speech of my host when what he was about to say had come from deep introspection.

'I know you have changed completely, and are a good man because you are born again, *Onye-ezi-omume*. You believe that

I should leave Ndali alone after I have suffered for her, because she is married.'

The other nodded to every word he said.

'I have heard all of that. I will not bother her even though, Nwannem, I have not lost a drop of love for her. My heart is still full, so full it cannot even be lidded. What I am going through, knowing she is alive and rejects me, is worse than anything I have gone through before.'

He paused because he'd seen a cockroach appear over the wall mirror. He watched it as it flared its wings, then flew down behind the chair.

'This is worse, my brother, I really mean it. It is an imprisonment not of myself, but my heart. It is held and locked up by her.' He moved to the edge of the bed and leaned against the wall. 'M.O.G., I don't want to love her. Not any more. She has spat on a man who sold everything he had to be able to marry her. I cannot forgive. No, I cannot.'

Even as he spoke, he knew that although he was bitter, what he wanted most of all was to have Ndali back – to spend those nights with her again, and to make love to her. He watched Jamike shake his head.

'At least, Jamike, I want to know what happened to her. I want to know at what time she decided to leave and get married. Do you see? I sold everything, I left for her sake, I want to know what she did for me, too. I want to know why, what sent out the wild mouse running into the street in broad daylight.'

'Yes, very wise, very wise,' Jamike muttered with the same intensity as my host's.

'I want to know what happened to her,' he said again, almost offhandedly, as if those words had been painful to utter. 'I wanted to write to her, but I could not find anyone who could help me post the letter in the prison.'

Chukwu, this was true. And it was this frustration that led me to try to get in touch with Ndali myself by performing the extraordinary act of *nnukwu-ekili* in which I attempted to appear in her dream to give her the information my host wanted her to have. Indeed, Egbunu, as I have already told you, her chi prevented this from happening. And, as I have already told you, many of the guards would not even respond to my host's request for help in sending a letter. And one, who spoke English, told him that if it was a letter to Cyprus, then he could help him, but for Nigeria, he couldn't because it would be expensive.

He looked upon his friend with terror in his eyes.

'I want to know what effort she made for me during those times.'

Jamike motioned to speak, but he continued.

'I want you to help me. And you must do this. See what you have caused me, see?' The other nodded with shame on his face. 'So you must help me, Jamike. You should go to her husband as a preacher, and tell him you have seen a vision for him. Tell him as if you know much about his life. Say, for example, that you know his wife. Tell him you have seen in a vision that someone in her past, a man, is after her, and will destroy the family if he does not pray.'

He looked at his friend, whose head was resting on his folded hands, eyes fixed on him.

'You see? Tell the man you want to know if she has ever told him about a man in her past before.'

'What if she has told her husband about the letter and that you are here?' Jamike, who seemed to have been rendered subservient by guilt, said.

'Yes? But he will not know, he cannot know you are coming from me. Be vague about me, say you see destruction, that the Lord showed you mourning and weeping caused by this man.'

He stopped now in the darkening room to replay the words he'd said in his mind, and when he had done it, the enormity of it struck him. Egbunu, please listen to these words of my host, for they are crucial to my testimony this night and a solid proof that he has not done harm to her knowingly.

'I am not saying I will hurt her, no. I love her too much to do that, even though I am angry, very angry with her. It is a strange, uncanny mix of feelings. Deep love that is beyond compare. But no, I will kill any man, her husband even, who lays a hand on her.'

Jamike nodded, with strains of discomfort evident in his countenance, moved in his seat, and said, 'I will do it, if you say I should. I will, my brother, even though this is sinful. You cannot say the Lord has said something when he hasn't.' Jamike shook his head. 'I cannot do such a thing, my friend, by lying. I will tell him that I want to pray for him, a special prayer when I go to the mountain, and I want to know everything about his relationship with his wife so I can pray against anything in their past trying to destroy their future.'

He did not know how to respond, so he kept silent, watching the man before him.

'I want you to be well again, my brother Solomon. This is why I'm what I have become. I caused all this for you, and I must fix it again. If this is all that will do it, I will go. As I said, someone who works near the pharmacy says her husband works at the Afribank at Okpara Square. I will go there and ask to see him – Ogbonna Enoka.'

My host nodded, his heart resting on the floor again.

Later, as he drove Jamike home, his spirit calmed, and it seemed that the anticipation of her story had healed him. He slept well that night and went early to his store the following day. So many people had come looking for him, the neighbours said. He contacted some of the customers and spent a good part of the morning transporting bags of millet to them. As the sun rose after the morning's slight shower, he returned to his store with a pickup from the major broiler feed distributor, AGBAM FEEDS AND SONS. As they offloaded the contents into his store, Jamike called. My host answered the phone with shaking hands.

'I spoke with him, my brother. I don't know, but I think I was able to convince him. I went there with Sister Stella, with my ministry badge clipped to the pocket of my coat.'

'I understand.'

'Yes, I will like to come talk to you about it, so that I can also greet you, since I will not see you until after we return from the mountain.'

'Yes, yes, you must come.'

'In the evening,' Jamike said.

'Why not now?'

'I will come, my brother. I will come in the evening.'

OSEBURUWA, when a man has sent for a healer, if such a man is sick, and he is told that the healer is coming, he begins to count the steps of the healer's trek towards him. I have spoken about what anticipation does to a man, and I have seen it many times. My host could not wait for Jamike to arrive that evening.

'When I got to his office,' Jamike began, 'I was afraid. I had also lied to my sister in Christ, Stella. I was sinning.'

'Yes, yes, I understand.'

'But it is for you, my brother Solomon. So I went in. The man is a good-looking man. He is tall and has Jheri-curled hair. Ogbonna Ephraim Enoka. Ephraim is his baptismal name. He said his grandfather was brother to Father Tansi. So with Sister Stella sitting there, we prayed for him. Then I asked if he believed in prophecies. He said yes, why not? "Am I not a Christian? Did the Bible not say shame on those who say they have faith but deny the power thereof?" I corrected him: "It is in the book of Timothy. *Having a form of godliness, but denying the power thereof: from such turn away.*"

'He said, "Oho, that is so," in Igbo, then turned back to English. "I believe in the power of God."

"'I am happy, sir. I will tell you, then. I was in the spirit praying as I passed this bank yesterday, and the Lord said, there is a man named Ogbonna here whose wife is in danger, in real danger. An enemy has appeared at their door and is knocking."

"'God said the name of the man is Ogbonna?" he asked.

"'Yes, yes. Father only gave me your first name."

"'Okay."

"'Is there another Ogbonna here?"

"'No, it is only me I know."

"'And my spirit confirms it right now as we sit here. I can hear the Ancient of Days, the Lion of the Tribe of Judah, saying this is the man. An old flame has come to your wife and can destroy your marriage."

"'God forbid in Jesus's name!" the man said. He snapped his fingers over his head. "God forbid bad thing."

"'Yes, brother. So can you tell me, is there any man your wife has offended? Anyone?"

'He seemed confused by this. I could see it on his face. He thought for a moment, and then said, "No, nobody."

"'Any man chasing her?"

"'No, I don't think so. She is a married woman with a child."

'At this point, my brother, I worried that this man did not know anything about you,' Jamike said. Having tried to distinguish his words from the words of Ndali's husband, his transition back to the language of the fathers was jagged.

'I asked him again. "Mr Ogbonna, is there any man whom she'd told you about?" and he looked at me, his face changing, and said, "Yes, because of God, only because of God I'm saying, because it is a secret." "Don't worry, tell it to the servant of God," I said. "She almost married a man who left her and went overseas," he said. "That man was the second person who had done this kind of thing to her." "So this man disappeared?" I asked. "Yes, no one heard from him again. That is all I know." I wanted to speak, but Sister Stella said, "So she never saw him again?" "That is all I know, Man of God," said Ogbonna.

'My brother, at this point, I was afraid if I pressed him more, he might become suspicious. So I said let us pray; that I will go to the mountain and pray, but that he should speak to his wife to see if there was a man after her.'

'Aye. Oh-oh, Jamike. This is insufficient,' my host said.

'But—'

'What if he asks her while you are away? And what if . . . '

He broke off his speech because one of the neighbours drove in on his motorcycle, vrooming as he parked it. The headlights of the motorcycle sent two beams of light through the curtains and illuminated the room, splashing their shadows on the wall as though calligraphed in thick black ink. When the engine went off, and the lights with it, he continued, 'What will happen if he asks her while you are away?'

'I doubt she will tell him. I think, and see, that she doesn't want him to know much.' Jamike slapped his leg to nip a mosquito. 'I doubt he would.'

'Yes,' he said again. 'But what if she decides to tell him after a man of God has spoken to him about it?'

Jamike considered it briefly. 'Then I will find out. I will find out when I return. Isn't what you want just the information about what she did about your going away? You will not do anything with it, except just know.'

He agreed.

'Then I will. Don't worry, my brother.'

When they went out, so that Jamike could return to church first before going home, it had become dark. They passed groups of schoolchildren trundling back home from school, crossing the street in cliques. A little boy stooped by the public gutter, vomiting into it, coughing, attended by his friends, who kept saying sorry. An adult stopped there and asked one of them to give the sick boy water. My host and his friend said sorry to the boy. Then Jamike placed his hand on the boy's head and began speaking in tongues – an act which I have come to understand is a strange aspect of the religion of the White Man and is like an incantation, *afa*, in odinala. When Jamike was done with it, he switched back to the language of the White Man. 'Thank You, Lord, Jehovah-jireh, the mighty healer, Jehovah-shammah, for healing this little boy.'

OKAAOME, he returned to his flat afterwards with the information he'd received from Ndali through Jamike. He was steeped in thought as he warmed the pot of jollof rice he'd made that morning. Insects gathered around the kerosene lantern as the pot hissed slowly to life. He was getting the pot off the stove when electricity was restored, and then, almost abruptly, it went off again. He returned to his room with the food and ate slowly, wondering why she had told her husband that he simply vanished and that she had not heard anything from him. How was it that he just vanished? How? Did Dimeji not take his message to her? He had asked that he tell her, that he contact her, just before he was sentenced. He had also asked Tobe to do so. Did she never hear what happened to him? It was, he resolved, improbable. There was a great chance she had heard and knew but was probably hiding the information from her husband. It puzzled him greatly. Why was she hiding it from him?

In such times, a man must be careful, for in a desperate state, his mind comes up with a lot of answers. There is a part of man that can be irrational, a part which exists exclusively in order to make him comfortable. Thus, in a situation such as this, it will reach for whatever it can, the lowest branch of the tree, and pick it up. What a chi must do is to try to pick the most reasonable suggestion and allow that to dominate others. So from the multitude of possibilities that came to him that evening, I picked that it could be that Ndali simply had never received a letter from him before the one he just sent to her. But what he settled on was different – that she had told her husband he vanished to deceive him, to make her husband think she didn't want him any more, when in fact she still loved him.

24

CASTAWAY

AGBATTA-ALUMALU, nothing cripples a human being more than unrequited love. Although Ndali once told him that she would not have drowned anyway, his act of generosity in trying to get her off the bridge was what first won her heart. And now her heart had been taken away from him by a man who worked in a bank and knew nothing of the sacrifices he had made for her. This was beyond what my host could bear. He was defeated in the days following Jamike's revelation. With Jamike gone in the following week, he became caught in the obsession of pursuing her. He fought hard against it at first by going to work and trying to focus on his store, but every day after closing, he would drive near the pharmacy and park on the side of the road. And from this vantage point, with his face concealed behind dark glasses, he would gaze at the pharmacy for a while.

Sometimes, the July rain would blur his vision, and he would sit there unable to see. Then, after he'd watched and thought about her so much that his heart would feel as heavy as a thing infused with lead, he would catch sight of her either walking out of the pharmacy or driving away in her blue vehicle. Catching sight of her was always enough for him to return home with a measure of relief. She was always in her white coverall, with whatever she wore under it showing. Most days, she wore a shirt and a skirt. Sometimes an ankara print blouse or an up–and–down. On those days when he saw her, he would return home, telling himself how beautiful she was, how her hair looked, or the colour of her fingernails. Once, she had painted them blue, and he could see them as she passed his car up close without noticing that the man in the car with the hat and sunglasses was my host. He stood think-ing about how he'd watch her paint her nails with cortex on the bench in the yard because she did not want him to choke on the strong scent of the nail polish. Once, she'd rubbed her fingernail on one of the white chickens, and the paint had stayed on its feather, a red splotch that could not be cleaned. It'd made her laugh so hard she'd cried.

He'd return home and long for contact with her. He'd think of all possibilities. He began to notice that the more he saw her, the more he raised the memories of their intimacy and the more his desire deepened. What would he do? She would disgrace him again if he came up to her and she would proba-bly hate him. She had read his letter, seen all he'd suffered, but showed no remorse. At the entrance of this kind of thought, his mood would change from desire to anger, then resentment. He would clench his teeth, stamp his feet and quiver with rage. He'd sleep in this mood and wake up the following day to the same routine: go to his store with the consolation that he'd devise a way to see her in the evening, then feel a flurry of conflicting emotions afterwards.

On one of those days, he followed her as she drove away, curious to see what she would do, for a thought had flung into his mind that she might have a lover. She drove to a school, a private primary school, where, at the gate, her son was waiting. He looked on from the side street, in his car, parked two hundred metres away. He noticed the boy's ears; how, by complexion, he resembled Ndali. He followed them on to their house, a duplex that stood grandly on Factory Road. It was fenced and had a gate as tall as the fence itself. He stopped by the house and surveyed its surrounding land, overgrown with bushes. On the other side of the unpaved road, a supermarket sat in front of what looked like a small clinic. A few metres from there was a shack under which a woman fried plantains, yams and akara every evening. He returned to his flat not knowing what to do with his new knowledge.

At the end of that first week without Jamike, on the Friday, he could not go to work. The bitterness of the previous night had lasted into the following day, and he'd found himself weeping for the pain her rejection had caused him. Egbunu, what I was witnessing in my host was peculiar and startling. It was the known alchemy of love – it is a thing that becomes alive and thriving in a state of decay. He swore to himself that he would confront her if she stepped out of the pharmacy that day. So that day, he decided to get out of his car and sit with the woman who operated the GSM phone stall across the road. As he fumbled with one of the service phones, the woman asked if he was the man who was always sitting in a parked car and looking at the pharmacy. My host was startled.

'Have you been seeing me?'

The woman laughed and clapped her hands in jest. 'Of course. You come every day, every day. How won't we see you? Maybe even the people in the pharmacy have seen you.'

He sat still. He turned to the street, to a cattle herder ferrying his cattle and slapping them with his stick.

'You have not answered my question,' the woman said again. 'Why are you always doing that?'

My host, astonished, knew he would no longer continue this venture.

'But I am always wearing sunglass, how did you know me?' he said.

'Because I saw you come out of that same car just now.'

'Okay, I was married to the pharmacist before,' he said. Then he told a lie about how her present husband took her away by casting a juju spell on her. The gullible girl felt sorry for him and, while trying to comfort him, brushed her hand against his. He'd felt nothing until then, but when her body touched his, it struck him that he was attracted to her. In a hurry to take advantage of the situation and drive my host away from his continuous, destructive obsession with Ndali, I flashed it in his mind that he could have this woman, and that she would love him always. As these thoughts floated about in his head, he observed her closely. Her features were common; she was cheaply dressed, and her skin was rough and coated with the kind of darkness that comes from privation. But on this day, she was dressed better than she usually was: in a good blouse and short skirt, her hair permed.

He sat there while she attended to those who wanted to make calls or buy phone credits, watching this woman, aghast at the sudden transference of his wanton desire. He developed an erection.

'I think I should take you to my house today, so you can come to know my place and we can be good friends,' he said.

The woman smiled and did not look at him. She fumbled with the cards, stacking them together with rubber bands.

'You don't even know me,' she said.

'You don't want to come, eh? Okay, what is your name?'

'I did not say that,' she said. 'My name is Chidinma.'

'I'm Nonso. So will you come, Chidinma?'

'Okay, after I close, then.'

Akataka, he stayed there until the woman closed the shop, then he drove her to his home, stopping to buy two bottles of Malta Guinness on the way. I did not flee at first because I wanted to see things go through, to see where it would end. Even though I had helped engineer it, I wanted to try to understand this new phenomenon: a man is wasting away only moments before in great desire for one woman, then suddenly he is burning for another with the same intensity. This was a mystifying thing. Aside from the woman's question about whether he would continue to look for his wife or love her instead – to which he said, 'I will love you instead' – there was no resistance. He tore at her hungrily, almost ripping her clothes. He plunged his hands into her brassiere and drank her breasts with mad haste. Many years had passed since he'd seen a naked woman, let alone touched one, so that when he came to the place between her legs, he was dazed.

It was at this point, certain the unexpected would unfold, that I left his body. But so monstrous was the clamour of Benmuo this night that I was forced back into my host at once, as if chased by some deadly beast. Thus was I forced to behold the mystifying alchemy of sexual intercourse. I came back when the woman's entreaties that he should use a condom, in the heat of the moment, became insistent. But he paid no heed. 'But don't release inside. Don't release inside, oh,' she'd begged as he thrust violently, his bed creaking. I witnessed him throw a shout and then relieve himself on the floor.

The woman lay by him and clutched him, but he faced the wall. As his heartbeat relaxed and his sweat dried, he began to feel different. He thought back to earlier in the day, how he'd sat there at the woman's table. What he saw now, Egbunu, was different. Different! He saw the spots on the woman's face, one peeled so that it had scabbed. He thought of the woman's missing teeth and what looked like a scar above her cleavage. He thought of the dirtiness of her nails, how she'd pick the mucus of her eyes with them. He thought of the dark pit of the woman's stomach as they lay to make love and the fortress of her vagina. He drew away and stepped out of the bed, opened the window and, looking up, recalled Ndali's body. He remembered the day she insisted he suck at her vagina and the revulsion of feeling that had seized him then.

When he turned back into the room, the woman had covered herself with the bedsheet. Resentment rose within him. For a reason neither he nor I, his chi, could determine, he found that he hated her. He sat on the chair and finished the malt, which he'd drunk halfway.

'Will you go home?' he said.

'Er?' she said, sitting up.

He regarded her, her ugliness more pronounced, and he convulsed with regret.

'I said, do you want to sleep here? I just want to know.'

'Eh, are you sending me away?' she said, her voice almost breaking.

'No, no, I'm saying if you want to go.'

She shook her head. 'So you have got what you want, and now asking me to go home?'

He gazed at her without words, surprised at his own sudden cruelty.

'*O di nma*,' the girl said, and snapped her fingers.

He watched her strap the brassiere back on, the line on her back almost unapparent, the plump of unremarkable flesh. Inwardly, he felt violated in a way he could not explain. Was it that he had known another woman and now Ndali would be defiled in his eyes? The fear rose with a mixture of anger. He closed his eyes and did not know when the woman finished dressing. The sound of the door broke him out of his reverie. He stamped to his feet, but she was out. He chased after her in the dark, barefoot, shirtless, his room unlocked, calling her name: 'Chidinma, Chidinma, wait, wait.' But she did not wait. She went on, sobbing, saying nothing.

He returned and sat down, only the smell of the woman left in the room. He did not know what to feel, remorse for how callously he'd treated the woman or anger at his own mysterious violation. He waited for an hour or so to pass, and then he rang the woman, but she did not answer. He sent a message that he was sorry. She wrote back: neva, neva in yr cum 2 my shop again! Neva in yr life!! god punish you!!!

He quaked in his seat as a possessive thought of violence perched on his mind, carried on the black wings of contempt. He deleted the woman's number, and that was it. That night, while he was asleep, two vagabond spirits broke into the house, fighting. They came through the wall, unaware they had crossed a human barrier. Chukwu, I must say that things like this happen quite frequently, but most of them are not worthy of recollection. But this particular incident moved me, for I could relate it to my host's situation.

One of the spirits was the chi of a man who had taken the wife of another man. The other spirit was the ghost of the woman's former husband. The chi was saying how exhausted he was, having been trying to fight off this ghost for years. 'Why don't you just go to rest?' it said. 'How can I be at rest when your host cheated me of not just my wife but my life, too?' the revenant said. 'But you should rest. Go to Alandiichie, return back in another life, and take back what was yours,' the chi replied. 'No, I want justice now. Now. Now. Tell your host to keep his hands off Ngozi. Or I will not let him alone. I will continue to haunt his dreams, attempt to possess him, cause him hallucinations until justice is done.' 'Well,' the chi replied, 'if you let it be, Ala and Chukwu will execute justice on your behalf. But you have taken it upon yourself to handle ...' Their conversation continued as I gestured at them to get out, and they, barely giving me and my host a look, returned back into the darkness through the wall. I did not know why I witnessed this – perhaps it was you who allowed me to see it as a warning to do more to dissuade my host from his pursuit of the elusive, a situation that could potentially cause him to become an akaliogoli, a vagabond spirit, without a home in the heavenlies or on earth.

ECHETAOBIESIKE, my host returned back to the way he was, a man of conflicting thoughts. He'd floated like some fluid element back into the thing that contained him. He stopped lying in wait near the pharmacy and turned his attention to her house. He would park his car a few stone throws away and walk up to the supermarket across from her house. He befriended the shopkeeper. He would buy biscuits and Coke and sit on the lone bench the man placed by the side of the shed, eating and drinking and chatting with the man in his mangled English. From this vantage point, making sure that his sunglasses did not once leave his face, he would first watch her arrive from work with the boy, then watch her husband. On the third day of this new routine, it struck him to ask about the family from the store owner.

'Mr Obonna?' the man, a Hausa who did not speak the language of the fathers, said.

'Yes, and his wife?'

'Oh, that madam? Me no know plenty about am, oh. She no dey talk at–all, at–all. Just only quiet like say she no get mouth. She dey come here plenty.'

He regarded the shopkeeper as the man scratched the two long scarifications on one side of his face. A man approached the shop in shorts, a shirt hanging from his shoulder.

'Well done, oh,' the customer said to my host.

'Well done, my brother.'

'Mallam, Cowbell dey?'

'Which one, na? Tin abi sachet?'

'Sachet. Bring four. Na how much, sef?'

'Tem tem naira. Four na four naira.'

When the man was gone, he asked the trader if he knew anything about Mr Ogbonna and his son.

'Ah, yes–yes. I sabi them well–well.'

Egbunu, I have told you that my host possessed the gift of good luck. True, many bad things had happened to him, but what his onyeuwa picked in the garden of Chiokike is potent. For how can I explain what he stumbled on by serendipity here? How, Ezeuwa? All he'd done was ask the man the corollary question to the one he'd asked about the family. 'Na only that son them get?' To which the man had responded thusly:

'Pickini kwo? Yes, Na only wan pickin. Chinomso, na only one pickin.'

Obasidinelu, my host jumped to his feet. For he had not told this man his name.

'Er, what?'

'The pickin naw,' the man said, astonished at his reaction. 'I say him name na Chinomso.'

He stood still now, unable to move his feet. He stared at the man, then in the direction of the house, then back again.

'Oga, wetin happen?'

He shook his head. 'Nothing.'

The man, easing up again, began to talk about how 'Mr Obonna' sometimes didn't take his change after purchasing and how, during Eid-El-Fitr, he brought him a goat. He listened with half his mind carried away. When he rose up and got back in his car, he became aware, as if his consciousness had been renewed, of the information he'd just received. How could it be that she'd named her son after him? How?

Nothing troubled him more than this contemplation. He sat, unable to do anything, helpless. It was a question that menaced him with its deceptive simplicity. For it seemed like it could easily be answered, as if the answer lay on some shelf just above his head. But any time he attempted to pick it up, he realised it was far away – a place he could not reach by merely stretching his hand. And it was this that troubled him the most. He slept little that night, and when he woke up, he feared he'd lost his mind from the unrelenting examination of his thoughts. He was hungry, shattered and dismayed, but there he lay, broken in bits. The people from the agricultural university called him two times, then sent a text saying they would no longer be buying feed from him as he was no longer serious about his business. They were the fourth or so regular customers who had abandoned him because he was now rarely at his store.

After he read the message, he snapped. He yelled into the hot day and stood up.

Why am I afraid of her? Why, after all I have done, after all I have done for her? No, she has to talk to me.

He paced the room, carrying the memory of the day she had rejected him in public, crying that she did not know who he was. Today, today, Ndali must give me answers.

He'd spoken so firmly that he was astonished at how

emboldened he'd become. He went out to the shared bathroom at the back of the flat to bathe. In front of it, the wife of one of the neighbours, a Yoruba man who spoke with a feminine voice, sat on a short stool, bent over a bucket, washing clothes. Soap suds were scattered about. The woman was swaddled in a wrappa, which hung over her bosom and was fastened into a knot beneath her hairy armpit. The woman greeted him, and as he passed, the portion of flesh exposed to his eyes annoyed him. He thought of the woman he'd slept with, how his feelings had surprised him. Instead of pleasure, he'd felt disgust, and that had shocked him. As he closed the bathroom door, made of zinc nailed to wood, and piled his clothes over the top, it struck him that what he'd experienced with that woman and his general apathy towards other women was because he still loved Ndali.

He drove again to her house and parked his car a few metres from it, on the side of the road opposite the direction from which her car came. He parked under a tree filled with birds tweeting, overlooking a fenced mansion from which the voices of children came in flashes. Then he waited, his eyes on the road, until at sundown he saw her car approaching. He'd thought and rethought things and made up his mind. He'd observed that cars seldom came this way, as the street that curved beyond this one did not give out on to anything beyond itself. It culminated in a dead end. But if there was a car trailing her own, and he could not block the road, then he would simply come out of the vehicle, chase after her car and interfere before she honked at her gate and the gateman opened it.

Egbunu, the moment came like something from his imagination. As soon as he saw her car, he started his car and drove it with a rush forward, then sideways into the path of the oncoming car. The cars almost hit each other, and the cry that arose as a result of this near hit threatened even his own disoriented mind. He sat for a moment to let his heart quieten. Then he got out of the car. He'd seen her, but he had not seen the boy who sat in the back. Now he saw them both, she turning back to the boy to say something. He walked to the front of the two cars and stood still. For a long time, months, ever since he returned, he'd wanted this moment. He felt himself shaking, something erupting along the base of his heart.

The person in the car behind his honked thrice and drove angrily past. But he stood there. Then she came out of the car. She looked at him and he at her. Life seemed to be there in that face, the life he once knew. But it was a face that was hard for him to recognise. Something about it was new, yet much of it was familiar.

'You?' she said, as if enquiring into the nature of his being.

He nodded. 'Mommy,' he said.

She stepped back towards the car, bent, and said something to the boy. Then she closed the door and stepped forward beside it.

'You, again? What do you want?'

He shook his head, for Egbunu, he was afraid.

'Mommy, I am sorry for everything. I am sorry. I am sorry. Did you read my letter? Did you read the—'

'Excuse me!' she cried. 'Excuse me!' She stepped back, put her hand on her face, and pointed the painted fingers at him. 'Why are you after me? Why are you coming to my chemist and my house? What is the meaning of this, eh?'

'Mommy—'

'No, no, stop! Stop it! Don't call me that, please, I beg you.'

He made to speak again, but she looked back at the car and the boy.

She turned to him again, and with her eyes closed, she said, 'Let me tell you, I don't want to ever see you ever again. What is this? Why are you following—'

'Ndali, listen,' he said, and stepped forward.

'Stop! Stop there!'

So violently had she moved backwards that it alarmed him.

'Don't you come near me at all. Listen, I beg you in the name of God, leave me alone. I am married now, okay? Go and find another woman, and leave me alone. If you come to my house again, I will arrest you.'

He saw that she had turned back towards the car, and he followed her. He'd come inches from touching her when she faced him again.

'Your son,' he said, panting from the rush. 'He has my name.'

In this memorable moment of life, when my host and the woman he loved were inches away from each other, a lorry started to approach the place where the two cars were fixed into a confluence. It was an instinctive moment, brief, like the last-minute glimpse of an assassin by his victim, but fraught with a grace that was imponderable to man. With one unwelcome step he had entered into her field of vision, and his legs had been caught in a loop from which he could not disentangle himself. He saw that she wanted to speak, but then, abruptly, she turned and went back in her car.

The men in the lorry had stopped and started to curse. He returned to his car and pulled it gently into a reverse. Her car coursed through and made for the gate to her house. He watched it disappear, the provoked lorry driver and passengers cursing at him as they passed.

EBUBEDIKE, I must not dwell on the thing he did afterwards too much, for it was something too difficult to watch. For my host was devastated by this encounter. The few words Ndali had said to him he carried in the weak sac of his stomach and digested them on the scene, weighing every word. But like a goat, he'd made them into veritable cud. And every night, when his life, which had acquired the restlessness of a pendulum, swung into a standstill, he'd bring up the cud and chew with fresh salivary intensity. But there was one thing that he could not shake off, that could not be chewed or broken down. For it was solid and complete in its composition. He'd seen it in her eyes, and even though he knew that his mind could become overreactive in such situations, he was convinced that what he'd seen in her was contempt.

It is hard to describe what this feeling did to him. He lay in the house for days, surrounded by the ghostlike, disembodied voices of the encounter. He ate little; he spoke to himself. He laughed. He cried. He stepped out wearily at night and ran back into his room again, drinking the rainwater that washed down his face.

I feared, Egbunu, that he was descending into madness. For even more, he was haunted by strange and persistent dreams, many of them of birds – chickens, ducks, falcons, and even hawks. They were dreams that exposed the inflammations of his afflicted mind. He became like a castaway – one rejected by earth and heaven. A living akaliogoli. I feared because I have come to know that the strongest kind of affection often exists in the heart of a man whose love interest is distant from him – the one he cannot have. That is the one his soul longs for with dying breaths, and the sublime dungeon in which his heart is caged. The only way to save him is to introduce a new affection as strong as the one he cannot get. But because no such woman was near, I feared.

His descent into this state continued for days, Egbunu, and

one evening, as he sat mumbling to himself that she hated him, he did not realise that his friend had returned.

He was almost thrown into a shock when he heard a loud knock on his door, followed by, 'Brother Chinonso, son of the living God!'

He rushed to open it.

25

THE SUBALTERN GOD

AKWAAKWURU, the great fathers in their unrivalled wisdom used to say that what a man is afraid of, that thing is greater than his chi. This is a hard saying. But it is true that fear is a great phenomenon in the life of a man. As a child, a man's life is ruled by constant fear. And once a person becomes an adult, fear becomes a permanent part of him. Everything a human being does is ruled by it. It is folly to ask, how may one be free from fear? Well, isn't it fear itself — perhaps the fear of having one's mind dominated by fear — that causes a person to ask such a question? Man must live by it. Man eats because he fears that if he does not, he will die. Why does he cross the street with caution? Why are that man and his child going to a clinic? Fear. Fear is a subaltern god, the silent controller of the universe of mankind. It might be the most powerful of all human emotions. Gaganaogwu, consider the story of Azuka, the man who killed his brother-in-law in a brawl three hundred and seventy years ago. That man was sentenced to death by the priest of Ala for having taken another man's life unjustly. My host at the time, Chetaeze Ijekoba, had been one of those who walked him to the forest and hanged him.

I had seen through him how this condemned man had been, how even his movement and his voice had been changed by fear, and it was clear that every moment of his life, from the time the judgment was pronounced, had been occupied by the fear of death. A man who persuades himself to live without fear will soon find that he has fled naked into the province of insanity, a place where he is without any acquaintances whatsoever.

When Jamike visited, he found my host consumed with fear – and desire, rage, love and grief. But most of all, it was fear that, in truth, he would never have Ndali again. Fear, Chukwu! The subaltern god, the tormentor of human-ity – that which holds a man on a leash and from which he cannot escape. Let him dart about the house, let him perch on windowsills, let him flap his young white wings as much as he wants, let him call and utter the orchestra of minorities; he cannot escape. For if he flies up, the roof will bring him back, and restore him to his place. Is the man at this point making merry? Is he drinking palm wine at his wedding? Is he receiving the benediction of his parents and the adulation of all his kindred? Is he making love to his wife? Is his wife in labour, and he is awaiting a child to be born? No matter, when he is done – when the party is over, when the wedding guests have all gone, when he has relieved himself and is calm again, when the child has been born and is asleep – fear returns with a presence more forceful than before and reels him back like a falconer does his bird.

So with this great fear my host needed help. He must at least try to know; he must try to find a way. A way? This was what he'd been trying to tell Jamike. And now, exhausted, he fell on his knee and held his friend who had returned to him from the mountain of prayers, filled with the spirit of the great deity worshipped in distant lands and also worshipped by the children of the pious fathers.

'Jamike,' he said. 'I know you are a man of God. I know God has changed your life, but I want you to do this one thing for me. I am sad, a very sad man still. I am still in a sloam. I will be saved only when I have my wife back.'

Even though he knew at this point that she had been lost, even though he could tell that he was now on the brink of insanity, he was worried by the consternation he saw on Jamike's face.

'Yes,' he said vehemently, gnashing his teeth and gripping Jamike's thin trousered leg even more firmly. 'She is my wife, Jamike. She is mine. We were going to get married. I suffered for her.'

His friend visibly seemed not to know what to say. He gazed on at my host, who loosened his grip. My host continued, 'About a week ago, I met her at the front of her house, Jamike. I saw her, so close, and her son. Do you know what his name, the name of her son is? It is Chinonso.'

'Your name?' Jamike said, and my most rational host became animated, for it seemed he'd struck something in the man with whom he sought help.

'That is so, that's the boy's name.'

'I can't believe it, my brother.'

'I think,' he said, but a deep chest-heaving inhalation silenced him, so that he began again: 'I think there is a reason why and I want to know. Did she think I was dead? Is that why she gave the boy my name? Or is it because of something else?' He coughed and spat into a handkerchief. 'The boy, I have seen him with my two wide-open eyes and my spirit tells me that he is my son.'

'It does?'

'That is so,' he said, and snapped his fingers. 'In fact, can you see the boy? He looks like he is about four years old. When did she marry this man? You said not long ago?'

'Ha, that is true. B–but when could that be?'

'I do not know. I do not know. I do not know, oh. Only God knows. But, my brother, my heart is broken. A dead person is better than me right now. I can't sleep. I can't eat. I don't know why my life is like this. But I want to know why her son has my name.'

'What you say is true, my brother Solomon. Ndiichie say that a toad in full daylight does not run for nothing. Either something is chasing it, or it is chasing something.'

True, Gaganaogwu: that was the wisdom of the erudite fathers!

'I understand, Nwannem Solomon,' Jamike continued. 'Ask me anything and I will do it. I want to help you.'

At this my host looked up and in that moment saw that he was kneeling on the ground and gripping the thin legs of his friend, his poor friend who had been without food for forty days and forty nights. The thinness of his friend's frame shocked him, and he withdrew his hands in a hurry and sat on the bed across from his friend. It was the word *help*, Egbunu, the promise of reprieve, hope, that did this to him. He sat up now, and shaking his head, said, 'I want you to go back to her husband, and say to him, "God has sent me to you, Mr Ogbonna, to warn you that they may be in danger."'

He waited for Jamike to speak, but his friend held his hand to his mouth, wiping the corners that opened into an O shape.

'It will not be a sin,' he said. 'All you are doing is trying to know if she is – whether she is safe or not. God will not forbid this. And, also, you are a pastor. So it is not a lie.'

Jamike shook his head. Although it seemed that it took a

great resolve for him to finally speak, he did not say, 'But the Lord has not sent me to him. That is a lie,' as my host had feared he would say. Rather, in a voice that seemed to cleave through the air like a sickle, Jamike said that he would do it. Then, as if he thought my host had not heard him, he repeated it again with the blunt force of a persuasion.

My host became calm. Then, lifted by a hand he could not see, he rose up.

CHUKWU, the great fathers often say that it was to the hunter's advantage that the antelope developed a bloated scrotum. For now the hunter with his poisoned arrow – even if he is an old man with a body full of old, weak bones – would be able to catch the antelope. Mr Ogbonna, my host's lover's husband, the evil man who had taken advantage of his absence and stolen his bride, the man who had ruined him, the man for whose sake he now suffered, the man who may be claiming his child, had already developed a swollen scrotum. He had given himself to a masked priest, a spy working for the damaged kingdom of my host. And now, on the evening of the following day, when the horizon itself wore a painted mask of thin grey and the bled-out red of a desert ant, my host and his friend drove to the bank where Ndali's husband worked.

He waited near a mechanic's workshop while Jamike went into the bank. The workshop was located under an old ugba tree, a tree that I immediately recognised. It had been there for many years. More than two hundred years before, as the heartless men of Arochukwu dragged my host, Yagazie, and other captured slaves along, their extremities bound with chains, a woman fell under the tree and fainted. The captors were forced to halt the march. Without a word, one of them, a stout man, signalled to the rest and said that the woman may be ill and might not make it to the seashore. So what to do? He cut her loose. But the woman did not move. They left her there, as if asleep, in a clearing with this single old tree.

My host came out from his car and stood under the tree with the men from the workshop, his eyes drawn to the Biafran flag, which was bound to a piece of wood inside the building. The flag was almost blackened with soot, with a hole at one corner of it. The men offered him a seat on a dirty bench by a big tyre, perhaps from a semi, with filing tools piled on it. But he stood by as the men worked, his arms folded over his chest, watching the street.

He had just bought a cold Pure Water from a hawker and was drinking it when Jamike returned. Jamike came with a certain muteness, as if something had silenced him. 'Let us go somewhere and talk,' he said to my host with haste in his voice, motioning towards the car.

They drove to his flat, and it was not until they had sat down, he on the bed and Jamike on his chair, that the conversation began.

'My brother, when I went in there, it was like he was waiting for me. He jumped up and said, "Pastor, Pastor, I'm in trouble." I asked what was the matter and he said, "Pastor, my wife, my wife." He was in anguish. He said Ndali had seen the man whom she almost married, and that the man had found out that the boy is his son.'

My host stood to his feet.

'Yes, it is your son, my brother,' Jamike said, looking up at him.

'How did that happen? How?'

'The man said she was pregnant before you left Nigeria. After you left, and she did not hear from you, she tried to find you. She called CIU.'

Ijango-ijango, you must wonder what this did to my host.
'Say again. *Isi gi ni?*' was all he could say.

'She called the university, she called Dehan, my brother
Solomon.'

He sat silent. I flashed in his mind two of the occasions when
she had held on to him and asked him to ejaculate inside her.
Then I flashed in his thought another one, that evening now
long past, when he'd been so carried away by it all that he'd let
himself ejaculate in her and pulled himself out only after much
had gone into her. And he hadn't told her, fearing she would
scold him. Then she asked him to put on the light so she could
clean herself with tissues. And he'd put it on, relieved that she
had not asked him if he'd pulled out effectively. He put the light
on and found, floating in the air, a white feather. Ndali had
been mesmerised by it. She'd asked where it was from and how
it had come to float in the air. And he said he did not know.
That was simply one of the many instances I reminded him of.
But on his own, my host recalled how, when he reached her
on the phone just after he'd received the promise of hope from
the nurse, she had said there was something she wanted to say
but she would tell him at a later time. I heard her voice still as
she said it to him on that phone many years ago: 'It is big, big
news, even me, I am surprised. But I'm very happy!'

'She could no longer hear from you, she was worried, my
brother. Child of God, she was with your child, and suddenly,
for many days no word. Then for weeks, she waited, no word.
She had the photocopy of your admission letter which you
had given to her. She called the school and was told of what
you had done.'

He was starting to speak, but Jamike went on.

'They told her you raped a white woman, and were going to
spend twenty-six years in prison. In fact, they told her that the

people were more lenient because in most Muslim countries, the penalty for rape was death.'

'Who told her that?'

'He did not tell me, but I think it was Dehan. He did not know the whole story; I don't think he did. But she tried. She looked for you, she tried to help you. He said she did not believe you did it, and had reported to the Nigerian embassy in Turkey, but no one did anything. I remember this, my brother, when I called my friends whose house you went to in Girne, they told me the Nigeria embassy in Turkey called the university. So I believe she tried, my brother. I caused this, but she tried to do something.'

'What else, what else happened?' my host asked, for the old rage had started to come upon him again.

'Her family,' said his friend, who had begun to weep. 'They were furious at it all. She was pregnant out of wedlock, then she was making international moves to rescue a man held as a criminal in another country. This was why they asked her to go to Lagos first. Ogbonna did not say this, my brother, but I believe she tried. Then she gave up.'

Ijango-ijango, something moved in my host's bowel, and he felt a warmth inside, as if something hot had penetrated it with slow ferality. She *gave up*. What does it mean? Akataka, it means that a person has tried something and then stopped. It may be that person has been trying to lift something, and then it occurs to such a one that they would never be able to lift it, so they resign and give up.

My host sat there, stunned, as if the world in which he'd been born, lived, made love, slept, suffered, healed and suffered again had been all along an illusion, the kind of sudden vision seen by the eyes of a blind old man: one moment radiant and aglow, and the next, a mirage that dissolves once it is seen.

26

SPIDERS IN THE HOUSE OF MEN

CHUKWU, your ears have been patient. You have listened. You have heard me recount all these things before the divine council here. You have listened while every tree in Beigwe wore the enchanting tunes like shiny garments. Even as I speak the music is pouring out of everywhere in the luminous halls like sweat from the pores of the skin. And all around are guardian spirits who must step in and render their respective accounts. But now I must hasten to fill the chasm that has opened in my story. And it will not be long, Gaganaogwu, till I am done with it.

To hasten, I must remind you of what the great fathers, wise in ways of war and battle, often say: that which must kill a man does not have to know his name. This was true of my host. For what he became, in the days and weeks after Jamike's discoveries, is painful to describe. But I must tell you the consequences of this change, because the cause for which I plead requires it. Egbunu, my host became a djinn, a man-spirit, a vagabond, a descaled wanderer, a thing creeping in the bush, a self-exiled outcast, shorn from the world. He refused to listen to the counsel of his friend, who begged him not to get in the fight. He vowed that he would, in fact, fight. He vowed, vehemently, that he would get his son back. He insisted that it was the only thing he had left in the world worth fighting for. And nobody, not even I, his guardian spirit, could persuade him against his will.

So he began again to lurk in the bush around her house, and when she drove home, he tried to accost her. She would not get out of her car but skirted around him and drove away. When this failed, he went to her pharmacy, shouting that he wanted his child. But she locked herself in the room and called on her neighbours from her locked window. Three men ran up into the pharmacy and dragged him out, punching him until his lips were swollen and the upper side of his left eye was split open.

But it did not stop him, Egbunu. He went next to the school the boy attended and tried to take him by force. And it was here that I think the seed of that which brought me here in this most troubling of human nights was sown. For I have seen it many times, Oseburuwa. I have come to know that a man who returns to that place where his soul was once shattered will not lightly forgive those who had dragged him there. And where am I talking about? It is that place where a man's existence stops, where he lives a still life like that statue of a man with a drum there at the centre of the street or the figure of a child with the gaping mouth near the police station.

Although the treatment by the guards this time was different, merely insults and slaps, he was tormented by the memory it unleashed in him. He wept in the cell. He cursed himself. He cursed the world. He cursed his misery. Then, Chukwu, he cursed her. And when he slept that night, a time in the past appeared, and he heard her voice say, 'Nonso, you have destroyed yourself because of me!' and from the bare floor of the dungeon, he sat up frantically, as if those words had taken years to reach him and he'd just heard them now for the first time, four years after she'd said them.

EZEUWA, Jamike came to bail him out the morning of the third day. 'I have told you, let her alone,' Jamike said after they had left the police station. 'You cannot force her to return to you. Get the past behind you and move on. Move to Aba, or Lagos. Start again. You will find a good woman. Look at me, all the years I spent in Cyprus, did I find anybody? I found Stella here. And now, she will become my wife.'

Jamike spoke to him, a man who seemed to be without a mouth, until they arrived at his house, and all Jamike's counsel came together with a combination of all the things he had seen and done. When the taxi pulled up in front of his flat, he thanked his friend and asked to be alone.

'No problem,' Jamike said. 'I will come and see you tomorrow.'

'Tomorrow,' he said.

OBASIDINELU, the great fathers in their diplomatic sagacity say that whichever tune the flautist plays is what the dancer will dance to. It is madness to dance to one tune while listening to another. My host had been taught by life itself these hard truths. But I had counselled him, too, and so had Jamike, his friend, on whom he now relied. And it was with these words in his heart that he unlocked the gate and made his way to his flat. He was greeted by his neighbour's wife, who was picking beans on a tray, and he mumbled a response under his heavy breath. He unlocked the padlock and opened the door to his room. Once inside, he was hit by a claustrophobic odour. Looking in the direction from which the loud droning of flies came, he saw what it was: the moi-moi he'd bought and half eaten the day he was taken away. Worms had filled the polythene wrap, and a milky substance ran down from the rotten food on to the table.

He took off his shirt and put the food in it, sending the flies into a frenzy. He wiped the putrefied substance off the table and took the shirt to the bin. Then he lay on his bed, his eyes closed, his hands on his chest, as he tried to think of nothing. But this, Egbunu, is almost impossible – for the mind of a man is a field in a wild forest on which something, no matter how small, must graze. What came he could not reject: his mother. He saw her, seated on the bench in the yard, pounding pepper or yam in the mortar, and he beside her, listening to her stories. He saw her, her head covered in a calico scarf.

He dwelt in this place, this veranda between consciousness and unconsciousness, until night fell. Then he sat up and let the idea flower that he should leave Umuahia and everything in it behind. He had thought about this in the police cell, even before Jamike said it again. And I had ensured that it persisted in his thoughts. The idea had come and gone out of his mind like a restless visitor those two days he spent there. Now something in the vision of his mother settled it, even if he did not know what it was. Was it that after she died he himself told his father many times that he should forget her? He had several times fought the man, told him it was only a child who hung on to what had been lost. Especially that night when his father, drunk, had walked into his room. Earlier they had cut up a chicken to supply to a woman whose daughter was about his sister's age and who was getting married. It may have been this that bothered the man. His father had staggered into my host's room in the dead of the night, in tears, saying, 'Okparam, I am a failure. A big failure. When your mother was in the maternity room, I failed to protect her. I could not bring her back. Now your sister, I failed to protect her. What is my life now? Is it just a record of losses? Is my life now defined by what I have lost? Who have I wronged? *Kedu ihe nmere?*'

In the past iterations of this remembering, he had thought of his father as weak, as someone who could not withstand hardship, who did not know how to turn his back. Now it struck him that he himself was clinging to what had been lost, what he could never again possess.

He would leave. He would return to Aba, to his uncle, and leave it all behind. He could not change that which has remoulded itself to resist change. His world – nay, his old world – had remoulded itself and could not change. Only forward momentum was possible. Jamike had left the province of his shame, made peace with my host, and moved forward. And so, too, had Ndali. She had wiped clean the board of the inscriptions he'd made on her soul and inscribed new things. There was no longer a remembrance of things past.

Also, it became clear to him now that it wasn't he alone who harboured hatred or a full pitcher of resentment from which, every step or so in its rough journey on the worn path of life, a drop or two spilled. It was many people, perhaps everyone in the land, everyone in Alaigbo, or even everyone in the country in which its people live, blindfolded, gagged, terrified. Perhaps every one of them was filled with some kind of hatred. Certainly. Surely an old grievance, like an immortal beast, was locked up in an unbreakable dungeon of their hearts. They must be angry at the lack of electricity, at the lack of amenities, at the corruption. They, the MASSOB protesters, for instance, who had been shot in Owerri, and those wounded the past week in Ariaria, clamouring for the rebirth of a dead nation – they, too, they must be angry at that which is dead and cannot return to life. How about everyone who has lost a loved one or a friend? Surely, in the depth of their hearts, every man or woman must harbour some resentment. There is no one whose peace is complete. No one.

So prolonged was his musing, so sincere his thoughts, that his heart gave the idea sanction. And I, his chi, affirmed it. He must leave, and his leaving would be immediate. And it was this that gave him peace. The following day, he went about looking for anyone who would buy his store's contents and take over the rent. He returned home satisfied. Then he called his uncle and told him all that had happened to him and that he must flee Umuahia. The older man was deeply disturbed. 'I t-told you no n-not to go back to th-that woman,' he said again and again. Then he ordered my host to come to Aba at once.

For days he packed the few things he had gathered, trying hard not to think about Ndali or his son. He would come back some day, in the future, when he had picked up his life again, and ask for him. That is what he would do, he thought as he stood in the emptied room that was once full, now with only his old mattress lying on the floor.

Agujiegbe, he would leave that evening and not return. He would leave! He had told Jamike this and once his friend had come to see him, he would begin his journey. He was waiting for the preacher to return from his evangelism and pray for him before he would go with all his things in his car.

Chukwu, at this point, I fear again that I must say that after Jamike had come, prayed for him, cried for him and embraced him, the old rage, the terror, the complex feeling that swallowed all things, came upon him again. He did not know what it was, but it seized him and plunged him into the abyss from which he'd been dragged out. It was, Egbunu, a single memory that did it: that one strike of a match that sets

an entire building on fire. It was the recollection of the day he
first slept with her and the day she had knelt on the ground of
the yard and sucked at his manhood until he toppled over the
bench. How they had both laughed and talked about how the
fowls had watched them.

Ijango–ijango, listen: a man like my host cannot leave a fight
just like that; his spirit cannot be satisfied. He cannot stand up,
after a great defeat, and say to his people, to all those who have
watched him being turned about in the sand, to all who have
witnessed his humiliation, that he has made peace. *Just like that*.
It is hard, Chukwu. So even when he said resolutely to himself,
'Now I will leave and go away from her for ever,' moments
later, as night fell, he gave in to the dark thoughts. And they
came crowding in, in their threatening fellowship, claiming
the entire world within him, until they persuaded him to go
into the kitchen and take a small can of kerosene, half empty,
and a matchbox. It was only then that they left him. But the
deal was sealed. He himself had sealed the can tightly and set
it on the floor of his car, in front of the passenger seat. Then
he returned and waited, waited, for the time to pass. And it is
difficult to wait when one's soul is on fire.

EGBUNU, it was almost midnight when he started the car
and drove into the night. He drove slowly, fearing that what
he carried was combustible and that he had all his possessions
packed into the car, ready for him to embark on his journey
afterwards. He drove on the empty roads past a vigilante
checkpoint, where a man flashed a torchlight into his car and
waved him to move on. Then he came to the pharmacy.

He parked his car and picked up the matchstick and box.

'I lost everything I had, Ndali, for your sake, only for you
to treat me this way? This way?' he said. Then he opened the

car, took the can of kerosene and matchbox, and went out into the dead of the night, dark beyond most nights.

'You paid me evil for all I did for you,' he said now as he paused to catch his breath. 'You rejected me. You punished me. You threw me in prison. You shamed me. You disgraced me.'

He stood now in front of the building, the world around silent, except for some church singing from somewhere he could not ascertain.

'You will know what it means to lose things. You will know, you will feel what I have felt, Ndali.'

In his voice now and in his heart, Egbunu, I saw that which has – from the beginning of time – always perplexed me about mankind. That a man could once love another, embrace her, make love to her, live for her, birth a child together, and in time, all trace of that is gone. Gone, Ijango-ijango! What do you have in its stead, you wonder? Is it mild doubt? Is it slight anger? No. What you have is the grandchild of hatred itself, its monstrous seed: contempt.

As he spoke, fearing what he was about to do, I came out of him. And at once I was hit with the deafening clamour of Ezinmuo. Everywhere, spirits ambled about or hung precariously from rooftops or on car tops, many of them watching him as if they had been pre-informed as to what he was about to do. I ran back into my host and put the thought in his mind to return home, or call Jamike, or travel, or sleep. But he would not hear me, and the voice of his conscience – that great persuader – was silent. He went ahead, once he'd made sure there was no human being around, and began pouring the kerosene around the building. When the kerosene had finished, he went to the boot of his car and brought out a small can, this one containing petrol, and poured it around the place. Then he lit the match and threw it at the doused building. And once the fire caught, he ran back to his car, started the engine, and raced into the gloom. He did not look back.

Gaganaogwu, I knew that no spirit would seek his body now that there was the food of vagrant spirits: a blazing fire. So I came out to bear witness, to see what he had done, so that when you enquired on his last day, I would be able to give a full account of the actions of my host. In the distance, as I stood in front of the burning building, my host drove away. By the time he was out of sight, almost a dozen spirits had gathered around the fire, floating like naked vibrations. At first I watched the beauty of the spectacle from the outside as discarnate bodies moved closer, past me. One of them, excited to the point of frenzy, ascended above the building and stood suspended at the point through which a black spiral of smoke levitated in a straight funnel. Others cheered as the smoke veiled the spirit intermittently and then revealed it again.

I was watching this when – I could not believe it – I saw Ndali's chi come out of the burning building, wailing. It saw me at once, and in a rush of words, it cried, 'You evil guardian spirit and your host! Look at what you have done. I warned you to desist long ago but he kept coming after her, chasing her, until he disrupted her life. And after she read his stupid letter two days ago, a thing she had been afraid to read, it disturbed her greatly! She began fighting with her husband. And this night, this cruel night, she left the house again in the heat of an argument and came here . . .'

The chi turned back now, for it had heard a loud, piercing cry from inside the burning building, and at once it vanished into the flames. I rushed in after it, and in the great conflagration, I saw, as a person was attempting to rise from the floor, a burning piece of wood that had been part of the ceiling fall on her back and send her out of her senses in pain. The impact her. But she made to rise again, seeing that a sudden mountain of fire had now erected itself before her from the other side of the room. A shelf of drugs had been thrown down and slowly collapsed into its wooden beams by the shattering fire, and a chunk of flame from it had caught the rug and was now coming towards the room where she was. She touched her neck and discovered that the liquid she could feel dripping down her back was blood. Only then did it seem that she realised the wood had lodged its nail-bearing head into her flesh, drilling the fire into her body. With hellish yelps and with the wood strapped to her back, she dashed through the yellowy theatre of fire that was replete with genuflecting tables, clapping windows, dancing curtains, exploding bottles. A chink of burned brick knocked her forward as she reached the door, and as she opened it, what remained of the burning wood fell off. The searing pain brought her to her knees like a caved priest lapsed into sudden prayer. It seemed to occur to her then that it was best she did not stand. So she began crawling out of the pharmacy like an animal grazing through a hamlet of flames.

By the time she escaped, people had gathered around the site of the conflagration – members of the vigilante group, neighbours and others. They met her with buckets of water, and as they poured them on her, she fell down and fainted.

I left her there then and ran to find my host. He was on the highway, speeding through the darkness, weeping as he drove. He did not know what he had done. Ijango-ijango, I have spoken many times this night about this peculiar lack in man and his chi: that they are unable to know that which they do not see or hear. So indeed, my host could not have known it. He was not aware. The Ndali that stood in his mind now as he drove was the Ndali that once loved him but who rejected him. It was the Ndali he'd lost. He knew nothing about the

Ndali who was engulfed in flames, the one who now lay on the ground in front of what had once been her pharmacy. He drove on, imagining her in the hands of her husband, thinking of how nothing he did could have brought her back. He drove on, crying and wailing, singing the tune of the orchestra of minorities.

Egbunu, how could he have thought that a woman who had a house would choose to sleep at her place of work? No. Why would she? There was no reason for him to think so. This is why a man who has just killed a person goes about his business without knowing what he has done. The august fathers likened this phenomenon to the spiders in the house of men by saying that anyone who thinks he is almighty, let him look around his house to see if he knew the exact time the spider began to weave its web. This is why a man who will soon be killed might enter into the house where those who have come to kill him are lying in wait for him, oblivious to their designs and not knowing his end has come. He might dine with these people, as the man in one of the books my former host Ezike once read. That tale had been of a man who ruled a land in the country of white people called Rome. But why look at such far-flung examples when right here, in the land of the luminous fathers, I myself have seen it many times?

Such a man walks into that room without any knowledge that what will kill him will have arrived – the way things come, the way change and decay encroach upon things with serendipitous strides and great transformations happen without the slightest hint that they have happened. But death will come, unannounced, suddenly, and perch on the sill of his world. It will have come unexpectedly, noiselessly, without interrupting the seasons, or even the moment necessarily. It will have come without altering the taste of plum in the mouth. It will have slipped in like a serpent, unseen, biding its time. A gaze at the wall will reveal nothing: no crack, no mark, no crevice through which it may have entered. Nothing he knows will give a hint: not the pulse of the world that will not alter its rhythm. Not the birds still singing without the slightest shift in their tune. Not the constant movement of the clock's ticking hand. Not time, which continues, unhindered, the way nature itself is used to, so that when it happens, and he realises and sees it, it will shock him. For it will appear like a scar he didn't know he had and inscribe itself like something formed from the inception of time itself. For it will seem to such a one that it has happened so suddenly, without warning. And he will not know that it happened long ago, and had merely been patiently waiting for him to notice.

AUTHOR'S NOTE

An Orchestra of Minorities is a novel that is firmly rooted in Igbo cosmology, a complex system of beliefs and traditions that once guided – and in part still guides – my people. Since I'm situating a work of fiction in such a reality, curious readers might decide to research the cosmology, especially as it relates to the concept of the chi. I must therefore declare that, like Chinua Achebe in his essay on the chi from which one of this book's epigraphs is drawn, 'what I am attempting here is not to fill that gap but to draw attention to it in a manner appropriate to one whose primary love is literature and not religion, philosophy or linguistics'.

This is to therefore say that this book is a work of fiction and not a definitive text on Igbo cosmology or African/Afro-religions. I hope that it can, however, serve as a sufficient reference book for such a purpose. The reason for this is that *An Orchestra of Minorities* has been resourced from numerous books on Igbo cosmology and culture, including *After God Is Dibia* by John Anenechukwu Umeh; *Ödïnanï* by Emmanuel Kaanaenechukwu Anizoba; *The Igbo Trilogy* by Chinua Achebe (this is often called *The African Trilogy*) and his essay on the chi; *Eden in Sumer on the Niger* by Catherine Obianuju Acholonu; *Leopards of the Magical Dawn* by Nze Chukwukadibia

E. Nwafor; and *Anthropological Report on the Igbo-Speaking Peoples of Nigeria* by Northcote W. Thomas, among others. These were augmented by field research my father conducted independently and some that I did in our hometown of Nkpa in Abia State, Nigeria.

As a matter of strict stylistic preference, I have chosen to write most of the spellings of the names, designations and honorifics of deities as one word instead of the more common compounds. Such words as *ndi-ichie* appear in my book as *ndiichie*. While I recognise the Union–Igbo agreement on the use of hyphens, I give fidelity to the way the people of Nkpa pronounce these words: in a fluid, uninterrupted flow. The same goes for the various names of Chukwu. Again, I recognise that *Gaga-na-ogwu* is the common rendering, but I chose *Gaganaogwu* instead. And there are names – *Egbunu*, for instance – that readers may never find anywhere else. For those interested in Union-Igbo spellings, I suggest they consult John Anenechukwu Umeh's beautiful book *After God Is Dibia* and the *Igbo Dictionary and Phrasebook* by Nicholas Awde and Onyekachi Wambu, among others.

Ya ga zie.

Chigozie Obioma
April 2018

ACKNOWLEDGEMENTS

This novel was inspired by various experiences. But its earliest source must have been my childhood name, Ngbaruko, the name of the man whose incarnation I'm believed to be. So I must thank my father; my uncle Onyelachiya Moses; my mother, Blessing Obioma; and others for creating curiosity in me about the chi and reincarnation early in life.

I'm grateful to early reader and helper Christina, my wife, for her generosity and for understanding my need to be reclusive while immersed in this great sea. Thanks also to my agent, Jessica Craig, who continues to be an early reader as well as a champion for my work, and never complains when I pester her. To my editors, Judy Clain and Ailah Ahmed, who revived the book from slumber. *An Orchestra of Minorities* would have been impossible without them and their teams at Little, Brown US and UK.

The support of Kwame Dawes and his wife, Lorna, was invaluable in ways only they and I could ever truly know. To Isa and Daniel Catto for the space in their castle to revise the book, and to the folks at the Aspen Institute. To early enthusiasts Camilla Søndergaard, Beatrice Mancini, Halfdan Freihow and Knut Ulvestad of Font Forlag, Thomas Thebbe and Pelle Anderson, and to my other publishers for their support. My colleagues at the University of Nebraska–Lincoln for their encouragement, and the university itself for providing an atmosphere for creativity. Also, thanks to Karen Landry, Barbara Clark, Alexandra Hoopes, and all those who have in one way or another helped make this book what it has become.

Finally, I owe my deepest gratitude to all the authors listed in my author's note and all who continue to ensure that the Igbo cosmology and philosophy do not die out. I must thank my dad again for being a researcher, a copyeditor and a champion, and for always reminding me what the great fathers said: *Oko ko wa mmadu, o ga kwuru mmadu ibe ya. Oko ko wa ehu, o gaa na osisi ko onweya o ko.*